GUARDIAN OF THE CROSSROADS

A Novel

Melanie Forde

Mountain Lake Press
Mountain Lake Park, Maryland

Guardian of the Crossroads: A Novel
By Melanie Forde

ISBN: 978-1-959307-42-6

Published in the United States of America
By Mountain Lake Press

Design by Jutta Medina

Author Photo by Picket Fence Photography

Cover image by the author

Printed in the United States of America

Also by Melanie Forde

Hillwilla

On the Hillwilla Road

Reinventing Hillwilla

Decanted Truths

The Quarryman's Girl

To Fauquier County, Virginia,
which graciously offered welcome
to a Damn Yankee

ONE:

A Reluctant Heroine

*T*ime and I have always had a complicated relationship. Ever since childhood. Little did I know back then just how complicated things could get.

Sure, when I was little, I shared my classmates' complaints about how long it was taking to be ten years old. Those kids couldn't wait to be taller and tougher and more independent of pesky parents. I, too, was taking forever to grow into a happier age. I hoped when I finally got to be ten I'd be less scared.

Those other kids probably didn't black out time. From an early age, I experienced isolated episodes when I'd just check out. When I checked back in, I had no idea how I'd spent the intervening half hour. Dr. Brown calls those "dissociative episodes," a fancy shrink way of describing how time can stand still.

By young adulthood, my contemporaries were flying through time. Not me. You know all those TV commercials showing buff young men and women, frolicking and perpetually smiling their incandescent white smiles? Time flies when you're having fun, the message goes, especially with the help of Product X.

The closest I ever came to that experience was when I painted, blissfully unconcerned about the hours passing. For most of my twenties and thirties, however, time had a heavy, viscous quality. Have you ever seen the small sculptures by Ernst Barlach? I identified with those bronzes and ceramics and wood carvings, heavy-footed and struggling to move forward. One college teacher claimed those figures somehow manifested Barlach's convictions about war and poverty. Professor Frankenheimer knew best, I guess. But I couldn't see it. To me, those little guys were just caught in time, slogging toward each new minute with enormous difficulty.

For me, the temporal mud only thickened with adulthood—especially in my thirties, when life boiled down to caring for Mother.

A few years after she died, my relationship with time got truly weird. The shift began slowly enough. But I can peg the start to Fauquier County, Virginia, where I had moved after finally selling my childhood home. I had hoped for a fresh start. But for quite a while, all I could see and smell and feel was that same old mud.

Fittingly, the start began in the mud of a roadside ditch, outside Leeds Manor Elementary School. There I was, hunched forward and miserable. With my eyes streaming and my left fist dug into the waist of my iridescent yellow-green vest, I threw up lunch, then breakfast, then what seemed like every morsel of food and every drop of liquid consumed the preceding week.

"Please, make them ignore me," I prayed.

"Them" was the crowd gathering to experience the miracle. Joining the chittering children outside the school was a stream of teachers summoned by the sickening squeal of tires leaving shadows on the pavement. Several motorists had pulled their cars off the road to extract phones and memorialize the spectacle. Click, click, click went the little artificial shutters. They captured the stunned but unharmed third-grader now standing safely out of harm's way; the silver F-150, sinking into the soft, aster-strewn ditch as baling twine competed with gravity to determine the ultimate destination of the pickup's load of hay; and the dazed driver, quizzically pondering the retches emanating from somewhere beneath his open passenger door.

The public awe was understandable. Leeds Manor Elementary School is an odd duck. In most schools, few pupils face any real danger of becoming roadkill because the only traffic they negotiate is in the parking lot where a big yellow bus deposits them in the morning and picks them up in the afternoon. Here, however, my duties as crossing guard were complicated by a series of countywide school closings in earlier decades. The original brick building was not large enough to accommodate the kids bused in from other areas. To handle the overflow, Fauquier County installed a trailer in a lot opposite the brick facility. A well-used country road separated the two buildings, with children crossing in both directions at the beginning and end of each school day. Signs with flashing lights announced a dramatic speed reduction, from forty-five to fifteen miles per hour, but every so often an oblivious or impaired driver would approach the crossing at a dangerous clip. I trembled every time I entered that crosswalk. Events on that October afternoon told me my collywobbles weren't baseless.

Life-altering events, like war or plane crashes, bring out the best and the worst in people, so they say. In my experience, moments of profound meaning merely brought out body fluids.

I experienced my first monthly blood, for example, on the day I lost my dad. Decades later, the discovery of Mother's dead body induced a hellacious nosebleed. And then there's my weird talent. Triggered by strong emotions, it has often been a handy coping strategy. Unfortunately, it has a bad habit of contorting my gut, generating tidal waves of sweat, or unlocking rivers of tears.

So it was no surprise how my body reacted after exercising that weird talent and preventing the silver pickup from pulverizing eight-year-old Marcy Boone. This time the fluid was vomit. Disgusting, smelly, decidedly unheroic vomit. Surely no one would want to focus on me in that state. But my whispered prayer went unanswered.

"You alright, hon?"

I recognized the voice of Ruth Levine, the third-grade teacher.

I nodded but remained hunched, turned away from her, just in case another retch was imminent. Meanwhile, I could hear a male voice somewhere above me. It was also asking questions, of someone else: "Can you tell me your name, sir? Do you know what day of the week it is?"

I must have been throwing up a long time. Long enough for the EMTs to arrive. Long enough for the cameras to start clicking. If I could have magically disappeared, I would have.

Eventually, the stomach spasms subsided. Gingerly, I eased into an upright posture, only to crumple from the sudden onset of the headache from hell. Pressing my knuckles into my jackhammering temples, I took a deep breath and eased upright again. As I awkwardly backed away from the ditch, I checked to see if anyone other than Ruth was focused on me. Spotting a clear path toward the staff parking lot, I moved forward warily. I was halfway to safety when the principal stepped into my path: Heather Hayes-O'Meara, a force to be reckoned with. She wore an angry expression. She was clearly displeased with me.

Heather never had much regard for me, of course. And why should she? I was just a crossing-guard and part-time art teacher. Worse, I wasn't very good at summoning the false cheer so many staffers mustered for her community-outreach projects. My passive indifference didn't help my finances any. I originally applied for a permanent position as art advisor with the county school system. When that didn't work out, I landed a part-time job as an art teacher at Leeds Manor, with the understanding that the principal had some discretion to add classes to my schedule. Principal Hayes-O'Meara chose not to exercise that discretion.

So I taught just two art classes a day to the littlest moppets.

Not much need for my fine arts degree there. To supplement my meager income, I hired on as a school crossing guard. I never would have kept afloat if Northern Virginia's real estate market hadn't skyrocketed over the decades, resulting in an outrageous sales price for Mother's modest house in North Arlington. A family friend helped me invest half of the net proceeds in a mutual fund, which was doing okay. I hoped to leave that nest egg untouched as long as possible. But the other half, earning a pittance in my savings account, was dwindling fast, despite my frugality. Thank heavens for the monthly annuity I still received from my father's life insurance policy. It was small, but essential. How, I often wondered, did he manage to keep paying into that policy during all those lean years? Did he sense he would die young? I guess it was a good thing for me he did. Golly, listen to me! A good thing? I'd rather have my dad than the maximum death benefit.

Anyway, there I was, disappointing my boss yet again, even if I didn't know why. Mrs. Hayes-O'Meara shielded her mouth from the vomit smell. Because of my throbbing temples, I was less than polite when I spotted her. I snapped, "Yes?" Golly, I was lucky I didn't slip and call her by her nickname. A while back, some snarky fifth-grade boys started referring to her as "Mrs. HO." The epithet spread like wildfire, even among the teachers.

The principal removed the protective hand from her mouth to warn, "You're not going anywhere until the police talk to you."

She waved theatrically toward the opposite sidewalk.

"My goodness, Heather, you'd think Cate had run over Marcy, not saved her," clucked Ruth, still hovering to make sure I was all right. As the eldest faculty member, just months from retirement, Ruth Levine got away with a maternal tone toward the boss.

She gently clutched my left elbow and guided me toward a sheriff's deputy, waiting impatiently on the sidewalk in front of the main school building. "C'mon, I'll go with you." she said. Once beyond the principal's earshot, she added conspiratorially, "I don't know why Heather's acting so pissy. Tomorrow she'll probably be fêting you as a heroine, if she thinks she can get some PR mileage out of this incident." She dug into a jacket pocket and extracted a roll of breath mints. "Here, hon, a couple of these will make you feel better."

Nodding, I unpeeled two of the mints and cautiously inserted them into my mouth.

The baby-faced policeman beckoned to us. "You're Catherine Devine, right?" When I nodded, he asked for my date of birth, address, phone number, and job title. Next, he fired off questions about the accident. When did I first spot the truck? How fast was it going? Was its course erratic or aimed toward the children? Did I smell any alcohol when I hopped into the passenger seat to pull the emergency brake and turn off the ignition?

I pointed to the left. "He turned from that side road. Looked like he was driving in a straight line but slowly or else I couldn't have caught up with him. And no, no alcohol. He just looked out of it."

The deputy nodded with self-importance. "EMTs think he probably had a TIA, a mini-stroke. You probably saved *his* life as well as the little girl's." He eyed my skinny, forty-something frame skeptically. "From what some of the witnesses said, that Ford was hustling. You must be in shape to run that fast."

"I don't feel all that great right now. I have a dreadful head-ache, and I'd really like to go home. If you're through with me, that is."

"You *are* through with her, aren't you, officer?" Ruth interject-ed, throwing a protective arm over my shoulder.

"It's 'deputy,'" he said peevishly. "Yes, that's all I need. Unless you have any other information you'd like to share."

I shook my head dully.

"Don't you worry about him," Ruth said, continuing to squeeze my shoulder and nudging me toward the parking lot. She added in a low voice, "He's so shiny new on the job, he probably thinks everyone's a perp."

The slang made me smile.

"What can I say? My husband controls the remote, and the TV is constantly blaring with police procedurals. But I'm glad I put a smile on your face. It's certainly better than that green color you were wearing a few minutes ago." She hugged me briefly then let me escape into my mud-encrusted, fifteen-year-old Jeep.

14

TWO:

OUT OF THE ORDINARY

Twilight was in full swing as I turned onto my driveway. How did that happen? Sure, I'd run some errands. But I gasped upon seeing the digital readout on my dashboard clock: "6:24." Shouldn't it have been just a little after five?

My confused musing was interrupted by a yodel of impatience from the gatekeeper's cottage, my rented home for the past two years. Hecuba, my Irish wolfhound, shimmied through the huge dog panel and loped toward the Jeep. Her brindle head loomed through the passenger window before I could roll it up.

"I'm sorry, Hecuba. I don't know where the time went, but I'm glad you didn't come to school with me today. That truck might have plowed into you. And even though I'm an awful person for saying this, you're a lot more precious than Marcy Boone. Now back off so I can haul in the groceries."

Hecuba spun around to face the hatch and, as soon as I opened it, thrust the top half of her body inside to inspect the grocery bags. Sniffing deeply, the wolfhound thumped her tail against my waist.

"Yes, I remembered your treats. Lord love a duck, you'll eat me out of house and home!"

Another hour passed before dinner. I carefully carried a mug of steaming soup into the living room. With my stomach finally settled, the jackhammer inside my head was now a Dremel, so I was looking forward to a light meal. Nestling into my worn leather sofa, I stirred dinner with a breadstick before setting the mug on a side table and reaching for the TV remote. My dog positioned her mass directly between the sofa and the coffee table.

"Hey! You've had your dinner. Let me have mine in peace, for heaven's sake!"

Dejected, Hecuba slumped heavily to the floor and rested bristly chin on bony knuckles, her yellow eyes still trained on the side table.

Click, click, click went the remote, as I dismissed one program after another. The noise induced an involuntary shudder, which made the dog stand and eye me with concern.

"Sorry, puppy. The clicking noise reminded me of the cameras from this afternoon. All those people taking pictures. I hope they didn't see anything weird."

Hecuba's ears pricked.

"It happened again," I explained. "But it was out of the ordinary, even my ordinary. Am I going nuts? I can't afford to go crazy. I can't afford much of anything, come right down to it."

Hecuba stooped to rest her head on my knees and receive some strokes.

"It started with that runaway pickup. I shooed the kids onto the sidewalk then worried they might not be safe even there. That willful Boone girl decided to cross anyway. Like she could contest road rights with an F-150! If I had any hope of keeping her safe, I'd have to do something about that truck. But moving a pickup isn't like making a pen skitter across a table, you know? I hoped I could remotely work the handbrake. Except I'd have to see the handbrake first.

"So, I dashed toward the oncoming truck, hoping to catch a glimpse of the emergency brake through a window. Unlikely, but I had to try. Then I thought maybe I could hop on the running board. But how could I intercept an oncoming truck before it hit Marcy? It was impossible!

"Except ... it wasn't. Suddenly, everything but me seemed to go into slow motion. Not just the truck. A bunch of fallen leaves got stirred up, but instead of swooshing by, they just hung in the air. I jumped on the running board, on the passenger side. It was like I had all the time in the world. Time enough to open the door, push the driver's deadweight leg off the accelerator, swing the steering wheel to the right, slam the gearshift into neutral, pull up on the brake, and punch the ignition button.

"How on earth did all that happen? How'd I get into the cab so fast? And what was all that slow motion business?"

Hecuba's extravagantly long tail curled into a loop, uncurled then looped up again. The swirls made me smile. They always do. She wanted to distract me from my confusion. I scrabbled her head gratefully, until it jerked upward. The hound sniffed the air, in the opposite direction from dinner. The doorbell rang.

"Nooo!"

Hecuba padded noiselessly to the front door and waited for me to catch up.

"Ah! It's just you," I told the peephole. The peephole image was familiar: the dramatically kohled eyes of fifth-grade teacher Morwenna Della Grazia.

"Way to make a girl feel welcome," grumped the muffled voice on the other side of the threshold.

""Oh, gee, sorry!" I said sheepishly as I opened the door. "Come in. Glad to see you. I thought it might be a cop or some-thing to do with that accident this afternoon."

Morwenna swept inside, silk scarf streaming from her neck. Her perfume acidified the air. She pressed a beribboned wine bottle into my hand, absentmindedly thumped my hound's flank, and tossed her coat on a nearby chair. Hecuba tiptoed toward the dog bed in the opposite corner of the living room.

"Well, it *is* about today's events," Morwenna explained, set-tling into the sofa and motioning me to join her. "I thought we should celebrate, you and I. It's not every day you save a life." She reached inside her purse and withdrew a folded piece of paper. "Here, this is for you. You'll probably see it in the Fauquier Times. One of their reporters was covering some event near-by—something about the county's largest pumpkin—and dashed over to the school to chat up witnesses. She heard about the runaway truck from the police scanner app on her cell. A real go-getter, that one. Anyway, I told her all about how heroic you were. I told her poetically."

I unfolded the paper and scanned the text. I must have looked confused, because Morwenna huffed in exasperation and snatched the paper from my hands.

"Oh, for heaven's sake! I'll read it aloud, then. Go fetch a corkscrew so I can toast you properly."

I trudged toward the kitchen and returned with the corkscrew and one glass. Before piercing the cork, I pointed to my mug. "Would you like some soup?"

Morwenna waved her hand impatiently. "I've eaten. Now give me my wine and listen. Sit!" She patted the sofa seat. "I've written a haiku, all about you." After clearing her throat, she read, "She is Woman: fierce/ And gentle. Bloodied./ Guardian of the crossroads." She laid the poem on her lap and looked at me expectantly.

"Gee ... thank you. Considering what happened after the truck stopped, maybe we should substitute 'puke-stained' for 'bloodied'?"

"Don't be silly! 'Bloodied' connotes the warrior goddess, battles, menstruation, the source of our womanly strength."

"I thought our periods just made us cranky."

"No, no! Don't buy into paternalistic stereotypes. Menstruation is a strength, not a weakness!"

"So, what happens when we hit menopause? Do we turn into

Samson, shorn of his locks?"

"We turn into the magic Crone, of course. Our strength comes from our life experiences, processed into generational wisdom. Honestly, Cate, don't you ever read? Some one of these days, I'll get you to attend one of our Wiccan meetings. We'll school you proper." She winked then frowned. "I probably need to explain how a haiku works, too. It has a seventeen-syllable structure, broken into three lines…"

I raised my palm. "Yes, I know, and you did a lovely job. Really. Thank you. I'm just in a fog. Haven't quite processed the events of this afternoon, I guess. I certainly don't feel as heroic as your poem—your haiku—makes me sound."

"Modesty never got anyone anywhere," Morwenna chided then gulped from her glass. "What, I'm drinking alone?"

"I really shouldn't, because of the methotrexate."

"The metho-what?"

"Remember me telling you I was diagnosed with rheumatoid arthritis last year? I went to the doctor because I was feeling so tired and achy. I thought it was just the cumulative stress of taking care of Mother those last few years and then losing her. But no, it was more than that. A little gift for the middle-aged. And the standard medication to treat rheumatoid arthritis—methotrexate—can be rough on the liver. So, no alcohol."

Morwenna pursed her lips. "Surely, one teeny celebratory glass won't hurt. And this is such a special occasion."

Shrugging, I rose to retrieve another glass from the kitchen. After hurrying back, I poured out a small amount of merlot and raised the glass toward my guest.

Morwenna reciprocated. "To the guardian of the crossroads. Glad I managed to work around my original version, where I was in danger of exceeding seventeen syllables. In that version, I called you 'guard.' Just didn't sound right. 'Guardian' has a mythic feel, don't you think? I'm gonna shop this little haiku around. I will absolutely, positively get it published. Somewhere."

Everyone who knew Morwenna knew of her publishing aspirations. She was determined to become a well-known writer. Not just of poetry. The other teachers at the school sometimes expressed skepticism about her talent. And I must confess, I shared some of that skepticism. But what did I know? After all, a feminist quarterly had accepted one of her poems and offered a free, year's subscription as remuneration. Morwenna was still lamenting her lack of full payment, because the journal went bankrupt six months later.

As she listed her latest writing submissions, I nodded and smiled and sipped soup. As tired as I was, I had difficulty focusing, especially when she quoted at length from a "patronizing" rejection email sent by one editor. Morwenna could be trying at times, but I owed her. It was she, after all, who had taken me under her wing nearly two years ago. She was the source of all sorts of useful information about the faculty, the students, local politics, the best farmers' markets. I may have been born and raised in Virginia, but the state's rural areas were new to me. I welcomed a guide. And I held out the hope that she might one day become an actual friend. Lord knows, I haven't had much experience with friendship. I'm probably too boring for someone like her, though. And I must confess, she's sometimes a bit too much for me.

As Morwenna continued her lament about publishing disappointments, I discreetly eyed her flamboyant jewelry, her flowered skirt, her flowing gestures. All so different from me. I regret that my initial read of her had been negative. She seemed false. It didn't help that I overheard a few stories about her. Several teachers snickered about how she came by her unusual name. Supposedly, she began life as "Mary Owens" but found the first name too tepid. Somewhere along the line, she began calling herself "Morwenna," without bothering about the legalities of the name change. She acquired her surname legitimately, though, from her second husband. After her first, brief marriage ended in divorce, Morwenna met and soon married Steve Della Grazia, a dentist nearly two decades her senior. Perhaps because he died just four years into the marriage, she tended to exaggerate his attributes, much to the annoyance of some colleagues. They would roll their eyes at anecdotes describing him as the most inventive lover, the gentlest caregiver, the most charming conversationalist, the most sensitive artist—a reference to his happy avocation as amateur cartoonist.

Yes, sometimes, Morwenna's anecdotes about her life could ring a bit false, but who am I to judge her for reinventing herself? Isn't that exactly what I tried to do after Mother died? Starting over is never easy.

Hearing Morwenna mention something about "The New Yorker," apparently the latest target of a poetry submission, I tuned back in quickly enough to cross my fingers and wish her the best of luck.

"Of course, it shouldn't take luck, should it?" Morwenna sighed. "Talent should speak for itself. But ours is often a disappointing world, is it not?"

As I searched for something validating to say, Hecuba rose abruptly from her pillow. She trotted past both of us and headed for the dog panel in the back door—leaving a pungent miasma in her wake. Since her tail was roughly at the level of our noses, the impact was overpowering.

"Golly! Hecuba H. Hound! Couldn't you have held it in until you got outside?" I fanned my nose and shrugged apologetically at Morwenna, who was pinching her nostrils.

She suddenly released the grip on her nose to gasp, "What did you call the dog?"

"Hecuba H. Hound. Why?"

"Did you come up with that name yourself?"

"Sort of. When I got her at the shelter, she already had a name, Heck. Her former owner had trouble keeping her in bounds when she was a pup. Apparently, the old lady got so used to yelling, 'Get the heck back here,' that the name stuck. But it just seemed too, I dunno, disrespectful. For all of her goofiness, this hound has dignity and deserved a more suitable name, but not too far removed from what she was used to. The poor thing had gone through so much trauma after her owner took sick and surrendered her. I didn't want to add to the confusion. 'Hecuba' was a nice compromise. Of course, when she gets rowdy, I call her 'Hellhound.'"

Morwenna's eyes widened. "Both names are telling. I don't think Hecuba is an accidental compromise. I suspect you were channeling some ancient energy, Cate. You do know where that name comes from, don't you?"

"Sure. Hecuba was the Queen of Troy. Priam's wife."

"Huh? Was she? Oh well, be that as it may. In Wiccan beliefs, Hecuba was the familiar of a powerful witch. Damn, I can't recall her name just now. I wonder what it all means." She tapped an incisor with a purple fingernail.

"Does it *have* to mean something?"

"It's just that ... you of all people ... you're the last person I would expect to have any association with things magical. Whoever would have thought? The universe must be trying to tell us something here."

It was hard to miss the implicit insult. Could Morwenna be jealous or resentful? Of *me*?

"I wonder... Does the dog have any special talents?" Morwenna prodded.

"She sure farts up a storm."

Morwenna erupted in laughter. I was relieved that a potentially contentious moment had apparently dissolved. She seemed happy to reconsider Hecuba's mythic connections. Perhaps my wolfhound was just an ordinary dog after all.

Three:

Wine, Wolfhound, and Song

A year of abstinence intensified alcohol's effects, good and bad. For the first time in ages, I didn't feel weighted down like those Barlach sculptures. I actually felt light. Light enough that I stopped obsessing over the afternoon's events and how I'd stopped that truck. What mattered was that I *had* stopped it. And perhaps saved two lives in the process. That was an event to be celebrated, not nitpicked. I didn't want the celebration to end and poured myself a generous second glass of merlot, before Morwenna could polish off the bottle. Once she learned there was no other alcohol in the house, she beat a hasty retreat.

I welcomed the opportunity to enjoy my lightness without any social obligations. I hoped to stay in this mood until sleep overtook me. I badly needed a whole evening free of anxiety. Perhaps because of the relative inactivity that darkness brings or because of the darkness itself, evenings were all too often spent focusing on everything wrong in my life. So much was wrong: precarious finances, strained health, no sense of purpose, no significant relationships, no clue how to make anything right.

The second glass of wine did not summon sleep. Instead, the lightness morphed into restlessness, demanding some kind of venting. A walk would do the trick, but it was a chilly, foggy autumn evening. As a city girl, I was still shocked by the full dark-ness of a country night. I was unlikely to encounter a mugger in this peaceful corner of Fauquier County. But I could fall over a tree root and break my leg. Or bump into a foraging bear. No, no, I would stay put.

For the first time in ages, I considered dusting off my few re-maining art supplies. Sketching and painting always soothed me. No, they did far more than that. They made me feel connected to something bigger than me. Art. That connection made me feel competent, like I deserved to take up space on the planet.

Most of my art boxes were in the cellar of this ancient stone cottage, but one was in the hall closet. Although I occasionally doodled, I hadn't picked up a paintbrush in more than five years, so I had no clear memory of what that carton contained—or why the contents were special enough to merit a worthier storage site than a musty old cellar.

With Hecuba padding behind me, I walked to the closet and pulled out the carton. It contained no supplies, only paintings and sketches I'd done over the years, many only half finished. They were in no particular order. A technically accomplished piece lay under something executed with a child's skewed perspective, for example. But even those childish efforts showed promise. Or so the merlot told me.

I lingered over one group of portraits, sketched and paint-ed from middle school through college. I didn't recognize most of the subjects but assumed they were classmates. One wonderful middle school teacher would assign pop sketches with a strict twenty-minute time limit. Those lessons knotted my stomach with anxiety. How could I ever produce something recognizable in such a short time frame? But the challenge forced us fledgling artists to focus more intensively. I thought I recognized a girl who was even more of an outcast than I. Jennifer Something. I had captured just a bit of her frightened rabbit expression. I also recognized Aaron Rappaport, a bit of a nerd who eventually transferred to a magnet school where he could develop his amazing aptitude for math and science. My watercolor sketch showed him still pudgy, with sensitive eyes that didn't pair well with his ridiculous red mullet. Oh, Aaron, were you trying to fit in? A sorry attempt. Especially since that hairstyle had passed its expiration date by the time we hit middle school. Ah well, he would go on to better things.

Next to Aaron's portrait were nude sketches dating from college. Scholarship students looking for extra money would hire on as models for art classes. As desperate as I was for money at James Madison University, I was far too timid to earn it that way. Admittedly, the subjects were usually draped in some way or turned away, affording limited views of genitals. But it was nonetheless amazing that I didn't pass out from embarrassment. I sure blushed though whenever a model entered the classroom and disrobed. But the pressure to create soon overrode my discomfort. To my middle-aged eyes, my execution looked skilled, even photographic. But there was something missing. I flashed on a comment made years earlier by an art teacher who described me as a good craftsman, but no artist. I would have to work hard to overcome my inhibitions, he said. For a while I tried. Then I stopped trying.

Now I was depressed as well as restless. I gathered up the nudes and returned them to the carton. As I scooped up some other works that had skittered onto the floor, I spotted another nude sketch, clearly done by my hand. The faceless subject had a flaccid penis with a hideous dark mole. The sketch made me extremely uncomfortable; why, I had no idea. I couldn't return the sketch to that carton fast enough.

I badly needed a distraction. I decided to take that walk, after all, despite the risk of tripping in the dark. Besides, it had been a week since I checked on the main house, More than that since I checked out the Ashwood family cemetery. I had an obligation to the Ashwoods, after all. The owners of this country estate were happy to rent me the gatekeeper's cottage for a ridiculously low price, because they wanted someone reliable to keep an eye on things when they were in Florida. No, I wasn't the gatekeeper. That job still belonged to Roy Washington, the former occupant of my cottage. But after Roy married his long-lost high school sweetheart, a widow living in a small ranch house ten miles away, his job as the Ashwoods' caretaker, groom, and gardener ended when the sun went down. So I became the estate's eyes and ears after dark.

It was comforting to have Hecuba accompany me. A wolfhound standing seven-feet tall on her hind legs would be one darned effective deterrent to any burglar or vandal. Sure, I knew Hecuba was an oversized teddy bear, but few people watching her lope silently through the woods would share that opinion.

I fetched my jacket and jingled my keys. In a flash, my trusty hound was beside me, golden eyes fixed on the door. Once outside, she waited impatiently to learn our route. When I waggled my small LED flashlight to the right, off she went, up the path leading to the cemetery. Dating back to the Revolutionary War, it was bordered on three sides by wild roses, honeysuckle, autumn olives, and poison ivy. Osage oranges, hickories, and hemlocks cast gnarly moonshadows over the brush. The relatively secluded hedgerows were well-warrened and a favorite hunting ground for my athletic hound.

When Hecuba loped beyond the scope of my flashlight, I shivered. Maybe I was channeling the fear of the bunnies tucking more deeply into their dugouts. Or maybe my youthful artwork had resurrected the fearfulness of my first two decades. There was no shortage of fearsome events. My father's fatal heart attack topped them all. After that, there were constant economic worries, my mother's repeated bone fractures, and her slow cascade of organ failures, with only me to look after her.

Other people went through sad and scary experiences, of course. Other people handled the difficulties so much better. Instead of learning from challenges, I let them wear me down. Would I have handled things better, I wonder, if I'd ever had a champion, someone to protect me, encourage me, teach me coping skills? My dad had his moments but died too soon. Besides, no one would ever mistake the mild-mannered owner of a failing hardware store for a superhero. My quirks alienated me from the kind of friends who might have included me in their alliance against a hostile world. Sometimes those quirks made me feel special. But always at a price.

I realized I was standing still. Literally and figuratively. Hecuba was long gone up the path to the graveyard. I stood in utter darkness. I didn't remember turning off the flashlight. Had my quirky talent kicked in? Maybe my mind shut it off. Why, I had no idea.

I rolled my thumb around the little metal cylinder in my palm, in search of the rubbery power button. An irrational panic seized me. I would never find the button. I would never find Hecuba. I would never find my way back home.

As I tried to exhale my fear, the moon nudged the treetops. Its fog-refracted glow now offered sufficient illumination to move ahead without artificial light. As I inched forward, I spotted Hecuba, standing at the opening to the graveyard, her tail held in an attentive, static curl. A lovely image. Why had I never tried to paint this scenery? It was all around me. Just waiting.

As I drew closer to my hound, the fog intensified, muffling sounds. Was that the mewling of a cat? The screech of an owl ... a human moan?

But Hecuba didn't appear agitated. She continued sitting, calmly.

Only then did I identify the melancholy notes of a penny whistle. No one making those lovely sounds could be a threat, right? Just then, Hecuba padded fluidly toward the piped lament. I followed but paused as a cloud passed over the moon.

"Sweet baby Jesus!"

Those words made me gasp. But there was something familiar about the voice uttering them. Besides, Hecuba had not barked or growled. I moved forward once again then jumped when a shadow rose from behind one grave marker. Next to the tall shadow was the silhouette of my seated hound attentive but still calm.

The wind moved moonlight through the overhanging hickory branches enough for me to see the tall shadow raise a palm. In greeting.

"That you, Miss Cate?"

"Roy?"

"Damned if your hellhound didn't just shorten my life a good ten years!"

"What are you doing here this time of night, Roy? You gave me quite the fright, too."

Shaking his head, Roy collapsed on the rough bench where he had been sitting. "Sorry. The missus had a meeting with those church gals of hers, so I figured I'd check on Sophie. This morning that white mare was worrying the wrap I put on her pus pocket. I got to fretting she'd do more damage to herself chewing at the duct tape. Came out here after dinner to have another look and take the dang thing off, if I could."

"Is she okay?" I perched on the edge of Roy's bench.

"Yeah. It looks good and drained, so I pulled off the dressing. She's a lot happier now. So then I just come up here to pay my respects to the dead folk."

"And serenade them, too. It sounded lovely. Once my heart stopped pounding, that is."

"You lucky. My heart's still thumping good. What y'all doing out here?"

"I just needed to clear my head."

"Heard you had one busy afternoon," Roy said, chewing on a thumbnail.

"How did you find out?"

"Aw hell, you can't spit around these parts without someone noticing. One of them IGA gals started babbling about the runaway truck when I was picking up some milk for tomorrow's breakfast. You a bona fide hero, I guess."

Hecuba groaned and lay down on the grass, chin on bony paws.

"Hecuba H. Hound!" Roy chided. "Don't you be doubting my words. The good Lord put your mistress in the right spot at the right time. And she rose to the occasion. That's a fact."

Chuckling, I jerked a thumb toward the dog. "At least all she did this time was groan to express her skepticism. Sometimes she makes her snarky little commentaries by passing gas."

Roy stroked the dog's head. "Well, the poor thing's gut was all messed up with them coccidia bugs, I do recall. How's her gut doing these days?"

Roy was quite familiar with Hecuba's health problems. A week-end volunteer at the local animal shelter, he was the one who put the giant wolfhound and me together. Working there helped him deal with his dogless state. His new wife was allergic. He was manning the front desk when an ancient woman surrendered the huge, skinny wolfhound. It was love at first sight for Roy, even if the dog was standoffish. There was no way he could let this majestic beast be euthanized. As he later told me, he hatched a plan right then and there. He recalled that I had asked about the safety of the area. He remembered how nervous I was about being far off the beaten path, with the lack of streetlights or any visible neighbors—at least in the cold-weather months when the Ashwoods were tucked into Florida's Gold Coast. Roy decided I needed a dog.

He was right. And not just to make me feel safe in my new home. I had always loved dogs, even if I hadn't had one in decades. A dog posed too much of a tripping hazard for Mother in her later years. But long before she became fragile, Dad brought home a cocker spaniel puppy. I was five at the time. One of his customers, after indulging an ill-conceived plan to become a dog breeder, was desperate to place her first (and only) litter of squalling, destructive puppies. Amazingly, Mother did not order the all-black puppy out of the house, even if she derisively called my Blackie a "devil dog." At last, I had a friend, one who didn't care if I was odd.

One week after Hecuba showed up at the shelter, Roy knocked on the cottage door to announce, "The Lord found you a security system, one that's tailor-made for you."

I would soon learn that Roy was always on the lookout for divine synchronicity. I was skeptical that the Lord was looking out for me, but I quickly warmed to the idea of a canine companion. Then I met her. Even at eighteen months, before she would acquire her full weight and stature, she was huge. She was also adorable and loving, and I was hooked. So, I took her in.

I had already loaded up with a stack of library books on dog training, made the acquaintance of a local veterinarian who patiently answered even my lamest questions, and I was well stocked in dog supplies from the Warrenton Walmart.

My first week as a dog owner was rough, thanks to Hecuba's

coccidiosis. But I decided that obsessing about her gastrointestinal distress was infinitely preferable to obsessing about every sound outside my door. By the second week, I couldn't imagine how I'd ever lived without her.

Breaking away from my reflections about the past eighteen months with Hecuba, I focused on Roy's question. "She's good." I responded. "The vet thinks we finally knocked those nasty bugs out of her gut. I still wonder how she got them in the first place."

"Don't know." Roy shrugged then speculated, "But that strange old gal who surrendered her didn't look like she was able to take care of herself, let alone a big dog like this. And skinny as Miss Hecuba was, I wouldn't be surprised if she was scavenging on all sorts of bad shit."

"Strange?"

"Sorry?"

"You said the old woman was strange. How so?"

"I guess anyone I don't know strikes me as strange, after living in these parts all these years. Thought you was pretty strange, too. All because you was a newcomer."

"It probably didn't help that I gave the dog such a strange name."

"Hecuba? Aw, I reckon I've heard that before. Wasn't there some loudmouth on that *Gilligan's Island* who had that name?"

I was never much of a television fan, but even I had heard of that particular TV show. I learned enough to know I had no interest in ever watching it. Despite Morwenna's reaction to hearing me say "Hecuba H. Hound" earlier this evening, my wolfhound's name no longer seemed weird.

"That old lady, she did say something kinda strange, come to think of it," Roy continued.

"What?"

"She said the hound was a queen in a previous life. I just nodded, figuring the old gal was talking ragtime. Not just broke up about having to part ways with her dog. Probably had a touch of the Alzheimer's, too."

"Hecuba was the name of a queen in ancient Greece. Well, in Troy."

"That a fact?"

"You don't suppose..." I hesitated about sharing the odd idea with Roy.

"Do I suppose the good Lord took some Greek queen and turned her into a scruffy old hound a bunch of centuries later? Now what for would He do that?" He shook his head dismissively.

Roy's certainty annoyed me. How could he dismiss Hecuba's name as pure coincidence, even as he viewed the timing of her surrender a divine blessing? How could he see a divine plan everywhere, while refusing to entertain even the possibility of reincarnation?

I didn't share my annoyance with him, of course. But I had little energy left for social niceties. It had been a long day, and escaping into sleep looked doable now that my restlessness had subsided.

I rose from my perch. "Guess I better check on the main house. It's been a while since I did."

"Don't you worry yourself none about that. I looked it over before I come up here. You go get yourself some sleep. Don't know why you're up this late with the day you've had. Go on home, now. As for me, I'll just set here a spell before I head out."

I sighed with relief, my annoyance gone. "G'night, Roy." I raised a palm in farewell then whistled for Hecuba as I trudged toward my cottage. Soothing penny whistle notes trailed after us in the fog.

FOUR:

MESSAGES FROM MORPHEUS

Blessed sleep overtook me just a few minutes after my head hit the pillow. Unfortunately, the dreams weren't quite so blessed.

That box of old artwork had dredged up old memories. So, my dreams transported me back to childhood. The first one was halfway pleasant, for a while. I was in my bedroom, with my dolls lined up on my bed. Sitting on the bed, I concentrated really hard on each plastic limb and willed it to move. Eventually, one doll raised an arm. And lowered it. Another kicked. Another looked at me expectantly, as if waiting for me to communicate what she should move. I felt giddy with power. Until the line of dolls began moving erratically, flailing their arms and moving forward. Toward me. The one marionette in the bunch began clacking his movable mouthparts. I yelled at the dolls to stop. They kept advancing. Closer and closer. The rusty squeaks of their moving limbs got louder and louder. The doll at the head of the line jumped into my lap and began marching up my chest. Her arms and legs made chopping motions as she advanced toward my face. "Nooo!" my dream-self screamed.

Hecuba chuffed sleepy concern from her pillow in the corner of my bedroom. I woke up hearing my vocal cords make a muffled protest.

"Sorry, puppy. Just a dream."

I lay in bed wondering what the dream meant. Yes, on several occasions as a child I had tried to will my dolls to move. With no success. Remember all those childhood tales about dolls and other toys coming to life? Well, they charmed me. Animated dolls seemed like a cure for loneliness. But there was another reason for my experiments. From an early age, I had isolated experiences where inanimate objects moved in my presence. Always when I was in the grip of some kind of negative emotion, especially fear. With each new experience, I suspected more and more that I was the reason those objects moved. As scary as those incidents were, I felt a small thrill. Just think how powerful I could become if I could intentionally and deliberately move objects remotely. Heady stuff for a little girl who felt utterly powerless.

It was some time before anyone witnessed me move something, intentionally or unintentionally. Mother dismissed the incident as a "quirk," a term that made me feel even odder than I already felt. It also took the power away from what I had just done.

I soon learned my quirks had a downside. Being able to change the trajectory of a rock some kid pitched my way was sure useful. But immediately afterward, I experienced an uncontrolled nosebleed, much like the vomit erupting after the runaway truck incident.

Instead of shaking off the crazed doll dream, I lay in bed

pondering which was the worse side-effect from my quirks: rampaging dolls or a rampaging gut? Like an idiot, I began making a list of pros and cons.

The list-making eventually wore me out. Enough to fold into another dream.

Hecuba's yellow eyes stared coolly at me. "I should be the narrator, not you."

"Why?" I complained. "It's my story, not yours."

"It's *our* story," the dream dog corrected me. "More importantly, you never give yourself sufficient credit. And who better to lay out your lives than I, who has served as your protector and companion for millennia? My path of service has wended through many cultures and times. On your behalf, I have padded thirstily through the sands of Giza. I have hiked, panting, up Mount Olympus. I have sounded the alarm at the gates of Rome. Frost-rimed, I have stood watch, at your side, over mist-obscured crossroads throughout the British Isles."

"Where were you when I was a scared little kid in North Arlington?" I challenged.

Hecuba snorted. "Have you so quickly forgotten the loyal cocker spaniel of your childhood? The dog with the 'liquid chocolate eyes,' as you put it?"

"Blackie? That was you?"

"Who else? I much prefer my current incarnation, of course. Of all the canids, none is nobler than the Irish wolfhound, a true dog of war. Are you aware that those of my bloodline were trained to pull an armored enemy from his speeding chariot? And decapitate him."

"Did you ever do that?" I asked.

Hecuba favored me with a wry grin. "That and more. But my feats lie humbled in the shadow of your own, my Goddess."

"Goddess?" I laughed.

"How else to describe She who shifts effortlessly among the realms of Heaven, Earth, and Hell? Among past, present, and future. Among your corporeal manifestations as Maiden, Mother, Crone. And yet you doubt yourself. You even doubt something as simple as your mind moving a doll's arm up and down."

"Wait a minute! Did I hear you right? You're saying I can shift time, too?"

Hecuba cocked her head. "What do you think?"

"I think I drank too much merlot."

The hound stood, stretched, and shook out her coat. She walked slowly away but turned her head to add, "By the way, as fond as I am of all your corporeal manifestations, the current one is perhaps my favorite. You call yourself 'spinster.' But you have no need of a mate. Indeed, what Titan, god or man would be worthy of you?"

A noise startled me and made the image of the departing wolfhound disappear. I blinked in an effort to resurrect that image. When I reopened my eyes, I could just make out my dark bedroom ceiling. The noise was Hecuba, the real Hecuba, scratching her pillow and circling three times before collapsing into a comfortable position.

"Wow! That was some dream! Some pep talk, too. Or should I pup-talk, huh?"

At the sound of her name, my hound yodeled softly.

"Sorry, girl. You go back to sleep."

I lay awake wondering whether the world would be a better place if dogs *could* talk. Would Hecuba sound as wise and articulate and full of herself as she did in my dream? Would she sound different if she were a cocker spaniel?

It was a silly way to spend my time, instead of sleeping. But it was a pleasant diversion. As I felt slumber's outriders rope me in yet again, I nestled into my pillow with the hope that the next dream would be equally amusing.

It wasn't.

The dream then featured Uncle Henry, Mother's older brother by a decade. Someone I hadn't seen or thought about in eons. Henry had not only helped raise his little sister but was also the source of financial largesse in some lean years. He'd visited a few times, when I was too little to remember. I didn't get to know him until he visited with us one whole summer, the summer before I started fourth grade. He was changing jobs and moving houses and needed a place to stay before his new life was ready for him. Far away in another part of the country.

In the dream, Henry was in my childhood house in North Arlington. He was holding a giant bottle of liquid. It was marked "Rx." And it was smoking. For some reason, Uncle Henry was taking care of me when I was sick. He smiled broadly, poured a big spoonful of smoking brown liquid from the bottle and extended the spoon to me. "This will fix your tummy," he said. I shook my head vigorously. "Don't want it," I protested. But he insisted and kept coming closer and closer with that smoking spoonful. Instead of running away from him, I fixated on the pictures on the wall behind him: small photos and sketches of flowers. I recognized them as the paintings that lined the upstairs hallway of my childhood home. As the spoon touched my lips, I focused really hard on those images of roses and Queen Anne's lace and lavender until they flew off the wall. They caromed around the hallway. One hit Uncle Henry on the back of his head. He yelped. And glowered at me, while he rubbed the back of his head. I saw blood on his hand.

"Now I'm in for it," I thought. And promptly woke up.

I was shivering. Had anything like that happened? I don't remember much about my uncle, apart from Mother's hero worship of him. She often bragged that, even as a youngster, he "ran with the in-crowd." He was always smiling. He had lots of clever jokes. But I never connected with him, any more than I connected with popular children. I couldn't remember ever seeing him angry, like he was in the dream.

I reached for the lamp on the bedside table. Hecuba grumbled as I turned on the light. "Go back to sleep, girl. I'm just gonna read for a bit."

In my current wired state, I knew sleep was impossible. Fortunately, the next day was a Saturday, so I didn't need to be sharp or well rested. Sleep wasn't appealing anyway, not if it brought more dreams like that one.

FIVE:

CO~CONSPIRATORS

The weekend was less than restful, with more weird dreams and painful walks down memory lane. It didn't help that I spent much of Saturday and Sunday dodging phone calls about the crosswalk incident. The dogged Fauquier Times reporter called repeatedly in hope of getting a phone interview. At least her messages were polite. A Washington Post reporter was clearly frustrated that she had to leave a message on my voicemail. She left three more messages within the next four hours. Her final one expressed annoyance at my "indifference" about "sharing" my experience in a "prestigious" media outlet. I assumed a meatier story would soon attract her attention, and both reporters would lose interest in my so-called heroic deed. Sure enough, my phone went silent before darkness fell on Sunday.

Although I was grateful to have employment, my part-time jobs hardly filled me with enthusiasm. So, gearing up for the work week, *any* work week, was a trial, all the more so on the Monday after the runaway truck incident. I prayed that Friday's events had dropped off the school's radar over the weekend. I desperately hoped I would not be the subject of gossip or stares. During my morning duties at the crosswalk, some children did stare. Most were halfway friendly. When Marcy Boone got off the bus, she marched across the road with eyes averted, pointedly ignoring me. I sighed in relief. Perhaps I would get through the day without attracting much notice.

But I wasn't quite invisible. When Nicu Radulescu showed up at the crosswalk, he gave me a big grin and raised both thumbs in salute. Unlike so many teachers who quickly form bonds of genuine affection with their students, I found it difficult to connect with the youngsters, whether I was shepherding them across the road or guiding them through finger-painting. Because art, like music, was an ungraded extracurricular subject, there was no pressing need to differentiate one student from the next. As a result, I had difficulty remembering names. Oh, I could recite the names of the troublemakers. Fortunately, they were relatively few.

Nicu did not number among them. But his name registered, nonetheless. Maybe it was because he was something of an outcast. He seemed to handle his outcast state far better than I did mine. But he wasn't managing all that great the first time I noticed him. That was just two weeks after I started at Leeds Manor. I was in the middle of the crosswalk, portable stop sign held high. After making sure the few cars on the country route had halted, I waved the waiting children forward. Some beefy boys were jostling one another and exchanging cheerful insults. The roughhousing continued all the way to the next curb. In their wake they left a gray blob in the middle of the crosswalk. The blob was Nicu. At first, I thought one of the boys had lost his backpack. As I approached, I saw sneakered feet sticking out from beneath the oversized bag. Nicu was curled into a crouch, head down, facing the pavement. Significantly smaller than the rowdies, he had apparently been the focus of all that jostling.

Alarmed that he wasn't moving, I bent forward, reaching for his shoulder. "You okay?"

His head bobbed up and down, and he staggered upright. Both fists were dug into his stomach. He headed for the opposite curb, but I nudged him to turn around so I could scan his face. He kept his head down, wheezing a bit. His hands remained clasped over his solar plexus. Gently, I pulled them away to search for some wound but saw nothing obvious.

"Did someone hit you?"

He shook his head, coughed, and only barely managed to utter, "Just ... fell."

"Just fell? My Aunt Fanny!"

I had my share of gut punches as a child. I knew how a well-placed jab could temporarily make breathing difficult and drain the blood from the face.

In mid-wheeze, Nicu raised his chin. The expression in his eyes transitioned from distress to amusement. "Your Aunt Fanny?" He erupted in giggles at my silly euphemism. The giggles triggered a series of coughs.

"Maybe I should take you to the school nurse?"

He waved me off, stood straighter, and smiled. "I'm okay," he said halfway believably. "You should see the other guys."

This time, I laughed. "Uh-huh. So, they'll be ratting you out to the principal, yeah?"

"It'll probably be a few days before they do."

"Huh?"

"I hexed 'em. Sometimes curses take a while to kick in," he whispered confidentially. Then he winked and smiled brightly before repositioning his huge backpack and dashing across the road. When he reached the opposite curb, he looked over his shoulder, grinned again, and flashed the peace sign. Chuckling, I responded with one thumb up.

Ever since then, Nicu and I enjoyed an amusing, largely non-verbal form of communication, punctuated by hand signals, winks, smiles, frowns, raised eyebrows, and head movements. This special relationship tickled me. Sure, it was ridiculous for a middle-aged woman to feel so gratified by a young boy's remote expressions of ... what, affection? Still, it was nice to feel like part of the in-crowd, even if the in-crowd consisted of just me and a bullied pipsqueak with delusions of grandeur. Inclusion was a new experience.

Then came another incident, last February. As I watched my charges skip, dawdle, plod, saunter, and run to the other side of the road, I felt a presence closing in on me. Normally the pedestrian traffic formed a magnetically repellent arc as it flowed past me. But this time one magnet deviated from the path. I felt a tug on my sleeve, followed by the soft plop of something landing inside the oversized hip pocket of my safety vest. Even without seeing the face beneath the mop of curly black hair moving away from me, I recognized Nicu by his gait, both determined and buoyant, with almost as much vertical as forward motion. Assuming he was unlikely to have planted a rodent or Morning Glory firecracker on me, I waited to investigate until the end of my morning crosswalk shift. From my pocket I pulled a small plastic bag. Inside was a bone-shaped cookie, plus a Post-it note bearing the scrawl, "Your dog is cool!"

Hecuba had obviously won another fan.

Back then, I was just starting to bring my dog to work, depending on the weather and my schedule. I discovered she was wonderful about snoozing in my Jeep. Since I usually had large gaps of free time between my crosswalk and teaching duties, I could hike to my car and take her for short walks. The school campus included both woods and fields that must have been filled with yummy smells to stimulate a canine imagination. Hecuba got more physical and mental exercise on days I took her to work than on days she stayed at home. Sometimes, she joined me for the crosswalk shift. She was a calm presence, sitting by my side and monitoring the traffic silently. I suspect that even without a neon-green safety vest, she was more visible than I to drivers. More than a few times, they would slow down to scope out the huge hound, even when I was waving them forward.

54

Nicu's interest in me and my dog tweaked my own curiosity in him, so I went to Ruth for information. She knew something about everyone who had ever set foot on the Leeds Manor campus. She told me his name and rank (at that time, the third grade). His family had emigrated from Romania when Nicu was just two. Of Romany heritage, they were used to discrimination, both in Europe and the States, and largely kept to themselves. More than once, Ruth witnessed kids goading Nicu as a "dirty Gypsy." His father, a metalsmith back home, soldered broken bracelet clasps and performed other repairs for a Warrenton jewelry store, with almost no customer contact. Nicu was a ho-hum student but showed an aptitude for music and art. During one show-and-tell, the normally withdrawn boy stunned Ruth and charmed some of the little girls in his class by playing an adept solo on a guitar borrowed from his father. She assumed the plaintive tune was a Gypsy folk melody.

After Nicu's gift for Hecuba, I muddled about an appropriate response. Recalling Ruth's anecdotes, I came up with an idea. My only problem was how to deliver my gift in low-key fashion, to avoid embarrassing the boy (and me). So, I asked Ruth to drop a large thank-you card on his desk one morning. Fortunately, she was no fan of the "collaborative learning experience" involving workstations instead of individual desks. Her third-grade classroom was old-school, with rows of desks, each designated for a specific student. So, I knew my envelope would go to the right addressee, more than likely without any of the other children even noticing. The envelope contained a mouth harp and the message, "Hecuba says thanks!"

A few weeks later, I heard an odd metallic riff from one cluster of children moving along the crosswalk. There was Nicu, harp to mouth, right index finger repeatedly twanging the thin reed. He suspended his playing briefly, spun around to catch my eye, waved, spun back then continued his dissonant tune.

My next actual verbal conversation with the boy occurred late one afternoon the previous March. The yellow buses had long since picked up their cargo and departed. As I headed for my Jeep, I spotted Nicu trudging toward the parking lot. He slumped down on a curb, elbows propped on knees, fists dug into cheeks. With the buses long gone, I worried that he was stranded.

"You miss your bus?" I asked as I settled on the curb beside him.

"Yeah. Had to see Principal HO."

"Uh-oh! You get in trouble?"

A weary nod.

"What did you do?"

"Got into a fight."

"That happen to you a lot?"

A shrug.

"Who won?"

Another shrug.

"So, you gonna whip up another curse?"

For the first time, he raised his head and looked at me. "I would if I thought it would work. They just laughed the last time I hexed 'em."

"I guess for magic to work, everyone's gotta believe in it."

He nodded dejectedly.

I knew firsthand the uselessness of the cheerleading mottos adults toss at children. So I wasn't going to tell him tomorrow would be a better day or even to hang in there. But maybe I could distract him from his misery.

"Unless you're my dog," I said. "She's magic. And everyone realizes it, sooner or later. Especially when she talks."

"For real?"

I nodded. "She can say hello. Well, okay, she sort of yawns the word. I taught her. Sounds kinda like 'Ha-rooow.' Sometimes she says it without my asking. Really freaks out the UPS guy."

Nicu looked disappointed. "That's it?"

"No. She tells me who I can trust and who I can't. If she doesn't trust someone, she gets between them and me. Really quietly and stares them in the eye. Makes them nervous as all get out. If she likes someone, she sniffs their behind. And if she thinks someone is silly or boring … well, she breaks wind at them."

The boy frowned in confusion. "Breaks wind?"

"She farts. Loudly and … unpleasantly."

Nicu executed a spit-take worthy of Jim Carrey. I didn't know whether he was reacting to my unexpected use of a crude term or to the nature of Hecuba's revenge. He erupted in high-pitched laughs. Finally, he said, "I knew that was one cool dog. I guess maybe farts *could* be magical weapons."

Smiling at the memory of that exchange, I snapped myself back into the present and watched the (now) fourth-grade Nicu disappear into the school. My smile broadened as I felt just a touch of giddiness at having a co-conspirator. Everyone else who commented on Marcy Boone's rescue made me uncomfortable. But this little boy conveyed his approval in such a sly way—not just with one thumb but two thumbs up!

I reflected on some other conversations with Nicu. There weren't many, and little of substance was discussed. Often, he interrogated me about the dog: Where did the name come from? How much did Hecuba weigh? How tall did she stand? Could she really kill a wolf? Had she said any other words lately? Occasionally, he hinted at elements in his own life: the bullying at school or his interest in music and drawing. He seemed to have difficulty opening up to anybody, so even this minimal effort at sharing charmed me. I understood his wariness. People could be treacherous.

And yet ... there I was, developing some kind of bond with this nine-year-old Gypsy, a boy who was almost as much of an outsider as I, hard-pressed to solve life's problems. Maybe Hecuba wasn't my only ally, after all.

Six:

Uninvited Guests

halloween didn't begin well, thanks to Morwenna. She had hatched a celebratory plan involving me and didn't get around to informing me until Halloween morning.

And how did I react? My usual way. Instead of expressing annoyance when Morwenna announced she was bringing a bunch of trick-or-treaters to my place, all I said was, "Umm, I guess I can get back home in time." Hopeless!

Never mind that I had zero treats for them. I lived awfully far off the road, so there was little reason to stock up on candy, all the more so since no little ghosts or goblins showed up the previous year, my first Halloween in Fauquier County. So now I'd have to dash to the IGA in between my late morning art class and my afternoon crosswalk shift. After dumping the goodies at home, I'd have to take Hecuba for an extra-long walk to knock some of the ginger out of her. Otherwise, she might be too boisterous around strange children. I also figured I should make sure the main house and stables were buttoned down before my uninvited guests arrived.

How did I let my schedule get so complicated? Didn't other people worry about consequences like I did, knowing that any single action could trigger multiple reactions and responsibilities? Why didn't other people realize that? Why didn't Morwenna realize that?

Spontaneity was her watchword, of course. Two weeks earlier she decided to organize a Halloween celebration at the school, after classes were out. She didn't factor in school bus schedules or the kids' reaction. As I later learned, her students balked at the idea of attending a "lame" school party. Many were eager to dash home, change into their Halloween costumes, and get an early start on cruising their home neighborhoods. Otherwise, the houses known for the best treats might run out of goodies before full darkness. So Morwenna bribed the protestors: If they attended her school-based party, in full costume, she would arrange a trick-or-treating caravan to affluent homes in the county. After recruiting several teachers to supply party decorations, cookies, and soda for the school celebration, she dragooned two minivan-driving mothers to chauffeur the kids to and from a likely neighborhood, yet to be determined. She didn't think of the Ashwood estate until a week before Halloween. She figured she could sell the kids on it because Civil War ghosts supposedly wandered about the estate. Mind you, I'd never encountered any. But what did I know? I just lived there.

Only half-a-dozen pupils signed on and produced the necessary parental permission slips. Morwenna managed to handle all the necessary consultations with students, teachers, and parents in halfway timely fashion but totally forgot to consult with her hostess presumptive. Until the eleventh hour.

"Oh, the kids won't stay long," she insisted after buttonholing me in a school hallway on Halloween morning. "And this will guarantee we both get into the Halloween spirit." Seeing my stunned expression, she added, "Oh c'mon! You know you don't have anything better to do." She winked and swatted my elbow playfully. I half believed she was doing lonely me a favor.

To sweeten her pitch, she leaned in conspiratorially. "Besides, I've got some very interesting information to share. I'll fill you in this evening." As she dashed off to class, she blew a kiss at me and called, "Thanks bunches. Blessed be!"

She succeeded in coaxing a smile from me. Morwenna was an excellent saleswoman. Colleagues often remarked on her energy. She was a "force of nature," they said. "Della Grazia gets shit done," they said. A few added, "Whether it needs doing or not."

My smile faded as I thought of all the chores awaiting me. As I watched her disappear into her classroom, I noticed she wasn't *zaftig* so much as fat. Was she charmingly flamboyant? Or was she just a bit trashy with all that makeup and perfume?

Immediately, those negative thoughts unleashed guilt. What contribution did I ever make to the school scene? What right did I have to criticize Morwenna for her spontaneity and enthusiasm? Besides, I knew all too well what triggered my criticism: envy, pure and simple. However appealing folks like Morwenna may be, I resented them because they were insiders.

Mother often chided me for finding fault with the popular

kids in school and on our block. A few times I made the mistake of carping about the "airheads" on the middle school cheerleading squad. Sometimes I griped about the "school spirit" assemblies organized by student government bigwigs. Occasionally I expressed annoyance with the fast-talking football players, the dramatic theater arts club members, and the pep squad dynamos in high school.

"Goodness, Catherine!" Mother would say, shaking her head sadly. "Imagine how dreary this world would be without the pretty girls, the athletic boys, the go-getters, the people who shine? Just what have you done lately to brighten this world? Don't begrudge your classmates the limelight. They've earned their popularity. Maybe you should try emulating them instead of envying them from the shadows. Maybe if you sought out those boys and girls basking in the limelight, you'd get a little glow yourself. Darkness does not become you, dear."

Such lectures ricocheted inside my brain as I dashed about my cottage readying things for Morwenna's imminent arrival. Mother's words stung. But they didn't change anything. Here I was having dark thoughts again. Here I was grumbling about the inconvenience of this Halloween celebration. I sighed and said aloud, "Mother was right."

"Mother is dead."

I spun around and gawped at Hecuba. Her yellow eyes had

been watching me as I poured the Halloween candy into bowls and tidied up. My sigh as I recalled those maternal lectures triggered a groan from the dog. Then she yawned. A long, bored yawn, containing multiple syllables. I chose to interpret those syllables as "Mother is dead."

"I must be losing it."

Truth be told, it wasn't just my dog's "words" that chilled me. I was already worrying about my sanity after those weird dreams and the resurgence of morbid memories I thought I'd sorted out years ago. My fantasy about Hecuba's three-word lecture was just the icing on the cake. Not for the first time since moving to Fauquier County, I considered calling Dr. Brown for an appointment. But this time, I felt more urgency about it. He was the psychiatrist I saw for precisely five sessions during Mother's last months. Based in Loudoun County, he was still within a reasonable commute and had been helpful enough for me to realize I needed far more sessions. Needing and affording were two different things, however. In my current job, part-time workers who logged at least twenty hours a week could buy into an (outrageously expensive) health insurance policy. It wasn't great but provided limited coverage for mental health care. I resolved to call him the next day. Maybe he'd have a slot before Thanksgiving. That possibility made me feel hopeful ... until it didn't. Therapy sessions, I recalled, could be daunting.

"Just what I need, more expenses, more scary things to handle," I griped, as I threw my dustcloth away. "I'll obsess about all that tomorrow."

Deciding to take a badly needed break before my guests arrived, I popped a CD into my ancient player. My choice was a collection of Bach organ pieces, leading with the "Toccata and Fugue in D Minor." Most people found it spooky, thus a suitable choice for Halloween. I found it soothing. Like all of Bach's music, it was orderly, composed with mathematical precision, offering me the hope that at least some part of this world made sense.

I collapsed into my sofa and rested my slippered feet on the coffee table. I cringed briefly, awaiting a maternal scolding: "Tables are not intended for feet. Goodness knows where those feet have been, Catherine," Mother would have said. But Mother was indeed dead, and it was now my coffee table, after all. Hecuba likewise settled, just barely fitting, on the floor beneath my legs. I breathed in her earthy scent, the soothing organ chords ... and peace.

But I wanted something more.

With difficulty, I hiked over my giant hound and headed for my kitchen counter, holding two bottles of cabernet sauvignon. While shopping for candy, I also bought a treat for Morwenna. Admittedly, two bottles were overkill, even for her. When I bought the wine, I had no intention of drinking any myself. But I changed my mind. A little alcohol might steady my nerves before company arrived. Besides, my earlier indulgence hadn't caused any wooziness or hangover. In addition, the previous week's routine blood test showed perfectly normal liver functions. On that occasion, I asked the nurse if alcohol was taboo for patients on methotrexate. She said, "As long as your liver enzymes are normal, an occasional glass of wine's not gonna hurt. Might even do you some good."

Those two glasses I drank the night after the runaway truck incident sure made me feel lighter, at least for a while.

Let's see if wine does the trick again.

I pulled one of Mother's crystal hocks from a kitchen cabinet, opened a bottle, and poured out a generous glassful.

Back on the sofa, I swirled the blood-ruby liquid with one hand while petting Hecuba with the other. My hound shifted position to see what was in the glass. Then she bobbed her head up and down. "Glad to have your approval, puppy," I chuckled.

One sip later, Hecuba rose and padded toward the hallway. She dropped onto her haunches and aimed her muzzle at the front door. I counted down from pinky to thumb and thumb to pinky. As the countdown ended, I could make out childish chatter. I groaned softly and rose.

The dog remained on alert as I peered through the peephole. Opening the door triggered a boisterous litany of "trick or treat!"

"Welcome," I said, too hesitantly. "Oh, golly! Wait!" I raised an index finger. "Forgot something!"

The bowls of candy were still on my coffee table. As I dashed off to fetch them, I left my guests at the threshold—facing cool, yellow-eyed appraisal from the biggest dog they'd ever seen. One of the mother-chauffeurs whispered to Morwenna, "Is that dog safe?"

Morwenna cleared her throat. "Of course." She didn't sound entirely convinced.

The little group huddled in suspended animation until one of the smallest children pushed forward, dropped to one knee, and extended a bone-shaped treat to Hecuba. The wolfhound ignored the offering but craned forward to snuffle the boy's dark hair. Nicu giggled, stood, and waggled the treat. This time, Hecuba snapped it up, slurped the boy's hand then stood, undulating her tail.

As I ushered everyone inside and dropped a Mars bar or Almond Joy into each plastic pumpkin, Morwenna challenged me, "Now you need to guess who everyone is. Me first."

She pirouetted. The purple veil descending from her pointy hat coiled loosely around her neck. The kids giggled as they searched my face for any sign of recognition. They saw none.

In a cartoonish German accent, Morwenna asked, "Zo, you do not know who I em?"

I scanned the black dress, the V-neck, the black-banged wig. And got nothing. Shrugging, I offered, "Well, I guess you're a witch. You look something like Anjelica Huston."

One youngster mumbled to her friend, "Who's Anjelica Huston?"

"Philistines! You're all just Philistines!" Morwenna complained, stomping her foot. "At least you got the actress right. But you have no idea of the character, do you?"

I shook my head. One of the mothers rolled her eyes. Two of the trick-or-treaters sniggered.

"Eva Ernst at your service," the witch said, with a zippy salute from a black-gloved hand. "You know, the grand high witch from the movie, *The Witches*. Honestly, it was a Halloween classic a few years back."

"A few centuries back," muttered the tallest boy, as he dug an elbow into a cohort's side.

How out of the loop I was! I didn't see many movies. But then I snapped out of my inertia. "Oh, wait! That's the Roald Dahl story, right? Golly, that scared the willies out of me when I read it as a child."

"Pree-Zisely," declared Eva Ernst triumphantly.

Why would a fifth-grade teacher, with students in tow, assume the persona of an evil witch who was determined to exterminate all the children on Earth, or at least turn them into rodents? Did kids like having adults play-act as their sworn enemies? Maybe normal kids did.

Morwenna exhaled deeply, clearly exasperated. "Well, let's see if the rest of you fare better. Let's see if our hostess can figure out who *you* are." She crooked a vaguely menacing black-gloved finger at one boy to approach me.

As I took in his costume, I experienced a rush of relief. I had actually watched one of the *Star Wars* movies on television a year ago but had no recollection of specific character names. "Umm, you're a Jedi knight, yeah? I'm sorry. I don't know which one."

The boy nodded with boredom and reached for another treat in the candy bowl.

After identifying Wonder Woman, Batman, a creepy clown ("Pennywise!" he corrected me), a zombie, and some kind of princess, I regarded Nicu, now positioning a three-eyed *papier mâché* crow on his shoulder and a broom between his knees. Skewered atop the broomstick was a Styrofoam wig stand. I desperately wanted to identify Nicu's Halloween persona but was clueless. I wondered if the broomstick indicated a witch but couldn't imagine a boy choosing a witch costume. I bit my lip, ostensibly deep in thought, as if I were within seconds of dredging up the character's name.

Seeing my confusion, Nicu adjusted the wig stand so it faced me directly. Then he pointed at a sign taped to the Styrofoam forehead. Leaning forward, I squinted at the felt-marker scrawl. "Hodor? Oh! Yes! I get it!" I silently thanked the local library for its generous assortment of DVDs. "The broomstick represents Hodor, the big guy who carries that kid around, carries you around. You're that kid from *Game of Thrones*, the kid who's..." I stopped myself from adding "crippled." The last thing Nicu needed was any association with someone even more vulnerable than he.

"What *is* his name? You're that boy with magic powers, right? And his name is … Brian? Bram?"

Nicu radiated delight. "Bran Stark, son of Winterfell. Only one other person figured it out."

A tiny princess jumped up and down, jabbing an index finger into her chest. "That was me! Ya know why? Because *Game of Thrones* is my favorite TV show ever. My parents don't know I watch it. But my big brother figured out how to stream it and he downloaded some episodes. He lets me watch them sometimes, at least the ones that don't have too much blood. Or naked ladies. I don't care about blood and naked ladies anyway. I care about Bran. He's so cute. Did you know he can see through the eyes of animals?"

"Like his direwolf," Nicu explained, turning to me. "Your dog would make a great direwolf. Can I borrow her?"

I looked at Hecuba, still scrutinizing the guests. "Sorry, but I need my direwolf around tonight. For protection against evil spirits."

The little princess flinched, and one of the mothers stepped in to explain, "Ms. Devine is just kidding."

I wasn't so sure. I was genuinely distressed at the idea of lending out my dog. To anyone.

"Now that all the trick-or-treaters have been identified, let the games begin," exclaimed Morwenna, perching on the edge of my sofa.

"Games?" I was stunned.

"Sure. Don't you have some apples we could bob for?"

"Apples? Umm, no."

"How you fixed for toilet paper? We could split into teams and have a mummy-wrap race."

"What?"

"Okay, then. Why don't we organize a treasure hunt? You stash something and we try to find it."

"How about playing spin the bottle?" offered Pennywise, nudging Wonder Woman, who tossed her dark hair, rolled her eyes dramatically, folded her arms, and sighed.

"Could we visit the graveyard?" Nicu asked.

The idea of trooping a bunch of sugar-crazed grade-schoolers up to a family cemetery had zero appeal. But I had no idea what else to do with my restive guests. It never occurred to me that they would require entertainment.

"I guess that would be okay. Just remember that this is the Ashwood family plot. Their loved ones are resting there. So, you gotta be on your best behavior."

Several kids groaned. One muttered something about a "lame party." But I heard a few appreciative "oohs," too.

Morwenna slapped her thigh. "The game's afoot. Let's go."

Seven:

Boundaries

he hike to the cemetery was uneventful. I was glad for the three other pairs of adult eyes watching over the boisterous youngsters. *Four* other pairs, if you counted Hecuba, although she had more in common with the kids as she loped joyously beside Nicu. He insisted on calling her "Summer," the beast's name in the book/television series. At one point, he exclaimed how perfectly Hecuba's coloring matched the canine character. "Even the same gold eyes!"

The two youngest children were tiring by the time we reached the graveyard. I hoped their fatigue would translate into a short visit.

One of the mother–chauffeurs was intrigued by the gravestones' age. Two barely legible inscriptions were of Revolutionary War vintage. Most of the markers dated from the Civil War era or late nineteenth century. Only one was from the twentieth century but still nearly one hundred years old. How sad. The estate must have lost its pull on most Ashwood descendants, now scattered far beyond Virginia's Northern Piedmont.

The minivan mom asked if she could return one day and make tombstone rubbings. Morwenna assured her she'd be welcome. I raised a timid hand in protest, like some kindergartener asking permission to use the girls' room. "I'd need to check with

Roy first," I said. "That's the caretaker. These markers are fragile. Acid rain and storm damage. I'd hate to see anything happen to this slice of history."

The requestor looked disappointed. Morwenna looked petulant. So, I added quickly, "But maybe it will be okay."

"Surely there'd be no problem if we took pictures," Morwenna declared. "You're right about this place being a piece of history. And a perfect teaching opportunity. Do you have your cellphones, Tobey and Karen? Yes? Good! Snap away, and tomorrow we'll discuss the history revealed in these stones. What fun!"

Pennywise and Wonder Woman pulled out their smartphones listlessly. Others followed suit. The peace of the little cemetery frayed amid electronic whirs and clicks, giggles and guffaws, as the photographers also memorialized one another, sticking out their tongues and forking their fingers. I shuddered.

One of the mothers stepped up. "That's enough! This is a cemetery, after all." Seeing the confusion on the youthful faces, she added, "It's like a church. You're supposed to be respectful. Honestly, people, haven't you ever been to a funeral?"

"I bet Gypsies go to lots of funerals," the creepy clown said, smirking and pointing at Nicu. "I heard they pick up lots of germs cuz they don't ever wash."

"Tobey!" exclaimed the other three adults.

Nicu balled his fists and took two halting steps toward his

tormentor, now slouching beside a smirking zombie. Despite the crack in his voice, the small boy mustered impressive volume. "At least I don't have a stupid last name like Drinkwater."

Tobey staggered backward theatrically. Clasping his hands over his chest, the clown sneered, "Ooh! That the best ya got, dickhead?"

"Stop it right now!" demanded one of the mothers.

Morwenna stepped between the two boys. Dramatically thrusting her palms sideways, as if she was about to dip into a plié, she cautioned, "Boundaries, boys, boundaries!"

Tobey folded his hands over his chest and chuckled. Nicu pivoted, retreating one step, then looked back over his shoulder. "Drinkwater? From all the trouble your mother gets into, it oughtta be just plain old 'Drunk.'"

Gasps circulated. Muffled giggles, too.

Nicu continued walking away, while Tobey's eyes glared. Morwenna whipped her head from one contestant to the other. "Do you not know the meaning of boundaries? Fine! You both got in your shots. Now leave it alone, or I'll get in some shots of my own. You paying attention?" She peered into the clown's rage-distorted face.

Morwenna announced we should all head back to the cottage and return to the business of trick-or-treating. Several children muttered, "about time" and "finally" as they trudged downhill.

I stood, watching them. Hecuba took up position by my right

hip. She sat with spine almost vertical. Her yellow eyes bored into the simmering Tobey.

No, it wasn't over.

Tobey finally began moving downhill, trailing the other children. He slowed to eye the tumbled-down fieldstone wall that had once marked the graveyard's circumference. In one fluid motion, he swooped forward, grabbed a flat rock the size of a dinner plate, wound his loaded arm, and cocked his entire body at the small, dark-haired boy downslope.

Hiking well ahead of the children, Morwenna was oblivious to Tobey's intent. Otherwise, she probably would have summoned just the right words to defuse the impending crisis.

The only word I could come up with was "nooo!"

Several heads turned toward me. When they did, they saw the locked and loaded Tobey. But no one was close enough to intervene.

In that instant, I knew what to do. I focused on the ground to Tobey's left. It was littered with fallen Osage oranges. Squeezing my eyelids, I imagined the nubbly green spheres beginning to move. Larger than softballs, they became a green river flowing into the path of the advancing boy. I imagined the balls rolling over and under his feet. I imagined him stumbling and falling, as his missile landed well short of its mark.

Which is precisely what happened. Okay, there was no "river" of Osage oranges. Just a few tumbled into Tobey's path.

But they were enough. He teetered, arms pinwheeling before he crashed to the ground. Ironically, his nose smashed into the fieldstone weapon he had artlessly tossed. He lay stunned on the leaf litter, a gush of blood erupting from his nostrils.

The blood at my own nostrils was much less obvious. No one noticed as I pulled a Kleenex from my pocket and dabbed at my nose. With minimal pressure, I stanched the flow. If anyone noticed, they'd assume I was having a minor emotional reaction to the boys' drama.

"Get up, Tobey!" Morwenna ordered. A slight tremolo undermined her tough demeanor. She now stood over the clown. He struggled to his feet, one hand cupping his dripping nose.

"I ting id's brogen," he whimpered.

"Well, if it *is* broken, that's karma." Morwenna dug her fists into her waist. "You could have broken Nicu's head if you hadn't tripped. What were you thinking, going after a little boy?"

Nicu groaned at the demeaning description. The zombie snickered.

"Well, I suppose someone will have to take you to the emergency room," Morwenna continued, making no offer to handle that chore herself. She stared at the two mothers.

"I've got to go into Warrenton anyway," one of them said dully. "Looks like trick-or-treating is over. I'll call Elsie Drinkwater first." She approached Tobey and waved his hand away from his face. Stooping to make a quick scan of the already swollen, dripping nose, she handed him several Kleenexes. Then she pulled a phone from her jacket pocket.

"Yeah, c'mon kids, let's head on home," said the other mother. "Some people just don't know how to behave. They spoil it for everyone else. She glared at the bloody clown then made a herding gesture toward the other children. They trudged peevishly but silently down the hill.

When the group reached my cottage, Morwenna asked if anyone had left anything inside. Several children nodded. Pursing her lips with annoyance, she added, "Go get your stuff then. And be quick about it. Tobey needs to get his nose looked at, and after all this drama, everyone would like to get home as soon as possible. Quick, quick! Like bunnies!"

I motioned toward the mother tending to Tobey. "I'll get you a towel, so your car doesn't get messed up."

"Thanks."

On my way to the linen closet, I daubed at my nose and was relieved to find only a drop or two of red. For once, this latest evidence of my psychokinetic quirk could be sniffed away inconspicuously.

Towel in hand, I headed back outside. In the hallway, I bumped into Nicu, the only other human in the house at this point. He carried the Styrofoam head tucked under his left arm and limply held his broomstick in his right hand. He stared hard at me. "You did that, didn't you?"

"What do you mean?"

"You made Tobey trip. I saw you looking at those big green nuts or whatever they were. Somehow you made them move."

"The wind must have moved them. Or gravity."

Nicu shook his head solemnly. "I saw how you squinted. Looked like your brain was gonna explode, you were concentrating so hard. And then the nuts started rolling."

"You're imaging things."

Eager to end this conversation, I brushed past him. He remained standing.

"It's okay," he called after me. "I won't tell. But I know you saved me. And I'm the second kid you saved."

I stopped in my tracks but had no intention of validating that observation. I waited until he plodded forlornly out the door. Then I went outside to raise my hand in limp farewell at the two minivan drivers. Suppressing the urge to bolt back to the safety of my cottage, I made myself watch the loaded vehicles for five whole seconds as they moved down the drive.

My relief at their departure was cut short when I spotted Hecuba, cocking her muzzle at the greensward to the left of the house. Morwenna's Mazda was parked there. Swell! I didn't have the energy for more conversation, not after the draining events at the graveyard. The only other human discourse I might have any stomach for at that point was a psychotherapy session, where I could spill out all my anxieties. Ah well, that would have to wait. With Morwenna, conversation would be more about listening. Bracing my shoulders, I reentered the cottage.

Immediately, I heard, "In the living room."

Morwenna sat on the sofa. "I don't know about you," she said, "but I need to chill out after all that nonsense." She patted the seat cushion.

As I plopped down beside her, she offered me a glass of cab. "Drink up. I slipped back inside as soon as the kids piled into the cars. I wanted to scour your kitchen in search of libations. *Et voila!*" She pointed to the wine bottle now on the coffee table. "I took the liberty of opening this. I knew you wouldn't mind. I figure we deserve it."

I took the glass in my hand. Initially offended at the trespass, I decided to be charmed at Morwenna's take-charge manner.

"Do you think that boy really broke his nose?" I asked.

"Don't know. Don't care." Morwenna tossed her hair. "I know we're not supposed to judge our little treasures, but that Tobey Drinkwater is a psycho. If he hadn't tripped, I've no doubt he would have cracked open the other boy's skull. A lot of kids are scared shitless of him. Rightly so. It doesn't help that he's older and bigger than the other fifth-graders. Little bastard was seven when he started school. Then he repeated second grade. He's smart enough, but trouble on the home front keeps getting in the way."

"So, what Nicu said about Tobey's mother is true?

"Sure is. Momma's a lush. She's been stopped for DUIs all over the place. The only reason she's not in jail is hubby."

"Hubby?"

"Alan Drinkwater. A county supervisor. And a partner in Warrenton's oldest law firm."

"I almost feel sorry for Tobey."

"Save your sympathy. Kid'll end up a serial killer. But, hey, the last thing I wanna do is talk about Tobey after spending a long day with wall-to-wall children. On to more interesting subjects. Remember me telling you that your dog's name rang a bell?"

"Yes?"

Morwenna eyed me eagerly over her wineglass rim. "Hecuba, the original holder of your dog's name, was the familiar of none other than Hecate." She waved one hand in a triumphant flourish.

Having no idea why this fact was so exciting, I sifted through my limited knowledge of ancient mythology for clues.

"Hecate! Hecate!" Morwenna prodded.

"She was a Greek goddess. No, wait! She was also a Titan, right? And didn't she show up in Egyptian mythology, too?"

"What is it with you and ancient cultures? Greeks. Egyptians. Move up the timeline. She's a lot more modern than that. And a lot closer geographically. Think British Isles."

The lecturing tone annoyed me. "Morwenna, I'm pretty sure she goes back to ancient times. Maybe Bronze Age or before? And yeah, Egypt and Greece."

My guest waved my words away. "Egypt, Shmee-gypt. It's the Celtic link that's important to us Wiccans. For us, Hecate is one of the most important mythic symbols, the queen of witches. In Celtic lore, she's the Crone, the wise old woman. And wasn't your hound surrendered by a wizened old woman? A coincidence? I think not!"

"Huh?"

"That old woman who brought this dog to the shelter? What if she was the reincarnation of the Celtic goddess Hecate?"

"Dumping your dog at a shelter doesn't sound very divine to me."

Morwenna tapped her upper lip thoughtfully. "What if she knew that the dog, her faithful familiar, would find its way to someone attuned to the Wiccan Way?"

"Me?" I scoffed.

"No, silly. *Me*. Maybe the goddess intuited the various connections that would link her dog to a Wiccan group. Maybe she knew the Ashwood caretaker worked at that shelter and would never let the dog be euthanized. With her wisdom, she could foresee all the connections that would lead from your caretaker to you and then to me."

"If Hecate's so magic, wouldn't she have found a less convoluted way to send the dog your way?" I reached down to give *my* dog's head a proprietary pat. "Besides, Hecuba isn't living in a Wiccan home. She's right here, with me."

"Oh, don't be so literal. Hecate may have wanted merely to surround her dog with protective Wiccan influences." Morwenna poked at her lip more vigorously as she parsed divine intentions. After a pause, she continued, "The Crone sees all and knows all. So, the complicated linkage would have been perfectly obvious to her. She sees multiple directions at once, after all. Britain is filled with statues of Hecate in wooded places where three paths intersect. Those statues typically have three faces—Maiden, Mother, Crone—each focused on one of the pathways, all guarding the crossro... Oh, my Goddess!"

"What?"

"I just realized. In my poem, I called you the guardian of the crossroads."

"But... I'm confused. It almost sounds like you're equating me, with my crossing guard duties, with some Celtic goddess. I thought the dog's previous owner, that old lady, was the goddess? Which I guess makes some sense if your goddess is portrayed as a crone. Except now you say she's also a maiden and a mother."

"Yes, yes, yes. Hecate is the culmination of the Eternal Feminine. She represents all stages of womanhood. As for the rest, well... I haven't worked it all out just yet. But I'm convinced a divine hand is at play here. How exciting!"

In her excitement, Morwenna splashed wine on her lap. As she paused to daub at the stain with a napkin, she added,

"I'll need to borrow your dog sometime. Take her to our Wiccan gatherings. Maybe Hecuba can serve as a medium to transmit a message from the Crone."

Hecuba raised her head and sniffed toward the spill. Then she rose and slouched silently out the back door's dog panel.

I suppressed a grin. It looked like Hecuba had zero interest in being loaned out to a group of Fauquier County witch-wannabes. "I don't know, Morwenna. Hecuba isn't all that gregarious. I don't think she'd be comfortable around a bunch of strangers."

"Nonsense! She just spent an hour or so around a bunch of strangers. She was fine. She really seemed to like that Romany kid."

"She knew Nicu from before."

"You're missing the point. Once you think about it, you'll understand. It's a great opportunity. Hecuba will be fine with the women in my little group. For one night. Maybe two."

Hecuba would be miserable, that much I knew. She had already been abandoned by that old woman. I was not about to inflict another abandonment on her, however temporary. Besides, I didn't much like the idea of being without my faithful hound for one night. Or maybe two.

Sensing that Morwenna expected a response, I dodged her eyes and focused on the wine glass in my hand. When I raised my head, I heard a quiet, firm, "No." It took a heartbeat to realize the voice belonged to me.

"What?"

"No, you may not borrow Hecuba."

Morwenna startled slightly and tried to read my face. After a minute, she shrugged. "No harm asking. But do let me know if your dog does anything unusual, 'kay?"

I dropped my eyes to my wineglass. I needed a moment to absorb what had just happened.

That's all I had to do? Just say no?

I felt downright empowered. Almost godlike.

EIGHT:

POWERING UP

Psychotherapy isn't much fun. It's work. I knew that when I scheduled an appointment— my first in three years—with Dr. Brown. So it didn't come as any surprise that there was sometimes a disconnect between what I wanted to talk about and what *he* wanted me to talk about. Oh, don't get me wrong. I have high regard for Dr. Brown. He's smart and compassionate. He also has a well-developed sense of humor, which can put things in perspective. Especially when it comes to keeping a molehill from becoming a mountain.

Nevertheless, there are times when I need to move at my own pace. And sometimes that's circuitous. Did you ever wish you could just open your mouth and vomit out all the stuff festering inside your head? Anyway, I wanted to talk about my fantasy of Hecuba speaking. But I needed to work up to that story, at my own pace. I briefly mentioned hearing the comment about Mother being dead. But somehow I veered off and started talking about the truck incident, which I characterized, perhaps incorrectly, as a psychokinetic incident. Psychokinesis was not a new topic in our therapy sessions.

Back in 2019, I told Dr. Brown just a bit about my experiences with moving inanimate objects with my mind. He didn't act like I needed to be committed. Which was a huge relief. He even cited studies of the "poltergeist phenomenon," typically involving an adolescent girl giving vent to inner turmoil by creating chaotic external surroundings. He never got around to explaining just how that troubled teenager caused the chaos, whether she was actually breaking glassware remotely. But he implied there was a "logical" explanation for how those things moved around. I was skeptical. After all, there was already one thing wrong with those studies. I wasn't a teenager when my mind first moved things around. I was seven.

So, I told him about that early incident in some detail. It all began with the medical encyclopedia handed down from my grandmother. While other kids were watching Freddy Krueger movies, I'd lug that book off the shelf and delight in all the gory pictures of swollen limbs and infected wounds. I was especially thrilled by the documentation of black widow spider bites. The photo of that poisonous spider was actually beautiful: her shiny black abdomen, her dainty legs, and that precise red hourglass. The black widow wasn't big like a tarantula, but as small as she was, she packed a punch.

One evening as I stared at that spider photo, I began to play with it. I made the image move, not just on the printed page. I felt powerful—controlling a venomous spider, even if it was only a virtual one. In the dim light of my childhood bedroom, my mind projected the photograph onto the wall. I made the spider grow bigger, making it move right, then left, then up, then down, then in circles on the bedroom wall. Except then the spider moved right when it was supposed to go left. It moved up instead of down, diagonally instead of in circles. And then, to my horror, it marched down the wall and onto my bed. I screamed. I sure didn't feel powerful anymore. No longer in control, I was a silly little girl in danger of being poisoned by my own fantasy.

My father dashed into the room. Through copious tears, I described what had happened. He saw the medical encyclopedia lying open on my bed. He saw the spider photograph. He saw no spider on my bed.

"Oh, honey, why do you fill your head with scary stuff like this? You just let your imagination run away from you."

My father's words were not comforting. It wasn't just "imagination." Why couldn't he believe me? When I asked Dr. Brown in 2019, he didn't have an answer.

His nonresponse made me stop from reporting another psychokinetic incident. One that happened when I was an adolescent, just like the patients in that poltergeist study.

By then, Daddy wasn't around to offer soothing words. He had died not too long before, and his calming influence on Mother was gone, too. She was testy that day because she needed to straighten out some problem with one of her many prescriptions. As she spoke on the phone with the pharmacist, I sat not too far away on the floor. Leaning against the sofa with my graying cocker spaniel's muzzle draped over my lap, I was watching an old movie on TV. It was *film noir,* a genre Mother had banned. She objected to the moral ambiguity. But she was preoccupied, and I thought she wouldn't notice my viewing choice.

I was wrong. Initially, the only problem was the television volume. Hearing a familiar hiss, I turned to see Mother glaring at me and making repeated jabs in the direction of one ear. Blackie, my sweet dog, got the message before I did. He tented his eyebrows, looked at me, then at the television set. He whined and nudged my elbow with his nose. By then, Mother's left hand formed a claw, rotating counterclockwise. I finally figured out that I needed to turn the volume down. Unfortunately, by then, Mother realized just what was on the screen: Humphrey Bogart, cigarette dangling from pouty lips. A bad boy if ever there was one.

Mother hissed again. Then she palmed something on a nearby end table. Without dropping the phone, she hurled the object.

Blackie whined, as if urging me to move out of harm's way. But I froze. I fixated on the incoming glass paperweight, shaped like a curled cat. I processed every nanosecond of its trajectory. How bizarre it was to hear Mother's calm, cultured signoff on the phone while I watched the violet hues of her launched missile brighten as it crossed a sunbeam. The paperweight got bigger and bigger, heading straight for me. Abruptly, illogically, it moved to the left, thudding into the bottom of the sofa. Missing both me and my dog. I retrieved the violet glass. Noting a small nick on it, I felt a sputter of exhilaration. I had saved the glass cat from worse damage, by changing its trajectory.

Moving the spider triggered tears. Moving the paperweight triggered blood. I didn't realize my nose was bleeding until Blackie began licking my face. A few swipes of that long tongue connected with my upper lip, where the first red trickles seeped from my nostrils.

That incident popped into my head again, during my 2022 session with Dr. Brown, after I'd described the near-disaster during the Halloween excursion to the Ashwood graveyard. In my head, for the first time, I zeroed in on the similarities between the two incidents: Mother hurling a paperweight at me as an adolescent; Tobey pitching a rock at Nicu on Halloween. I had prevented both missiles from reaching their targets.

Dr. Brown interrupted my unspoken, internal analysis. "Cate?" he called with a note of concern. "Are you still with me?" Leaning forward in his leather armchair, he peered over his reading glasses.

I desperately tried to recall the last thing he had said. "Umm, you wanted to know something about Morwenna?"

"I asked that question two minutes ago. Where did you go?"

My pulse rate went into overdrive, and I'm sure my cheeks

reddened. I had tuned out. Not for the first time. "Hmm? Oh, gee," I said lamely. "I guess I got lost in thought. I'm sorry, that was rude of me."

"Don't be sorry. Tell me where or when you got lost."

"Halloween, I guess. And how it all started with Morwenna." That wasn't a total lie. But resurrecting all the details of both the Halloween and childhood incidents seemed too daunting.

Dr. Brown looked skeptical. "Okay, then let's go back to Morwenna. Earlier you seemed reluctant to talk about your friend. Why is that?"

"Is she my friend?"

"You tell me."

I felt exasperated. I wanted to examine the psychokinetic incidents. Mother's paperweight. Tobey's rock. To say nothing of that truck heading for Marcy Boone. But it was all somewhat frightening and more than a little complicated. Where to begin? Morwenna might be a less satisfying subject of discussion. But at least she was a safer topic. Or so I thought.

I told him she was the closest thing to a friend that I had. And why wouldn't I seek out her company? So many people did. She was popular because of her flamboyance and assertiveness. Admittedly, I didn't always feel good around Morwenna. Sometimes, she made me feel... Sometimes, I felt absolutely powerless around her. Well, he sure zeroed in on that.

He wanted to know why. When I said she could be annoying,

he wanted examples. I came up with some and admitted that, sometimes, when in Morwenna's presence, I felt like a godhelpus. Had to explain what that meant.

That opened up one fat can of worms. Dr. Brown smiled encouragement. And waited. A psychiatrist, I had already learned, is very good at waiting. That must be part of their residency training. Just wait out the patient. Until the silence becomes so intolerable she'll spill her guts.

I finally said I spent time with Morwenna because otherwise I'd be all alone. But that didn't feel quite right. I don't mind being alone. I'm pretty good at it. I guess the expression on my face conveyed unease with my answer. So, Dr. Brown prodded, "Your motive is loneliness?"

Was it? "Maybe I just want to look normal," I speculated. "Normal people have friends. And since Morwenna kind of took me under her wing, I look like I have a friend. I look normal."

"How's that working for you?"

Dr. Brown can be something of a smart aleck. I wanted to tell him so. But all I said was that he was giving me a headache.

I tripped myself up with that one. He teasingly reminded me that he didn't have the power to give me a headache. Not unless he had some kind of psychokinetic power, too.

"Now you're making fun of me," I complained. Amazing! I actually protested!

Dr. Brown dropped the teasing tone and asked, "Have you

ever thought about your own power? Where it comes from? How you lose it? How you grow it? How it makes you feel?"

"You mean my ability to move things with my mind?"

"Well, sure. But more than that. We all have power, Cate. Virtues, strengths, abilities. The only time I've heard you talk about feeling powerful is when you describe these psychokinetic incidents. And they're few and far between. What's more, they come with some drawbacks. So, do you spend the rest of your time feeling impotent?"

I probably did.

"How about when you're with your dog?" he suggested.

I felt a smile on my lips. "No, I don't feel impotent around Hecuba. But why would I? She's a giant and protects me."

"Someone else might find that giant threatening. Hecuba might make someone else feel powerless. Sounds to me like you've developed a good relationship with that huge dog. Does the dog obey you?"

"Well, yeah. She comes when I call. She sits when I tell her to."

"And this dog weighs, what?"

"One ten."

"And what do you weigh?"

"One-o-eight."

"And when Hecuba stands on her hind legs, is she as tall as you?"

I couldn't help chuckling. "Taller, by a good stretch."

"So, you have a really tall dog that weighs more than you. And you can make it do your bidding. I doubt you're muscling Hecuba into sitting or lying down on command. I suspect there's something authoritative and appealing in your personality that makes your dog want to please you. Wouldn't you agree? I don't know, Cate, but that sounds pretty powerful to me."

"Yeah, but Hecuba's a love. And so smart. Anyone could train her."

"Really? Didn't you laugh earlier today about how standoffish your dog can be around other people, including the powerful Morwenna? Could she make your dog heel?"

What suddenly popped into my mind was how Hecuba had farted out her annoyance with Morwenna's visit. I blurted out, "No, Morwenna can only make Hecuba break wind."

"Another psychokinetically gifted person?"

I frowned and folded my arms. "Very funny."

"I try." He smiled then glanced at his mantelpiece clock. "Unfortunately, our hour is up. I want to assign homework. I want you to think about situations where you feel good about yourself, if not actually powerful. What are you doing? What time of day is it? Where are you? Who else, if anyone, is present? How long does the good feeling last?"

"New situations? What if there aren't any? What if I can only come up with stuff that happened in the past?"

Dr. Brown rose from his chair slowly. As he rubbed the

stiffness out of his lower back, he shook his head gently. " We're not grading here. Past, present, hypothetical. Doesn't matter. Just think about it."

Homework! I wasn't expecting that. But at least the assignment was halfway interesting. And I was nothing if not a diligent student back in the day. So, I promised I'd think about it.

NINE:

LASSITER BROWN, M.D.
SESSION NOTES, 16 NOVEMBER 2022

Devine, Catherine (Cate): Established patient (cf. session notes from fall 2019)

Recorded with patient approval. Stated reason for resuming therapy: Increased anxiety, two recent incidents moving objects with her mind (cf. childhood history of perceived psychokinesis), possible delusions involving pet dog.

General observations: Patient is neatly groomed 42 yo woman. Dressed conservatively, subdued colors, no visible makeup, no jewelry apart from watch. Posture slightly stooped. Pale, thin. Reports only medication as methotrexate for RA. Well tolerated. Patient is highly articulate, with normal affect, if minimal eye contact. Gesticulation increases with anxiety. Frequent self-soothing tics like plucking nubs in her sweater, smoothing sofa cushions, playing with her braid. When avoiding uncomfortable questions, patient sometimes hums briefly, apparently unaware of doing so. One possible dissociative episode, preceded by humming, with patient appearing briefly unfocused, disoriented.

Highlights from transcript: Cate exhibits anxiety when discussing her dog's function as an apparent counterpoint to the internal scolding voice of her late mother. On Halloween, Cate felt peeved at being coerced into celebrating the holiday. Her annoyance triggered memories of her late mother, who often chided her for being negative. Cate reacted to those memories by embracing the maternal criticism. "Mother was right," she uttered out loud, in the presence of her pet dog. The dog reacted to the utterance with a "skeptical expression," interpreted as a reminder the mother had died and that the internal scolding voice should cease to have any power.

While relating this anecdote, Cate seems quite upset, manifesting multiple tics. Is there more to this story? Did Cate perhaps hear the dog say the mother had died? Why the need for follow-up rationalizations? Cate speculates, for example, that she may have been projecting her own thoughts onto the dog. She wonders if she herself uttered, "Mother is dead." Nothing remarkable about either version of the story, so why does it trigger agitation?

I focus on the proximate cause for her negative thoughts about the Halloween celebration. She explains that a "work friend" (Morwenna) foisted the party on her, inviting not just herself, but a group of kids to Cate's home for trick-or-treating, with the expectation of entertainment. I suggest that anyone might react negatively to such an imposition. Cate shrugs off that observation (preferring to believe the internal scolding voice?) and claims to see only good intentions on Morwenna's part.

When I ask for more info about the work friend, she shuts down. Hums, zones out for several minutes.

Me: "Where did you go?"

Cate's facial expression suggests confusion, then annoyance, then embarrassment. Is she worried I have witnessed her dissociation? Worried that her worst fears about her mental health might be true?

Cate quickly apologizes for her "rudeness" for tuning out then explains she really doesn't want to talk about Morwenna.

Me: "What _would_ you like to talk about?"

"My psychokinetic experiences. The recent ones."

I assure her we will but add, "Why don't you want to talk about your friend?"

Response: "Is she my friend?"

Me: "You tell me."

Flips braid several times. "Well, she's probably the closest thing I have to a friend."

I wait a few minutes for her to continue.

Cate picks up a throw pillow and plops it on her lap. Pats it. Hums a few seconds. Finally: "It's just that when I'm around Morwenna... When I'm around Morwenna, I often feel like what my mother used to call a 'godhelpus.'"

"Colorful expression. Care to define it?"

More braid twisting and pillow patting. "Oh, you know, what we middle school kids used to call a feeb."

Me: smiling and nodding encouragement.

"Morwenna ... has a certain flair. And people are really drawn to her. No, it's more than that. She has this ... power." Punches pillow. "And when I'm around her, I feel powerless."

"Are you among the people who are drawn to her flair, her power?"

"Well, who wouldn't be?"

"Again, you tell me."

Bites lip, closes eyes briefly. Begins slowly, "I'm not sure. Maybe not? No, I don't think I find Morwenna's power, her flair, all that attractive."

"Does she have other attributes you <u>do</u> find attractive?"

"Well, she can be funny and sarcastic, but it's hard to get around all that flamboyance. Sometimes it comes across as, I dunno, artificial. And that's annoying, you know?"

"So, why do you think you hang out with Morwenna?"

Cate frowns, shrugs, strokes braid, pats pillow, averts eyes.

Me: "What's in it for you to spend time with someone who annoys you and makes you feel powerless?"

"Are you saying I'm a masochist?"

Me, chuckling: "Are you diagnosing yourself?"

Cate punches pillow again. "Oh, c'mon! I'm looking for a straight answer!"

"Me, too. Why hang out with the annoying Morwenna when spending time with her makes you feel bad about yourself?"

Cate, slumping against the sofa back: "Because I haven't got anyone else to hang out with?"

"So, your motive is loneliness?"

"I guess. Or maybe ..." Pauses to twirl braid. "Maybe I just want to look normal. Normal people have friends. And since Morwenna kinda took me under her wing, I look like I have a friend. I look normal."

"How's that working for you?"

Cate, looking frustrated: "Dr. Brown, you're giving me a headache."

"Gee, I didn't know I had so much power. Maybe I have telekinetic gifts, too."

Cate folds arms and looks down. "Now you're making fun of me."

"Just a bit. Have you ever thought about your own power? Where it comes from? How you lose it? How you grow it? How it makes you feel?"

"You mean by ability to move things with my mind?"

My comments on above: Patient seems more comfortable talking about psychokinesis than everyday life. The psychokinetic episodes may scare her, but they please her at some level. Because she feels empowered? Contrast that with the lack of power she feels in her everyday life, i.e., around Morwenna.

At the same time, in our dialogue, Cate exercises adversarial power, shows anger.

Follow-up questions: Is Morwenna a surrogate for the domineering mother? Why does Cate hold on to the internal scolding voice? Anger toward mother redirected against herself? Thus avoiding filial guilt. How common are dissociative episodes? How long do they last? Do they pose a threat to everyday functioning? Discuss meds.

TEN:

BATHROOM INTERFACING

Dull purple swirled around the sink drain. I was glad to be alone in the teacher's lounge bathroom. No adults were around to witness yet another Devine Disaster. That was Mother's way of describing the consequences of my physical and social clumsiness. Once the purple cleared, I filled the basin with warm water, bent awkwardly, and swished the end of my long braid in the water. I managed to grab some paper towels from the dispenser without leaving paint speckles on the counter. As I swathed the wet braid in the towels and squeezed, I mumbled, "You were right, Mother. I am a klutz."

"What's that, hon?"

I whipped around, leaving a purple arc on the sink rim, the floor, the front of my beige sweater.

Smiling, Ruth entered the bathroom, grabbed a handful of paper towels, and mopped up the drops on sink and floor then looked at the splotched sweater. "Now that's a rookie mistake, wearing light-colored clothing for an art lesson. Which one of the little Van Goghs got you?"

"No, it was my fault. One of your third-graders decided her Thanksgiving turkey needed a purple tail-fan and was so delighted with it she waved the dripping artwork at me. In my effort to dodge it, my braid ended up in her paint jar."

"Let's get a little soap on this. Good thing God made tempera paint washable." She squeezed a dollop of liquid soap onto an index finger then rubbed the stains on my upper chest. "Here now, don't squirm," she ordered, chuckling at my blush.

"No, really. It's okay."

"It will be, once I'm done." Ruth grabbed another towel, wet it, and handed it to me. "You sponge off the soap and ... oh for heaven's sake, your hair is still dripping stains! We need reinforcements." She dashed to a locker and extracted a fluffy cotton towel. "Mavis is going through the change, poor thing. A sweat factory. She keeps real towels on hand to mop herself up every few hours." Ruth sniffed the green cotton. "Don't know how clean this is, but..." She wrapped the towel around the wet braid and squeezed it with both hands.

"I don't want to stain Mavis's towel."

"She's got others in that locker." Ruth kept her death grip on the wrapped braid. "I'll take this one home and launder it. Mavis will never know the difference." Releasing my braid, she eyed her work. "There. Only some clear, wet spots on your sweater and they'll dry quick enough. Which one of my third-graders was the culprit?"

As I looked down doubtfully at my sweater, I struggled for the right name. "Gee, I can never get the names straight. I was subbing for the other art teacher. Ms. Carpenter? She's got the flu. This is the first time I've had any of these kids. Little blonde.

She was a princess for Halloween."

"That really narrows it down."

"Wait. I think her name is Lily. Yes. That's it. She kind of looks like a lily. Very pale and delicate."

"Oh, Lily's a sweetheart. Very enthusiastic." Ruth took the wet paper towels from my clenched hand and dumped them in the trash bin. "I understand you're scheduled for a command performance in a few weeks."

"What's that?"

"Don't tell me Heather hasn't mentioned it yet?"

I shook my head warily.

"For heaven's sake, it's a wonder that woman... Well. Fauquier Partners in Service is holding its annual holiday affair. In between Thanksgiving and Christmas. It's where they celebrate this citizen and that for do-gooding. Like volunteer firefighters, EMTs, and people who raised pots of money for some charity or another. And, ta-da! This year, you made the list of honorees." Seeing my puzzled expression, she prodded, "You know, for saving Marcy Boone. No one's called you?"

"Oh, no, no, no." I waggled both palms in protest.

"Now, now. Look at it this way. Heather really wants the publicity. She figures a countywide feel-good moment for the school might pry some extra bucks out of the board of supervisors when they debate the school budget. So, if you agree, she'll be in your debt. And if she's in your debt, you can probably wangle some extra teaching hours."

"But I'd be so uncomfortable. I don't like being the center of attention."

"Oh, hon, you'll be just one of multiple honorees. If I know anything about people—and I assure you I do—most of them will be only too willing to talk up their deeds. You'll spend maybe a minute in the limelight. Some club leader will read a paragraph about how you stopped the speeding truck. He'll shake your hand, give you a certificate. Applause, applause. Then everyone's attention shifts to the next honoree. Easy peasy."

"Sounds awful."

"Hey, you get a free dinner out of it. And probably some kind of gift card for the local Walmart or maybe for a local restaurant. Who doesn't like swag?"

"Swag?"

"See how trendy I am? My daughter taught me that one. She got swag—skin care samples—for attending some promotional lecture at the Warrenton Holiday Inn. She gave me one of the samples. Pretty good stuff for old skin. But I'm still mad at her."

"Why?"

"Joanie, my youngest, won't be coming home for Thanksgiving like she has for the past decade. She's gonna trek to Chicago to visit her fiancé's family. I guess I shouldn't complain, since Joanie and Mark are using the visit to announce their engagement, something I've known about for a month. So, I haven't lost the inside track. But it's a worrying sign, don't you think? I'm starting to lose my baby."

"Just because she's about to start her own family doesn't mean she'll forget where she came from."

"I hope not. But the house will feel so empty. Deborah's brood always alternates Thanksgivings between the grandparents, and this year it's her in-laws' turn. So, it will be just Arnie and me. Which brings me to why I tracked you down—before I got diverted by the purple paint. I know it's awfully late to ask, but I only just heard about Joanie's cancellation, and it got me thinking... Oh, listen to me, what a way to extend an invitation! I'd love to have your company for Thanksgiving, stuff you full of turkey, put some meat on those bones. And just wait till you see the desserts. I take great pride in my baking. And I can guarantee top-shelf libations. As for the company, meh. You'll probably have to listen to some of Arnie's corny anecdotes. He'll be delighted to have a new audience, though. Please say you'll come. I mean, if you don't have any other plans?"

"Well, I'm not sure."

"Oh, silly me. You've probably received a million invites already, haven't you?"

"Well, no, but..."

"But nothing. Say you'll come!"

"It's Hecuba. I can't leave her alone on a holiday."

"Oh, honey, bring that big hound along. I'm planning on

stashing my little Fluffy in the barn anyway. She's such a pest when turkey's roasting. The two dogs can keep each other company. And when we're done with dinner, we'll fix 'em up with some nice turkey treats."

"Gee, I don't know if…"

"Sure you do. The dog will be fine. I won't take no for an answer."

"Umm, I guess so. Okay. Should I bring anything?"

"Just yourself and a big appetite. Come around three, and we can relax with a few drinks before dinner. I'll text you the directions to our farm. Oh, heavens, look at the time! I'd better take a wee fast and get back to my little ones before they trash the place." Ruth disappeared into a stall as I pulled at my sweater front, trying to circulate air through the wet spots. When she emerged again, we exchanged waves and she dashed out, Mavis's towel in one hand.

I continued fanning my damp sweater when the lounge door opened again.

"Whatever are you doing?"

Someone loomed in back of my mirror image: Principal Hayes-O'Meara, stout arms folded over chest.

"HO! No!" I groaned at my gaffe as I turned around. "I mean, oh, no! I must look awfully silly."

"Just a bit." She smirked.

"I got purple tempera on my sweater. Think I got it all out. But now I'm trying to dry the wet spots." I billowed the sweater front in and out.

"Uh-huh. Listen, I need your cooperation on something very important to our little community." Heather walked closer. "We have a valuable opportunity to interface constructively with TPTB, thanks to the incident with the speeding truck and Marcy Boone. Your apparent reluctance to talk to reporters may stem from misplaced modesty, but we absolutely cannot fail to capitalize on the imminent Citizen Star awards."

Heather looked like she was expecting some response, but I had none. Unless I cared to share my dread with her. Even I wasn't that clueless.

"You look like you've never heard of it?" she continued. "It's sponsored by Fauquier Partners in Service. I suppose you've never heard of them, either. Honestly! They're a big deal, Cate. And you're on their list of Stars this year. They want to give you a certificate. A club spokesman tried contacting you multiple times, but for some unknown reason you never returned her call. If she doesn't hear from you in the next day or so, the award will go to one of the semi-finalists.

"Now this may mean nothing to you, but it's of crucial importance to all our stakeholders, and I need you to step up. This is our chance for positive countywide exposure. Maybe for statewide publicity. All of which will maximize funding opportunities. Staffing opportunities, too." Heather emphasized the last point by sliding her right hand forward, in thumbs-up position. "I've shared this insight with Superintendent Marshall, who hopes to increase his leverage in the ongoing budget negotiations with the board of supervisors. The Citizen Star awards could mean serious leverage, Cate."

"Gee, there was a message on my voicemail a while back. I recall something about the Citizen Star, but I thought it was some local newspaper. Didn't listen all the way through. Thought the call was a sales pitch for a new weekly. So, I blocked the number."

Heather squeezed her eyelids and exhaled forcefully. "You blocked...? Well, water under the bridge. I have the name and number of the Fauquier Partner who called you. You absolutely must interface with her, sooner rather than later." She thrust a Post-it note at me. "Do you have your mobile with you? Perhaps you can call her right now?"

"It's in my Jeep." I squinted at the multi-looped scrawl on the note.

Leaning forward, with one hand positioned conspiratorially at the side of her mouth, Heather whispered. "And when I referred to staffing opportunities, I meant increased hours for teaching associates. Associates who help our youngsters blossom artistically."

"Uh-huh." I was still trying to decipher Heather's penmanship.

"You'll interface with that club spokesman as soon as you

get in your car, right?"

"Umm, I may have to charge my phone first."

The principal strained to extract something from the back pocket of her stretch trousers. "Here, mine's fully charged. Make the call. Now."

ELEVEN:

GAUDEAMUS IGITUR

Say what you will about television dumbing down culture. I have learned some useful things even from sitcoms aimed at the lowest common denominator. So, it was liberating to hear the term "stress fest" applied to Thanksgiving and watch all those sitcom families celebrating the holiday by arguing with their relatives, tuning them out, and judging one another. As a little kid, before accumulating sufficient exposure to sitcom tropes about Thanksgiving, I assumed I was to blame for putting the stress in the fest. Because I didn't stir out the lumps in the gravy. Because I didn't pick up Blackie's toys, causing Mother to trip over a squeaky bone as she carried the turkey platter to the table. I never lived down that Devine Disaster, let me tell you.

But according to TV sitcoms, I'm not all that abnormal after all. Thanksgiving is apparently stressful for many families. How would I know? I never celebrated the holiday any place but my childhood home. Joining the Levines for Thanksgiving would be a first for me.

So, I braced myself for stress. But both Ruth and her husband Arnie seemed relaxed. No one cared that the mashed potatoes had some lumps and the white meat was a little dry. The atmosphere was warm and friendly and welcoming.

I stressed through the main course, nonetheless. Mainly

because of Hecuba. I hated cooping her up in a barn with a dog she'd never met. Since Fluffy was about one-tenth the size of my wolfhound, I certainly wasn't concerned for Hecuba's safety. But she's a sensitive soul.

Ruth must have sensed my unease. When no one wanted seconds on the turkey, she announced a relocation to the barn. She stashed the perishables in the fridge. Then she focused on the after-dinner treats, dessert plates, and libations. The task of transporting everything fell to Arnie and me, while Ruth wrapped pieces of turkey in foil. And off we went.

As we approached the closed barn, I stopped briefly to listen for any sounds of canine distress. I heard none. Before Arnie slid open the large barn door, he peered through a little window to one side of the door then motioned to me. "You gotta see this," he whispered.

Inside, I saw a tiny white furball sound asleep between Hecuba's two front legs. The little dog's head was draped over one of my hound's paws. Hecuba was most definitely not asleep. Although her chest was on the ground, her head was raised, and her golden eyes fixed on the exit. When Fluffy snuffled in sleep, Hecuba lowered her nose to investigate. Her expression radiated resignation. Which made me feel guilty, but I couldn't help chuckling a bit. Arnie was chuckling, too.

By the time he slid the heavy door open, Fluffy was hopping in circles on her hind legs and squealing with happy excitement.

Hecuba remained in her alert down-stay. She probably had yet to spot me, because I brought up the rear, dwarfed by Arnie, standing well over six feet.

"Did you think we'd forgotten about you ladies?" Ruth gushed, raising her turkey packet well beyond the reach of the little dog's jumps. "Oh, shush now, you'll get yours. Close the door, will you, Cate?"

As I put my shoulder into the door—ineffectually—I felt a soft poke in my lower back. Of course, it was Hecuba, her world-weariness replaced by an expression of joy. I laughed as she snuffled various parts of me and pretty much forgot about closing the door.

Arnie came to the rescue. "It can be tricky," he explained, pointing to the railing that held the sliding wooden portal.

"I told you, Arnie. That top rail needs oil."

Once the door was closed, we humans extracted our cargo from our respective tote bags: glass goblets, dessert plates, forks, a bottle of wine, a corkscrew, paper napkins, a foil packet containing fruitcake. We deposited everything on an overturned metal trough, standing high enough to frustrate the hopping Fluffy.

"Settle down, there, Fluffmeister." Ruth wagged her finger at the excited dog. "Yes, I know you'd love some of this fruitcake, but it has raisins, and raisins are no-nos. You sit."

To my surprise, the little dog complied. My own dog,

meanwhile, was glued to my side, more interested in me than the food.

As Arnie circled around us to fetch two folding chairs from a far corner, he shook his head admiringly. "Jesus, that's one big dog."

"Park it here, hon," Ruth told me, pointing at a rough wooden bench. "Don't worry. It may look rough, but it would support an elephant. One of Arnie's creations. Ripped the boards himself from an oak he felled years ago. Back when this place was infested with Gypsy moths. Who knew I married a woodsman?"

"Wow!" I exclaimed, patting the bench appreciatively. Hecuba signaled her approval by sniffing the seat before lying next to it.

Reaching for the wine bottle on the trough, Arnie explained, "I have fun playing in the woods, especially since I retired. Later, I'll show you my *shiitake* stash. Got one log left to harvest before the weather gets too nasty."

"You would not believe how good they taste!" Ruth said. "This wonderful earthy flavor. So much better than those limp, slimy things in Giant's produce section. But first things first." She plunked pre-cut slabs of fruitcake on each plate, while Arnie wielded the corkscrew. "Now, I know a lot of folks turn up their noses at fruitcake, but this is different. None of that awful candied stuff here. No ma'am. I use the plumpest dried fruit. And whole Brazil nuts."

Pouring out all the wine into the three goblets and handing

one to me, Arnie added, "Then she soaks the thing in brandy for ages. Watch out it doesn't knock you on your keister, a little thing like you."

"My goodness, Fluffy! Stop prancing. You're gonna trip me." Ruth managed to deliver the dessert plates without falling over the excited dog, shadowing her every step. After resuming her seat, she raised her glass. *"L'chaim! We* couldn't exclude the furry ones entirely. Oh, my, I'd better feed them first." She reached for the second foil-wrapped package.

"Wait! Wait! It's bad luck to interrupt a toast." Arnie raised his wineglass. "Thank you, Lord, for the good food, the good company, and for getting us through another year without too much grief." He waved an encouraging hand toward his wife and me then swallowed a large gulp of Valpolicella Ripasso.

After sipping from her glass, Ruth extracted two slabs of turkey from the foil. Fluffy's hopping resumed. "Can I just toss it to your hound?"

"Umm. It would be better to call her to you. Make her sit. Then stay. Then say..." I mouthed "okay." "When you have a dog this big, enforcing manners is important."

"Come here, Hecuba." The hound complied. "Well, look at that, Arnie, the beastie obeys me. Alrighty. Now both of you, sit! Wow, this is fun, I've never felt so powerful." Ruth picked up the two slabs and suspended them over the sitting dogs. "And now I want you to stay and..."

Fluffy launched herself skyward and snatched one of the slabs. Hecuba remained sitting, while the little dog gnawed at the meat, now between her front paws.

"Look how you embarrass me, Fluffy! Your turn, Hecuba. Okay!" My seated hound raised her head ever so slightly and gently clamped her incisors over the turkey, swallowing it in one gulp.

"That dog whisperer guy got nothing on you, hon." Arnie grinned at his wife.

"I'd happily take the credit, but that honor belongs to our guest here. You're obviously an excellent dog trainer, Cate."

I beamed and marveled at how easily the conversation was flowing. Even from me! The chatter continued well after the last fruitcake crumb disappeared.

"Full darkness has descended," Arnie said suddenly, pointing toward the barn window. I'd better hike up to the house and turn the floodlights on for you gals."

"Good idea, hon." Ruth nodded at her departing husband then turned to me. "And I've got another good idea. I hate to see you drive home in the dark. The roads out your way are so twisty, and we've all had a few drinks. So crash in our guest room. You and Hecuba."

"Oh, no. I couldn't put you out. We'll be fine."

"You'll put me out more if I have to worry about you making it home safely. There's no school tomorrow, and you don't have to go home to tend your dog. She's right here. So there's no reason not to wait until tomorrow, when the sun's shining and you've got a clear head."

"No, really. But before I leave, let me help with the cleanup." I stood up, too abruptly, and—darn it—wobbled slightly.

Ruth waggled an accusatory finger. "See? I've over-served you. It's final. You and the heck-hound are staying. And since you are, we can have a little brandy in our coffees as we sit by the fireplace. Then I'll pour you into bed."

I was nervous about staying over. Not really sure why. Being away from my refuge too long, maybe. Worried I'd wear out my welcome. But I really didn't feel up to the drive in the dark. And it felt so comfortable here. "Well, I guess so. If you're sure I wouldn't be in the way."

"I'm sure. Ah, Arnie's put the lights on, so let's gather up here and head for the house."

As Ruth and I cleaned up in the kitchen, under Hecuba's watchful eyes, Arnie tended to the den fireplace. By the time we all arrived, the hearth was casting a cheerful glow on three rocking chairs, arranged in a semicircle. An antique end table held a coffee-maker, creamer, sugar bowl, mugs, spoon, and brandy bottle.

"Take your pick." Ruth pointed toward the chairs. "They're more comfortable than they look. I scarfed them up at an estate sale years ago. Arnie loves 'em cause they're extra-large."

"Cream or sugar?" he asked, as he poured out the coffee, followed by a dollop of brandy in all three mugs.

"Just a splash of cream for me, thank you."

Ruth retrieved her and my cup and cautiously stepped over the snoring Fluffy to take her seat.

"Mind if I open the window a crack? Ruth and I like to listen for the owls around this time every evening."

I nodded and waited. All three of us sipped our well-laced coffee and listened. The only sound was Fluffy's snoring and the crackling fire.

"Oh, for heaven's sake! They're not going to perform on command," Ruth sputtered.

Arnie raised a staying hand.

After a few minutes, a soft "hoo-hoo-HOO" sounded in the distance. Hecuba tented her ears but remained lying by my chair. A few minutes later, a more sonorous chorus of triple "hoos" filled the den. Nodding, Arnie explained, "That's the great horned guy. He likes to park in the big hickory by the front door. That first one was probably one of our barred owls. Got a bunch of them."

The silence returned. As did Ruth's impatience. "Arnie, you can't expect us to be quiet the rest of the evening."

His resigned nod made me smile. Then came a protracted, tortured scream varying in pitch and intensity. I flinched. Arnie grinned and said, "That will be one of the resident screech…"

Before he could finish, the screech owl's utterance was

drowned out by a new sound. Hecuba, still lying down, slowly pointed her muzzle toward the ceiling and howled … for a full thirty seconds before diminishing. She lowered her head then raised it again to summon forth another mournful wail. Then another. And another. Fluffy, startled awake, joined the chorus with a few higher-pitched howl-lettes of her own.

Arnie and Ruth gazed wide-eyed at my hound, then at me. I shrugged, embarrassed. Finally, Hecuba's wailing stopped, punctuated in a yawn.

"What, in the name of God, was all that about?" Arnie asked.

"Did the owl's screech make her howl?" Ruth asked at the same time.

I shrugged again and reached down to pet my hound's head. "Wolfhounds just howl. More than many other dogs. Sometimes it's to alert to danger, sometimes because they're lonely. But sometimes, they seem to do it to express a joyful connection with nature. I think maybe Hecuba is feeling happy, at peace." My dog turned her yellow eyes on me and blinked. Then she settled her head back on her front paws with a contented sigh.

"Wow!" said the Levines in unison.

Wow, I thought. *Looks like I'll finally have something positive to report at my next session with Dr. Brown.*

Just like Hecuba's attunement with the natural world, I felt at peace, accepted in this warm household. I was glad I was staying overnight. I wanted to stay. Forever.

Twelve:

Dizzying Events

Unfortunately, another event would overshadow the happy report I planned to give to Dr. Brown the next time I saw him.

It all began with the Citizen Star awards ceremony at a Warrenton banquet hall, as I dreaded my time in the limelight. The spinning light-globe overhanging that hall made me light-headed, as I waited to be introduced by the emcee. The next thing I knew, I was jolted back in time.

Just like that, I'm in Russell Hofstadter's physics lab in high school. We're measuring the speed, frequency, and length of ripple-tank waves. The lighting is dizzying since the teacher killed the overhead fluorescents. All those ripples of shallow water, illuminated by tiny halogen bulbs, are casting weird, undulating images on the classroom walls.

I have another reason to feel dizzy, however. The school's star quarterback has just slipped his arm around my waist. No one can see in the darkened lab, but I can feel the warmth of Joe Scanlon's palm resting above my left hip. Then I feel light pressure on my right thigh. It's coming from the denim-clad exterior of Joe's left thigh. His well-muscled thigh.

This is impossible! Girls like me do not stand hip-to-hip with all-star athletes who turn even the prettiest, most popular cheer-leaders into gibbering fools.

Then I notice my bangs fluttering. They're being stirred by warm breath. Breath smelling of Altoid mints and Joe Scanlon.

"So, whaddya say, Devine? You in?" he says, grinning lopsidedly.

I notice his eyes are brown. And warm. And no, they're not mocking me. I try to recall what preceded this question. I was far too preoccupied with our physical contact to focus on his words.

Joe clarifies things: "You wanna be my partner for the sci-ence fair?"

Incredulous, I look up at the ceiling, half expecting a bucket to overturn and dump pig's blood all over me. I look back at Joe. "You want me as your partner?"

"Didn't you hear what Hofstadter said? We gotta pair up for our projects. And I sure don't want to get stuck with someone like Randazzo." He nods toward a beefy boy picking his nose at the far corner of the lab table. "I really need to pass this class. Got a lot better chance with you than with Lamebrain over there."

Okay, this isn't exactly the balcony scene from *Romeo and Juliet*. But it's not some mean-spirited prank, either. Joe wants to benefit from my academic skills. And he's being quite open about that. No shame there.

But why not team up with someone like Billy Chu? He's nothing short of a math and science genius. Sure, I'm an A student in the humanities, but I struggle to get Bs in the sciences. Of course, it might be hard for a boy to ask for help from another boy. But there's at least one science whiz among the female classmates. What about Emma Singh? She's not only brilliant, she's also witty and not bad looking.

Why choose plain, weird old me? Unless he actually does like me, and the science fair project is his way of making an overture. A face-saving way. If I say no, he hasn't been rejected as a potential boyfriend.

I don't say no. Looking into those warm brown eyes, I stutter, "Umm, hmm. O-okay. Sh-sure."

Joe slaps me on the back. Hardly romantic. But it is physical contact. And it's friendly. I can work with friendly.

"Umm, what will we do for our…?" I begin as the fluorescent lights flicker back on. Mr. Hofstadter motions for us to return to our lab stools. As Joe heads for his seat, he smiles and holds a make-believe phone to his ear. I guess we'll work out the details of our new partnership over the phone.

Immediately, I obsess about the details. Why didn't I think to give him my phone number? Will he be able to find my last name in the ginormous Arlington phone book? How many Devines are there in that directory? Should I slip him a note containing my scribbled number? No, no, I could never do that discreetly.

126

A few days pass. Fretful days. Joe calls. Somehow, he has tracked me down. One problem solved. But the bigger problem of what we're going to do together is unsolved. Joe doesn't focus well. Our phone conversation is scattered. Most of it involves his sports schedule.

As the deadline approaches for submitting science fair topics, I realize I'll have to take action. I come up with a possible project: the scientific application of moiré patterns. I suck up the courage to call Joe from home one evening. I fortify myself first by beckoning Blackie to sit by my side on the sofa. He's old and gray and sick from kidney disease by now, but he struggles up beside me.

With one hand holding the phone and the other petting Blackie, I tell Joe my idea. He sounds befuddled. "You mean those big creepy eels?"

"Huh? Oh, you're thinking of morays. No, this has a different spelling. I'm talking about repetitive, overlapping patterns. Mr. Hofstadter talked about them a few weeks ago, how moiré patterns can be used in X-ray imaging and microscopes. It's an old technology that makes anomalies stand out."

"Anomalies?"

"You know, tumors or damaged cells. I don't think we'd have to build a moiré imaging tool. We could just explain the process, with lots of visuals."

"Are you kidding me? That sounds way too hard."

"I'm sure we could find the visuals in the library, maybe even on the Worldwide Web, using the library's computer."

Joe chuckles. "I was right to pick you. I could never come up with something that sounds so rad but doesn't involve that much work. So, you got it covered, then?"

"Well, no. We'll both need to do a lot of research. Study the various applications. Figure out which ones we want to highlight. Collect the visuals. Write up the explanations."

"Jeez, I'm getting a headache already."

"It shouldn't be too hard. We can each study up a bit then pool our ideas. Maybe at the main library?"

Joe groans.

"Well, if not there, maybe we can get together during a study period."

Another groan.

"How about meeting in the cafeteria after class one day?" I suggest.

"After class I hit the gym."

"I thought football season was over."

"I have weight workouts. Gotta stay bulked up. They don't give football scholarships to skinny-ass wimps."

"Oh." I've exhausted my options. This partnership is looking less and less doable. So much for acquiring some social status from hanging out with the high school heartthrob. What's more, I'm also worrying that the silly partnership idea might have unpleasant academic consequences.

"Look," Joe says, "why don't I come over to your house next weekend? I'm free Sunday afternoon. That work for you?"

"Umm. I guess that would work. Maybe around..."

"Great. See ya at three on Sunday." Joe hangs up.

I look at the phone in my hand. I look at Blackie and moan. He chuffs sympathetically. My stomach starts roiling as I wonder just what I've gotten myself into. I don't have the opportunity to obsess about it, not just yet, because Mother is suddenly in front of me.

"You're seventeen years old, Catherine," she says. "You're old enough to know that the hostess is the one to set the time and date. Not the guest. I assume that was your science fair partner? He's using you, dear. He's coming when it's convenient for *him*, with not one thought for *your* convenience. To say nothing of mine. You might have consulted me first. I warned you, Catherine. Never say I didn't warn you.

"What does a boy like that want with you, anyway? From what you've told me, he could have his pick of science partners, of girls. There are only two reasons I can think of why he'd ask you: to pick your brain or pluck your cherry. Catherine, Catherine! Are you so spineless you can't stand up for yourself when someone is using you?"

Tears are very close to erupting from my eyes. Blackie licks my chin then looks at Mother. And growls.

"Is that dog of yours growling at me? Hmph, even the dog has more backbone than you. It will earn him a one-way ticket to the pound if he keeps it up."

I place a protective palm on my spaniel's thin shoulders. "No, that was just a groan. He's been doing that a lot since he got sick."

"Whatever. I had plans for Sunday afternoon, by the way. Not that you asked. A visit with Mrs. Haley. I expected you to come with me. You know the difficulty I have negotiating stairs with this osteoporosis. Well, fine. I'll manage by myself. Somehow. But don't think my absence will give that boy a free hand to do whatever he wants in this house. I don't want the neighbors clucking about you anymore than they already do."

The hurtful words reverberate inside my brain. I want to cry. I want to curl up into a little ball. But then … I want to scream. And I do. I scream out everything I'd overheard one day earlier from two neighbors sitting on their porch as I passed by. The two elderly sisters weren't clucking about me. They were clucking about Mother. About "what a tyrant that mother is."

"Horribly judgmental," one sister said.

"Expects the world to do her bidding," said the other.

"She acts insulted if you say good morning, like you're not good enough to address her."

"And the daughter, poor thing! She'll never have any kind of life unless she gets out of that house, sooner rather than later."

Yes. That entire eavesdropped exchange is coming out of my mouth, at full volume. Every last wounding word, aimed straight at my mother.

When I finish, I take some satisfaction from the redness in Mother's face, from the way she's clutching at her chest.

"How dare you speak to me like that!" she wails, close to tears. "And you said not one word in my defense? How could you betray me so?"

I can't believe this is happening. I can't believe I mouthed off at my mother. I can't believe it when my mother collapses, hitting her head on the hardwood floor, blood trickling from one ear. This isn't the history I remember. This isn't my life. Is it?

THIRTEEN:

FRAGMENTED

Suddenly, I realized Mother wasn't the one trickling. It was me. I looked down in horror as a small puddle of urine formed on the floor. With even more horror, I realized it wasn't the living room floor in my childhood home. It was the floor of a Warrenton hotel, the banquet hall that was the venue for the Citizen Star awards ceremony. There was no Mother. There was no Blackie. Just me…

And about one hundred people, all staring at me. I reeled. The emcee rushed toward me. What was his name? Ah, yes, Chad Baumgartner. Chad rushed forward and took my elbow to steady me.

I felt gratitude. Then I felt nausea. I vomited on his proffered arm. Oozing fluid from two orifices, I dashed to the ladies' room.

Mercifully, it was unoccupied. I ducked inside a stall and mopped myself up with toilet paper. Then I sat down, fully clothed, and tried to piece together what had happened. What on earth had triggered that bizarre trip down memory lane? Except it wasn't all memory, was it? That last part was new: me mouthing off at Mother; her collapsing. What in heaven's name was wrong with me?

I took a few deep breaths. They helped a bit.

The first pieced-together memory: I saw myself entering the hall earlier that evening. I was greeted by Chad, who reminded me of someone, but I was too nervous to figure out who. He ushered me to my seat at a linen-covered table. A table peopled by other Citizen Stars and their plus-ones. I certainly had no appetite for the dinner that preceded the awards ceremony but figured I could have a nibble or two so I'd look normal. My companions exhibited none of my anxiety. There was lots of conversation, but no one seemed to expect anything of me. So, I nodded and smiled at appropriate points. The menu did not stick in my memory, any more than how long dinner lasted.

The next fragment: Someone at my table complained about problems gearing up for his speech.

"Speech?" I asked suddenly.

"Yeah, the five-minute spiel we're all supposed to give."

"Oh, uh-huh. Sure," I remembered saying, as I gulped down the acid now searing the back of my throat.

Ruth was so wrong. I wouldn't just receive some certificate, easy-peasy. I'd actually have to speak—for five whole minutes—in front of one hundred or more people. How had I missed that detail? My public speaking experience was limited to guiding elementary school children through the mechanics of applying tempera to paper.

134

The third resurrected image was of Chad breezing by our table to tell us honorees the order in which we'd be speaking. It was then that I figured out whom he resembled. He had the same wide-set brown eyes, the same large frame, the same lopsided grin as high school all-star Joe Scanlon. As I analyzed the resemblance, Chad asked me if I minded being the last speaker.

Minded? Lord love a duck, no! Maybe a meteor would incinerate all of us before I had to address this crowd.

If a meteor didn't hit me, maybe inspiration would as I waited for my turn at the lectern. Maybe I could pick up some cues from the three speakers preceding me. Maybe they'd be as clumsy as I felt. Maybe expectations would be quite low by the time my turn came.

The next memory consisted of shards from the speeches made by the other honorees, who dashed my frail hope of low expectations. The first "star," a volunteer firefighter, spoke for almost fifteen minutes. His self-deprecating humor kept the audience grinning—when they weren't gasping at his account of jumping from a second-story window while holding a baby swaddled in a wet bath towel.

The second honoree was no less endearing, although I did not absorb one word he spoke or what he did to receive his award. But I had hopes for the third, a twelve-year-old girl who had plunged into the frigid Rapidan River to save a classmate. What tween has public speaking experience or stage presence? Mind you, I wasn't hoping she'd bomb and embarrass herself. I just hoped she'd lower the bar a bit so I wouldn't prove quite so disappointing.

No such luck. She was as articulate as she was brave. She electrified the audience with her wide-eyed descriptions of the icy river, the victim's bluish complexion, and her own anxiety about correctly recalling her CPR lessons as a lifeguard-trainee.

Now the bar was even higher than it had been. Worse, I had yet to come up with any idea of what I would say about the speeding truck and Marcy Boone.

The next memory fragment was the panic flooding my brain as Chad introduced me. As I hyperventilated, trying to avoid fainting or otherwise disgracing myself, only a few words from his speech registered: something about his pride that a fellow Free-Stater numbered among the honorees. I'd lived in Fauquier County long enough to hear the history of the Free State, the area where I—and apparently Chad—lived. Its rolling hills were once notorious for moonshiners, folks who bitterly and violently resisted the arrival of tax collectors following victory in the Revolutionary War. In some eyes, the Free State was an embarrassment. But others saw what Chad saw: a region known for "rugged individualism and resourcefulness."

The final resurrected recollection featured my first minute at the lectern. In a quavering voice, I began: "Well, umm. I'm kinda new to Fauquier County." I paused to clear my throat. "So I don't know if I can take any credit for Free State resourcefulness." I saw the audience members closest to the lectern shift in their seats. Were they bored already? After another cough, I continued, "But maybe it was osmosis." More fidgeting. And not just from the audience, because some muscle in my hip had started twitching, and it was making my skirt quiver. I clutched the microphone with both hands, for support. "I mean, maybe you can kind of, I dunno, absorb something of the local culture, you know? So maybe I did absorb some Free State resourcefulness, and it came in handy at that crosswalk."

Audience members actually smiled. I paused, hoping to figure out my next few words. I turned to Chad, to gauge his reaction. He smiled encouragement. The smile was so like Joe Scanlon's...

As I pondered in that bathroom stall, I could remember nothing about the rest of my speech, assuming it continued. I had absolutely no idea what went on in that banquet hall as my mind trekked back to my senior year in high school.

So, was this an example of the dissociation Dr. Brown had

mentioned? And if it was, I must be in more trouble than I thought.

How much time had passed at that lectern as I relived—and partially rewrote—my seventeenth year? Did I pee my pants immediately after uttering those first few, halfway successful sentences? Did I freeze up at the microphone? Or did I continue talking? I had no clue.

Huddled in that bathroom stall, I visualized Chad's face again. Not the shocked expression after I'd disgraced myself. But the earlier, Scanlonesque smile as I first stood at the lectern. And without planning on it, as I sat on that Warrenton, Virginia, toilet, I lurched back twenty-five years, to Arlington, Virginia. Again.

Joe arrives and slumps into an easy chair. He asks for a Coke. When I return from the kitchen, Coke in hand, he groans, "How long is this gonna take?" He looks at his watch and grumbles, "If I'm late, Sandy's gonna kill me."

"Sandy?" I ask.

"Sandy Reynolds. My girlfriend. She keeps me on a short leash." He chuckles, glugs from the can, burps, then chuckles again.

I take in his pleasing dimples but do not feel pleased. I notice the crookedness of his top incisors. I feel anger. He scheduled a date during the time allotted for our science fair collaboration? Really? But I soldier on, sharing some of my research findings.

Joe interrupts me as I propose how we might divide the

workload. "Enough! I'm getting a headache. Sounds like you got everything taken care of. I'd just screw things up anyway. Why don't you keep handling the research? I can help set up the displays on fair day."

He checks his watch again. "Jeez. Gotta go." He slurps more soda, slopping it onto the side table. Mother's side table.

I notice the tiny puddle. I notice the smug expression on Joe's face as he walks to the door. I watch the nonchalance of his stroll down my street. I see the cavalier way he waves at the blue Mustang waiting for him. Then I glare up at the sky, which suddenly fills with ominous dark blue clouds. Thunderclouds. Highly unusual for March. Suddenly, a lightning bolt rips out of those clouds and makes straight for Joe's head.

Chatter from two women entering the ladies' room jolted my brain back into that Warrenton bathroom stall. I bolted upright, turning around just in time to vomit into the bowl. Once. Twice. Thrice.

What the heck had just happened inside my head? How much of it was the memory of actual events? And how much had I edited? I flushed away the noxious smell and focused on the conversation bouncing between two other stalls. Apparently, the two occupants had not heard my latest eruption. Or didn't care. Their conversation continued without pause.

Unfortunately, they were talking about me. About my earlier

disgrace.

"One of the more interesting ceremonies, wouldn't you say?"

"You got that right. S'ppose it was some food allergy?"

"Since when do food allergies make you piss yourself? Looked like some weird nervous reaction to me. She was terrified when she started her speech."

"Yeah, but she recovered from that wobbly start. Talked for damn near five minutes about what happened with the truck, the kid in the crosswalk. And then boom!"

"Yeah, I know, at first, I thought she'd had a stroke."

"I thought Chad Baumgartner was gonna have a stroke."

Laughter.

"Couldn't have picked a better person to barf all over."

More laughter. Then two flushes. Sounds at the sink. The door opened and closed.

I reached for the latch on the stall door, in hope of making an inconspicuous exit. Halfway out of my hiding place, I saw the door open again.

"*There* you are!" said Morwenna.

Only then did I recall that some school staffers planned to attend the Citizen Star awards ceremony. I hadn't seen Morwenna in the hall before I stepped up to the lectern. Then again, I was too nervous to focus on much. She would not have been my first choice of post-disaster encounters, but things could have been worse.

"I'm glad you're not Principal HO," I said, with genuine relief.

"Oh Goddess, no!" Morwenna laughed. "You don't want to be anywhere near Heather right now. You okay? You gave everyone quite the scare. Suppose you got that flu that's making the rounds?"

"Let's go with that story. It's much better than some humiliating panic attack."

Morwenna flapped a hand. "They'll have something else to gossip about soon enough. Especially with all the heavy drinkers out there. They're just a heartbeat from humiliating themselves." She abruptly raised a finger then dug into her tote bag. "Hey, I picked up your certificate."

"Thanks. I doubt I'll be framing it. No desire to commemorate this evening. Look, can you do me another favor? Can you get my coat from the coatroom? I've got a stain on my skirt. I'd like to make as discreet an exit as possible."

Morwenna circled around me. "I don't see anything. Oh, there it is. Phooey! It's so small no one will notice." She took me by the shoulders and pushed me toward the door. "Best to get it over with. I'll tell them you've got the flu, with a raging fever, and I'm taking you home. The patient needs to lie down, stat. No time for talk. Sound like a plan?"

I nodded, inhaled deeply, and exited the ladies' room, with Morwenna's arm around my shoulders.

Fourteen:

A Rutted Memory Lane

Monday morning came all too quickly. I braced myself for snide comments about Friday evening's disaster. The youngsters straggling across the road avoided eye contact. But that was hardly unusual. An adult with little power over children was often invisible. But I did catch a few sniggers.

Of course. My humiliation would have circulated via the Fauquier County grapevine, especially because some school employees had attended the Citizen Star event. Suddenly, from somewhere in back of me, came the sound of dramatic gagging. The source was Tobey Drinkwater. Egged on by his buddies, he staggered in front of me then clutched his belly with one hand while covering his mouth with the other. As he bent forward, he ejected a rubbery disk through the upper hand. Tobey's gang bellowed approval when the fake vomit splatted onto the pavement. I rolled my eyes. So did several passing girls. They weren't signaling solidarity. They were merely expressing disgust at the hopelessness of boys.

When Marcy Boone walked by, she stared at me and guffawed.

I heard myself mutter, "Shoulda let the little rugrat become roadkill."

I shocked myself, not merely because I'd uttered those nasty words aloud. I knew I didn't mean it, if only because Marcy's death or injury would have devastated that truck driver. He had sent me a touching letter, addressed care of the school. In it, Colby Shifflett thanked me for saving not just one life, but two. He didn't have to deal with the "guilt of hurting a little girl," on top of the rigors of post-stroke rehabilitation. He was expected to make a full recovery, thanks, in part "to your miraculous intervention."

Focused on Shifflett's kind words, I was oblivious to the presence of yet another youngster until I felt a tug on my sleeve. Bracing for more insults, I looked down and saw a conspiratorial smirk.

"'Roadkill,' that's a good one," chuckled Nicu while handing me the plastic puke. "I swiped it when they were busy laughing."

I quickly stuffed it into my safety vest. "Thanks. I think."

The small boy walked a few steps away then turned and said, "Hope you feel better."

I narrowed my eyes briefly, searching for sarcasm in his words. I found none. He was sincere. His kindness nearly triggered yet another outflow of body fluids, tears. I limited my grateful response to a shy nod.

As the last stragglers cleared the crosswalk, Tobey circled back. Stepping right in front of me, he unfurled a supine palm. "Gimme back my property."

"What?"

"I saw that dirty little Gypsy steal my puke and give it to you."

144

I was tired of feeling shame. Now I felt merely weary. I sighed and shook my head. But when Tobey glared at me and thrust his palm close to my face, my fatigue morphed into anger. "So, you're admitting you just littered? Surely you know that's against school rules."

"Huh?" Tobey's palm retreated a few inches.

"More importantly, it's against county ordinances. Why, did you know that the police can arrest people for littering? Golly, I'd hate for your parents to have to bail you out at some filthy police station. There'd probably be a really big fine to pay, too."

"Yeah, like the cops are gonna bother with littering."

"I dunno. It's not up to me. Your litter is evidence now. At very least, I'll have to turn it in to Principal Hayes-O'Meara."

"You just wait till I tell my parents!"

"I imagine the principal will tell your parents herself. That will probably be a painful conversation for your mother to hear. Especially since she's been ... ill so much."

Tobey flinched. He stomped away to join his buddies watching the proceedings from the curb. He turned briefly to flip the bird and shout, "Fuck you!" His friends guffawed their approval. One of them, however, whined, "You lost the puke?" Tobey shoved him roughly to one side and trudged into the school.

Then came another chuckle. Behind me. From an adult larynx.

"You handled that like a real pro, hon," said Ruth.

"Glad to know I can do something right. You heard about my

miserable performance on Friday evening, I suppose?"

"I heard you gave a good speech. Got more than a few chuckles and applause before you became ill."

"Really? All I remember is barfing a few seconds into my speech. And all over Chad."

"That's not what the online edition of the Fauquier Times reported, with a few quotes from each speaker. Yours was self-effacing. You refused to take credit for saving Marcy. You said it's human nature for instinct to kick in, to do the right thing. You said lots of Free-Staters are resourceful. Lots of people, period. Anyone would have reacted the same way, you said. And that was just an excerpt. Sure sounds like you spoke for more than a few seconds."

All I could do was shake my head. "I don't remember any of that."

"Your embarrassment over getting ill probably eclipsed the good stuff. Some people have difficulty focusing on the positive. See only the negative. It'll come back to you once you fully recover. You're looking awfully pale, by the way. You sure you should be at work? When Gabby and Dan got the flu, it took them a good week to get over it. I doubt you kicked it over the weekend. Maybe you should go home. At very least, stay home tomorrow."

"Maybe I will. The weekend was just a blur."

"See? You take care of yourself." Ruth looked at her watch.

"Oh, Lord! I'd better get in there before they tear the classroom apart."

My hand flailed in the direction of the alarm clock. It wasn't easy making contact, because I was buried, head and all, under the bedcovers and had to claw my way out. That bit of calisthenics overtaxed my weary body, and I considered staying right where I was. But a new noise followed the silenced electronic hum. A much more persistent noise: Hecuba launching into a full-throated howl. Then another and another and another.

"Awright, awright, I'm getting there," I protested thickly.

She stopped howling but chuffed impatiently until I made eye contact. Her yellow eyes radiated concern. I assumed she was lobbying for breakfast, but I had no idea what time it was. It didn't help that her head and shoulders were now blocking my view of the alarm clock. I raised my head enough to look around her brindle muzzle and gasped.

"Two o'clock?" I turned toward the window, filled with daylight. "Are you kidding me? Oh, puppy, you must be starving! I'm so sorry."

With effort, I sat up in bed and promptly slammed a palm into my forehead in a futile effort to stop the throbbing in my sinuses. "Lord love a duck! How can it be so late?"

As I gingerly swung my legs over the side of the bed, I was

grateful the back dog door was open. One of the few things I remembered from the previous night was deciding to do that, so I could sleep in—maybe all the way until nine or ten—without straining Hecuba's bladder. I knew I was still suffering the physical and emotional repercussions of the awards ceremony fiasco and figured sleep was the best healer. Yeah, I was taking a calculated risk with the security of my little cottage, but Hecuba is one heck of a security system all by her ginormous self. I also recalled texting Heather late Monday to tell her I was taking sick leave for three days. If I felt better quicker, I'd let her know. I figured that should give me time to heal. To vedge out without any obligations apart from Hecuba. And since this would be my last sick day, well, I'd best cram in as much sleep as possible.

The gratitude for my foresightedness was short-lived. As soon as I stood, I realized sleep hadn't cured me. After all that time prone, my sinuses felt like they were filled with cement. The congestion made me so dizzy I needed to steady myself by leaning one palm on Hecuba's withers. "Sheesh, you'd think I'd been drinking all night. But what the heck *was* I doing?" I hoped my sleep fog would clear soon. I hoped I was not in the throes of yet another blackout.

I braced myself against the walls to make my way first to the bathroom then to the kitchen to feed my hound. Hecuba dogged me every wobbly step of the way. Her tail thumped against my hip as I opened the cabinet containing her kibble.

When I bent forward to fill her bowl, I unleashed a howl of my own. The pain under one eye was intense. The dizzying effort to resume a fully vertical posture unlocked a stream of fluid inside my nose, face, forehead. I dug into my pajamas pocket for a wad of Kleenex while simultaneously staggering to the kitchen table.

I sat down with a thud. Seeing my cellphone and laptop on the table, I figured I should make at least a cursory check for any news that couldn't wait. On my phone were two texts from Heather. The first was a peevish acknowledgement of my sick leave. The second was a group text, alerting staffers to a heating malfunction that would necessitate closing shop on Friday. I could hardly believe my good fortune. I had another day to recover!

My next task was to jog my memory about the previous evening. Perhaps my laptop contained some clues. As I flipped the lid open, my memory cleared a bit. There on the screen was the last article I'd read: the Fauquier Times account of the awards ceremony, including snippets of the speeches. I shook my head.

"Ruth was right. I clearly talked for a lot longer than I realized. Darn, I said that?"

Next, I scrolled through my viewing history. Clearly, I'd been in full research mode the previous evening, regarding Joe Scanlon. But I hadn't gotten very far. I'd tried to download an ancient article from The Washington Post but needed a subscription to access it. In my sleepy state, I must have lacked the energy to pursue the lead, with its alarming implications. The headline read, "Arlington Youth Struck by Lightning." The date was March 15, 1998. If I couldn't get the Post readout, surely I could find the news elsewhere. My hunt began and, within a few minutes, yielded several short accounts from other news sources. They told me "Joseph Scanlon, 18, of Arlington" had indeed been struck by lightning on March 15, 1998. Incredible! That shocking news bore no semblance to my perception of how my senior year in high school played out.

Until reading these reports, I would have sworn that the lightning bolt image was a fantasy, a vengeful indulgence on the part of someone still steamed over Joe's cavalier behavior all those years ago.

I began babbling to myself. "He suffered a brain injury from the lightning strike? And look! There's a quote from Coach Bayliss saying what a tragedy it is to see a promising football career cut short. How can that be? I remember Joe getting a football scholarship to Old Dominion University. Did he have some miraculous recovery?"

I needed to continue my research. If my "fantasy" about Joe and lightning actually happened, what about the other fantasy I indulged in while I was dissociating from the painful events of Friday night? If I reimagined a new reality for Joe Scanlon, what of the fantasy I'd created about Mother?

I logged onto the bereavement page for the funeral home

that handled Mother's death—three years ago, after a heart attack (not something that makes ears bleed) finally claimed her. Bereavement pages remain accessible for a long time. But I found no listing for Helen Devine. Even though I clearly remembered posting her obituary there.

"Has history changed? Did she die years earlier, when I was a senior in high school? That day when I supposedly sassed her, shocking her so much that she fell and hit her head?

I looked for any article mentioning "Helen Devine" in March 1998. I found nothing. I felt relieved. No evidence of that fantasy morphing into reality. Until I realized the Internet offered no evidence of Mother's death in 2019, either.

"But if Mother died decades ago, wouldn't my life be completely different now? I wouldn't have spent a decade taking care of her. Certainly, without that experience, my life would have followed a different path."

I looked around my little cottage. Everything was where it should be. Not that that necessarily meant anything. It was reassuring, nonetheless.

The soggy Kleenex in my hand suggested something bizarre had happened. That river coming out of my nose felt like the typical aftermath of a psychokinetic episode, not the flu or some pedestrian sinus infection. But what physical objects had I moved in the past few days? None. Unless what I moved wasn't physical. What if those recent trips down memory lane, especially the ones coinciding with apparent blackouts, were a form of psychokinesis? What if I had moved time itself?

I shuddered. Then I jumped in my seat. This time, the cause was perfectly ordinary: a knock. As I followed Hecuba's path toward the door, I wondered if whatever awaited me outside was some blowback from Friday night's humiliation. I exhaled relief at the peephole's wide-angle distortion of a familiar, friendly face.

"Wait a minute, Roy! I gotta get decent."

"No rush," came the muffled reply.

I retreated to the bedroom, donned sweats, and returned. Opening the door only halfway, I apologized, "I'd ask you in for some tea, but I don't want you to catch this miserable bug I've got." I pointed to my red nose.

"Don't you worry none. Just wanted to make sure you was okay. That Jeep of yours ain't moved from under that big hemlock for five days now. Figured you got that flu been going round and stayed home from work. But I worried some last night, when I was late heading home, and this cottage, it looked all dark. Couldn't see no lights at all. Didn't want to bother you if you was sleeping, but that worry started eating at me. So, when I finished with the horses today, I said, 'Roy, you get yourself down to that cottage and find out if that little gal needs anything.'"

"That's really sweet. I'm sorry I worried you, but apart from my sinuses, I'm feeling better. Stomach's not so wobbly as it... Wait a minute, five days? It's Thursday, just my third day of sick leave. I

152

had planned to go back to work tomorrow, but it turns out..."

"Mnm, mnm, mnm," Roy interrupted, shaking his head slowly. "Don't know how many kids gonna be going to school on the Lord's Day."

"Tomorrow's Sunday? So, today's Saturday? Not Thursday? Golly, how did that happen?"

"Fever." Roy nodded gravely. "It can play tricks with your head. You think you need to go to the hospital? Or maybe that medical place not too far down this road? I could drive you in my truck."

I tried to contort my lips into a reasonable facsimile of a reassuring smile. "Oh, no. I don't need the urgent care center or the hospital. I guess I've been sleeping so much I just lost track of time."

"Well, that can happen, too. You been eating? Gotta keep up your strength. I'm a-go to the IGA later this afternoon. Want me to pick up some cans of soup for you? Hot soup's good for flu."

This time, my smile was genuine. "Thank you, but no. The pantry's always well-stocked going into winter. I'm good. But that's nice of you to offer."

"If you say so. But you just call out, you need something. I'll probably be back here tomorrow afternoon to check how that Sophie horse is healing. Send up smoke signals. Okay?"

I cocked my head toward Hecuba, sitting calmly by my side.

"I'll send out puppy paws, here. But seriously, I'm okay."

Roy stroked my hound's head. "You keep a close eye on Miss Cate, you hear?"

Hecuba unfurled an extravagantly long tongue, slurping snappily on the recoil. Roy and I chuckled.

"Thanks for checking on me, Roy. I appreciate it."

"You get yourself back inside. Shouldn't-a-kept you talking so long in this cold air. Take care of yourself, now!" He tugged on the visor of his cap.

"Will do. You, too, Roy."

After easing the door shut, I leaned against it and patted my chest. Hecuba stood, prodded my elbow, and softly yodeled concern.

"Am I losing it, puppy? Man, I must have been sicker than I thought."

Was I trying to reassure my dog? Or me? I couldn't shake the feeling that something more than a virus was scrambling my brain. Something involving unintended walks down memory lane, a rutted lane leading to conflicting realities and a decidedly non-linear timeline.

Fifteen:

Brain Fog

The mist was animate, swirling through the moonlit woods like some languorous snake, over, under, and around the brush. More than merely animate, given the seemingly sentient choices as it navigated obstacles. Sometimes it decided to filter *through* a shrub, temporarily disappearing before reforming on the other side. Sometimes the milky wisps hitchhiked on air currents to gain sufficient elevation to curl around my shoulder in a sepulchral greeting. Fog normally unsettles me, because it obscures and distorts reality. But not this time. Maybe because my own reality had been distorted so much lately, I felt right at home.

More than that. I felt protected by the white shroud that rendered my legs invisible from the knees down. The mist felt like a trusted guide, escorting me on a journey of unknown purpose. And before I knew it, the fog guided me to a waystation. Thin wisps that had been moving along with me suddenly swirled upward, circling first my knees then torso, then head, before merging with the denser mist in the woods. I felt like I was supposed to stop at this junction of three wooded pathways. So, I paused, gazing for several minutes at the narrow track coiling through the trees ahead. Next, I swiveled left to scrutinize the second trail. Then I turned right to ponder the third alternative.

Each path seemed to beckon me. But I had no desire to choose any of them. I just wanted to stand where I was and monitor what might come out of the mist—from the front, from the left, from the right. Although alert, I was unafraid of what might materialize. It certainly helped that I had my faithful hound at my side. She had stopped when I stopped. She, too, was curious.

I stroked her head. "Why does this feel so right?"

Hecuba's long nose swiveled toward me. "Because you guard the crossroads. Always have. Always will."

I experienced absolutely no surprise that my dog could talk—and so articulately. Her words validated the comfort I was enjoying at this juncture. Everything felt so familiar, as if I had often taken up this station.

Hecuba just stared as I absorbed these odd feelings. Then I heard these words: "There are always at least three routes to choose from. Always at least three different versions of reality. Sometimes many, many more."

Again, I was utterly unsurprised by a talking dog. I simply nodded, suspecting the words held wisdom.

The moment disintegrated abruptly. The mists that had lazily swirled with soft, yellow innocence fractured into strobes of intense white. My body tingled unpleasantly. For one second, I wondered if I had been struck by lightning. Just like Joe Scanlon.

But it wasn't lightning. It was the high beams of a car jostling down the rutted driveway of an adjacent property, hundreds of yards away. The visual intrusion, magnified by the fog, jolted me out of my dreamy state. The tingling was probably nothing more than fight-or-flight hormones kicking in, raising the hairs on the back of my neck and arms.

The next sensation was cold moisture numbing my toes. Looking down, I saw flannel slippers. *Soaked* flannel slippers. Only then did I realize I wasn't dressed for a hike on a winter's night. I wore a flannel nightgown, with nothing underneath. Shivering, I reached for Hecuba, who nuzzled my waist.

"Thank God you're with me, puppy! Where the heck am I?"

Hecuba yodeled softly then aimed her muzzle upward and to the right. It pointed at the Ashwood family cemetery, recognizable in the moonlight. What on earth was I doing here?

Only one explanation made any sense. Sort of. Sleepwalking. I hadn't done that since I was very small and remembered little about it. Were there rules to sleepwalking? If there were, I had no clue what they might be. But sleepwalking would explain the talking dog, my lack of surprise, and my sense of comfort with what would otherwise be an eerie setting. Dreams—not just mine, I suspect—often distort perception.

That explanation didn't comfort me for long. Do sane adults sleepwalk? Panic washed over me. Rotating in a full circle, I looked for my cottage, not quite sure where it might be, not certain it existed at all. The mist was making it hard to orient myself, but I finally spotted a fuzzy yellow glow. My back porch light.

I began hiking in that direction, with Hecuba padding by my side. The only sounds were my anxious panting and the sucking squeaks from my soggy slippers. After perhaps one hundred feet, the ground fog regathered and completely obscured the porch light, indeed the whole cottage. I gasped then chided myself for thinking my home may have somehow disappeared. Then again, this was a night for strange occurrences. Hecuba loped ahead, as if to guide my way. Before she herself became engulfed by the fog, she turned and chuffed at me. I nodded. "I'm coming, girl."

As I changed out of my fog-dampened nightgown in the safety of my cottage, I marveled that I didn't have full-blown hypothermia. I seemed to be all right physically. My mental health was another matter. My distress intensified when I spotted the date glowing blue on my alarm clock.

"Monday?" I groaned. "What happened to Sunday? Wasn't I just talking to Roy?" I shook my head to clear out the cobwebs. "No, no, no. It was daytime when I chatted with Roy. And now it's …"

Leaning closer to the clock, I gasped. "Five o' clock? Lord love a duck! I have to get up in ninety minutes! I absolutely cannot miss another day of work! What in God's name is going on with me?"

Hecuba hefted herself from her pillow in the corner of the bedroom and moved to the side of the bed. She laid her muzzle over my chest, and I stroked her wiry fur. "I'm okay, I think. Just awfully confused."

I stared at the dark ceiling and willed sleep to come. If it did, maybe everything would make sense come daylight. Or so I hoped.

Morning offered little illumination. Sleep-deprived, I went through the motions of feeding myself and my dog. I started out the door three different times before realizing I'd forgotten something—keys, phone, coat. Taking Hecuba with me would have required far more organization than I could master, so my disappointed hound was left behind.

Despite all the false starts, I arrived at the crosswalk five minutes before the first school bus arrived. My arms were barely able to raise the stop sign. I had the grim thought that if another runaway truck bore down on one of my charges, the kid would be toast. Me, too, most likely.

Both of my art classes were uninspired. I checked my plan book and quickly scotched what I had penciled in for that day's exercise. If I'd been at work for more of the previous week, I would have printed up a bunch of acorn, pinecone, and star stencils then cut them out so the kids could color them and glue then onto cardboard wreaths. In my current state, arming kindergartners and first-graders with scissors—even the blunt-tipped kind—seemed like an accident waiting to happen. For that matter, I wasn't up to the mess of all that glue, either. Fortunately, I had a sizable stash of autumn leaves. I told the kids to pencil outlines of the leaves onto white construction paper then color them in with crayons. When several children protested that they had performed this very task not all that long ago, I told them to come up with fantasy colors this time. Go beyond the burnt oranges and browns and reds. They looked at me like I was insane. I probably was. But several gleefully wielded black and purple and silver crayons until the bell rang.

I often ran errands between my last morning class and my afternoon shift at the crosswalk, but I didn't trust myself to drive more than absolutely necessary in my foggy state. So I retreated to my Jeep, discreetly parked at the far end of the staff lot and thus beyond the range of passersby. From my glove compartment, I extracted a mylar blanket, unfolded the loudly crinkling material, wrapped it around me, locked the doors, and levered my seat as far back as it would go. At the last minute, I remembered to set an alarm on my cellphone. Then I prayed that I would be able to catch two whole hours of naptime—boring, conventional sleep, without any forays into foggy woods, any revising of my personal history, or any tinkering with time.

Some kindly deity must have been watching over me. For a change. My alarm went off as planned. I woke up feeling marginally better. I recalled some dream snippets, none in any way remarkable, and saw no evidence that I had sleepwalked out of my mylar cocoon. Everything seemed normal, or as normal as a two-hour nap in a Jeep can be. I noted nothing more disturbing than bed hair and a bladder in need of emptying. I had enough time to remedy both problems in the staff lounge.

On the way, I bumped into first Ruth then Morwenna. Both made a point of asking if I was all right. So much for my reclaimed sense of normalcy. Ruth scolded me for coming back to work too early. Morwenna teased, "You really shouldn't go on a bender on a school night."

Mercifully, my crosswalk duties were uneventful. As I returned my safety vest and stop sign to my locker, I crossed paths with Heather, who glared at me. Was she still peeved about my sick days? Or was she showing disapproval of my hungover appearance? Great, nothing like being even more out of favor with my boss. And I really couldn't blame her. I wasn't acting very reliable—or sane—these days.

Upon my arrival home, I had more reason to doubt my sanity. I had failed to lock the doors. That security lapse apparently didn't cost me anything. Hecuba wasn't acting distressed, like she'd fended off burglars or vandals in my absence. But she did look a bit out of sorts. Instead of mischievously lobbying for a walk or an early dinner, she sniffed me—appraisingly, cautiously—from head to toe.

"That's it. Even the dog senses something off with me. I need to figure out what's going on. Soon."

I tossed my jacket on the hall coatrack, pulled my cell from my back pocket, and thumbed in Dr. Brown's number. I waited impatiently for the beep after his voicemail message then blurted out, "This is Cate Devine. It's not really an emergency, I guess. But some weird stuff has been going on. Sleepwalking and losing a few hours here and there. I'm just a little anxious about waiting until my next appointment. Maybe you could see me sooner? If you have any openings, that is?" I shook my head over my apologetic tone.

Watching Hecuba exit through the dog panel to take care of business, I felt the phone vibrate, still in my hand. "Dr. Brown? Wow! That was fast. You just had a last-minute cancellation? Terrific. Umm, no, not for you, of course, but for … oh, never mind. Yes, I can be there by four-thirty. No problem. Thank you. So much."

Before I could pocket my phone, Hecuba burst back inside. She pranced around me and whined.

"Yeah, I know. I haven't taken you for a walk or a ride in ages. I'm sorry, but you'll have to be lonely for just a bit longer. I can't take you with me. I really can't. It will be dark soon and cold. You'll get chilled in the car, while I'm in talking to Dr. Brown."

Hecuba chuffed disapproval. The next thing I knew, she bolted back outside and circled my Jeep. She obviously felt she had a better plan. I was already feeling like an unreliable caretaker of my loyal beast, and the thought of abandoning her yet again, even if only for two hours, weighed on me.

"Oh, all right. I guess I can place Daddy's old army blanket on the deck. You should be warm enough curled up there."

Sixteen:

Baby Steps

As I parked outside Dr. Brown's home office, I was surprised to see him walking across the small paved lot with a canvas log carrier in one hand. He raised his free hand in greeting and did a double-take when he saw Hecuba's head protruding from a rear window of my Jeep.

"It's a little chilly in my office today," he called as I climbed out of my car. "So I've got a fire going. You can bring your dog inside if you want. Kinda cold out here."

"Really? Hmm. I guess. She's pretty well behaved."

"Maybe she'll have a calming effect. You sounded upset over the phone." He diverted his eyes to Hecuba dismounting. "Wow! You said she was big."

We all trooped inside. I motioned Hecuba to settle on a braided rug in front of the couch where I sat down. After depositing his load of wood on the hearth, Dr. Brown proffered the back of his hand to my hound's nose. I liked that. She apparently did, too, because she unfurled her tongue and slurped his hand.

"Sounds like you've had an interesting few weeks," Dr. Brown said as he sat in his easy chair.

Where to begin? Weeks ago, when anticipating my next therapy session, I actually looked forward to recounting my happy Thanksgiving experience with Ruth and Arnie. Now, Thanksgiving seemed far, far away. I seemed almost healthy back then. Well, there was no doubt when that changed.

So, I began my session by talking about that horrid awards ceremony. My anxiety. How I blacked out shortly after beginning my speech. I didn't know what else to call it. I told Dr. Brown how I apparently kept right on talking, with no subsequent memory of what I said, while my conscious brain—was that the right term?—hiked back to high school. First to physics lab with Joe Scanlon. Then to my phone conversation with Joe, which Mother overheard. Then to my sassing Mother and her passing out and hitting her head. I told Dr. Brown how that last part, with Mother, didn't happen in reality. At least I didn't think it happened. Then I told him how I came to at the speaker's lectern in the Warrenton banquet hall, peeing on the floor and then throwing up on the emcee.

He listened patiently. Without any sign of alarm. He encouraged me to continue.

So, I told him about hiding out in the bathroom stall in that Warrenton hotel, only to have another trip down memory lane. For all I know, that was another blackout, too, because I had no sense of how much time I spent there. I must have been doing more than reliving old events in that stall, because those events didn't quite play out the way they should have. I told Dr. Brown about remembering the meeting Joe and I had at my childhood home, to talk about our science fair project. How Joe expected me to do all the work. How he'd made a date for that same afternoon. How annoyed I was when he left to meet his girlfriend. How I watched him get hit by a lightning bolt. How that never really happened.

I told him how I came to in that bathroom stall and threw up all over again. I wondered if the vomit was triggered by some kind of psychokinetic episode.

Then I fast-forwarded to my sick days. How awful I felt. How I lost track of time, didn't even know what day it was. How I researched Joe's and Mother's history, and it looked like Joe really had been hit by lightning, and Mother died decades before she actually did.

Finally, I recounted the day's earlier events. How I sleepwalked my way up to the graveyard and heard my dog talk. By the time I finished, I was hyperventilating. I was surprised there was still time left in our session. I looked at my therapist to gauge his reaction.

He said, "Pet your dog."

"What?"

He nodded encouragement, while Hecuba rose to a sitting position and, stooping slightly, draped her head over my knee. Automatically I began stroking her rough fur. "Tell me why I'm doing this?"

"It sounds like even the memories of these events are causing anxiety. So, getting to a calmer place might not only make you more comfortable, but more focused, too. There's no shortage of data establishing how effective just petting a dog can be. It can lower pulse rate and blood pressure, for example. And I've personally found dogs to be wonderfully nonjudgmental. You can tell them anything, and their opinion of you won't change one bit."

I nodded and kept stroking all that unruly fur.

"So, what troubles you most about these events?"

"Hard to decide. There's the lost time. Do you call them blackouts? Or what was that other term? Dissociation?"

"Does it matter what we call them?"

I shrugged. "Then there's the creepy way memory collides with reality. I 'remember' something different from the way things really went. And when I do a little research, the altered memory looks realer than the established memory. Does that mean I'm changing history somehow?"

"Lots of studies have established how unreliable memory can be. Witnesses have been absolutely sure they saw somebody commit some crime, but the evidence proves otherwise. We can certainly explore how some of your memories may have shifted with time and experience. But it would be a much more productive exercise if you started out in a calm frame of mind. That's where medication might help. Especially with the gaps in time. If you're experiencing a lot of stress from a given situation, zoning out of that situation can be a protective reflex. To some extent, that reflex can be healthy. But we don't want it do get out of hand. Medication could relieve the anxiety, so you don't disso-ciate."

"Gee, I hate the idea of more medication, given the heavy-hitting stuff I'm on for RA. Is this something I'd take permanently or just as needed?"

"Right now, I'd recommend a daily regimen."

"I dunno. The idea of adding more chemicals to the soup worries me."

"Sit with the idea for a while. We can always revisit it later. Meanwhile, I'm curious whether your recent experiences have any precedents."

"I don't understand."

"Have you ever zoned out before? And what about sleep-walking? Have you ever experienced that before this morning?"

"I'm not sure. A few times as a kid, after going to bed, I'd be surprised to find myself someplace else. But then suddenly, I'd wake up in my bed, as usual. So maybe I just dreamed about being in that other place. Except…" I paused, struggling for the right words.

The antique mantel clock seemed to tick more loudly than usual.

After a while, Dr. Brown prodded. "Sometimes, we feel a mem-ory before we intellectually retrieve it. Maybe focusing on your emotions as this memory hovers in the background can bring it forward."

Unfortunately, I had no clue what I felt at the moment, apart from frustration at being unable to conjure a fuzzy shadow hovering in the back of my brain. In my effort to concentrate, I fingered one of Hecuba's ears and closed my eyes. When I reopened them, there was Dr. Brown, calmly waiting in his easy chair, a patient smile on his face. How could he be so calm? I certainly wasn't. Not for the first time, I speculated about shrink training. I imagined "Patience 101" classes, involving a professor placing a chocolate truffle on a student's desk and making the psychiatrist-in-training execute the same sit-stay I demand of Hecuba before she gets a treat. The silly image brought a smile to my lips. And, weirdly, that distraction allowed my half-memory to emerge from the shadows.

"I got it!" I almost shouted. What I got was an image of Uncle Henry reading some book in our dimly lit kitchen in Arlington, as I entered the room. In that scene, I poured myself a glass of orange juice and asked him if he wanted a bowl of cereal for breakfast. He laughed and told me it was just past midnight, and I must be sleepwalking. Next thing I knew, I was back in bed. I thought I had dreamed the whole inconsequential scene from my bed. But the next morning, I overheard Uncle Henry chuckling to Mother about how cute it was that I had sleepwalked my way into a breakfast ritual.

"Any other sleepwalking incidents?" Dr. Brown asked.

I shrugged. "How would I know, if I didn't wake up in the midst of sleepwalking? I'd just think it was an ordinary dream."

Dr. Brown smiled. "An astute observation. What about losing chunks of time? Anything like that happen in childhood?"

I splayed my palms in frustration. "All kids daydream, don't they? Me probably more than most. Wasn't like I had a bunch of friends to distract me. So I distracted myself."

"A concrete example would be nice."

The rigors of the day were weighing on me. It would be a struggle to dredge up a worthy example. Besides, I didn't see the point. I hadn't ever "gone elsewhere" until I zoned out of that Warrenton banquet hall.

"Had I?" I was surprised I'd uttered that question aloud.

"Think of something?" my therapist prodded.

I flipped a hand dismissively. "Only how bored I used to get when I was sick as a kid. You know, mandatory bedrest, with no TV to watch, nothing to do. And for a few minutes, I'd visit someplace other than that boring bed. Don't remember any actual place I imagined in those daydreams. That's all they were."

He nodded. "How old were you when you 'visited' away from your sickbed?"

"I dunno. Maybe nine?"

"How did you feel when you zoned out back then?"

"Don't remember. I'm guessing it was better than feeling bored out of my mind in bed."

"So, none of the anxiety you experienced with your recent

episodes of dissociation?"

"I think I'd remember if that were the case. Of course, the way my memory has been playing tricks on me lately, who knows? I mean, in the last two weeks, I've experienced so many different versions of my past. Hard to know what's real and what isn't."

"Earlier you expressed concern that you might be doing more than just misremembering things. You expressed concern that you might be altering history—not just yours, but your mother's and a classmate's—simply by reimagining it."

"Yeah, I know. Sounds crazy. Especially when I hear you say it." I tugged on Hecuba's ear roughly enough for her to chuff at me.

"I've heard crazier."

I frowned. "That's less than encouraging."

Now he was the one to splay his hands. "Look, talk therapy isn't supposed to be a sprint to the finish line. More like a marathon, made up of baby steps. And you've taken some productive ones this afternoon." He paused to glance at his clock. "Before our next session, consider how you'd feel if you were indeed changing reality by reimagining your past. Scared? Empowered? Something else entirely? Also, think about medication. Just to make it easier to explore all these issues without triggering even more stress."

"Or more dissociative episodes?" I asked, shuddering.

"That, too. If you're reluctant at this point to use medication to ease the anxiety that triggers those episodes, or the anxiety involved in exploring troubling memories, you might try some relaxation techniques…"

"You mean … yoga?" I interrupted, a pained expression on my face. "I could never see myself in a yoga class, surrounded by all those buff, spandex-clad women."

He chuckled, "I doubt the average yoga class is quite as buff as what you see on television. But sure, if you were comfortable with yoga, that might help. Just taking a few moments to inhale into your abdomen, with a long exhale, can do a lot, too. Not all that dissimilar to petting your beast there."

I scrabble Hecuba's cowlick. "I'd rather pet a dog."

"Okay, what about taking your dog for regular walks? Exercise releases endorphins that can help you de-stress. Or maybe just set aside fifteen minutes of quiet time every day—in a comfortable, safe environment. With no one else around, no agenda, no music, no gimmicks, no distractions. Just sit and listen to the sound of your breathing."

I shuddered.

"I take it you're not reacting to the dog walk?"

"No. The dog walk sounds fine. But if I sit and listen to my own breathing, my heart will start racing, and my brain will fill up with chores that need doing, worries, self-doubt…"

"That happens all the time in meditation. Folks who do it regularly let the distracting and disturbing thoughts come and go. Just don't focus on them." He paused and chuckled again. "By that deer-in-headlights look on your face, I gather you're not sold on that idea. So, walk your dog more often. That's not gonna work here, of course. But there are some other relaxation techniques we might try at some point."

"Like?"

"Well, there's hypnotherapy. In the calm state of hypnosis, you could access memories without stress. No drugs would be involved, and you'd be very hands-on throughout."

"How on earth would I be hands-on while hypnotized?"

"It's not a nightclub act," he said, shaking his head. "You'd fully participate in the process, examining events you may not be able to remember in your current state of awareness. You'd just be relaxed enough to explore what triggered the memory shutdown. You'd have full recall of what happened under hypnosis. And we wouldn't go too far in any one session, so you'd have the chance to digest the experience."

"That doesn't sound bad. Could we try it today? Right now?"

Dr. Brown cocked his head at the clock. "Our session is almost over. Besides, we don't want to rush the process. Meanwhile, you might consider coming here more frequently than once a month. Most insurance companies operate on a calendar year basis, and here it is December, so you've got latitude with your quota of covered visits." He closed his notepad. "Oh, one more thing. Bring your dog with you to future sessions." He pointed at Hecuba.

174

"Really? Why?"

"You seem more in touch with your emotions when that massive beast is at your side."

"Yeah?"

"Yeah."

Hecuba's golden gaze ping-ponged between Dr. Brown and me. At his last statement, she stared at him, opened her mouth, and panted.

"Is she smiling at me?" he asked.

I bent forward to scan her face. "She is! I think she just decided she trusts you."

"I'm honored. Definitely bring her next time. I'll bring dog treats."

Seventeen:

Lassiter Brown, M.D.
Session Notes, 12 December 2022

Devine, Catherine (Cate). Last session 16 November 2022

Recorded with patient approval. Patient requested earlier session than scheduled (on a monthly basis, at her insistence because of limited insurance coverage) to address possible panic attack during recent public speech, several "blackouts," more delusions about talking dog, sleepwalking and/or other sleep disturbance, perception that she might be changing history by misremembering it.

General observations: Patient very pale, drawn, blue circles under eyes, somewhat lethargic. Reports she had been ill with flu or bad sinus infection. Grooming not up to previous standard: may have slept in her clothes? Hair somewhat out of place. But her powers of articulation still at very high level, although she occasionally struggles to find just the right word. Displays some tics, like tugging on braid and humming, but less so than in previous session. Because she's less intimidated by therapy, after last session? Or because her dog (gigantic wolfhound!) is at her side, at my urging after seeing the dog in her car? (NB: this is same dog she hears "talk.") Petting the dog (well behaved, gentle, calm) seems to ground her (recommend including the animal in future sessions, when possible).

She views as "humiliation" her recent public speaking event (awards ceremony for saving little girl from runaway truck at school crosswalk), even though she apparently gave a competent speech, lasting perhaps 15 minutes. Has no memory of that, apart from opening lines. Focuses instead on "coming to" when she lost bladder control and later vomited in public. (Fixation on the negative, as depression symptom? Combined with difficulty integrating positive experiences).

Patient reports that, while making the speech, her mind wandered back to her senior year in high school. Apparently triggered by physical resemblance between awards emcee and Joe, a high-school classmate (romantic interest?). One of those memories concerns "Mother," who appears yet again as unsympathetic, harsh judge, perpetually focused on Cate's failings. The other involves Joe, her partner in science fair project, portrayed as exploitative (dumping workload on Cate and ditching their planning session to meet with another girl). Patient reports that in the "real" version of both interactions, she failed to stand up for herself. But in the revisited version, she exacted punishment, having deus ex machina elements: Joe got hit by lightning; Mother suffered possible hemorrhagic stroke just because Cate "sassed" her. Grandiose delusions? Any parallel to empowerment derived from "psychokinetic" episodes?

At the same time, she reports guilt over altering Joe's and Mother's history. And vexation that her own history remains unaltered, regardless of how she reacted to unfair treatment from Joe and Mother.

Cate's focus on rearranging memories may be a distraction from the more serious problem of dissociation. No indication (so far) that another personality is taking over during these blackouts. But blackouts, as well as sleepwalking incident, could jeopardize her health (hypothermia, e.g., from sleepwalking in just a nightgown on a damp winter's night) and pose long-term consequences. (NB: Continue urging medication to reduce likelihood of dissociative triggers from anxiety.) Meanwhile, look for childhood trauma that set her on dissociative path.

At my prodding, patient recounts possible early blackouts and sleepwalking incidents, although she is quick to rationalize, dismiss both as daydreaming or normal nighttime dreaming about being in another place. Cites boredom as dissociative trigger. Her affect while making this claim is calm, neutral. Given her high intelligence and creativity (BFA), she may have low threshold for boredom. Explore whether childhood "daydreams" posed any threat to overall functioning.

Re sleepwalking: Does she associate these possible episodes with stressful times? After father's death? Family financial worries? Arguments between parents? Physical illness?

How traumatized was she from father's death at early age, on threshold of sexual maturity? The parent she was closest to? A benign presence? Weak? Physically absent? Need more info.

Mother? Portrayed as non-nurturing, critical, judgmental, domineering. Source of emotional abuse. Any indication of other kinds of abuse? Is emotional abandonment enough to trigger dissociation?

Little mention of other relatives, close contacts, childhood friends, influential teachers, clergymen, neighbors, apart from sparse mention of "Uncle Henry" and two neighbor sisters, apparently sympathetic toward Cate.

When I raise the subject of medication again, patient resists again, worried about combining anxiolytics with the "chemical soup" she's already on (methotrexate, well tolerated, for RA). I suggest possibility of hypnotic regression, as nontraumatic way of accessing memories, sources of trauma. She initially expresses skepticism but acts much more receptive to idea of hypnosis than to medication. I'm troubled that she may see hypnosis as a quick fix, not an ongoing process, concomitant with talk therapy. I remind her that the whole process is a marathon, not a sprint.

She agrees to increase the frequency of sessions, after learning the limited number of psychotherapy visits is calculated on the calendar year. Next session scheduled for ten days.

EIGHTEEN:

HOLIDAY DISPIRIT

I still don't know whether what decked me was the flu or something beyond the scope of modern medicine. But the flu bug was sure going around. Amber Carpenter, Leeds Manor's other "associate" teacher, was the latest casualty. She recovered just fine but learned, too late, that her weakened state was no match for her weekend indulgence in alcohol. Even I knew that Amber was a fixture at Warrenton's bars every weekend. Heather knew, too. The principal was not a happy camper when she strode out to my crosswalk on Monday morning to recruit me to cover for the "probably hungover" Ms. Carpenter. Amber had texted in sick at the last minute, much to Heather's annoyance. Also on short notice, the principal expected me to guide Ms. Carpenter's fourth-graders through their holiday-themed art project that morning.

I wasn't feeling great myself. Not from too much fun, alas. But there was no reason not to pick up the much-needed extra teaching hours, especially since frigid weather dictated against bringing Hecuba to work with me. So, I told the principal I would step up.

She nodded curtly and pressed a folded piece of paper into my palm. In a low voice, she warned, "Just don't let them draw any of these subjects." Without any explanation, she marched across the road and into the school.

I waited to read Heather's list until after the last moppet was on the sidewalk. The long roster of banned themes made me groan. I was grateful Santa Claus was not among the taboos.

On my way to the classroom, I passed a large produce crate on the display table in the main hallway. It crowded out the usual sign-up sheets, event brochures, safety tips, and healthcare propaganda. The crate was squeaking.

When I peered inside. I saw an undulating cloud of black, tan, and white fur. Closer inspection turned up six ridiculously pink noses. In that furry pileup, it was tricky to figure out which feline butt belonged to which feline head. Although not much of a cat person, I cooed to them.

I became so engrossed with the kittens that I didn't realize I was not alone in my admiration until I felt something brush against my right elbow. It was black curly hair, belonging to Nicu Radulescu, now also peering into the crate. "I'm bringing one home," he announced.

"Gee, they look too young to be weaned. Wonder where the mom cat is."

"She got run over. Ms. Della Grazia is taking care of them. Says they'll be ready to go to their new homes by New Year's. I got dibs on the black one with the white chest. Right there." He pointed to the tuxedoed kitten who had been jumping on a tawny tabby before rolling off into instantaneous, drunken slumber.

I laughed, wondering if the cats had alphas like dogs did. "He's adorable. Is it a he?"

"Ms. Della Grazia thinks so. But I don't much care whether it's a boy or a girl. That's the cat I'm gonna get."

"That's the cat you're gonna get if I see a permission slip from one of your parents—before Christmas break, you hear?" said Morwenna, wedging in between Nicu and me. The boy nodded, but his attention was focused on the inside of the crate. He was whispering something in Romany to the sleeping tuxedo.

Rolling her eyes, Morwenna turned to me. "What about you? Want one? Like now? I'm so tired of the constant feedings and mess that I'm entertaining the idea of dumping the whole damn box in the woods."

Nicu's chin rocketed up. "You wouldn't!"

"No, of course, I wouldn't," Morwenna told him, then mouthed "maybe" at me. "Seriously, you want one?"

"Have you met my dog? Hecuba might inhale the whole litter with one gulp. I have no idea how she'd be around cats. Kittens. Don't want to find out."

"Rats! It's hard to find likely suckers as we head into Christmas. Everyone's so busy." She paused to place both hands briefly over Nicu's ears, as he returned his gaze to the squeaking carton. "So, I figured I'd conduct a little psy-ops here. Get the rugrats hooked and have them pester Mummy and Daddy into giving them a furry Christmas present. Or New Year's present. I guess I can't dump them on anyone until they're finally on solid

184

food." She sighed heavily.

"But you were okay dumping one of them on me before then?"

Morwenna snorted and nudged my side. "Sure. I know a patsy when I see one."

Nicu looked up at us. "What's a patsy?"

Morwenna swatted his shoulder. "Off to class, before you're late. Remember, it's the art room this morning."

The boy waved at the kittens then trudged off.

"How'd you end up with these guys?" I asked.

"My idiot neighbor. She rescued them after she saw the car hit mom. She kept them overnight then dumped them on me, saying she's afraid of their cooties. She's preggers."

"Ah, the old toxoplasmosis excuse," I snickered.

"Look at you, being all snarky." Morwenna nudged my ribs again.

The warning bell rang.

"Jeez, we better run," she said as she stepped away from the display table.

"Better take the menagerie with you," I warned. "If you leave them here, God knows what will happen to them."

She nodded. "Yeah, gotta worry about one of our serial killers in training." She slipped her canvas tote bag from her shoulder to mine then hefted the crate. "C'mon. Open the classroom door for me. Goddess knows, none of the little rugrats would get off their butts to help me."

Escorting Morwenna made me late to class. I was relieved and surprised at the quiet inside the art room. Heather had failed to tell me that a student teacher was scheduled to shadow Ms. Carpenter. I knew the shadows were circulating through the school for the entire month of December, but I had yet to work with one. The young woman had things well in hand by the time I arrived. I saw twenty fourth-graders, eyes closed, hands folded on their desktops, apparently zenned out as their mentor guided them through breathing exercises.

"This is how we call in our creativity, boys and girls," crooned the twenty-year-old. Her palms came together in front of her chest as she inhaled loudly. Then she pushed them outward while stertorously exhaling. "In through the nose, out through the mouth. In with creativity, out with all the silly reasons why we think we can't draw."

Amazingly enough, all the kids complied. No way I could have inspired such uniformity of performance. Of course, anyone would find it hard to sell this yoga-like exercise if they thought it as silly as I did. Children can always tell when adults are merely going through the motions. The young woman at the head of the class seemed totally committed, even if she managed to interrupt her sweeping gestures to waggle her fingers at me.

"Are we all ready to show Ms. Devine what wonders we can

paint? Yes? I think we are!"

Many of the kids nodded eagerly. An exception was Nicu who rolled his eyes at me. I couldn't suppress a smirk and winked back at him. Immediately I felt guilty. What business did I have begrudging this student teacher her youthful enthusiasm? I should be glad she had yet to become jaded.

A minute later, the young woman approached me and introduced herself as Sally Slomkowski. "But you can call me Sally," she added, pointing at the blackboard, which was overwhelmed by the huge, chalked letters, "Miss Sally."

I nodded and smiled weakly. "Welcome. Maybe you can pass out the materials. They're in that cabinet."

Miss Sally beamed. As she fetched materials, I told the kids, "Okay, guys, let's draw something cheerful for the holidays. Maybe something showing how your family celebrates."

"I don't know what to paint," whined a towheaded moppet, dragging the heel of her palm across her forehead."

"Well, there's always Santa Claus. Or maybe a snow scene. Umm, or elves? Or..." My brain frantically tried to resurrect the list of taboo themes. Were Christmas trees okay? I thought so but couldn't remember for sure.

Sally interrupted, "How about wreaths with big red bows? Or candy canes! Or menorahs, all lit up! Or a solstice candle decorated with holly and ivy! I know, how about a stack of presents all wrapped up? Oh, there are so many pretty holiday decorations to draw!"

"I want a puppy for Christmas," shouted one red-haired boy. "Can I draw a puppy?"

"Sure, you can draw a puppy, Ethan!"

I was stunned. Sally already knew the kids' names!

"How about a rat? Can I draw a rat? With big sharp teeth?" asked one of the larger boys.

Befuddled, the student teacher looked to me for help. I shrugged and said, "Why not? Just give the rat a big red bow."

Sally and I walked around the workstations to make sure the children had enough drawing utensils, ranging from colored charcoal pencils to glitter pens. As the children dug into their assignment, we fielded questions and complaints like "I forget what a wreath looks like." Sally frequently stopped to exclaim over this and that rendition of Christmas decor. I chuckled appreciatively over the fanged rat, which the large boy was feverishly outlining in dark purple gel-pen. The kid deserved an A for effort. I feigned enthusiasm when one little girl pointed with excitement to her sketch of a wreath, or maybe it was a donut. When I spotted Nicu's work, however, my admiration was genuine. His two elves were remarkably well executed.

"Is that a hammer you're putting in this guy's hand?" I asked. "So he can make toys for Santa's workshop?"

"Not toys," Nicu said without looking up. "Tanks."

"Tanks? Like, battle tanks?"

The boy nodded and kept sketching. "They're at war with

another clan of elves."

"Warring elves?"

"Why should they be any different from us?"

"You got a point, Nicu," I sighed, saddened that someone so young could have such an insight. "So much for sugar plums dancing in your head."

"What are sugar plums?"

"Come to think of it, I don't know. Probably went the way of cookie-baking moms."

"My mom bakes cookies," Nicu looked up, solemnly correcting me.

"Well, I'm glad. But don't be so literal."

He rewarded me with an impish grin before refocusing on his militarized elves.

As Sally and I circled back to the front of the classroom, she whispered to me, "That kid gives me the creeps."

"Really?" I whispered back. "Clearly, you haven't met Tobey Drinkwater."

"What grade is he in?"

"Fifth."

"Oh, I haven't worked with any fifth-graders yet. But that one..." She cocked her head in Nicu's direction. "He's just ... I dunno. My meemaw would say 'fey.'"

Shrugging, I made an effort to mask my annoyance. I wondered what adjective Miss Sally would apply to *me*, if I moved a few colored pencils around with my mind. Oops. There I was having negative, antisocial thoughts again. That realization promptly induced guilt then annoyance, as I internally chided myself for chiding myself.

"Where'd you just go?" Sally asked.

She was staring at me oddly. Had I zoned out for more than a heartbeat?

"Sorry. It's the holidays," I covered. "So much on my to-do list. I was thinking of all the chores waiting at home."

Sally nodded. "Don't I know it! And I still have to cram in a few more teaching practice hours before Christmas break. How did you do it? Back in the day, when you went to college?"

I felt my shoulders stiffen. "I don't have formal teaching certification. My degree was in art, not education."

"A BFA? What are you doing here?"

"Kinda hard to translate a BFA into a job that will keep a roof over your head. For a while, I was selling some of my paintings. In the art shop where I worked 'back in the day.'"

"Yeah? What medium?"

"Oil and acrylic, mostly. Sometimes watercolor, but that's so unforgiving."

"You still paint?"

"Not for five years or more."

"How come?"

The twenty-year-old was unlikely to empathize with my

reasons—like my overall lack of self-confidence, or the often-crip-pling doubts about my talent, or the time-sucking demands of an ailing mother. So, I just shrugged and said, "Life."

Sally shook her head vigorously. "I'm not gonna let anything get in the way of my goals. No ma'am! Nuh-uh!"

I found myself staring at a nearby jar of tempera and won-dering if I could remotely dump it over the student teacher's head. The sight of purple paint trickling down Sally's pert nose might be worth the resulting nosebleed or bladder eruption caused by a psychokinetic tantrum.

Red-headed Ethan interrupted my fantasy by waving his artwork in the air. "Look at my puppy! I wish he was real."

"Why, it's just adorable, Ethan!" Sally responded. "What a good job!"

I nodded supportively, even if the muddy blob on the con-struction paper bore little resemblance to anything canine.

By the time the bell rang, my face was no longer capable of a pleasant expression. But Sally was still filled with cheer and heartily wished the departing students the happiest of holidays. I managed a half-hearted wave in their direction, while stowing the drawing implements and sponging off the high-pressure lam-inate desktops.

"What's got you so bummed out?" Sally asked, after seeing the last child out of the classroom. "Bet it was that Romany kid with the warring elves, huh?"

"What? Oh… No. I guess I was just thinking of those tedious chores awaiting me."

"I hope you knock them off fast so you can enjoy the holidays." She thrust her small hand toward me. "It's been a pleasure working with you. You have yourself a great holiday break!"

I shook her hand and said, "Same here. Merry Christmas."

The young woman giggled. "Don't let Ms. Hayes-O'Meara hear you say that. But don't worry. I won't tell."

She actually skipped out the door. *Skipped!* Lord love a duck!

Nineteen:

The Dread of Dredging

1 felt extravagant seeing Dr. Brown just a few days after my last visit. But he was right about the insurance coverage. I considered it high irony that—on the day of my appointment, at least— I was feeling halfway normal. The downside of improved mental health was less grist for the therapy mill. I hoped to get inspiration during the late afternoon dog walk after work. And sure enough, I realized my angry feelings toward that student teacher probably rated as worthy of exploring. It was decent grist but not too intimidating. Some people, I gather, can blurt out their most embarrassing or frightening experiences in their very first therapy session. Not me. I needed to work up my courage.

Of course, moments after entering Dr. Brown's office and settling Hecuba by the therapy sofa (as I'd come to think of it), I had second thoughts. My interaction with Sally would cast me in a bad light. I'd been unkind and judgmental. And that really wasn't me. Was it?

So, I opened with a diversion. "Can we try that hypnotic regression stuff today?"

"What's the rush?"

Rats! He wasn't gonna let me off the hook. So, I soldiered on after punching the throw pillow I'd positioned over my stomach. Energetically enough that Hecuba briefly raised her muzzle from the carpet. "It would be nice if my hypnotized self could dredge up all the things that trouble and scare me, while I just observe and learn."

"That would be nice, wouldn't it?"

"Doesn't work that way, huh?"

"Doesn't work that way." He chuckled. "So, what is it you're reluctant to dredge up, as you put it?"

"I'm starting to wonder if this whole process I've started—not just therapy, but those weird trips down memory lane where the memories get distorted—might change me into someone I don't recognize. Or like."

"An example would be nice."

I punched the pillow again. "Okay. Well, I didn't much like how judgy and cranky I got with this young student teacher. You know, I even fantasized about seeing if I could consciously initiate a psychokinetic episode to put her in her place. I imagined moving a paint jar and upending it on her."

"And did you move the jar?"

"No, but I enjoyed the fantasy."

"Tell me what bugged you about this student teacher."

Sighing, I recited the most obvious annoyances in the conversation with Sally, and I confessed to feeling jaded around all that youthful enthusiasm.

After a pause, Dr. Brown said, "I might have wanted to toss something at Miss Sally myself."

"Really?"

"Look, none of us is perfect—or supposed to be. It's human to feel annoyance when a twentysomething repeatedly reminds you how much older you are and reacts insensitively to your honest admission that life can get in the way of goals. It's how you channel your annoyance that's important. Sounds like you didn't behave inappropriately, but I'd like to know why that interaction is still troubling you, X days later."

"It wasn't just *that* interaction. Earlier that morning, I was grumpy with Morwenna. She said I was being snarky."

"Were you?"

I explained how she'd tried to fob off a kitten on me and called me a "patsy." I also confessed to feeling judgmental about the woman who dumped the kittens on Morwenna in the first place.

"Sounds like you accurately identified exploitation. Morwenna's effort to coerce you into doing something you didn't want to. The neighbor's successful guilting of Morwenna. Those efforts, like the student teacher's insensitive remarks, triggered anger. Sounds perfectly normal to me.

"But it's not *my* normal. Typically, I'd just ignore such comments. I can't really recall many incidents when I felt anger."

"Really? Hurtful words and actions just roll off your back?"

"Umm, well, not exactly. But I don't show my anger."

"And how's that working for you?" Dr. Brown leaned forward in his easy chair.

I shrugged, defeated.

Still leaning forward, the therapist asked, "Cate, why are you seeing me?"

"So, you can fix me?"

"Wow! I didn't know I was so powerful."

"Okay, okay. I'm here so I can fix myself."

"And wouldn't that presuppose change?"

"But what if I *had* thrown paint at Sally?"

"What if the sky had fallen? That didn't happen either."

"Huh? I don't understand."

"Tell you what. I'm giving you another homework assignment. I want you to recall some negative interaction from your past where you didn't stand up for yourself. Think of ways you might have expressed your anger, disappointment, hurt feelings con-structively. And we'll talk about it next time. Okay?"

"What if I can't think of any constructive ways?"

"What if the sky falls?"

I frowned. "You're being annoying."

"Yes, I am. And you're honestly expressing your annoyance. Keep up the good work."

There was no doubt about which "negative interaction" to choose. I probably should have discussed that incident during my very first session with Dr. Brown, back in 2019. Of course, the confusion following Mother's death was crowding out earlier misery. No, no, that's not true. The shameful incident was always with me somewhere, no matter how far down I stuffed it—proving that hurtful words and actions most definitely do *not* roll off my back.

Dr. Brown was right: What am I doing in therapy if I'm not willing to do the work? And work it would be, not just the effort to figure out how I might have stood up for myself. Just dredging up that memory, to say nothing of sharing the humiliating details with another human being, would be a dreadful effort. Yup, dread. That's what I felt the whole drive home.

Twenty:

Lassiter Brown, M.D.
Session Notes, 21 December 2022

Devine, Cate. Last session 12 December 2022.

Recorded with patient approval. Patient agrees to schedule more than monthly appointments. Main focus this session: anger-inducing interactions with colleagues.

General observation: Cate's appearance healthier than at last appointment. Not as pale. Looks more rested. Grooming standards up to her norm. Usual high level of articulation. At my suggestion, dog is with her, but with less interaction than previously. Frequent tics: twisting braid; punching throw pillow. Some humming. No zoning out. Less anxious than before but more restless. Frustrated with pace of progress? Angry? At whom?

Patient has difficulty recognizing her own angry feelings. (Her own emotions in general?) At one point asserts she might feel anger, but never shows it, as if this were a virtue.

She relates her interaction with a coworker earlier in the week, a young student teacher, Sally, "shadowing" her art class. Reports Sally's ability to control and inspire the children in class. Patient asserts she is incapable of exercising the same degree of authority, inspiration. Implies feeling of impotence, a theme in earlier sessions. Ditto negative self-image.

Cate does NOT appear to envy Sally's enthusiasm during

class. Rolls eyes describing some examples. Perceives of this enthusiasm, at least the degree of enthusiasm, as false? Low tolerance for inauthenticity?

Relates insensitive comments made by Sally, underscoring how much younger she is than Cate and how much more motivated. When Cate admitted that life got in the way of her artistic aspirations, Sally claimed she wouldn't let anything obstruct her goals.

As Cate describes this interaction, she manifests physical agitation, punching the pillow, gesticulating more forcefully, raising her voice, rolling her eyes, frowning, grimacing. Manifestations of anger, but only toward Sally?—or also at herself for failing to express her annoyance at the perceived slights, in real time?

Homework for next session: recall earlier negative interaction when she felt slighted, wounded, angry, belittled—and how she might have stood up for herself or changed the outcome of that interaction for the better. (NB: pay attention to her choice of counterparts for this negative interaction; will Mother come up?)

Cate's only complaint about homework assignment is concern that she might be unable to figure out a remedy. Ties into negative self-image, perception of impotence, incompetence. Apparently has no trouble recalling past incidents that angered her—in contrast to earlier claim that she never gets angry.
Progress?

TWENTY-ONE:

HOMEWORK

There was no way I could put off this homework assignment. If I waited, I'd dither and lose the courage to revisit a very bad point in time. Courage? Not a word I associated with myself, but that's exactly what I needed to summon.

So, after getting home, I fed Hecuba and settled into my recliner with her. "Before I walk down this crooked memory lane, I want you nearby, girl. To ground me. Okay?" I tousled the fur on her head. Hecuba nodded and slurped my hand.

I leaned back in the chair, folded my arms over my chest, closed my eyes, and concentrated hard on an evening early in my sophomore year at James Madison University. It all began with Kimmie. Kimmie of the raccoon eyes from too much mascara, the tight skirts, the perpetual smile, the claim she never met anyone she didn't like. Yeah, especially if the other person had XY chromosomes.

On that particular evening, as I vividly recalled, Kimmie was recruiting girls to accompany her to a "totally rad" frat party. You know, I still don't understand the pack mentality so many girls have when on the prowl for dates. They seem to need to enter the fray as part of some female posse, only to desert the pack at the first sign of male interest. Well, I didn't understand that mentality and had no interest in being part of Kimmie's posse. I politely declined, saying I needed to study.

"C'mon," Kimmie wheedled. "College is more than books," she continued. "It's the social experience, too. When's the last time you had some action?"

Only then did I sense someone in back of Kimmie: Emily, a short, sour-faced girl, snorted derisively.

"Don't be bitchy, Emily," Kimmie chided. "Cate's just a little shy. She loosens up when she gets a drink or two in her."

I groaned inwardly that Kimmie would blab a secret few knew. I had discovered alcohol freshman year. I didn't have the money to indulge often, but I occasionally ventured into the Burg, as my cohorts called downtown Harrisonburg, to patronize the local ABC store. For some unknown reason, no one ever asked me for ID. I was often mistaken as older. Maybe because I was so serious or dressed much more conservatively than my contemporaries. Or maybe the local store was manned by shiftless employees. For whatever reason, I never had any difficulty buying a pint of bourbon. I didn't buy it to score points with my peers. Drinking was a solitary endeavor, with the sole goal of dulling the constant anxiety that plagued me. My peers would never have known about this habit of mine if not for Kimmie.

After trudging through a howling snowstorm to get back to her residence hall one winter evening, Kimmie discovered the dorm's heating system was down. She knocked on my door in search of extra blankets. I felt sorry for her, shivering there in the

204

doorway. I also was feeling the first signs of lightness from alcohol. I offered her a shot to warm herself. Kimmie's eyes widened with admiration. And so began one of the few convivial evenings I would experience at college. Wrapped in afghans, Kimmie and I sipped bourbon and chatted and watched the wind-driven snow assail my windowpanes.

Despite her inability to keep a secret, Kimmie wasn't so bad. Far too different from me to be a friend. But because she was so open about her own life, she was easy to chat with. And she didn't seem to care that I was a social outcast.

After her indiscreet comment about alcohol's beneficial effects on me, Kimmie pointedly mentioned that the party venue would have plenty of booze. My sophomore year had yet to feature the anodyne blessings of bourbon. I'd been too darn broke to buy any. My summer job, cleaning hamster cages at a pet supply store, wasn't as lucrative as hoped, and my textbook expenses were higher than expected. I found myself worrying about splurging on a lousy candy bar. So, when I heard about the free liquor at the Kappa Something or Something Kappa frat house, joining Kimmie's posse suddenly had appeal.

Once we arrived at the party, I immediately regretted my decision. The lighting was so low I was in danger of tripping over unseen furniture. The music volume was excruciating, and what lyrics I could understand featured lots of obscenities. Like a dummy, I complained about the music to my companions. Emily shot back, "Whaddya want? Some cheesy ABBA songs from a million years ago? Jesus!"

My need for alcohol, of any kind, became urgent—to numb me to the chaotic atmosphere and the judgment of my peers. I spotted a bar setup in another room. Kimmie was right about Kappa Something's generosity. I saw a couple of coolers with beer and ice on one table. On another were bottles of wine, vodka, and cheap, blended whiskey, plus stacks of tall, clear plastic cups. I poured myself a modest amount of whiskey. Kimmie grabbed a Miller Lite, and Emily dredged her plastic cup through the ice cooler then filled it with Sly Fox wine.

Now that I had a drink in my hand, all I wanted to do was retreat to some isolated corner. But doing so would certainly madden Emily, maybe annoy Kimmie, too. So I dithered, as usual. Could I pick up some coping cues from my companions? Unlikely. Emily was scowling at her surroundings. And Kimmie wore a dreamy smile as she swayed to the music and scanned the room. In the haze of weed, it was hard to avoid getting jostled by dancers. So I suggested we move to a less crowded spot. Surely that was a reasonable idea?

Not in Emily's playbook. "Don't you know anything?" she groaned. "The idea is to get noticed, not hide in some corner. Oh, fuck me! Look who I'm talking to! Mole-girl!"

I averted my eyes from Emily's sneer and focused, stupidly, on my feet. When I risked looking up again, Kimmie was swirling her bottle and beaming at everyone around her. Emily flipped her hair and licked her lips. But her still-sour expression undercut the provocative intent. What boy would risk approaching her? Just as that thought popped into my head, one boy did indeed approach—to ask Kimmie to dance.

"This party is so lame," huffed Emily, as Kimmie and the boy departed.

I shrugged and took a sip of whiskey. I nearly lost that sip, because I was startled by a tap on my right shoulder. Whipping my head to the right, I saw Emily, rolling her eyes in disgust. The reason for the tap stood at my left shoulder. Grinning, he asked, "Wanna dance?"

"Umm. Gee. I guess so. You mind, Emily?"

Emily rolled her eyes again. "What do I look like? Your mother? Jesus!"

The boy grabbed my free hand and sprinted toward a somewhat less crowded area of the makeshift dance floor.

"What about our drinks?" I asked.

"Let's park 'em on that side table. Don't worry. I'll remember where they are." He grabbed my plastic cup and placed it and his beer bottle on the table. When he returned, he placed my arms around his neck, circled my waist with his hands, and pressed into me as a slow-tempo tune began. I looked downward in hope of mirroring his steps. His shoulders slumped with disappointment. When the slow dance was over, he broke from our desultory hold, raised a palm in farewell, and dashed off in search of a more agreeable partner.

I limply returned his wave then squinted through the stinky haze in search of my whiskey cup. After retrieving it, I spotted an empty armchair, sat down, and focused on my drink.

The next thing I knew, I was waking up, gagging from some awful smell, worse than before. Was I asleep? Did I black out?

My nostrils were overwhelmed by a nauseating blend of alcohol, cannabis, peanut butter, and chemical preservatives. It took a while to identify those different sources. The chemical stink must have been the spill-proof sofa upholstery, since my nose was buried in the fabric. When I tried to put distance between my face and the fabric preservatives, a lightning bolt exploded inside my brain. Bracing the back of my head, I tried again to sit up, to survey my surroundings. Where was I? I saw various undulating sofas, chairs, tables, and candles. I squeezed my eyelids and took several deep breaths. The double vision subsided a bit. Gingerly, I moved my head in a slow arc. I saw a small room containing one sofa, one armchair, and an end table topped by a pillar candle, the only source of illumination. I was the room's only occupant, for now, although I was dimly aware of people in other small rooms. Feeling for my watch, I squinted at the shimmering numbers and finally made out "two o'clock."

"My purse!" I was surprised at the thickness of my voice. I flailed at the sofa cushions. My hands knocked something off the sofa back: a large piece of folded cardboard, bearing crudely scrawled letters. Bringing it closer to my face, I read, "Box Lunch, Free!"

What did that mean? The cardboard reeked of another chemical, vaguely familiar: a Sharpie marker. The smell suddenly triggered a memory of a sour-faced girl smirking and scrawling on cardboard with a pen, before balancing the cardboard on the sofa back.

Both the memory and the Sharpie odor faded. Now the dominant sensory input was the sweet, earthy scent of peanut butter. I raised my upper body a bit more. From this angle, I saw that my feet were bare. My legs, too, apart from something swaddling my knees. Panties.

Shaking, my left hand reached for the panties. As I pulled them up my thighs, my fingertips spasmed from encountering something alien. Something sticky: peanut butter.

I brought my fingertips to my nose and sniffed. And gagged. They were smeared with peanut butter. Traveling down my still-buttoned shirt, my hand hovered nervously over my crotch. And made contact with gobs of peanut butter.

Lurching fully upright, I whimpered at the pain in my head then looked at the mess between my legs. Nausea erupted. I vomited over the side of the sofa. Shaking, I managed to sit up again. With considerable effort, I pulled the panties all the way up and shuddered as the sticky gobs oozed between my labia. I desperately wanted to remove every molecule of peanut butter, but my priority was escaping from this horrid, smelly room.

My first effort to stand failed. Panting, I braced my palms on the seat cushions to try again, but something dug into my backside: my purse, wedged between the seatback cushions. I had no idea how many minutes passed before my uncoordinated hands extricated the small shoulder bag. My fingers dug inside and were rewarded with the feel of wallet and keys. The rush of relief emboldened me to try standing again. This time, I raised my rear end two whole feet off the sofa before falling back again.

"Okay," slurred that heavy voice. I decided to find my clothes before trying again. I groped around the cushions then leaned forward—cautiously, dizzily—to search the floor. My hands recoiled at the feel of vomit. Flying upward, they brushed against the cardboard sign. I picked it up and read it again. This time I understood. With horror, I realized I was the box lunch.

With difficulty, I hung my purse around my neck and willed myself upright. I no longer cared about my shoes or jeans. I had to get out of there. Music was playing, and voices were buzzing from another room. I couldn't let anyone see me like this.I lurched around the sofa and, using the back for support, stumbled toward the door farthest from the music.

Clutching at various pieces of furniture, I reached the doorway. A draft of cold air refreshed me somewhat. Enough to see a hallway leading to an exterior fire door, left ajar beneath a red exit sign, the hallway's only illumination. Bracing first one hand, then the other, against the hallway wall, I made my way outside. And promptly fell off the two steps leading into an alley. I crawled on all fours, until broken glass stabbed my naked knees. I dug my fingertips into the mortar on the exterior brick wall and wobbled upright. Using the wall for support, I finally reached the sidewalk, mercifully empty.

What now? I had no idea how to get to safety.

An approaching car triggered panic, the urge to run. But all I could do was brace myself against an exterior wall as the car pulled up, and the passenger window rolled down.

"You need help, Miss?" called the driver.

Shaking my head, I mumbled something inane about catching the campus bus.

"Don't think the campus bus is still running. I could take you home. You don't look like you can walk too well."

"Noo! Just gonna keep…"

I wobbled along the sidewalk, groping for support from another wall. I managed twenty feet, while the car rolled alongside. Then I stubbed a toe on uneven pavement and fell, crying.

An emergency brake ratcheted. A car door opened. Footsteps approached. Two hands gripped my upper arms and pulled me upright.

"Cate? Cate Devine?" said the owner of those two hands, as he examined my face, visible under a streetlight. His gaze dropped. "Aw, jeez, you're bleeding. Your knees are a mess. And look at your... Who did this? Maybe we should go to the hospital?"

I groaned in protest, with surprising volume. I tried pulling away from his firm grasp, but that was laughably impossible.

"It's okay. It's okay. It's me. Aaron Rappaport. From the old neighborhood in Arlington? Remember?"

Squinting, I saw something familiar about him. The unruly red hair. The thick glasses miniaturizing his blue eyes. The pale complexion. The slight twist to his prominent nose.

"We went to the same schools for a while," he continued. "Before I switched to Thomas Jefferson? Sometimes, we rode the bus together, ate lunch, walked home together. Remember?"

Incongruously, I almost chuckled at the memory of a heavy-set boy complaining how that twist messed up his sinuses. Made him need nasal sprays. Made him even more of a nerd. Yes, yes. I knew him. He was a nerd. A safe nerd. He was...

"Aaron?" I croaked.

He smiled, nodded, and edged me toward his car. He leaned me against the right front fender so he could open the passenger door. Apologizing as he clumsily stuffed me inside, he grabbed my shirt collar to keep my head from colliding with the gearshift. "Sorry," he repeated as his hand grazed my breast to pull out the shoulder harness before engaging the seatbelt.

Once behind the wheel, Aaron said, "I'd feel a lot better if we went to the hospital."

"No! Just a couple. Cuts. On my knees."

"I'm not talking about your knees. You're only half-dressed and you're acting really out of it. Like maybe someone..."

I tried to convince him, convince myself, that I'd just been the target of a stupid joke.

"A joke?" Aaron raised his voice. "Someone did something to your... You reek of peanut butter ... down there."

Tears welled in my eyes. "Why can't I remember? Only one drink. Less."

"Did you leave that drink unattended?"

I didn't understand.

"Did you leave the drink someplace where you couldn't keep an eye on it?"

Now the tears really flowed. I nodded.

"I think you got roofied, Cate."

"Roofied?"

"A guy slips a drug into a girl's drink to make her pass out. So he can ... do stuff to her. Which is why we really should go to a hospital."

"No! No guy."

"Huh?"

"That face! I see a face. A girl. Smirking. Standing over me. On a sofa. Something in her hand. A jar? Uck! It smells. Peanut butter! She's bending ... over me. Laughing. Sticky feeling. Between my legs."

"Jesus!" As Aaron started the engine, he added, "That's really twisted."

At a stoplight, he cleared his throat. "Look, if you won't go to the hospital, I could take you to my apartment. My roommate's gone for the weekend. You could clean up. Take some of my sweatpants. They'll swim on you, but I'll give you a pair with a drawcord, so they'll stay up. Don't know what to do about your shoes, but heavy socks would help? Yeah?"

I nodded. And sniffled gratefully.

"Okay, we got a plan."

There was little talk for the rest of the ride. I leaned my head against the window. Exhausted, I wanted to sleep but was afraid to. I struggled to remember more details of the evening.

At one point, I made Aaron white-knuckle the steering wheel by shouting, "I threw up! On the floor."

"Good. Maybe you didn't get the full dose in your system. Have some water." He took one arm off the wheel and fished around behind his seat. He pulled out a half-empty plastic water bottle. "Here. To flush out the drugs."

Removing the cap and positioning the bottle at my lips was tricky. I took a cautious sip.

Aaron nodded approvingly then frowned. "Why would a *girl* do that? To another girl?

I gulped back more tears. "Doesn't like me."

"You know who it was?"

214

"Emily. I think."

"Where was this sofa you were on?"

I turned my head to look for the scene of my humiliation. With considerable relief, I realized we were far away from it now. "Frat house."

Aaron sighed. "Figures. Didn't anyone try to stop her?"

I shrugged. Then a fuzzy vision came to mind. Several boys were snickering. One said, "Not me. That's just nasty looking." I erupted in tears but continued. "She made a sign. Put it on the sofa. Oh, God!"

"That doesn't sound good. What did the bitch write?"

I choked out the hateful words.

Aaron slapped the steering wheel. "Jesus! What is wrong with people? Did anyone take her up...? Oh, fuck it. That may not be as important as getting this bitch. She needs to be punished."

"Nooo! I can't. Just can't. Couldn't handle it."

Aaron reached over as if to pat my thigh. Realizing it was bare, he paused then went ahead anyway. I felt a warm, firm, re-assuring squeeze just above my bloody left knee. "Maybe things will look better tomorrow."

TWENTY-TWO:

HOME IS WHERE YOUR DOG IS

ecuba launched herself onto my recliner. Because the back was as horizontal as possible, the giant wolfhound fit, but just barely. Straddling me, she looked down with profound concern.

"I'm okay, puppy. Sorry if I worried you. I probably gasped and groaned a few times, huh? That was some trip down memory lane. But that's all it was, just a dark, scary memory."

I reached up to stroke Hecuba's long nose. The dog slumped down on top of me. Draping her muzzle over my throat, she sighed.

"Oof, Hecuba, I can't breathe. You gotta get off. Got more work to do." I pushed my palms against her chest. Reluctantly, she rose and half-slid onto the floor. She settled on the rug beside the chair and yodeled softly until I reached down and petted her head.

"See," I told her, "I just revisited that memory. The way things actually happened. But that's only the first part of my homework. Now I have to figure out what I'd change. This may take a while, so I better open your dog panel. C'mon, girl, go pee."

Hecuba eyed me skeptically. She seemed to be on guard duty, and I was the sheep that needed protecting. In my case, the wolves were all internal. To encourage her I rose and walked toward the door. Finally, she headed in that direction. As she stooped to exit the dog panel, I called, "I need some fortification first. Gonna make some cocoa."

Hecuba returned a few minutes later. Seeing me in the kitchen must have reassured her, because she did a one-eighty and went back outside. Most nights she needed to patrol the back perimeter of the house before she settled down to sleep. I chuckled when I heard a few short, sonorous barks, her way of telling raccoons and foxes and coyotes and possums that they had best keep their distance.

Sipping cocoa in my recliner, I focused on the second part of my homework assignment. How would I change what happened to me back in 1999? Would I be a different person if I'd acted on my first impulse, back when it all started, with Kimmie showing up at my door? Would I be a different person if I'd gone to that humiliating frat party but done something to make Emily pay for what she did to me?

The more I thought about it, the more I wondered if this could be more than a speculative exercise, which surely was what Dr. Brown had in mind. He wasn't telling me I could change my past. He was asking me to learn from it, think of different ways of reacting to it, in the hope that I could employ those techniques when bad things happened in the future.

Which made sense. But wasn't very appealing.

Was Dr. Brown even right that we cannot change our past? Wasn't it possible that I had already changed history? And not just mine. There was some evidence, however inconclusive, that I had altered Joe's and Mother's reality, simply by traveling back in time and fantasizing punishments for both of them. I laughed at that cavalier "time travel" term. I meant it the way people usually do: When we immerse ourselves in memory, we travel back in time. But … is that *all* it was?

I didn't have any proof that my fantasies had indeed summoned a lightning bolt to fry Joe or a brain hemorrhage to kill Mother. But I did have proof of a sort that my actions or thoughts prevented Marcy Boone from ending up as roadkill. Because of me, that runaway truck didn't hit her in the school crosswalk. The explanation other people embraced didn't seem very logical: There was no way I could have run fast enough to intercept the truck and—whether remotely or directly—pull that emergency brake and punch that ignition button. The more I thought about the incident, the surer I was that I had somehow manipulated time in that crosswalk. My time sped up. Or earth-time slowed down. Because of something I did. And since I had already chalked up experiences moving physical objects with my mind—objects like Mother's paperweight or the Osage oranges that tripped Toby Drinkwater—how much more far-fetched was the idea that my mind could somehow move time, too?

My therapist would disagree. But it felt right. It felt like that crosswalk incident was a turning point in my life. Look at all the craziness I'd experienced since then! As if a new power was awakening in me, but I had yet to get it right. If I could just get it right, I could redress all sorts of wrongs. I would start with the frat party humiliation.

Resolutions are all well and good, of course. Implementing them is another matter. I closed my eyes and thought hard about that party. If I could move time to save Marcy Boone, couldn't I move time to save myself from the humiliation of all those years ago? Wasn't I as worthy of rescue as Marcy?

But what exactly had I done to manipulate time enough to get to that truck before the truck got to Marcy? I had focused. Intently. Every single detail in those nanoseconds at the cross-walk. So that's what I would do now.

I remembered the knock on the dorm door in the fall of 1999. I envisioned the scowl on Emily's face and the stringiness of her hair. The bold pinkness of Kimmie's sweater, juxtaposed with the blackness of her tight skirt. I could see the little blob of eyeliner in the outer corner of Kimmie's left eye. My ears pricked at her Tidewater accent, which turned "frat house" into "frat hoose." As I lay on that recliner, my soles absorbed the heavy bass beat from the boombox playing decades ago in the neighboring dorm room. I sneezed as I experienced yet again the clash of perfumes: Kimmie's White Shoulders and Emily's Chloe. My tongue suddenly went dry, craving the sweet, oaken sharpness of bourbon after Kimmie mentioned "free booze" at this "totally rad" party.

220

"No, I can't," I explain. "I have a poli-sci paper due on Monday. Gotta hunker down and write it."

"C'mon, Cate. College is more than books. It's the social experience, too, right?" Kimmie leans in to give me a friendly nudge. "Besides, when's the last time you saw some action?"

Emily, standing behind Kimmie, snorts and eyes me up and down.

My spine tingles with anger. White, hot anger. I feel it and can't suppress it. No, I don't *want* to suppress it. I hear my voice, tight and loud: "None of your goddamned business when I last saw some action! And Emily? Your perpetual scowl is oh, so attractive. Gonna give you mannequin mouth before you hit thirty-five. Not a pretty sight."

I slam the door, savoring the stunned expressions on both girls' faces. From the other side of the door, I hear Emily's comeback: "Cunt!"

That all ya got, bitch?

I don't need to actually say those words. I feel terrific. Powerful. I stood up for myself. I won. So, what now? I lean against the closed door and wait. I'm waiting to see if, having accomplished my mission, I'm transported back to my Fauquier County recliner. Or maybe to a completely different life in the twenty-first century? That possibility scares me. Nor am I looking forward to whatever body fluid will gush forth, as it always has after psychokinetic incidents.

But nothing happens. No transport. No fluid leaks. And my feeling of empowerment vanishes. I'm scared. Am I stranded? How do I get back to my fortysomething self? Panic roils my gut. "Lord love a duck, what do I think I'm doing, playing with time?"

Maybe I need to apply the same focus to my twenty-first century realities as I did to my 1999 dorm room. Desperately, I try to envision Hecuba and my cottage. But panic disrupts my ability to concentrate. Maybe I just need to rest before summoning the proper degree of focus.

I pat my gut to calm its spasms. It feels flaccid, like you'd expect of a middle-aged abdomen. I run to the mirror. The face looking back lacks the taut smoothness of teenage skin. Didn't Kimmie or Emily notice how old I look? Of course, from seventeen on, I was always mistaken for a lot older. Even as a young adult, I looked serious, grave. It probably helps that the forty-two-year-old weighs the same as the nineteen-year-old, that my hair is as dark as it ever was, that I've worn it the same way for decades: long and straight. But it's more than that, I suspect. I've always been invisible to most people. "Mole-girl," as Emily called me. Maybe I'm too invisible for Emily and Kimmie to notice details about my appearance. Or maybe they see what they expect: a nerdy nineteen-year-old desperately needing style. Who knows, maybe I'm seeing what *I* expect to see in the mirror, too.

222

What are the rules? How can I play this game if I don't know what they are?

My pulse rate is soaring. So I sit at my desk and take deep breaths. What was it Dr. Brown said: Breathe into the abdomen? I do. My heart stops thudding. Maybe a distraction would help. Scanning my desk, I zero in on a well-scribbled legal pad, with five pages rolled back over the cardboard. Even with all the cross-outs and lousy penmanship, it's obvious this is a poli-sci paper, probably the one due in three days. For the life of me, I can't remember the subject. I flip the yellow pages forward to read the title: "Mismanaging the Iran Hostage Crisis." Now I re-member. I got an A-minus.

The panic returns as I wonder if I'll have to write this paper all over again. It looks like it's half done, with underlined copies of source material lying to one side. I suppose I could write the rest of the paper if I have to. And maybe I *do*. Who knows how long I'll be stranded here? Who knows the consequences of not submitting this paper? Besides, this is something for which I *do* know the rules.

I settle at my desk and concentrate—not on my wolfhound or my cottage or Leeds Manor Elementary School. Not on all those things I don't know how to get back to. I'm grateful for my temporary situation as a singleton in a double dorm room. My roommate had transferred out of JMU two weeks into the first semester. Eventually, I guess I'll be assigned a new roomie. But for now, I'm alone. I can hole up in this room, without needing to talk to anyone. The dorm is sparsely populated on weekends. So, I should be able to make the odd trek to the hall lavatory without bumping into anyone. Food is another matter. But maybe I'll be long gone before I absolutely need to eat. I hope.

I read my notes and scribble. Read some more. Scribble some more. After the last page, I look at a small clock on my bookcase. It's late morning. Saturday morning. Which should raise all sorts of new concerns. But I'm too tired. I stumble toward my bed and let sleep envelop me.

When I wake up, the room is dimly lit by a streetlamp outside. There are no streetlamps within miles of the Ashwood estate. So, it's a safe bet I'm still in Harrisonburg, still in 1999. I need to pee, but in my groggy state, moving out of that narrow bed proves too daunting. I'll lie here a few more minutes, wake up more fully, and maybe my brain will figure how to get out of this increasingly claustrophobic dorm room.

Inspiration doesn't move me. Voices do. Girls talking rapidly in the hallway. One is crying.

I tiptoe to the door and listen.

"They took her to UVA?"

"Yeah, she was in a coma. Needed more care than the Burg could handle."

"I'd fucking go comatose, too, rather than remember that."

"Oh, stop, Beth!"

224

"How would you feel if you woke up with peanut butter all over your twat?"

"I heard some guy went down on her. Munching all the way. Yuck!"

"Well, that sign did say 'box lunch.' Tee-hee."

"Gross!"

"Gonna be a while before any girl gets near *that* fucking frat house again."

"I just heard! Lacey's in a coma?"

"It was alcohol poisoning."

"Can you imagine drinking that much? Not even *you* could manage that, Cindy."

"Didn't y'all hear? Wasn't alcohol."

"She was on drugs?"

"Not voluntarily. Some kind of sedative got slipped into her drink."

"Rohypnol. They call it the date-rape drug."

"Jesus!"

"Knocks the girl out. Doesn't even realize she's being raped. Usually doesn't remember, either.

"But Lacey got more than knocked out."

"Mixed with alcohol, it can kill you."

"Christ!"

"Bet she woulda died if that guy didn't call nine-one-one."

"One of the frat brothers?"

"I guess. He's also the guy pulled the munching asshole off Lacey."

"I heard some of the other guys tried to stop him from calling an ambulance."

"No! Really?"

"Fucking frat boys!"

"Cops are probably all over that fraternity house now."

"Good!"

"Fuckin' A!"

"They know who did it?"

"Gave her the drug? Or smeared her with peanut butter?"

"Whatever. They're both crimes, aren't they?"

"Oughtta line up all those asshole frat boys and take a good sniff. See who reeks of peanut butter."

"Might not be a frat boy."

"You mean, a townie?"

"I heard it was a girl."

"Oh, get real! What girl would roofie another girl?"

"Well, someone saw a girl with an open jar of peanut butter."

"Did they see her putting it on Lacey?"

"Don't think so."

"That doesn't mean anything then."

"Maybe not. But how many girls at a party have a drink in one hand and peanut butter in the other?"

"So, who's the girl?"

"Dunno. It was pretty dark."

226

"The witness was probably out of his mind drunk anyway."

"I still think it was some douchebag boy."

"Me, too."

"I just heard about Lacey!"

"Yeah, we heard she snorted so much coke she landed in the hospital."

"No! Lacey doesn't do drugs."

"Not willingly."

"Huh?"

"She got roofied."

"Huh?"

"She gonna be okay?"

"Poor Lacey."

As the conversation enters a new loop, with new girls joining in, I ease away from the door. Would they be sympathetic, if they were talking about "mole-girl" Cate Devine? Or would they find a way to blame me? I wonder how long the victim will be defined as "poor Lacey."

Then it hits me. Lacey would probably be just fine if I hadn't slammed the door in Kimmie and Lacey's face. Maybe I was supposed to go to that stupid party, after all? Why, I have no idea. Am I more expendable than poor Lacey?

I gotta get outta here!

All I want is the comfort of my Irish wolfhound. Feeling the rough fur on Hecuba's head would be the best Christmas gift I could get. It's nearly Christmas in 2022. Not late October, like here. Heck, I'd settle for the simple pleasure of watching Roy trudge solidly to the Ashwood barn. Or even the sight of Morwenna winding one of her ridiculously long scarves around her neck. I nearly smile as I recall the feeling of little Nicu tugging at my sleeve to show me something. I can see myself in that baggy, neon-green safety vest. How I long to return to that world.

If only my sinuses would stop pulsing, maybe I could figure out what to do.

"Lord love a duck! Where'd all this blood come from?"

A faucet was dripping. Inside my nose. I heard each droplet. I watched red blobs trickle down my shirt. "Darn! I'm gonna stain my recliner!"

My recliner? I grasped the blood- and snot-smeared arm of the big chair. My recliner! Something that didn't exist in my dorm room. I rubbed the arm to make sure it was real. It was real! I didn't care that I was making more of a mess. I didn't care about anything but the blissful realization that I was back home.

As I gave thanks, I heard a crash. It was Hecuba, bolting through the dog panel. Within seconds, one hundred-ten pounds of wolfhound pounced on my torso. She proceeded to clean up the nosebleed from Hell. As she slurped, I kneaded her coarse fur. "Yes, I'm really home, puppy. Home with you. Thank God!"

TWENTY-THREE:

NORMALCY, THEOLOGY, AND COOKIES

Do you realize what a blessing our electronic devices are? Yes, yes, we waste a lot of time on them, and some folks say they signal the decline of Western civilization. But after that exercise in reshaping my past, all those blue numbers grounded me in my twenty-first century, Fauquier County realities. They told me what day it was: Thursday, December 22, the last day before Christmas break. They told me what time it was: two in the morning.

That last piece of digital information raised some questions. While I was spending more than twelve hours in 1999, only six hours passed in 2022. Did that mean I had slowed time in my Fauquier County reality? Did it mean I accelerated the passage of time in my college reality? I had no clue.

The other question was how on earth would I able to go to work on just four hours sleep. I've never been on a plane, but I suspect the way I felt was very like jet lag. Serious jet lag. I couldn't afford another sick day. And quite frankly, I needed the normalcy of fingerpainting Christmas trees and Santa Clauses. Figuring out just what had happened in my last visit to 1999 could wait. I needed sleep and a clearer head before I had any chance of undoing what I'd apparently done wrong.

My pre-bed rituals were complicated by Hecuba. That

hound would not leave my side—not to pee and not to settle into her usual pillow on the bedroom floor. As soon as I tucked beneath the covers, she leapt onto the bed. I lacked the energy to scold her off. Besides, that large presence sprawled beside me was comforting. And soporific.

When the alarm sounded, Hecuba rose with me, followed me into the bathroom, and lay on the tile floor throughout my shower. She was never more than three feet away as I dressed and fixed breakfast. Clearly, this was a day when my hound would join me at work, at least in the crosswalk. So, off we went. Together.

Nicu was delighted to see her standing guard in the crosswalk. After he scrabbled her ears, he waved a cellphone at me.

"What? I can't see with the sun in my eyes," I complained.

"Lemme brighten the screen." He pressed some button and tried again, raising the phone to my face. "Can you see it now?"

"Your cat?" I asked, squinting and shielding my eyes with one hand. "He's a cutie. What are you gonna call him? I assume you haven't picked him up yet, right?"

Nicu shook his head. "After Christmas break. And he's a she. Gonna call her Percy."

"Unusual name. Especially for a girl. Where'd you get it?"

"The Percy Jackson movies. Kinda old, but I got the DVDs from the library. Cool stuff. See, Percy is a superhero. Then he finds out he's the son of some Greek god. Name begins with a P..." He chewed on his lower lip as he tried to recall the name.

"Poseidon?"

Nicu beamed. "Yup. That's it."

"But this superhero is a boy, right? Why name a female cat after him?"

He sighed wearily, as if I'd just asked the world's dumbest question. "Ms. Della Grazia thought all the black kittens were males. So I made a list of cool names for boy cats. Then the kitten I liked best turned out to be a girl. By then, I'd already decided on 'Percy.' So, I asked my mom if she knew any girls with that name."

"Did she?"

"Not really. But when I told her about the Greek gods in the Percy Jackson movies, she started thinking about this one girl god who had a name that sounded a lot like 'Percy.' So, once she remembered it, I figured I could keep the name."

I tapped my upper lip in thought. "I wonder what goddess your mother had in mind. Can't think of anything close to... Oh, wait! Persephone?"

Nicu nodded. "That sounds like what she said. What did Percy the goddess do?"

"If I remember right, she was queen to Hades, king of the underworld."

"A queen? Cool! And Hades, that's like Hell, right?"

"Sort of. Hades was the guy who ruled the underworld, the place where people went after they died."

"Like a cemetery?"

I didn't have the energy to explain the difference. "Close

enough."

"Awesome name for a black cat."

I nodded halfheartedly.

"Over Christmas break, we gotta buy a bunch of stuff for Percy. You know some pet store where I should go?"

"You'll probably find everything you need at Walmart. You'll need food, and make sure you get kibble for kittens, not adult cats. And a litter box. And litter. Better get some toys, too. And have your mom call a vet about shots."

"Wait, wait!" Nicu's thumbs were working overtime, logging info onto his phone.

"Taking care of a pet is a big responsibility. You up to it?"

Nicu looked up from his device. "I'm up to it." He nodded gravely. "And some day, I'll be up for a big, beautiful dog like this, too."

He hugged Hecuba's neck. She slurped him from chin to forehead. He laughed and palmed off his face.

"Good sign. You're not grossed out by dog slobber."

"Nah, I'm tough. Bye, Hecuba!" He skipped a few steps away then turned and called, "Merry Christmas!"

I smiled and waved. Then I beckoned a few latecomers across the road. My crosswalk chores done, I headed for my Jeep, with Hecuba ambling beside me.

As I opened the back hatch, I caught the wary expression on the wolfhound's face. I guessed she had no intention of leaving my side. So, I resorted to subterfuge. "Ready to go home, girl?" I opened the driver's door and sat inside, with my legs still outside. For added inducement, I dug into my pocket, extracted a dog treat, and tossed it over the back seat onto the deck. Hecuba bolted inside. As she wolfed down the treat, I scurried outside and closed the hatch.

Hecuba howled. Indignantly, piercingly. Then she scratched at a rear window.

"Settle down, puppy! Look, I've gotta pee, gotta dump my stuff in my locker. And get things ready for my ten o'clock class. How about you chill here a few minutes? I'll take you for a walk when I get back."

Hecuba was having none of it. She howled in protest. She scratched at the window.

"Lord love a duck, Hecuba H. Hound." I climbed behind the wheel, and the unruly behavior stopped. "Okay, we'll wait ten minutes. If everyone's in class, we should be able to sneak inside. But you better be on your best behavior."

Fifteen minutes later, we entered the empty bathroom adjoining the empty teacher's lounge. "You sit here, while I make a pit stop. Don't move. Don't make a noise."

Inside the stall, I groaned at the sound of footsteps. Expecting some expression of horror at the massive canine presence, I finished up hastily. When I opened the stall, I saw Ruth sponging off her sleeve while a wagging Hecuba snuffled her back. Ruth's mirror image smiled at me.

234

"Phew! I'm glad it's you. Heather would have a fit if she saw a dog in here."

"What Heather doesn't know won't ruffle her feathers any. Besides, in a few days it will be Christmas Eve. Isn't that when animals get free rein?"

Joining Ruth at the sink, I asked, "Free rein? Oh, you mean the myth about animals conversing on Christmas Eve? How do *you* know about that?"

She dried her hands and placed them on her hips. "I've only been teaching little kids for a million years. I doubt there's a kid-oriented myth I haven't heard."

"Oh. Yeah."

"I'm Jewish. Not deaf, dumb, blind, and stupid."

"Oh, gee, I didn't mean... Sorry."

"Relax. I'm just jerking your chain. I'll have you know I trim a Christmas tree, and I used to leave cookies for Santa. No way my girls were gonna do without all that fun when they were growing up. No way *I* was gonna do without. I love Christmas. I love all the happy holidays. I'd celebrate Diwali if I could just remember when it comes round. I even have a bonfire for Novruz. I just tell Arnie it's time to burn the pile of garden debris."

"Arnie doesn't share your ecumenical spirit?"

"Not so much. But he did spin a prayer wheel when we visited Nepal two summers ago."

"When in Rome?"

"Something like that. It doesn't hurt to cover all the bases, I figure."

"My mother would be shocked. She was big on the first commandment."

Ruth shook her head. "I never could understand why the creator of the universe would feel insecure if little old me wondered occasionally about other gods and religions."

"I wonder, too. Especially when it comes to the multi-god religions that believe in reincarnation. The whole cyclical nature of time, you know?"

"C'mon, let's continue this theological excursion in the next room, where I have a tin of Christmas cookies with your name on them. Along with some *rugelach*. Because, why would you *not* add *rugelach*?"

We laughed and headed for the lounge. Hecuba followed close on our heels.

As Ruth sorted through a large shopping bag containing several cookie tins, I asked "You think there's anything to reincarnation?"

"A few billion people believe in it. As for myself, if there is such a thing, I'm gonna tell whoever that I'm through."

"Huh?"

"I'm old and tired and the thought of starting all over again is not appealing. I mean, would you want to be a teenager all over again?"

"No, but if there's something to be learned from going back to the beginning, well, maybe… I don't know."

"Mind you, I'm no saint. But I've lived a decent life. I think I'm a good person. I've raised two good kids and like to think I've helped a lot of little ones in my classes over the years. How much better am I gonna get in some new life? Who knows? Maybe I'd just screw it up."

"That worries me, too. What if going back to the start … I mean starting all over again, would just make things worse?"

Ruth nodded. "I had a friend in college. Philosophy major. One of his professors threw out a hypothetical. If you could go back in time with a fail-safe opportunity to kill Hitler, before he came to power, would you? Most of the students said, yes, of course. They'd be saving six million Jews and God knows how many million more who died in the war. But my friend? He was skeptical. What if killing Hitler only paved the way for an even worse monster? Would Stalin, without Nazi tanks rolling into the Soviet Union, have become even more lethal? Or what if all those millions saved from the death camps and the bombings and the fighting generated a population explosion, one the planet couldn't handle? Would the competition for scarce re-sources have translated into more wars, more atrocities, more disease, famine, crime, pollution than we have today?"

"I guess we can't foresee the consequences we might un-leash. Or whether we could handle the resulting guilt."

"Well, isn't this just the chirpiest subject as we head into school break? Here, open your tin and have a cookie. Or better yet, a *rugelach*. It won't bring world peace, but it will lighten your spirit for a bit."

Hecuba rose abruptly as I opened the tin. I aimed a warning finger at her as I sampled a sugary Christmas tree. "Mm, you make good cookies. And you're right. This is the best I've felt all day. But darn it, I'm sorry. I didn't get you anything. I've been so out of it lately."

Ruth waved dismissively. "You still look awfully pale, hon." Turning to Hecuba, she added, "You gotta take better care of your mistress. Don't let her overdo it, okay?"

Hecuba looped her long tail cheerfully.

"Hey, talk about feeling spacey," I said. "It only just occurred to me that you're not in your classroom. Aren't you afraid the kids will be climbing the walls?"

"I got ink on my sweater and came in here to wash it off. Got a student teacher shadowing me today. She can handle the kids for a few more minutes."

"I had one of those the other day when I was filling in for Amber."

"Was yours as earnest as mine? Good heavens, was I ever that young and naïve?"

Laughter made me choke briefly on some crumbs. "Mine was a bit trying."

"Yeah? What'd she do?"

238

"Made me feel old and incompetent. Come to think of it, she was more than trying. She was a perky little shit."

Ruth erupted in laughter. "I don't think I've ever heard you use bad language before."

"Oh, golly. I'm sorry. I shouldn't have said that."

"Don't be ridiculous. I cuss plenty myself, even if I have to watch it around here, with all the little ones. Cussing is probably what keeps us from murdering each other. Gotta vent all those negative feelings somehow. I've even been known to toss out the occasional f-bomb. Arnie thinks it's cute, which is a sure sign I'm doing it wrong. It's absolutely maddening when I tell him to eff off, and he just laughs."

Hecuba pricked up her ears and aimed her muzzle at the door.

"Oh, Lord love a duck! Are those footsteps? I better get the dogness out of here."

"Go out the other door," Ruth said. "I'll chat up whoever's coming so you two can make a clean getaway."

Stashing the cookie tin under my arm and picking up Hecuba's leash, I whispered, "I owe you. Thanks for the cookies. And thanks most of all for lifting my spirits. Have a great break!"

"Merry Christmas!" Ruth whispered back.

TWENTY-FOUR:

LIGHTING THE WAY

ecuba was calmer by the time we finished our walk around the Leeds Manor campus. I got her into the car without too much difficulty and promised I'd be back in an hour, after my ten-o'clock class. She protested with just one mournful howl. A long one. But then she settled down. After the morning class, I ate my lunch in the Jeep and shared some sandwich meat with her. By the time I had to leave for my afternoon class, she seemed reassured that I would return. She enjoyed our crosswalk shift, wagging her entire rear end when several children wished her a Merry Christmas. Her enthusiasm put smiles on the kids' faces. Mine, too.

My smile lingered all the way through the errands that needed doing on the route home. But the dimming of the light, as the sun dipped below the hillscape, also dimmed my mood. I shivered as I steered into the dark twists of my long driveway. I did not look forward to trudging in the dark from my parking space to the cottage. Frugality prevented me from turning my porch light on before I left for work. Halfway into the last bend, dominated by giant hemlocks on either side of the driveway, I was surprised to see the darkness receding. Surprised and concerned. Did that glow signal some intrusion?

Hecuba did not share my anxiety. Staring into that glow, she chuffed and wagged her tail. Somewhat reassured, I parked, shut off the engine, and popped the latch for the back hatch. Hecuba exploded outside and romped toward the light. I wasn't convinced her happy mood was justified but figured she was far more capable than I of scaring off any prowler.

With a small flashlight illuminating my way, I caught up with my wolfhound. She was joyously inhaling a small spruce tree, festooned with multicolored lights and ropes of cranberries and popcorn. An extension cord connected the tree to an outlet on the side porch.

"What the...?"

I trained the flashlight beam over every square foot of the cottage's exterior. Nothing amiss. The inside was dark, as it should be. I tested the main door, back door, side door. All locked. Everything was as it should be, except for that riot of colors radiating from the spruce.

After unlocking the front door, I urged Hecuba to patrol each room. When I turned on the hall light, I noticed a business-sized envelope on the floor. It had apparently been shoved under the door. Thready lettering was on the outside: "Miss Cate." In a healthier state of mind, I would have identified the author long before I extracted the envelope's contents.

"Of course! Roy." I patted my chest as I read the message aloud:

Wanted to give you a jump start, since you been

sick and not up to holliday preperations. Hope you dont mind. Will check in on yall tomorrow. Merry Christmas, Roy.

I went onto the side porch to admire the tree and chided myself for constantly whining about what's wrong in my life—when quite a lot was right. I thought of my conversations with Ruth and Nicu, snippets of warmth and fellowship. And now this Christmas gift. What had *I* done lately to make the world a kinder place?

I also thought back to the kindness shown by Aaron Rappaport on that ghastly night, decades earlier. What serendipity that an old childhood friend should turn up years after I'd last seen him—and just when I needed him. He did more than drive me back to safety. He patiently waited as I showered in the bathroom of his tiny apartment. He dug out extra towels, probably the last clean ones he had, so I could follow up with the steaming hot bath I craved. He lent me fleecy sweatpants, a sweatshirt, and heavy wool socks. He made me scrambled eggs and flooded me with tea, in hope of flushing the drugs out of my system. He insisted I catnap into the afternoon, to ensure I was reasonably sound before he took me back to my dorm. And after making his original case, he never pressed me again to get the police involved.

What had I ever done for him? Yeah, I laundered the loaned sweats and returned them with a long letter of gratitude. Over the next few months, we got together for lunch a few times. I commiserated with his failure to win a scholarship to the Massachusetts Institute of Technology straight out of high school and his reluctant enrollment at the much more affordable JMU, much less appealing for a budding tech genius. I expressed awe at the work he'd done the previous summer as an intern at the Naval Research Laboratory outside D.C., even if I understood not one word of his discussion of nanotechnology. I assured him that summer job experience would impress MIT, in his renewed application for admission and financial aid. And somewhat later, I expressed my elation when he produced his acceptance letter, with notification of a full scholarship. But once he transferred to MIT, our connection waned, mainly because of me. Aaron was an unfortunate reminder of what happened in that frat house. After we both graduated from college, his emails stopped altogether. He was understandably busy launching his global software firm. Why on earth would he have any interest in maintaining a link to a girl from another era, an era that had been much less happy and prosperous for him?

Hecuba grew impatient with my wool-gathering. She pranced around the porch and yodeled softly. "Yeah, I know. You're overdue for dinner. And I'm done thinking about what a lousy friend I was." Before heading to the kitchen, I looked once more time at the Christmas lights. To reassure myself they weren't an illusion.

Once both tummies were full, I sat down on the sofa, where I could see that cheerful Christmas apparition. I dreaded the process that lay ahead but feared I'd lose courage if I waited too long. To face my mission, I needed all the illumination I could get. Literally and figuratively. Perhaps sensing my tension, Hecuba jumped on the sofa and sprawled across my lap.

All those memories of Aaron reinforced my will to try one more time to get the past right. "Funny," I told Hecuba as I stroked her head, "but until his hunk of junk showed up outside that Harrisonburg alley, I'd totally forgotten my old middle school buddy was at JMU, too."

I suddenly realized that my semi-reclined position on the sofa was all too similar to the way I was arranged on another sofa twenty-three years earlier. The realization made me queasy. But perhaps the parallel would facilitate the focus apparently needed in order to bend time.

"No!" I said abruptly, causing Hecuba to twitch. I could not go back to that frat house. I could not experience that scene all over again. My goal of righting an old wrong didn't necessarily mean starting from scratch. My first rectification effort focused on events *before* the frat party. But avoiding the frat party only hurt someone else: "poor Lacey." Maybe I should focus on my actions *after* my humiliation. So, there was no need to go back any further than my conversation with Aaron, when he urged me to get the police involved. And that conversation took place shortly after Aaron and I drove away from the frat house.

Focus on the car, Cate.

I reconstructed exactly how rough the engine sounded. I recalled the drumming of my heart as I heard the car approach. I felt the pain from the glass shards digging into my knees, as I crawled along the sidewalk. I could feel the warm blood trickles meeting the cold night air.

It felt so real. And then it *was* real.

And here I am: back on that sidewalk, unable to navigate without bracing against the brick wall. I'm horribly dizzy and confused. And terrified that another predator is about to pop out of the approaching vehicle.

"You need help, Miss?" calls the driver.

I shake my head. "Going home ... gonna catch ... campus bus."

"I don't think the campus bus is still running. I could take you home. You don't look like you can walk too well."

"Noo!" I continue staggering down the sidewalk. I manage about twenty feet as the car rolls alongside. "Owww!" I stub my bare toe on uneven pavement. I lurch forward, but my fall is interrupted by the arrival of a huge dog. A wolfhound. I steady myself on the dog's withers.

"I can take the dog, too, if you promise he won't bite my head off."

"She," I hear myself slur. Somehow, I know this is a female dog.

I know this dog is my friend. "No. No bite."

Maybe it's the dog's presence, but the car no longer scares me. I stop trying to flee.

"Cate? Cate Devine?" the driver asks suddenly.

After introducing himself as an old acquaintance, Aaron Rappaport, the driver gets out and begins the laborious process of folding my ragdoll self into his econobox. The huge dog complicates matters. While making no attempt to bite or even growl, she seems determined to position herself between Aaron and me.

I'm finally in the passenger seat. The wolfhound is mostly in the backseat, but her head looms between the two front seats. Awkwardly looking over the dog's head, Aaron notes for the first time the peanut butter now oozing onto the passenger seat. He asks lots of questions about what happened to me. It takes a while for me to dredge up the details. Those I can remember, anyway. Aaron expresses outrage. Shock. Sympathy.

He says I should go to the hospital. I shake my head vehemently, but he persists. He's pretty sure I got "roofied." Just a tiny amount of blood is all the nurses would need. If it contains the date-rape drug, they'll call the police. "And maybe the cops can track down this pervert girl and any of her accomplices. Make sure they never do this to anyone else."

"Lacey!" I shout. Why, I don't know.

"Is that the girl who drugged you and smeared you with peanut butter?"

"No. Emily."

Aaron doesn't understand. "You can tell everything to the nurses in the hospital. Okay?"

There's some reason why I know I should go to the hospital, talk to the police. But my brain is too drug-addled to know precisely why, except it has something to do with "Lacey."

"Will you go?" Aaron prods.

"Scared."

"I know, but I'll be there. Maybe we can take the dog, too. Tell 'em it's a service dog. Will that make you feel better?"

I nod. A hot tear trickles down my cold right cheek.

"Good girl!" He reaches over to pat my thigh, hesitates, then goes ahead anyway. I feel a warm, firm squeeze just above my bloody left knee. "Things will look better once you get checked out and cleaned up."

The checkup is a nightmare. The nurses banish both Aaron and the dog. Even in my foggy state, I realize they're wondering if Aaron was the source of my distress. As one of them wheels me into an examining room, a burly policeman strides toward Aaron.

"No!" I shout. "Saved me. Aaron ... saved me!" I try to point back toward my savior. The effort is too challenging. I look up at my chauffeur. "Tell the police? Please?"

"We'll let them know sweetie," the nurse says. "Let's worry about you first, okay?"

In the examining room, she asks dozens of questions. Then:

"We're gonna help you up on that table and see what's going on. I'm Nancy, by the way. I'll be with you the whole time. Let's get you into a gown first, okay?"

I protest feebly as Nancy starts unbuttoning my shirt.

"Gonna put your clothes in a bag. We won't lose anything. I promise. And I've got a nice, clean gown here that will cover you up."

"No. Dirty."

"Nancy holds up the gown. "It's just out of the laundry. See?"

I shake my head. "*I'm* dirty. Will get it dirty."

Nancy laughs. "That's why God invented washing machines, sweetie. We want to see what's going on down there. After that, we'll help you clean up."

A minute later, I jump as a warm hand gently pats my (now gowned) shoulder.

"I'm Dr. Mishra," the hand's owner says. "I'll be examining you. Can you tell me your name?"

I look at Dr. Mishra: a tiny woman, with a long gray ponytail. Not intimidating, but still... Why am I doing this? I shoot a panicked glance at Nancy.

"Dr. Mishra's good people. And I'm staying right here."

I nod and let Nancy help me up onto the table. A lightning exchange follows, between her and the doctor. Words fly over me: tox screen, altered, contusions left patella, no bruising on thighs, vulva, peanut butter.

A rubber band girds my left bicep as something sharp pokes into the crook of that arm. With a harsh snap, the elastic disappears, replaced by a black cuff that gets tighter. A black clothespin imprisons the tip of my left index finger. Someone's apparently offering explanations. Hands grasp my ankles and position my feet in cold, metal stirrups.

"Okay, Cate. Can you scooch your butt down a bit? Ever had a pelvic before?"

"A what?"

"We need to look at your pelvic area. See what's going on. You ever had a pelvic exam?"

I shake my head and whimper.

"It won't hurt. Won't take long."

It *does* hurt. And it takes forever or feels like it, anyway.

Time passes. How much time I have no idea. Next thing I know, I'm in a different cubicle, cordoned off by a white curtain. Light is bouncing in from somewhere outside. The rising sun? I feel for my watch but find only a plastic bracelet reading "Devine, Catherine," followed by numbers I'm too weary to parse. My other arm is hooked up to an IV bag.

"Your watch is in the plastic bag beside this chair," says a male voice nearby.

Turning in that direction, I recognize Aaron. "You're here?"

"Where else am I gonna be?" he shrugs and grins. "It's seven a.m., in case you're wondering."

250

"I'm in the hospital? Still?"

He nods. "In something like a recovery room. They cleaned you up and pumped fluids into you. To flush out the drugs. And yeah, you were drugged with Rohypnol. They figured you could sleep it off here. When you feel okay, I can take you home. There's a detective just itching to talk to you, too. I told him everything you told me, after his henchman, some big scary cop, figured out I wasn't Jack the Ripper. But the detective needs to hear everything from you, so he can go after the creep who did this. Oh, you're fine, by the way. You already sound halfway normal, too."

"Hecuba?" I have no idea how, but I know that's the big hound's name.

"That's the dog, right? She's at my apartment. I went there to pick up some sweats for you to wear back to the dorm. I took her for a short walk so she could pee. She howled when I left the apartment. Not a happy camper being separated from you. I gather she was not inside that frat house with you? Otherwise, the peanut butter pervert would be lying in a pool of blood."

"No. She was outside." I assume.

"Poor dog's had a rough night. But not as rough as yours."

I manage a smile. "Doesn't look like you've had a great time, either. Thank you for hanging around."

Aaron shrugs again. "Like I said, where..."

"Miss Devine?" interrupts a voice on the other side of the curtain. "It's Detective Kruger. I spoke with your friend earlier. Okay if I come in?"

"Okay."

Aaron rises so the policeman can sit in the cubicle's only chair. After taking ownership of it, Kruger announces, "The good news, as you've probably heard, is there was no rape. But you were drugged, and that counts as assault. And the business with the peanut butter counts as sexual battery. We want to get the perp. You saw a young woman. Someone you know?"

I regurgitate everything I can remember. I'm relieved at how lucid I sound.

"I'm hoping more of your memory will return. The docs don't know whether that will happen. Gotta be honest with you. We have a less than solid case against this Emily Denmark." He pulls his glasses down his nose to examine his notebook. "Because you were under the influence, your testimony isn't all that reliable. I know, I know. It's ironic that the drug this chick gave you could end up protecting her. But I'll see what I can ferret out from other kids at that party. At very least, I'll chat with little Miss Emily and scare the shit out of her. I'll also need a formal statement from you, young man," he adds, turning to Aaron. "You can testify to Miss Devine's condition coming out of that frat house. And if this comes to trial, you may need to appear as a witness. You okay with that?"

Aaron pauses. "Would that be in the next two months?"

"I doubt it. Why? You going someplace?"

"I'm transferring to MIT in January."

"A young Einstein, huh? Last I heard, even far-off Yankee-land is connected to Virginia by interstates. Just keep yourself available for questioning in the meantime. I've got your phone number. And is this the right number for you, Miss Devine?"

Not long after entering Aaron's car, to retrieve Hecuba from his apartment, I fall soundly, blissfully asleep. By the time we arrive, my brain feels almost normal, although I'm still not steady on my feet. My brain is functioning well enough to understand that I have made another trip from 2022 to 1999, this time with my dog. I also understand that going to the hospital and talking to the police were essential to my mission: to right an old wrong and prevent Emily from victimizing Lacey or anyone else. But I have no idea whether I've accomplished that goal. The fact that I'm still in 1999 makes me wonder if I've failed.

As he opens the door to his apartment, Aaron asks, "How about a cup of tea before I drive you home? The more fluids, the better, according to the doctor."

"Okay. Thanks." I settle onto a ratty sofa. Hecuba leaps up beside me.

"Are you allowed to have dogs in your dorm?" Aaron calls from the kitchenette.

"No, I'm just ... I was just keeping her for the weekend. For a friend. A friend who had to go out of town. On short notice."

I stroke Hecuba's shoulders and wonder how I can get both of us back to the appropriate time. Apparently, the fact that she had glued herself to my body, way back on that Fauquier County sofa, guaranteed that the wolfhound would be part of my time-bending journey. I silently vow to make sure the same conditions apply for the return trip. No way I'll chance Hecuba getting lost in time. But it sure is nice to have her here with me. For however long it takes for me to complete my mission. I shudder briefly. Will we be stalled in 1999 until Emily's trial? Lord love a duck! I just want to go home.

When Aaron returns with the tea, I say, "Congratulations, by the way. You said you're transferring to MIT. I remember you talking about MIT back in the old neighborhood. That was your dream school. And you finally made it. Way to go!"

"Thanks. I got accepted my senior year in high school, but the financial aid wasn't near enough. That's why I'm at JMU. But when I reapplied this summer, MIT gave me a full scholarship. They liked the stuff I was doing over the summer for the Naval Research Lab."

"Wow! You must be excited."

He just shrugs.

"You're *not* excited? Isn't this a dream come true?"

"I guess. But I'm scared, too."

"Of what?"

"Remember when that cop called me an Einstein? I'm no

Einstein. I'm good at some stuff, but there's a boatload of stuff I'm not good at. That cop also made Massachusetts sound like it's at the end of the universe. I'm doing pretty good here. Know my way around. What do I know about Cambridge? How will I fit in around all those guys who really *are* geniuses?"

I'm stunned. I'm not the only one wracked by self-doubt and paralyzed by the fear of taking risks? I try to assure him. "You probably didn't know anything about this corner of Virginia, either, when you started at JMU. And you figured it out. Don't you think you'd figure it out up there, too?"

"It sounds so far away: 'up there.' Besides, I should stay available in Virginia so we can nail Emily."

"No! That cop didn't say you had to stay in Virginia. If there's a trial, you can drive down. Or maybe... Aren't there ... depositions? Maybe you wouldn't have to be here at all."

"Whatever. If you've finished your tea, we should probably take off. I gotta prep for Monday's lab work. Can use some extra shuteye, too."

It's clear that Aaron isn't ready to explore his fears about MIT and Massachusetts. And I don't have the energy to help him right now. I'm feeling the need for some alone-time to process this new version of my sophomore year and figure out just how—and when—I can journey into my future. Or do I mean my present tense? A chill snakes up my spine. Is time itself relative? Oh my God! Speaking of Einstein...

TWENTY-FIVE:

PAINTING THE ROAD OUT OF OZ

1'm back in my tiny dorm room by Saturday afternoon. Funny, how I once thought of it as so spacious, at least during that period when I was without a roommate. Right now, however, it's inducing claustrophobia. Partly because I'm sharing it with a giant wolfhound. Mostly because I'm trapped. Not merely trapped in 1999, but trapped in the room, since I'm loath to venture beyond it. Who knows how bumping into another dorm resident might screw up history? Will she narc me out for having a dog in my room, perhaps resulting in a disastrous separation from Hecuba? So, I wait until the hallway is silent before I dash down the hall to use the bathroom. And forget about going to a dining hall. I'm keeping hydrated with the six-pack of apple juice I found atop my bookcase. A search of my desk drawers produces a stash of vending machine snacks—loaded with preservatives, but beggars can't be choosers. I'm sharing my food and drink with Hecuba, who has been a lamb about our confinement. She's so happy smelling all the new scents she hasn't so much as whimpered. Since we knocked out her coccidia infection, her toilet habits have been exemplary. She can get by with very few bathroom breaks.

Does something need to happen in the police investigation before I can return to my proper time? It feels like these two treks back to my sophomore year have been about moving time forward, moving the traumatic experiences of that year into my fortysomething consciousness, so my more mature brain could handle the experiences better. My mature brain didn't do such a bang-up job during my first rectification effort, however. Avoiding that frat party didn't stop Emily from committing a crime, once again without punishment. And it's still anybody's guess if I've done any better with this latest effort.

Once again, I realize I have no idea what I'm doing. Or how I'm doing it. For lack of any logical plan, I wait to see what happens.

Late Saturday evening, I overhear a conversation in the hallway. Two girls are whispering. With difficulty, I catch the name, "Emily." Other girls soon join in the conversation, and the volume improves.

"Yup, she got in that cop's face and told him he had no right to be on our campus."

"Classic Emily. She'd mouth off at God Almighty."

"Fucking lot of good it did her."

"I wish I'd seen Emily in handcuffs."

"They cuffed her? Like some criminal?"

"What she did *was* criminal!"

"Who'd she do it to?"

"Cops aren't talking."

"Suppose they would have cuffed her is she'd kept her

mouth shut?"

"Lawyer up. That's what you need to do."

"I still don't get how the cops could come here and arrest her. They can do that without her parents? Without the permission of some university official?"

"She's nineteen. Gets treated like any adult perp."

"You know that cop practically slapped her in the face with his warrant?"

"Fascist fucker!"

"Yeah, well the fascist fucker had a lot of justification."

"Sure did. Someone at the party saw Emily doing it. Knew her name and everything."

"Drugging the other girl's drink?"

"No, smearing her twat with peanut butter."

"But they'll get her on the drug charge because of what they found in her room."

"What'd they find?"

"A prescription for Rohypnol."

"Get out!"

"But if a doctor prescribed it, how is it a crime for her to have it?"

"Rohypnol's illegal in America."

"The prescription was filled in Mexico."

"I heard the Bahamas."

"Can get a lot of good shit in either country."

"Yeah, like you'd know, Mary Ann!"

"All I know is, there were lots of pills in that bottle. I'm glad the cops took it."

"Shit, yeah! She coulda roofied this whole dorm."

"Well, I still don't like the idea of storm troopers charging into our residence hall."

"I don't like the idea of Emily dropping drugs into our drinks."

"Doesn't sound like we gotta worry about that anymore."

"No, ma'am. That girl's headed for the slammer."

"Buh-bye, Emily."

A wave of pure unadulterated glee washes over me. It feels so good knowing that Emily will get punished for her perverted little joke. No! It was more than a joke. It was assault, a trauma that would stay with me for decades. I wonder if I'm the only one Emily has assaulted.

"Supposed we can go home now?" I whisper to Hecuba.

I sit tailor-style on the floor and beckon the dog onto my lap. Hugging her furry neck, I close my eyes, in an effort to focus on my Fauquier County realities. I think of the hardwood smoke scenting the chilly December air. The ground fog blurring the wooded trail above my cottage. The gentle whickering from the stable.

Hopefully, I open my eyes. I see none of what I've imagined. I smell none of it. Hear none of it. I'm still stuck here.

My elation long gone, I begin obsessing about all the complications of "fixing" my past. What good does Emily's punishment do me, if I have to relive even more of my sophomore year? And even if I do manage, somehow, to get back to 2022 sooner rather than later, will Emily's punishment have some beneficial effect on my life in my forties? Will I suddenly become more confident, more trusting, more comfortable with myself? Or, will I still be me with the same crappy job and dim prospects for the future?

Hecuba whimpers softly and paws at the door. Sighing, I open it a crack. Seeing the hallway empty, I beckon the dog to follow me. We dash to the fire doors and walk down the stairs. Once on the ground floor, I jam a pencil in the doorframe, so I don't lock us out of this exit. Hecuba immediately finds a grassy area and relieves herself. We retrace out footsteps and return to the room. I stash the dog inside while I make my own trip to relieve myself.

I dig an extra blanket out of the closet and place it on the floor as a makeshift dog bed. "Go lie down," I whisper. "I'm sorry, puppy. I'll try again tomorrow to get us home. Meanwhile, we both need sleep."

Within a few minutes, a soothing rhythm of breaths emanates from the folded blanket. I'm not so lucky, however. Sleep eludes me as I consider various ways of summoning the focus that seems to be essential to my time-bending journeys. Staring at the gray ceiling triggers no brilliant insights. Nor does churning from side to side or punching my pillow. Well, if I can't conjure any solution or get the rest I need to get my brain to focus, the next best thing is to divert myself from my worries. I get out of bed gingerly, fearful of waking Hecuba. But the snoring hound is dead to the world. I turn on my desk lamp, in hope of seeing some novel that might calm me. Nothing but textbooks. I spin around and spot my rickety easel. It holds an acrylic landscape, something I was apparently working on all those years ago. Was it an assignment for one of my studio art classes? Or was it something I was doing for pleasure? I have no idea.

I turn on the tiny tensor light affixed to the easel to look more closely at the half-finished, vaguely impressionistic painting leaning on it. "Hmmpf. Pretty underwhelming. The craftsmanship is okay. But wow, is it timid!"

Once again, I recall that critique from a high-school art teacher: "You show promise as a painter, but you need to over-come all that inhibition."

Those words stung. At the time, I didn't really understand what he meant.

But now I'm seeing my work with new eyes, after decades spent as a thoroughly inhibited, timid adult. I see the rigidity of execution. And those pale color choices! Everything—from the trees to the clouds—is just too orderly. Despite some pointillist splashes, I was clearly intent on realism. Except even in that re-gard, I failed. There's no hint, for example, of Mother Nature's constant swings between chaos and order.

I remove the tacks holding the painting to its cardboard

backer. As I toss the canvas onto my desk, I spot a watercolor pad on my bookcase. Grabbing it, I pull back the cover and shiver with delight as my fingertips graze the delicious texture of the topmost cold-pressed sheet. I carefully extract it from the binder and tack it onto the cardboard. Then I hunt for tools. In one corner of my desktop is a small coffee can holding an assortment of brushes. On the lowest bookshelf I find tubes of watercolors, a small plastic palette, and a roll of paper towels.

"Water! I need water."

On my bureau, I spot the plastic water bottle Aaron gave me. What else do I need? Yes! There's my paint-smeared step-stool! After shoving it next to the easel, I gather all my tools and place them on the topmost step. Then I pour a small amount of water into a reasonably clean coffee mug. And freeze, as I experience that all too familiar terror of the blank canvas.

Then muscle memory kicks in. Even before I know what I plan to paint. My fingers deftly squeeze blobs of color into the small palette wells. They test the brush tips before choosing just the right instrument. A brush slips between right thumb and first two fingers as if it were a natural part of my hand.

Hecuba's head bobs up, sniffing toward the paints. She scans my face. Deciding there's no cause for worry, she sighs and tucks her muzzle beneath one knee.

And suddenly I know what I should paint. What I *need* to paint. My right hand darts in and out of the tensor beam. As if wrist and fingers had minds of their own. Only occasionally do I pause to rub my lower back. It's weary from standing, bent slightly forward. I've no idea how much time has passed at my easel. This is hardly a new sensation. Painting has always demanded my total attention, wiping out both past and future. This is one obsession that's rewarding.

During one pause, as I rub my lumbar region and gaze at the work before me, I notice thin gray light illuminating the room beyond the range of the tensor beam and desk lamp.

"Brilliant, Devine. Your body really needed sleep."

Sighing, I step back from the easel to take in the totality of what I've been painting. Until now, I've been focusing on the component parts: the wash, the shadows, the fog, the blend of colors. I'm stunned. Anyone familiar with the Ashwood family cemetery would recognize the giant hemlocks and white pines and hickories standing vigil over the gravestones. For all the realism, however, what I see is something more than fog-shrouded trees and graves. What I see is foreboding and hope intertwined, light and dark jostling for dominance, hushed stillness with just the suggestion that some storm could be brewing. I see something more, too: a cry of yearning. The yearning for home, for belonging somewhere. This painting has power. It's evocative, it's…

"The best thing I've ever done."

For reasons I don't understand, I know I could stare at this painting forever. But life won't let me. A shriek interrupts my reverie. It takes several heartbeats for me to identify the noise of an old-fashioned landline. Then I hear the drone of my recorded voice.

I rush to my desk. "Hello? Oh, wait a minute. Let me turn off the darn answering machine. There. Sorry. I'm here."

A snort of impatience crashes into my right ear. Then: "Bill Kruger here. Detective Kruger. You doing okay?"

"Oh. Hi. Gee. I'm surprised to hear from you … this soon." Squinting at my alarm clock, I read seven-thirty. On Sunday morning, I assume.

"Yeah, well, I probably should have waited. But I wanted to be sure and catch you at the dorm. Got good news. I figure you shouldn't have to wait for good news."

"Uh-huh?"

"It's about that Emily Denmark chick. You probably heard she was arrested yesterday afternoon. Searched her room. Found Rohypnol. Have a witness who saw her doing stuff to you at that party, when you were passed out."

"I overheard some of the girls talking about it. Didn't know how much of what they were saying was true. So, she'll be charged?"

"Yes, ma'am. But it gets better. Little Miss Emily crumpled like a cheap suit. When she heard what we had on her, she stopped mouthing off about the Fourth Amendment and student protests on her behalf. Gone was the attitude. She actually whimpered! Luckily, I managed to dragoon someone from the Commonwealth Attorney's office, weekend or no. Got him to offer Denmark a plea deal. She'll be wearing an orange jump suit, at least for a while, but not as long as she would if she went to trial. We assured her any trial would end with a guilty verdict. Little snot couldn't wait to take the deal. Even before consulting with the lawyer mommy and daddy hastily arranged. I just love these know-it-alls who talk about 'lawyering up' then can't wait to spill their guts. Makes my day." Kruger chuckled.

"Wow. Gee. That *is* good news. But … um, what do *I* have to do now?"

"Not a whole helluva lot. You won't need to testify, since there won't be any trial. Your friend, what's his name … Rappaport? He won't have to testify, either. There'll be an allocution hearing. Not sure when that will be yet."

"Elocution hearing? What's that?"

"Allocution. With an A. That's where Denmark fesses up, laying out her misdeeds. Then she tells the judge all about her sterling qualities, in hope of reducing the sentence. But don't worry. This prosecutor has a good rep, and his plea deals generally stand up. Sometimes, the judge wants input from the victim—that's you— to weigh the harm done before he hands down any sentence. But it's pretty much a slam dunk. I'll be in touch about the time-frame and any other details, once I know them. Okay?"

"Okay. Gee. Thanks. Bye."

A second after I hang up, I realize all the questions I didn't ask. Like, would my identity as Emily's victim become common knowledge? I shudder, thinking of possible ramifications, not just on campus, but at home. With Mother. With the neighbors. Wait a minute! Is Mother still alive? Or did I cause her premature death in that earlier bit of time travel, when I tried to rectify another wrong?

My brain is too tired to compute all these potential consequences. So I decide—for once—to focus on that one brilliantly positive detail: Emily's wrong will be righted.

And suddenly, fatigue kicks in. So intently that I nearly pitch forward onto my desk. "Better place," I mumble, as I lurch toward my unmade bed.

On the way, I pass my still illuminated easel. I stop. Look at the painting. And I practically shout, "That's my ticket out of here."

Despite my fatigue, I remove the (mostly dry) painting from the easel, cardboard backing and all, and relocate to the floor, right next to Hecuba, who has been watching my every move. I plunk down, tailor-style. One hand has a death grip on her collar. The other steadies the painting on my lap. I stare hard at those gravestones and trees. I recall every detail of the Ashwood cemetery. The acidic scent of fallen pine needles. The ground fog chilling my bare ankles. The shrill lament of a screech owl. The chiaroscuro play of clouds scudding past a full moon.

"Ouch!" I cried, plucking a sharp pine needle from my ankle. I twirled my head, dizzying myself with a kaleidoscope of tree branches. Even though I was sitting solidly on the ground, I felt the need to steady myself. Thrusting out one hand, I felt cold, damp soil. The fingers of my other hand were wedged between a rolled leather collar and Hecuba's rough neck fur.

"Looks like we're back in Kansas, Toto."

Twenty-Six:

Solstice Visitors

1 hugged my giant beast of a dog so hard she groaned.

"Sorry, puppy. I'm just so happy we're back where we belong. Everything okay with you?" I asked, cradling her muzzle in both hands. "What's this? Look at all the gray in your face. It wasn't there before, was it?"

Hecuba slurped the tip of my nose. As I wiped the slobber away, I said, "That's the last journey for you, my graying hound. I don't want you using up your dog years any faster than absolutely necessary. It's travesty enough that you guys walk the planet for such a short time."

Only then did I take a moment to assess any damage my latest journey might have cost *me*. I touched my nose. Nothing was dripping there. My gut wasn't rocking or threatening some outpouring from one end or the other. "Hmm, don't tell me I actually get a pass."

No sooner were the words out of my mouth than a shiver snaked up my spine, and cold sweat erupted from head to toe. Since we were outside, and I was hardly dressed for a late December night, my teeth started chattering. I needed to get inside as soon as possible. But when I turned my head around to figure out where we were, I experienced horrible vertigo, so bad I nearly fell.

"Okay," I panted. "W-we're in the Ashwood cemetery. Now if I can only h-hike down that long h-hill before keeling over. You go ahead, p-puppy," I said, pointing downhill. "I'll c-catch up."

Hecuba had a better idea. She positioned herself by my left hip then nudged my left palm with her nose. Understanding, I grasped the fur on her tall withers to steady myself. And we made our slow, cautious descent.

Another gust intensified my shivering but cleared most of the fog obscuring my path. As we circled a huge hemlock, visibility improved even more, and we caught the first glimmer from those lights Roy had strung on the little spruce off my back porch. My first—idiotic—reaction was to chide myself for wasting electricity. Who knew how long those lights had been on? How long had I been gone, in terms of Fauquier County's twenty-first century realities?

"Who cares!" I suddenly shouted. The lights were cheerful, welcoming. Besides, I was tired of constantly chastising myself.

Which is why I restrained from self-criticism minutes later, when I realized I hadn't locked the back door. I let Hecuba scope out the interior of the cottage first, to make sure no interloper had taken advantage of my security lapse.

Once inside, I headed straight for the bathroom. With my wolfhound keeping close watch, I turned on the overhead heat lamp and cranked up the shower's hot water faucet. While waiting for the bathroom to steam up, I scrutinized the pale face looking back from the mirror.

"Lord love a duck! I look like Dracula's been nibbling on my neck."

After the shower, I swathed myself in flannel pajamas, topped by my heaviest sweatshirt and a quilted, ankle-length bathrobe. But I was still shivering. "Hot tea. I need tea."

On my way to the kitchen, I grabbed my cellphone from the bureau. It read eleven o'clock on December twenty-second. I was stunned that only a few hours had passed here, while nearly two days had played out during my latest visit to 1999.

When the tea was ready, the dog and I relocated to the living room. Hecuba ignored my hand signal to settle on the floor beside the sofa. Instead, she hopped up on the couch and wedged herself beside my hip. "Oh, all right. I can use your warmth." I grabbed the afghan draped over the sofa back and wrapped it around both of us.

Once my shivering eased, I leaned my head against the sofa back. Sleep soon overtook me. I was dimly aware of the windows rattling in the wind and the soothing snoring of the wolfhound beside me.

Hecuba was the first to wake. She harrumphed briefly then lumbered off the sofa. I opened my eyes to white light moving across the otherwise dark interior walls. A car was pulling up the drive. And it was continuing uphill, past the cottage.

"What now?" Hecuba was doing her best to bark down the back door. I clutched the afghan around my shoulders as I stumbled toward the nearest window to investigate. Sure enough, there were the red taillights of a large SUV approaching the graveyard.

Anger overrode any anxiety. How dare someone intrude on us at this time of night!

I grabbed a down parka from the coatrack and opened the back door. Hecuba charged out the dog panel while I slipped into the rubber shoes I keep nearby. I pulled a small flashlight from one pocket and trained its beam on my hound, loping through the shadows up the hill. Her silence spoke volumes. I almost felt sorry for whoever was up there.

As I wearily hiked after her, I saw the SUV stop just short of the graveyard, its exhaust still swirling in the cold air. Hecuba got in front of the vehicle, lowered her head, and glowered into the headlights, frothy saliva leaking with each growl. When the headlights turned off and the engine went mute, the driver's door opened slightly. My wolfhound dashed around and slammed the door shut in one pounce.

Now only a few yards away from the car, I heard whimpers from the rear seat. Then a vaguely familiar female voice called, "Cate? Help?"

"What the hell, Morwenna!" I exclaimed angrily.

The driver's window whirred down a few inches. "Jesus Christ! You're almost as menacing as that, that behemoth."

"What in God's name are you doing here this time of night?" I shot back. Scanning the front and back seats and seeing three wide-eyed passengers, I added, "All of you?"

"It never occurred to me you'd mind. I tried to call you for the past day or so, but you never answered. I wanted to let you know our plans. This graveyard, you see, is the perfect spot for our annual winter solstice ritual." She whirled her fingers toward her companions.

Only then did I notice that all four women were dressed in what looked like choir robes, in different colors.

Morwenna continued, "I had hoped we could borrow Hecuba for the ritual, but seeing how protective she is, maybe that's not a good idea. Unless you'd care to join us and keep her behaved? Pretty please?"

"No. No borrowing Hecuba. No borrowing me. And find another place for your ritual. The Ashwoods would be livid if I let their family cemetery be used for something like that."

Morwenna's eyes widened. "Really? I was sure it would be all right."

"You were wrong." For emphasis, I dug my fists into my hips. That triggered another chill, so I hugged my parka to my chest. "Look, I feel like dirt. Can you turn around, please, and head on out? I need to go back inside where it's warm. And I badly need sleep."

274

"Oh. That's why you're being so bitchy." Morwenna nodded knowingly.

"*That's* why? No other reason you can think of?"

"Okay, okay. We'll go back to Meg's car. It's parked at the start of the driveway. But I really gotta pee. Can I come back after I dump them off. Just for a few minutes?"

I shook my head and clicked my tongue. "Oh, all right. But only for a few minutes. Besides, you might catch whatever I've got."

I grabbed Hecuba's collar in case she tried to follow Morwenna's car, lurching forward then back a few times before finally facing downhill and starting its slow descent. The dog and I veered off to the cottage.

Once inside, I fired up the teakettle again, in hope a steaming cuppa would cure the new wave of cold sweats. I stared at the "68" reading on the thermostat and muttered, "A low electric bill isn't gonna help me much if I die of pneumonia." I punched the digital device until it flashed "72."

Teacup in hand, I settled on the sofa, wrapped myself in the afghan again, and waited for headlights to train across the living room wall, signaling Morwenna's return from seeing off her companions.

"Door's open!" I yelled in response to the tepid knock. Hecuba, sitting alertly by my feet, growled softly but did not move.

"Jesus Christ, I need to pee!" Morwenna complained as she

gathered her purple robe and dashed to the bathroom.

On her return trip, she stopped to eye several handwritten envelopes on the kitchen counter. "I haven't seen a thirty-four-cent stamp in quite some time. Come to think of it, I haven't seen handwritten letters in quite a while, either. That's what these are, right?"

"Fix yourself some tea if you want. But I was serious about needing sleep. As soon as I finish my tea, I'm heading to bed."

"I'll pass on the tea. Hey, you don't look so good." She plopped down beside me. Hecuba groaned and relocated to a pillow on the opposite end of the room. Morwenna pointed toward the kitchen. "You been hiding some secret admirer? Those aren't old love letters, are they?"

"Just a friend from college. We corresponded for a while after he transferred to MIT. I was thinking of him a few days ago and pulled out his letters. They date from way before he got famous, of course."

"Famous? Maybe I'll have some tea after all."

Morwenna rose abruptly and nearly tripped over her robe. From the kitchen, she called, "A. Rappaport? Who's that?" Clearly, she was scrutinizing my letters from Aaron.

"Aaron Rappaport. You know, the founder of that big Internet software firm. He's to virus protection what Bill Gates is to Windows."

"Never heard of him," Morwenna shouted back.

276

"You never heard of Rapp-Support? I had it on my old laptop. My new one came with McAfee. Not as good."

"I've always used the free stuff, whatever it's called." She yawned, loudly enough for me to hear in the living room. She was losing interest in my proximity to fame.

Teacup in hand, Morwenna walked into the living room. "I suppose this Aaron guy looked like every other computer nerd? Honestly, I can't tell the school's tech-support guys apart. They're scrawny, have greasy, thinning hair, wear clunky glasses, and smell."

"Actually, Aaron was kind of cute, after he lost weight. Tall. Nice hair. A nice guy." I was annoyed at myself for sounding defensive. So, I switched the subject: "What were you doing out there tonight? Wasn't the solstice on the twenty-first?"

Morwenna lowered herself onto the sofa before answering. "Yesterday's forecast called for freezing rain at night."

"Isn't the timing important? How can you celebrate the solstice after the solstice has come and gone?"

Now it was Morwenna's turn to sound defensive. "Well, it's the intention that counts, isn't it? And I can't help it if Meg and the others wimped out. Fine bunch of Wiccans. They're still soccer moms at heart."

I chuckled. "So, what's involved with this ceremony? And why do you look like members of a Baptist church choir?"

She looked down at her gown. "I do *not* look like a choir

member. Do I? Damn. Maybe we should have ordered the robes with the cowls."

"Maybe so."

She pursed her lips in annoyance. "In the solstice ritual, we celebrate the rebirth of the sun and the turning of the Wheel of the Year. And we pay homage to all three phases of the Eternal Feminine, transitioning from Crone all the way back to Maiden. We gather in a circle under the moon. One of us, dressed in black, assumes the role of the Crone. Another, wearing red, is the Mother. Meg, in white, represents the Maiden. So, we start off by..."

"You're wearing purple. Who are you supposed to be?"

"The high priestess, of course," she explained, tossing her hair. "As I was saying, we start off with me lighting the Crone's candle, who then lights the candle held by the Mother, who then lights the Maiden's candle."

"Your candle-lighting would have been tricky tonight, with all the wind out there."

Morwenna folded her arms over her ample breasts. "We Wiccans are very in tune with natural elements, and the wind is..."

"Cold?"

"Oh, you're just being..." She sighed heavily. "Fuck it! Mother Nature can be a bitch. I hate to admit it, but I'd rather be warm in here with grumpy old you than freezing my ass off outside. Maybe we'll do better celebrating the summer solstice."

278

"Sounds like a plan," I chuckled. "And my plan, as I said before, is to sack out under a pile of blankets. So, drink up."

"I'm not sure I like this new side of you."

I gathered the afghan more tightly around my shoulders, rose, walked to front door, opened it, and waggled my fingers at Morwenna.

She stood up, hiked her purple robe a few inches above her ankles, and trudged toward the door. "We Wiccans don't get no respect." But she smiled as she returned my wave. "Hope you feel better soon. For all our sakes."

Twenty~Seven:

No Little Things

Amazingly enough, I awoke feeling much better. The chills were gone, and I had some energy, at least for pleasant tasks. I began the day by writing Roy a thank-you note and attaching it to Ruth's tin of cookies. I hiked to the barn and put the regifted tin where he was sure to see it.

Then I turned my attention to artwork. The watercolor I'd done in my dorm room, as I waited to journey back to the twenty-first century, had resurrected a long dormant yearning. I hunted through various closets and boxes for old brushes and canvases and paints. Ideas for paintings and sketches flooded my brain. But first I needed to reexamine the artifact I'd brought back from 1999. My original assessment of that watercolor was accurate. It was indeed good. So good, it needed hanging. I dug out an old picture frame. Its matting wasn't properly sized but would do for now. After finding appropriate wall space in the front hallway, up went my moody painting of the Ashwood graveyard. I just stood there, admiring it.

I was so transfixed that noises from the front door didn't register for several minutes. Hecuba sure heard them, though. She went into a happy dance, tail slapping against the wall, as she urged me to answer those knocks. Right now.

Finally opening the door to Roy, I apologized for the delay.

"No problem," he said, as he gave the dog's flank a solid thumping. "You happy to see me, huh, Hecuba?"

"Of course, she is. She remembers who saved her from the pound. Besides, she's an excellent judge of…"

The ring of my phone, abandoned in the kitchen, cut off my words. I beckoned Roy inside then raised a finger and dashed to the kitchen.

"You go get that. I'll just set my old bones here in the living room a minute. Don't you hurry now."

When I returned, grumbling over yet another telemarketer, Roy was staring at the newly hung painting on the hallway wall. "This is beautiful! You do it?"

I smiled and nodded. "Couple of days ago. I was … sick and couldn't hike up there so I did it from memory. Not sure I got everything right."

He returned his gaze to the watercolor. "Got everything right and then some. It's kinda soothing to look at, you know? Soft, but just a little, I dunno, mysterious, too."

"Really? Gee. Thanks. I haven't painted for such a long time. I thought maybe it was good. Good enough to hang."

"You mind if I take a photo of it? I'd like the Ashwoods to see it. I think they'd really like it, too."

"Yeah? Sure."

Roy pulled his phone from a rear pocket and photographed

282

the painting from several angles. "Mnm, mnm, mnm. That's one nice picture."

"I hope you got my cookies okay. I put them on the top shelf in the tack room. Figured the horses couldn't get them there."

"Sure did. That's why I'm here. To thank you. Whaddya call them little twisty things?"

"*Rugelach*."

"Best cookies I ever et. What's inside 'em?"

I closed my eyes briefly to concentrate on the taste of Ruth's baked goods. "Dried apricots and walnuts and spices."

"Apricots! That was it! Great stuff. Mighty nice of you to part with them."

"Mighty nice of you to string up those lights on the little spruce out back. I've been laid up a lot lately and haven't had much chance to prepare for Christmas. Like I said in my note, I was really touched. What a cheerful sight to greet me after a long day."

"My pleasure. You feeling any better? Still look awful pale. And I ain't seen you around much these past few days."

"Whatever bug I caught a few weeks ago made a brief return. But this morning, I woke up feeling better than I have in a while. Maybe it's because I was playing with my water paints. When I was younger, that always made me feel better."

"I don't wonder. That picture over there makes me feel good just looking at it. Well, I won't keep you. Just thought I'd stop by before I head home. The missus kicked me out this morning. Already cooking up a storm for Christmas, and I was getting in her way. Kept swatting my hands as I tried to sample this and that. I figured I'd stay out of trouble by checking on the horses."

"I hope you have a very Merry Christmas, Roy. You and your wife."

He tugged on his visor. "Merry Christmas to you, too, Miss Cate." His smile suddenly vanished. "You gonna be spending it with family?"

"A friend invited me for Christmas dinner," I lied.

"Well, that's just fine. You enjoy. And thanks again for them cookies."

"Thank *you* for my Christmas tree."

Roy headed for the door but turned once again toward the painting. "Mnm, mnm, mnm," he repeated before leaving.

In the kitchen, I placed my sketch pad and a woefully limited assortment of pastel chalks on the table. I knew exactly what I had to draw: Aaron. Thanks to my recent trips back to college and my perusal of his letters, I was confident I could capture him from memory alone. My right hand seemed to move independently of my brain. And just as in the dorm room, I felt wholly in the moment. Unfortunately, when I finally paused to assess my efforts, the image inside my head wasn't emerging on paper. "Something's wrong about the nose," I muttered. "The eye color, too. But there's some sense of his personality, at least."

My subject was peering into a computer screen, which cast a blue haze on his face. A nineteen-year-old face, radiating intelligence and gentle concern.

The jaw wasn't quite right, either. I added more shading there, only to realize his jaw was becoming more angular, stronger than it actually was. Was I overcompensating because Morwenna had made him sound like an ugly nerd? How could she form such a concrete, erroneous image of someone she'd never met? Preconceived notions. The very instincts that made people steer clear of odd girls like me. I had to admit, however, that those instincts were often useful. They tell us to steer clear of the serial killer, even though he has a lovely smile.

I continued finessing Aaron's face, darkening his eyelashes, bringing out the depth in his blue eyes. Then my hand froze. If Morwenna's preconceived ideas about Aaron were annoying, it was downright disturbing that she had never heard of him. Sure, she had zero interest in technology. But she was attracted to fame. Aaron's name and picture appeared often in all sorts of media. Did they just not register with Morwenna? How likely was that?

I retrieved my laptop from the coffee table in the living room, plunked down on the sofa, opened my browser, and typed "Aaron Rappaport" into the search box. The battery was low, so the search engine was slow to deliver. What finally popped up were the names of numerous lawyers, physicians, professors. But not the Aaron I had known. The closest result was an engineer, but the accompanying info was too thin to pinpoint him as my old school chum.

Then I remembered that "Aaron" was his middle name. He found his first name embarrassing. Maybe the search engines would list him under the first name? Unfortunately, I couldn't remember it. Then it hit me: Why not search for his virus protection software.

I typed in "Rapp-Support." Nothing resembling virus protection popped up. But I did see an incomprehensible blurb about a network optimization tool called rAPP. Could that have any connection to Aaron?

A low battery warning suddenly flashed on screen. Could a dying battery be the reason why I was striking out with my online search? I closed the screen and plugged the laptop into a power source. "I'll try again when you're feeling better," I said, patting the lid.

Back at the kitchen table, I couldn't concentrate on my sketch. I couldn't shake my queasiness over Morwenna's unfamiliarity with Aaron's name, to say nothing of my failure to find him online. Had I somehow altered Aaron's life path during my second trek back to JMU?

I flashed on our conversation in his apartment, before he drove me back to my dorm room. He was talking about his full scholarship to MIT. But instead of sounding happy, he sounded scared. Scared of all the challenges he'd face there. Scared of a whole new area of the country. What had he said about Massachusetts? It was at the "end of the universe." Then he cited the potential need to testify at Emily's trial. He seemed to be using that obligation as an excuse to stay at JMU, to avoid all the scariness associated with transferring to MIT. When I pointed out that he could do both—testify and transfer—he changed the subject.

But that was before Detective Kruger called me. I left 1999 before I had the chance to tell Aaron that Emily had pleaded out and there'd be no trial, no need for him to testify. Surely the detective would have told Aaron? Or maybe not.

What if Aaron didn't go to MIT? What if his MIT education and all the contacts he would make there were essential to his career path? Without that experience, did Aaron become just another one of those faceless computer nerds Morwenna mocked? And was I to blame for all that, by tinkering with history?

I slapped a palm against my forehead. "The letters!"

If Aaron's letters had a return address in Cambridge, then all was well. I dashed back to the kitchen. On the counter were two letters. I was sure I'd pulled out more than that.

One was a Christmas card dated December 1999, before Aaron would have transferred to MIT. Sent from his home address in Arlington, it contained little more than "best wishes for a better year than you had in 1999."

I pulled the notepaper from the second envelope, also bearing the Arlington address. The postmark was blurred, and Aaron had not headed his message with the date. He began by praising some baked goods I'd sent him, my way of thanking him for his help after the frat house disaster. When did I do that? October or November of that year? In other words, well ahead of the date of his transfer to MIT. But surely he would mention the upcoming transfer in the text.

I continued reading. He wrote about a temporary job landed during some school break. Thanksgiving? Christmas? I couldn't tell. The job involved commuting more than an hour to a hay farm well west of Washington. He had to scale twenty-foot stacks of hay, toss the bales into the customers' truck beds then pack and tie the bales securely. He joked about sliding off those tall stacks, causing a major collapse and earning ridicule from his coworkers. They also teased him about the "deer in headlights look" he'd get whenever a customer asked him which bales were third-cut orchard grass. "What the heck is third-cut orchard grass?" he wrote. "Guess I better do well in school. Doesn't look like I have much of a future working with my hands."

What school did he mean? JMU or MIT?

In hope of finding the missing letters sent from MIT, I lifted the flour and bean canisters to see if an envelope somehow got shoved underneath one of them. Nothing. I stooped to examine the kitchen floor for fallen letters. Nothing.

Maybe this was a small matter. But the disappearance of correspondence that would have confirmed Aaron's transfer to MIT felt consequential. Suddenly I flashed back to a history term paper I'd written about American isolationists in the 1930s. That paper began with an intriguing quote from Congressman Bruce Barton, "Sometimes when I consider what tremendous consequences come from little things, I am tempted to think there are no little things." The quote stuck in my head because my history professor sneered at it, finding it "irrelevant."

It sure didn't feel irrelevant twenty odd years later, as I stood in my Fauquier County kitchen. "What have I done?"

Twenty-Eight:

Metamorphosis in Oils

1couldn't sit on this. I couldn't live with myself if my effort to get justice had somehow robbed Aaron of his success. Aaron, the guy who rescued me. If I had my druthers, I would have launched myself back to 1999 as soon as possible. But there was Hecuba to consider.

She was lying by my feet as I called the vet, just half an hour before closing time. During our last visit, the office manager reminded me that time was running out to cash in on the animal shelter's offer to cover half of certain veterinary expenses for adoptees. Animal rescue groups of all stripes, I learned, often did this to make their foundlings more adoptable. The coverage would run out at year's end.

"Any chance you still have that opening for a dental cleaning the day after Christmas?" I asked. "I know this is short notice, but Dr. Fry has been after me about the tartar problem."

The vet tech clicked her tongue. "Huh! We have two open slots. So-called animal lovers have other things to spend their money on over the holidays. You wouldn't believe how many cancellations we get this time of year. Want early or late morning?"

After opting for the earliest appointment, I learned Hecuba should be sufficiently recovered from anesthesia to go home mid-afternoon. "Umm, there's a slight chance I might not be able to get there before you close. Would you have room to keep her overnight if I run late?"

I breathed a sigh of relief to learn there should be room, since several boarders would be going home on the twenty-sixth. I was already winging it on the timing. The more skinny-room I had for my next bout of time travel, the better.

Clicking off my phone, I shivered guiltily over Hecuba's concerned gaze. "Nothing to worry about, puppy," I lied. "We're just gonna make sure you keep your chompers for a long time. And think how sweet your breath will smell when all that nasty tartar's gone."

I looked at the to-do list I'd scribbled an hour or so earlier. "Okay, that's done," I said, crossing off one item. "Now to stock up on provisions. Gotta do something to keep myself sane until the twenty-sixth."

When the dog angled her head inquisitively, I said, "Wanna go for a ride?"

Hecuba's tail sketched happy figure-eights.

A few minutes later we were on the road to Warrenton, Fauquier County's seat and largest town. My wolfhound joyously inhaled every passing scent through the halfway-open rear window. I was considerably less perky. Facing the crowds at Walmart two days before Christmas was a daunting prospect. But I needed to divert my attention from the next trip back to 1999, when

I would do my best to persuade Aaron to go forward with his transfer to MIT. There was no guarantee I would succeed. Every new time-bending excursion seemed to raise new problems, like Hecuba's visible aging when she joined me on the last journey. There was no way I would take her with me this time. But leaving her at home was also risky. What if a day spent in 1999 translated into a week for Hecuba in 2022?

My pulse rate ticked up as all these worries crowded my brain. I slapped the steering wheel to shut them down. "And that's why I'm braving the crowds at Walmart."

My plan was to immerse myself in artwork for the next two-and-a-half days. But my surviving art supplies were meager. I had almost no usable oil paints. The few remaining tubes had dried up. And oil—a rich, more forgiving medium than watercolors—would work best for that portrait I wanted to create of a youthful Aaron.

The sun had set by the time I pulled into Walmart's humungous lot. The only available parking spaces were acres from the store. "You stay here, my hound. I won't be long. I hope."

I quickly found what I needed, including a folding easel of Chinese manufacture, cheaper than the one I'd used in college eons ago. I had tossed that artifact when the den of my childhood home became the bedroom for my increasingly non-ambulatory mother. Once upon a time, the den was where I stored all my art supplies—and too infrequently put them to use. No sense getting all rueful now. I had a mission and tackled it with surprising efficiency. It wasn't long before I was ready to check out and, miracle of miracles, an idle register opened as I passed by. I ignored the glares of people standing fifth or sixth in line at other registers and wheeled my cart into place.

Just two hours after I'd launched this excursion, Hecuba and I were back home. I took care of her growling tummy but had no interest in feeding my own. Feeling like the little kid who dashes downstairs to unwrap the presents under the Christmas tree, I couldn't wait to try out my purchases.

I unpacked the tarp and spread it on the floor. I set up the easel on it then placed a pre-primed canvas on the easel. A nasty voice inside my head told me if I were a real artist, I would have cut several lengths of premium cotton—or, better yet, linen—canvas, stretched them, and primed them myself. Never mind that Walmart didn't carry rolls of canvas. A real artist would have trekked however long it took to a good art supply shop. A real artist would be awash in ideas for flexing her creative muscles, before working her way up to the project at hand.

"Stop it, Cate!"

For an instant, I thought the scolding came from Hecuba, not me. But that would be ridiculous. Wouldn't it? My hound sat near the tarp, monitoring my setup activity with a low level of curiosity. I saw nothing unusual in her body language. When her golden eyes met my gaze, she lifted her eyebrows in anticipation of some words of wisdom, or perhaps a tossed dog biscuit.

294

Deciding I had nothing to offer, she sighed and lowered her upper body onto the rug.

I returned my gaze to the canvas. The dreaded blank canvas. A distant memory stirred. Once upon a time, a teacher talked about his summer gigs conducting art therapy seminars for people working through emotional trauma. When his traumatized clients froze at their easels, he'd urged them to feel their way into painting, first by choosing colors that best reflected their mood at that precise moment.

"Worth a shot," I mumbled, resolving to warm up to my portrait plans with some abstract painting exercises. I squeezed a blob of alizarin crimson onto my palette. I had no idea why. Nor could I have identified whatever mood that reflected. I just wanted to look at red. I played with the blob on the palette, thinned it out with some drops of mineral spirits. I dipped one of my fattest brushes into the bloody pool and boldly moved it diagonally across the canvas. Then I curled it halfway back, like an upside-down checkmark. I grabbed a tube of mars black. Inside my head, a former professor chided me for using a color straight from the tube. It was "pedestrian" and "puerile" not to mix one's colors.

"Lord love a duck! Maybe I *feel* puerile!" I said, squeezing black onto the palette and attacking it with a medium-width brush. The brush zigzagged horizontally across the canvas. Then my palette knife smeared the zigzags. The effect was crude but oddly satisfying. My next choice was a blob of titanium white, into which I squeezed a tiny bead of cadmium yellow and a drop of mineral spirits. After randomly smearing that concoction just below the zigzags, I played with a blend of red and yellow and randomly applied the mixture in small, swirling circles. Next came exclamation points of brown, red, and yellow, intersecting with triangles of purplish green.

Stepping back for the broad view, I was horrified. The canvas was loud, garish, and confusing. "No one would want to look at this thing!" Immediately I began softening the colors, blending in daubs of white here and there and thinning the heaviest smears.

When I finished, the sharp contrasts had been eased. Pastels now crowded out the bold-hued slashes. The work was still an incomprehensible abstraction, but it was easier on the eyes. It wouldn't offend anyone.

And why was that so bloody important? I stepped back from the work once again. And realized how dull and inhibited it was.

I stomped into the kitchen and pulled a plastic trash bag from the cabinet then marched back to the scene of my crime. I was about to bury the canvas in the black plastic but stopped. At very least, this piece would remind me what *not* to do. And who knows, maybe it would help me find my way back to whatever it was I had started to paint.

I set the tepid abstraction on the floor tarp and placed a

new board on the easel. This time I played with several colors on my palette before applying them to the canvas. I wasn't buying into that art teacher's prejudice against ever using color straight from the tube. I just wanted to give myself the time to decide which hues appealed to me and which repelled me at that precise moment—all without judging myself or even wondering why.

After a minute or so of mixing this color and that, I looked down at the mixtures. Not one spot was pastel. The palette temperature was decidedly hot.

After thinning one of the bright yellow blends, I used my entire arm to wash it across the top two-thirds of the canvas. For the lower third, orange—applied with more pressure—dominated the underpainting. While the paint dried a bit, I hoped the piece would tell me where it wanted to go. Maybe half an hour passed. I received few glimpses of the painting's future. Then, after plunging a brush into a bold crimson puddle, with just a touch of black, I shut my eyes as I stroked across the piece. I alternated between closely examining my brush-strokes and blindly conjuring the painting's bones.

Finally, I discarded the brush and pressed my fingertips into the canvas. My hand swept right, then up, then back, with varying degrees of pressure—a tactic better suited for acrylics. My fingers would be stained for days. But it felt right.

When Hecuba chuffed and headed for the closed door, I

mopped up my hands in a clean rag and rose stiffly. Knees and ankles popped as I limped across the living room. After letting the dog outside, I looked at the clock: "3:10."

"Yikes! How did it get so late?"

Fatigue won out over artistic ambition, so I capped the paint tubes and spirits and daubed at spills on the tarp, before Hecuba could spread them around the cottage. Only after folding and stowing the tarp did I examine what had occupied me for the past few hours.

"Really?" I clapped a spotted hand over my mouth. "I did this?" It didn't look like something I would do. It was so angry. So spirited. So filled with contrast. Violent slashes of red and orange and black set off melancholic purples and grays, with the occasional glint of white or soft gold, which came across as both vulnerable and hopeful. The painting was confusing and more than a little crazy. But it certainly wasn't dull or inhibited. Most important, it spoke to me, I had no idea whether it would speak to anyone else. Surprisingly, I didn't care.

I awoke to Christmas Eve when the sun was as high in the sky as possible for late December. I'd not only slept in. I'd slept the sleep of the dead, with not one thought expended on my imminent return to 1999. The cathartic nature of my painting exercise must have facilitated sound slumber. I resolved to play with color and canvas as much as possible over the next two days.

I also resolved to lavish attention on Hecuba before packing her off to the vet. With the temperature edging toward the mid-fifties, a long dog walk had more appeal than usual. After a very late breakfast, I leashed my hound, and off we went. Combining deer trails with an old skid road, I charted a roughly four-mile course around the Ashwood estate. As we approached the horse pasture, I unclipped Hecuba and let her lollop around the fencing. Several herd members ambled over and exchanged breath with the joyous hound through the wooden rails. After a few minutes of this communion, I whistled for the dog to join me in a nearby clearing, where I picked up a fallen hickory limb of just the right size. I tossed it in the air and marveled at Hecuba's mid-air catch. Repeated tosses of the stick triggered all sorts of goofy balletics. Often the hound snared the stick at its apogee. Occasionally, she tumbled upon her return to earth, all while keeping the chunk of hickory firmly behind her canines. The slobber on the wood enhanced the happiness of Hecuba's smile.

Inevitably, our excursion took us to the Ashwood cemetery, where the hemlocks and hickories shielded us from the uptick in wind, while allowing sunlight to brighten the bench that overlooked the graves. I sat down and patted my knee, beckoning Hecuba. She sat on my right foot, facing away, but periodically angled her head backward over my knees to smile at me, tongue lolling from her mouth.

"Life's not so bad, is it, hound of mine?"

Folding my arms over my chest, I leaned against the back of the bench. After freeing my foot from the dog's bony rump, I stretched my legs forward, and closed my eyes, enjoying the sun's warmth on my face. The red blurs inside my eyelids reminded me of my painting. I smiled.

The next time I opened my eyes, the sun was warming my shins. "Isn't it funny, Hecuba, how comfortable this old graveyard feels? Not spooky at all. Kinda feels like I belong. Maybe the dead people like that we're keeping watch for them."

Lying like some *au couchant* lion sculpture, Hecuba kept her gaze on the edge of the woods. But she heard what I said.

And I heard what *she* said: "Well, of course, you're comfortable. You've been comfortable among the dead ever since you kept Persephone company all those centuries ago, after Hades carried her off to the underworld. Of all the gods, you're the only one who can transition through all three realms: the ambrosian heights, earth, the underworld. And often you've had me at your side when you do."

I liked the sound of that and nodded.

Then I bolted forward and stared wide-eyed at my dog, still faced away from me. "What? Did that come from you? No, no, no! I must have been dreaming."

Hecuba turned her head to yawn at me. She stretched herself upright then ambled downhill toward the cottage.

I followed, rubbing the sleep from my eyes and shaking my head. "That was some dream. Either that, or the old Christmas Eve legend is true."

Once home, I opened my laptop. The dream's Persephone reference nagged at me. Wasn't there some recent conversation about that bit of Greek mythology? As I read the search results for "Persephone," the conversation with Nicu came back to me. That was the name of his kitten. At the time, I recalled little of Persephone's history. But Google filled in the gaps.

Persephone had indeed been abducted by Hades. Her mother Demeter was so distressed she solicited the help of another goddess, Hecate, who could hear the young maiden's screams. Grabbing her torch, Hecate set off in search of the kidnap victim. The search took her to the underworld, where she found the young goddess. But Hades wasn't about to lose his trophy bride. A deal was struck, requiring Persephone to return to him for half of the year. He would, however, allow her protector Hecate to keep her company during those dark days.

Sometime earlier, I must have learned those snippets from Greek mythology. And promptly buried them in my brain—only to regurgitate them during my afternoon nap.

Satisfied to have a halfway logical explanation for my dog's mini-lecture, I started to close the laptop. "Wait a minute, didn't Morwenna claim to have some special connection with Hecate? But Morwenna's version wasn't about ancient Greece. It was about guarding crossroads in the British Isles. Huh?"

So I typed more words into Google's search box and learned that Hecate figured in lots of different myths in lots of different cultures. She was worshipped in ancient Egypt, Greece, and Asia Minor and was enjoying a renaissance in modern Wiccan circles. In the Dark Ages, she supposedly protected travelers against whatever evils lurked in Britain's wooded pathways.

"Girl got around," I chuckled. "And look at that! She was often accompanied by her hound." Turning to Hecuba, I added, "Just like you, puppy!"

At that moment, my "puppy" was generating seismic-level snores. Her gangly limbs were stretched at odd angles on the hallway floor. She didn't look like the reincarnation of some god-dess's noble canine companion. Even more ridiculous was the notion that I could have been some goddess in a previous life. As if I had power to protect anyone from anything!

As I closed my laptop, however, the memory of Marcy Boone abruptly stifled my self-deprecating laugh.

Twenty-Nine:

Gut Feelings

Neither Christmas Eve nor Christmas Day was traditional, even by my standards. Normally, I'd have some kind of turkey-themed dinner, if only a frozen turkey pot pie. I'd watch some version of *A Christmas Tale* on TV or maybe *The Bishop's Wife*. I'd play carols courtesy of my father's ancient vinyl records, where the hissing from all those scratches enhanced my enjoyment. And I'd place the tree-topping angel, handed down from one set of great-grandparents, on a table, surrounded by some votive lights. Not this year. I subsisted on cereal and sandwiches. Neither the angel nor Dad's records made it out of the closet, and the TV never got turned on.

I was too busy painting. My productivity was manic. I soon ran out of the six-pack of canvas boards from Walmart and made do with sheets from a painting tablet dating back more than a decade. The works were variations on the same theme. I guess you could classify them under abstract expressionism, although Pollock and company might disagree. Funny, I never liked the abstract expressionists when I studied them in school. They struck me as self-indulgent and pointlessly obscure. But here I was, being self-indulgent and obscure, and rather enjoying it. I was tapping into emotions I didn't understand, couldn't identify. The process felt therapeutic, even if it solved nothing. I still had all the same old worries and insecurities.

After a ham sandwich for Christmas dinner, I forced myself to put down my brushes and clean up, so I could write a detailed plan for the next day. Precise details might guarantee a speedy and successful roundtrip to 1999. With forethought, I'd have a better chance of correcting my earlier missteps, which just might have messed up Aaron's life.

As I made room for my new art supplies in the box containing older sketches and paintings, several spilled out: nude studies from college. Included among them was the creepy sketch of a penis with a mole. I still had no memory of painting it, even though the work was clearly mine. What's more, the portrayal was far too graphic for the typical studio exercise. Yes, the other models were nude, but their poses obscured most of their genitalia. Most significantly, the other sketches and paintings had faces. This exception zeroed in on the subject's crotch.

The more I examined the charcoal sketch, the more anxious I became. No, I felt frightened. How could I be frightened of something I had crafted with my own hands? Wasn't that one reason why I was so drawn to art? For a few hours, I created my own reality, even when I was trying to replicate external reality as precisely as possible. I was in control.

I felt out of control as I looked at the mole. The hideous mole on the hideous penis. "I hope it was cancerous," I said suddenly. I had no idea why. No idea who I was cursing.

All the good feelings of the past two days drained out of me. I was becoming a powerless puddle. And that was the last thing I could afford before the next day's daunting excursion.

I shoved the troubling sketch back in the box and took a series of deep breaths. What was it Dr. Brown had advised? Breathe into the belly? So, I tried making my abdomen expand with each ragged inhale. And I exhaled long and noisily through my mouth. After about twenty of these, my heart rate slowed a bit. That alone gave me some semblance of control. I could do this.

I grabbed the notepad used for grocery lists and sat at the kitchen table. However much effort might be involved, crafting my plan for the next journey back to 1999 felt like a welcome distraction. As scary as time travel might be, it felt far less scary than whatever backstory that mole drawing held.

I started scribbling. I had no intention of reliving the sexual assault, the immediate aftermath, the version where I slowly came to my senses in Aaron's apartment, or the version where I went to the hospital. Those points in time didn't need revisiting, I figured, if my sole goal was to remove whatever spanner I'd thrown into Aaron's life. The day after that horrid frat party, I had somehow enabled his fears of inadequacy at MIT. So maybe all I needed to do was deprive him of any excuse to stay in Virginia—like a trial requiring his testimony. I hoped to arrive in 1999 one hour after Detective Kruger called me in my dorm room, to report Emily's plea deal. That should give me plenty of time to contact

Aaron, share the good news, and tell him he had no reason not to head for Cambridge and the bright future awaiting him there. Once that item was resolved, I decided against making a list of the sights and sounds in my 1999 dorm room. Just writing down those details might launch me before I was ready, before I could take care of Hecuba.

That night I slept fitfully, caroming from one plotless dream to the next. They were a series of disjointed, jarring images filled with garish brushstrokes, two-dimensional nudes that moved, lots and lots of moles. The visual cacophony segued into monochromatic reality when I awoke. Dense cloud cover prolonged the pre-dawn gloom. The heavy mood was further weighed down by Hecuba's grumpiness upon realizing there would be no breakfast (no food before anesthesia). But we made it without incident to the vet's office, where a cheerful tech got Hecuba's tail wagging. As the dog trotted off to the holding crates, she looked relieved to get away from gloomy me.

Once back home, I tidied up the cottage and turned on a few lights to prevent me from crashing into something if I returned in full darkness. I placed my cellphone on the kitchen counter so it wouldn't get lost on the journey. I left a housekey inside a fake rock on the porch, so I could lock out burglars but still have a way back inside after my return. I didn't want to take my keys. They were just something else that could go missing in 1999.

Satisfied that nothing looked amiss, I went outside, locked

the door, and trudged uphill toward the Ashwood graveyard. I'd decided that site should be my departure point. After all, it was already a kind of portal where the dead had their final earthbound stay before heading for a different reality. So, why shouldn't I treat the graveyard as my own portal before heading into my past-altering reality?

Fortunately, there was no sign of Roy. His appearance would disrupt the concentration needed for my visualization process. I parked on the bench closest to the grave markers and filled my brain with sensory images of my dorm room. Precisely how it looked on that morning in the fall of 1999. How the early morning light weakly entered the window. How I heard the girl next door stumble into some piece of furniture as she got out of bed. How the light on my answering machine flickered redly, signaling the message begun by Detective Kruger before I picked up the receiver.

And there the red light is, flashing with excitement over the detective's message. When I push the button, I hear his voice and then my own. I don't yet know how much time has transpired—in 1999—since that call came in. But that's easy to check, with the help of the Timex watch lying on my bureau. Its little window verifies the date. The time is still early morning, thus not long after Kruger's call. I congratulate myself for my precision. I'm getting better at this.

308

Then, for the very first time in all my peregrinations, I wonder where my younger self is. Would the world explode if two versions of me collided? It's surprising it hasn't happened yet. Unless it *can't* happen? Maybe it's impossible for more than one version of me to occupy a given space at any one time. Or maybe there really aren't multiple versions of me? How on earth does any of this work? Clearly, I don't know as much as I—very briefly—thought I did.

"Well, no sense thinking about that now. I've got a call to make."

On my desk I find the note paper where I'd jotted down Aaron's phone number. I punch the numbers into my Ma Bell landline.

Aaron answers on the first ring: "Cate? You okay?"

"How'd you know it was me?"

"I sprung for Caller ID. You haven't answered my question. Are you all right?"

"Better than all right. That detective just called me. He said Emily took a plea deal. There won't be any trial. You won't have to testify. No need to put your plans on hold. You can head off to MIT early next year, just as scheduled."

"Wait! Slow down! Is Emily going to jail?"

"Yes. For less time than she would if found guilty at a trial. But Kruger assured me she'll spend some time behind bars."

"Good. Maybe she'll think twice about drugging someone else after she gets out."

"Let's hope so. Anyway, I wanted you to know immediately. And I also … well, I'm troubled by something. That conversation we had about your transfer plans. Sounded like you're suddenly disenchanted with your dream school."

"I just wonder if I'm making a mistake. I'm doing okay here. Know my way around. Have a few friends. Why start all over again?"

"Isn't MIT *worth* starting all over again?"

"But it will be so hard! Not just starting over. The curriculum. What if I'm not as sharp as I thought I was? What if I bomb out? At least here, I'll graduate near the top of my class."

"Sounds like you're settling. What if you find out you're even *sharper*? The only way you'll know is if you challenge yourself. How challenged are you at JMU? And how can you grow into your potential if you're not? Right? Don't you owe it to yourself to stretch your wings? Don't you owe it to your parents?"

I wince at that bit of emotional blackmail. But I don't try to smooth things over, like I normally would. I let the awkward silence lie between us.

Aaron finally responds. "Jeez, thanks for the guilt trip."

"You remember Mr. White, our chemistry teacher in middle school? Remember him saying that the biggest regrets adults have involve the stuff they didn't do, the chances they didn't take."

"Uh-huh. I also remember Ben Toddman wishing he hadn't

wrecked his old man's Buick. I bet that joy ride is one thing he'd take back if he could."

"Yeah, and you always thought Ben Toddman was a jerk. He probably never made a wise decision in his life. You're not him. You had a positive, attainable dream: going to MIT and using it as a launching pad for a great future. Well, you've made that dream come true. So why not go for even bigger dreams, dreams that an MIT education can help you realize?"

"You really think I have a great future ahead of me?"

"Not if you stay at JMU."

"What about you, Cate? Maybe JMU isn't good enough for you, either."

"It's good for the arts, and that's what I want. But there's no comparing JMU and MIT when it comes to science and technology."

"I guess."

"I can see you getting your undergraduate degree from MIT, near the top of your class. And after you get your Ph.D., you'll launch some gazillion-dollar company producing, I dunno, tiny byte-thingees. Hundreds will owe their jobs to you. Who knows what technological advances your company will give the world. And your face will be on the cover of TIME magazine. Man of the Year!"

"Tiny byte-thingees?" Aaron snorts. "Stick to the arts, Devine. For all our sakes."

"I will if you promise to stick to your transfer plans."

"Okay, okay. I give. Sheesh, you're worse than my mother. I'll go to MIT. But you gotta promise me something, too."

"What?"

"You gotta send me a postcard from Paris when your artwork gets exhibited at ... what's the famous art museum there?"

"The Louvre?"

"Yeah, that's the one."

I laugh. "It's a deal."

"Gonna hold you to it, Devine." He pauses. "And thanks for talking me off the ledge."

"After everything you did for me the other night? Least I could do."

"Happy to do it. And it's been good seeing you again, Cate. Well, um ... *why* we reconnected was pretty crappy but ... oh, hell, you know what I mean."

"I do. And it was good seeing you again, too. You take care, now."

I hang up, feeling pleased with myself. No, I don't know for sure that my fix worked, but I gave it a good shot. Aaron seems headed in the right direction, now that he's "off the ledge."

My sense of satisfaction fades as I remember two other missteps needing correction, the ones that may have altered Joe's and Mother's life. That realization triggers cramping in my gut. Is it even possible to make a lateral move: journeying from JMU in

1999 to my Arlington home in 1998? That feels risky, especially given my responsibilities toward Hecuba. Better to head back to my Fauquier County reality first.

So I sit on my bed and start breathing deeply, while visualizing the Ashwood graveyard. How peaceful it is there. Each deep breath gets easier as I envision that space, smell the crushed pine needles, hear the distant whickering of horses, feel the crispness of the late December air.

Crisp indeed! I rubbed my arms briskly to warm up. It was awfully cold outside. A cold winter's afternoon, by the angle of the sun. Not early morning in autumn. Looking around, I saw the familiar, rain-worn gravestones and smiled. I made it back. In record time. I trudged in the direction of my cottage. With every step, the cramping in my gut intensified. What now?

Once inside, I dashed to my phone to check the time and date. It told me I'd been gone only a few hours in twenty-first-century time. It also told me I had one new voicemail.

"Miss Devine? It's Callie at Dr. Fry's. Hecuba's just fine, but we had an emergency with another dog. Needed surgery. Dr. Fry won't get to Hecuba's dental cleaning until this afternoon. Which means she'll still be loopy from anesthesia by close of business. So we'd best keep her overnight. You can pick her up tomorrow. Give us a call if you have any questions, okay?"

Well, none of that was bad news, nothing to cramp up my innards. Now that I suddenly had a free afternoon and evening, maybe I could squeeze in some more time travel, to address whatever I'd done wrong with Joe and Mother. I felt impatient, eager to make things right as soon as possible.

But first, I had to address whatever was physically wrong with *me*. In the bathroom, I discovered I'd started my second menstrual period in one month. Maybe perimenopause was to blame. More likely it was time travel. Did I really think I could get away with a journey, however short, without some body fluid issuing forth? Silly girl.

Thirty:

Cleaning Up Messes

1 cleaned myself up, popped two aspirins, and hiked up the hill once again. Given the relative ease of the time travel just concluded, I hoped this next excursion would be easy. I certainly had no trouble visualizing my childhood home or Mother's outraged appearance that day in March 1998. Sure, it might be tricky getting the timing right: just after Mother overheard my phone call with Joe to set a date for discussing our science fair project. But I had a clear memory of the wan sunbeam infiltrating the half-shaded living room. I also recalled quite specifically how I had to grab Blackie's collar as he growled at Mother. That was a rare occurrence, which should help pinpoint the time of my arrival.

Nevertheless, my visualization of Mother, Blackie, and that living room was in danger of getting displaced by another image: a mole on a penis. I knew without a shadow of doubt that going back to wherever and whenever that image originated would spell disaster. So every time the mole would intrude on my concentration, I curled my toes and clenched my fists and focused on the white fur covering Blackie's muzzle and eyebrows in the last year of his life. As I recalled the sadness of losing him the summer of 1998, it grew easier to banish that bizarre nude study.

I'm in my childhood living room again, holding onto Blackie's collar as Mother scolds me.

"I had plans for Sunday afternoon, by the way. Not that you asked. A visit with Mrs. Haley. I expected you to accompany me. You know the difficulty I have negotiating stairs with this osteoporosis. Well, fine, I'll manage by myself. Somehow. But don't think my absence gives that boy a free hand to do what he wants in this house. I don't want the neighbors clucking about you anymore than they already do."

Her words sting, just as they did more than two decades earlier. Just as before, I recall the conversation I'd overheard of two neighbors clucking, but not about me. They were gossiping about what a "tyrant that mother is." How "judgmental." What a "snob." They expressed sympathy for "the daughter, poor thing."

I'm pretty sure that, in the original version of this scene, I bowed my head, begged Mother's forgiveness, and said nothing about the neighbors' criticism. Although I don't want to sink into spineless contrition this time around, I don't want to trigger a fatal shock, either. So I resolve not to sass her, as I imagined doing during my apparent blackout at the Citizen Star awards ceremony.

I decide on a middle course.

"I'm sorry if I inconvenienced you, Mother," I say calmly. "But this science project is an important part of my physics grade.

My scholarship to JMU depends on at least a three-point-oh average when I graduate from high school. I know how pressed you are financially, and that burden will ease somewhat if I'm out of the house, living at the dorm. Your grocery bill will certainly go down." I offer a self-deprecating smile.

"All well and good, but you might have consulted me first."

"Sorry, but it was hard pinning Joe down. Of course, you know you have nothing to worry about when he's here. I've always behaved responsibly and don't plan to stop now."

"Responsibly?" Mother snorts.

"Don't you think a solid record of school attendance and good grades show responsibility? When other kids are out partying, I'm studying or handling household chores."

"Are you complaining?"

"Not at all. I've always known how hard things have been since Daddy died. I've always known my future wouldn't be handed to me on a silver platter."

"Well, don't expect me to police this young man. It's all on you. Do you really think you're up to it, Cate? You know how you get around strangers."

"I'm up to it," I say nodding. "Thank you for understanding."

Mother harrumphs and heads for the kitchen. Before leaving the living room, she eyes me with curiosity. I look up and smile. Mother shakes her head and leaves.

I'm shaking. With disbelief, relief, a sense of victory. Okay, for most people that scene would hardly classify as a triumph. But it feels pretty darn good to me. I've actually "managed" my mother, like an adult. And unnerved her in the process, although without drama, petulance, or a catastrophic health incident.

I head upstairs to the bathroom, to tidy up and plot my next journey. Although the visualization process that sent me here was difficult, I have ended up exactly where I wanted to be and have done exactly what I wanted to do. Feeling like I'm getting the hang of bending time, I debate whether I should trek back to my Fauquier County reality before haring off to undo whatever I'd done to Joe. But this time, a lateral move seems like a reasonable risk. After all, Joe's visit would take place just days after my ever so adult discussion with Mother.

I don't have an appropriate portal from which to launch my next journey. But the bathroom of my childhood home is the only place with any semblance of privacy. So, I sit down, fully clothed on the closed toilet lid and start visualizing Joe's entry into my living room that Sunday in March 1998. I see his dimples, his slightly crooked top incisors. I see him sprawled in Mother's favorite armchair, slurping from a can of Coke. I hear him complaining that my outline of the science fair project is giving him a...

"Headache! How long is this gonna take?" He looks at his watch and groans again. "If I'm late, Sandy's gonna kill me."

"Sandy?" I ask, even though I already know the answer.

"Sandy Reynolds. My girlfriend. She keeps me on a short leash."

He chuckles, glugs from the can, burps, then chuckles again.

"Sounds like you got everything taken care of. I'd just screw things up anyway. Why don't you keep handling the research? I can help set up the displays on the day of the fair."

I feel the same surge of anger I felt the first two times I experienced this scene. I will not take this insult lying down. But I won't summon a thundercloud, either. As big a jerk as Joe is, he doesn't deserve a fried brain.

"You're acting like a jerk," I tell Joe as he rises from his chair, downing his Coke and spilling some on Mother's side table.

"Huh?" he says, wiping his mouth with the back of his hand.

"If you leave me to do all the work, I'll claim all the credit. Makes no difference to me. But I doubt you can afford a failing grade in physics. That might just kill your plans to land a football scholarship to ODU."

"Huh?" he repeats, slumping back into the chair.

"So how about we spend half an hour or so breaking down who's gonna do what? You can keep Sandy waiting. Or you can make your date and flunk physics. Which is it gonna be?"

Joe's jaw drops and his eyes widen.

"So," I continue, grabbing the notepad lying beside me on the sofa. A million years earlier, I filled it with my organizational ideas for the science project. "Here's the list I made of ten tasks we need to do. You decide which five you can handle. I'll take the rest."

Biting his lip, he squints at the pad. "Umm, I don't know what the third item means. Or the fifth. Or the seventh."

"Fine. I'll handle them. Now you pick the five you *do* understand. Numbers one, two, and ten are pretty easy. Now pick two more."

"You're one tough girl," he says flashing his most endearing smile. "Can't you handle a couple more?"

I fixate on his crooked front teeth and shake my head. "Nope. Not unless you want Hofstadter to know how you welched out of this project."

Groaning, he eyes the list once again. "Crap!" After a heavy sigh, he adds, "I guess I could handle numbers four and six."

"Terrific. You take care of one, two, four, six, and ten. Get them done in two weeks. After that, we'll meet again to see if we've covered all the bases. Central Library is a more convenient place to meet. How about the first Saturday in April? At ten?"

"Saturday? That's the only day I can sleep in."

I splay my hands and stare at him.

"Okay, okay. Jeez, you're worse than Hofstadter."

I rip off a blank piece of paper from my notepad and scribble down the tasks Joe is supposed to handle. "So you don't forget," I say, handing him the paper.

Joe pouts and thrusts the list in his pocket. Head down, he trudges toward the front door, which I open wordlessly. As he plods down the front walkway, he grumbles softly, "Ballbuster."

Smiling, I look up at the sky. No thunderclouds. I don't need any bolts of lightning. I did what needed doing. My smile broadens as I watch Joe approach a blue Mustang parked at the end of my street. He gesticulates wildly at the driver's window then trudges dejectedly to the passenger's door and slumps inside. The Mustang burns rubber as it takes off.

I chuckle gleefully. My glee is cut short by a cramp that doubles me forward. I head for the bathroom where I take a while to clean up. I've felt better, but, hey, handling the red tide is a small price to pay for the satisfaction earned from these last two treks to 1998.

And as long as I'm back in the "portal" that is my Arlington bathroom, I might as well start the visualization process sooner rather than later to get me back home.

THIRTY~ONE:

GOOD NEWS, BAD NEWS

Cramps and profuse menstrual bleeding weren't the only reasons undermining my elation at accomplishing what I'd set out to do. The face looking back at me in the hall mirror of my cottage seemed downright haggard. I was used to the purple stains under my eyes. The white streak at the right temple was new. No wonder. Taking three trips back to the 1990s in just one day was bound to take a toll on my body. Giving my hair a mournful pat, I said, "Oh well, the hellhound and I will be a matched set."

Even though the cottage felt hollow without Hecuba, I was relieved to have more than eighteen hours before I needed to pick her up. My laptop told me it was late afternoon on December 26, 2022, so I had plenty of time for online detective work.

I promptly tapped "S. Aaron Rappaport" into Google's search box. A dozen listings came up, all recognizable as the Aaron I knew. Did my earlier failure to include his first initial, standing for a name he hated, explain why no hits came up during that search? I was too impatient to test that theory. It was enough to know that my time-bending excursion hadn't deprived Aaron of his success.

Next, I filled the search box with "Joe Scanlon," "ODU," and "football." Two relevant listings appeared, referring to Joe's athletic career in college. Clearly, he had not been disabled by a lightning bolt in high school.

Finally, I searched for Mother's obituary. And there it was, the very item I'd sent to The Washington Post three years ago: "Helen Purcell Devine, age 70, died peacefully at her home in Arlington, Virginia." If she'd had a fall giving her a fatal brain hemorrhage in 1998, she would have been forty-seven when she died.

"Phew! Everyone's where they should be, *when* they should be."

My relief had a positive effect on my cramps. My stomach actually growled from hunger. Deciding on an early dinner, I fished a mac-and-cheese from the freezer and turned on the oven. As I waited for the temperature to slog up to three-fifty, I wondered if some universal good was served by Aaron, Joe, and Mother living their lives exactly as I'd first remembered. That might certainly be the case with Aaron. After all, his tech company had generated lots of economic benefits for lots of people. But was the world better because Joe Scanlon had been a college all-star and Mother lived another twenty-three years? How odd that none of my time travel triggered changes in *my* life. I always had the same job and lived in the same place in Fauquier County, regardless of any tinkering with time. Was I somehow predestined to be in this time and place?

"To what end?" I snorted derisively.

Truth be told, I hadn't revisited the late 1990s to restore the cosmic balance. I made those trips first and foremost for me, to relieve me of guilt from tinkering with anyone's life. Pretty narcissistic, when you get right down to it. Funny, I never thought of myself as a narcissist before. The label didn't sit comfortably. But it was preferable to labeling myself a spineless wimp. I wondered if Dr. Brown would agree.

Then I wondered if I should share with him the craziness of the past few days. For therapy to work, I should be totally honest with my therapist. But too much honesty might land me in psychiatric lockdown.

As I popped the frozen dinner into the oven, the phone interrupted my musings. "Lavinia Ashwood" vibrated on the screen.

"Mrs. Ashwood?"

"When *will* you remember to call me Lavinia, dear? Ah well, never mind. I trust you had a pleasant holiday?"

"Oh, yes. Just fine. And you?"

"Splendid. Splendid. The reason I'm calling is because, well, I didn't realize you were such a talented artist."

"I'm sorry?"

"Roy. You really impressed him, Cate. He texted me several photos of the painting you did of the family graveyard. Just breathtaking! Harland was over the moon when he saw them."

"Golly. Thank you."

"Not at all. It got me to thinking … Harland's health is the main reason we spend part of every year in Florida, but he gets horribly homesick. At first, it was just the horses. It's much more than that now. Harland feels divorced from his very soul. Those Fauquier County acres are his ancestral homestead, after all. It's getting harder and harder to keep him from heading north on Groundhog Day—a date that rarely sees even the hardiest crocus bloom in northwestern Fauquier. Lord knows, Easter is no guarantee of gentle weather, either."

I chuckled. "It certainly wasn't gentle last year."

"My point precisely. So, I thought Harland might feel less homesick if he was surrounded by mementos of the old homestead. And I would face less risk of being prematurely catapulted out of the Florida sunshine. Will you help?"

"Help? I don't follow."

"Cate, I'd like to buy your painting and commission more. Would you part with it for two-hundred-fifty dollars?"

"Two-fifty?" I gasped.

"All right. What would you say to three hundred, then?"

"Umm, sure."

"Excellent. Could you take the painting to that frame shop in Warrenton? Marcia has done work for me before, and I trust her to find an appropriate frame. I'll have her bill my charge card for the frame and the cost of sending the painting down here. Would you get in touch with her as soon as possible? I'd like the painting to arrive for Harland's birthday. That's January seventeenth."

"Sure."

"Excellent. That takes care of my first request. Now, could you select other scenes around the property to paint? I'd like at least one additional piece evoking the old homestead before, say, March? I don't know how your creative process works, but I'd be interested in however many you could produce. I'd want to see photos of the paintings, of course. Most likely, anything you create will be lovely, but just to have an idea how much I should offer."

I placed a palm over my suddenly racing heart, gulped, and said, "I could do that. As for how quickly any other artwork would come, it kinda depends on the flow, you know?"

"One must be in tune with one's muse."

"Uh-huh. Yeah. That. Do you have any preference for media?"

"Media?"

"Oil, acrylic, watercolor, pen-and-ink, charcoal, pastels?"

"I'll leave that entirely up to the artist, my dear. Just keep me posted on your progress, won't you? You have my email address, right?"

"I do. I'll start looking around to see…"

"Oh dear, there's Harland at the back door. I want to keep this hush-hush until his birthday. So, I'd best sign off. I'll pop the check in the mail tomorrow. You have yourself a Happy New Year!"

The line went dead before I could return the wish. I stared, disbelieving, at the phone in my palm. "Three hundred dollars?

Maybe half a dozen commissions? Happy New Year to me!"

I pulled out all my art boxes. Would I need more supplies? I wouldn't really know, of course, until I had a better idea of just what "scenes" I would choose. Certain media just wouldn't do for certain subjects. I knew that much, regardless of how long my artistic aspirations had been withering. Like a kid on Christmas morning, I continued pulling things out of those boxes and imagining what projects might come forth. Yes, a dark internal voice doubted that I could pull this off. But I absolutely, positively would not let it ruin this moment. "I can do this!" I shouted. Halfway convincingly.

And then I saw it. Again. Picking up that horrid nude study, I whispered, "What are you doing? Following me around like some dark cloud?"

I stared hard at that stupid penis. At that wretched mole. Why on earth would I paint such an ugly thing? And then ... something began to shift, ever so slowly inside my brain. Wisp by wisp, the fog obscuring ancient memories began to dissipate.

I hurled the sketch from me, as if it were burning my hands.

I grabbed some craft shears and attacked the jettisoned drawing. The first cut went straight across the penis, neatly dissecting the mole. Not satisfied, I kept cutting until the shreds were unrecognizable.

"Ignorance actually *was* bliss, wasn't it?" I whispered, as a single tear rolled down one cheek.

329

THIRTY-TWO:

FINDING THE RIGHT WORDS

A part from retrieving Hecuba and seeing to her basic needs, all I did between the evening of the twenty-sixth and the afternoon of the twenty-ninth was obsess about finding the right words. How could I possibly tell my complicated story to Dr. Brown, when I saw him for my next appointment? My homework assignment for him—thinking of the ways I might have reacted differently to troubling events—had raised all sorts of issues. Talking about time travel and my humiliation at that frat party would be challenging enough. How on earth would I tell him about the repugnant memory that suddenly and savagely slouched out of the shadows of my brain? How could I begin to talk about it, as I surely must if this whole therapy business was to have any point?

Time seemed more malleable and unpredictable than ever—not only because of my own ability to bend that construct. As events from my childhood—long suppressed, apparently—capriciously replayed in both my dreaming and waking moments, I felt caught in some kind of time loop. Nevertheless, time behaved predictably enough for December the twenty-ninth to arrive exactly when it was supposed to.

So, there I was, sitting on Dr. Brown's sofa, kneading Hecuba's fur so roughly she occasionally groaned, while words spilled out of my mouth in no coherent order. There was no way to craft a rational progression. How could any of this make sense to my therapist when it made no sense to me? But Dr. Brown soldiered through my verbal diarrhea with a calm, thoughtful expression. He probably uttered no more than two words during this first phase of the session, however long that was. Finally, I paused to gulp air. I was hyperventilating.

Dr. Brown used the pause to comment. "We've got quite a lot to unpack. And we will. There's no rush. Of everything you've just told me, is there any one feeling you'd like to focus on right now?"

I blurted out, "Yeah. What's wrong with me?"

"How is that a feeling?"

I groaned, struggling to find the words. "It *feels* like there must be something inside me that brings out the worst in people. It feels like there's something that puts a target on my back. Something that makes otherwise normal people want to hurt and humiliate me."

"Do you really believe that your college classmate—Emily, was it?—would never have had cruel instincts, never have acted on them, if she hadn't met you? When someone runs a stoplight and t-bones your car, are you responsible? Hardly. As for your uncle … well, he just sounds like the soul of normalcy, right?"

"But my mother worshipped him. During his rare visits, she got downright chirpy, almost youthful. Maybe because he was her father figure? He had been kind to us, giving us money when times were really hard. He could be charming and witty and had "lots of skills."

"Especially those hidden medical skills. Let's talk about the enemas in more detail. You said they were prescribed by your pediatrician, for some GI trouble?"

I nodded, digging my knuckles more deeply into Hecuba's scruff. "Except, I remembered it as an offhand suggestion. But what do I know? I was only nine."

"What do you remember him saying?"

"Something like, 'If the cramping and nausea don't go away with the pills, maybe an enema will speed things along.' I asked Mother about that days later, when she told me I'd need twice daily enemas until I got well."

"Did she explain why she wouldn't be the one administering the enemas?"

"Mother was disgusted by body fluids. Of any sort."

"Did she use that word?"

I nodded. "She'd often tell me how disgusting I was if she had to use the bathroom after I'd done my business."

Dr. Brown shook his head ruefully. "Okay. Can you reconstruct the first enema? What did Uncle Henry do? Where did it take place ... stuff like that."

"It was always in the hallway leading from the bedrooms to the bathroom. Uncle Henry lined the hallway with newspaper, so the floor wouldn't get messed up. He told me to take off all my clothes while he took the enema bag to the bathroom."

"*All* your clothes?"

"Uh-huh. When he came out of the bathroom, he was holding up the filled bag and wearing some kind of blue gloves. Latex, I guess. Then he'd attach the bag to a hook on the ceiling. My mother sometimes hung a spider plant up there. It had lots of babies and they had room to cascade downward from that height."

"Did your uncle try to make you feel less scared?"

"He was all business. Not mean. Just efficient, I guess. He'd squat down beside me and tell me to part my legs. Then he'd stick the tube inside. I didn't like the feeling, but it didn't hurt. I guess he put Vaseline or something on it first. But then it did hurt. A lot."

"When?"

"As soon as he opened up the clip on the tubing. The water would rush in. I remember the cramping. Felt like my insides were gonna explode, all the way up here." I patted my diaphragm.

"Once the bag was empty, how would you relieve yourself?"

"Uncle Henry would tell me it was okay to dash to the bathroom. Where I'd just explode."

"You had to wait for his okay?"

I nodded. "But it was right away."

"Uh-huh, but he was still the one who had control over your body function." He shook his head. "Okay, I'd like you to imagine something. Imagine Hecuba here has some tummy trouble. The vet tells you to administer an enema. How would you go about it?"

I shuddered. "Well ... gee. I guess I'd pet her a lot. Tell her she was gonna be okay. Ask her to lie down. Or no, maybe it would be easier if she was standing? Yeah, I guess I'd cradle her belly with one hand and stick the nozzle in with the other. Oh, wait. First, I'd put Vaseline on the nozzle and hang the enema bag someplace."

"Where do you think you'd hang the bag?"

"Huh? I dunno. Maybe hook it onto a coat hanger and stick the hanger over the back of a chair? I don't get it, Dr. Brown. What does any of this matter?"

He raised a staying palm. "Listen to what you just said. You've described several ways in which you'd minimize the dog's fear and discomfort. And you'd hang the bag maybe only a foot above the dog."

"Yeah? So?"

"So the water wouldn't rush into her with a ridiculous amount of force. The way it would when that enema bag was hanging from a seven- or eight-foot ceiling."

"Oh. Yeah. Was that why it hurt so much?"

Dr. Brown nodded. "Sounds like your uncle was bent on turning an unpleasant but nonthreatening procedure into a sadistic exercise."

"Why?"

He shrugged. "My professional assessment? He was nuts."

I actually laughed. Dr. Brown laughed, too.

"Okay, so that's the rough outline for the first enema. You didn't say anything about what he was wearing, apart from the latex gloves. What was he wearing?"

"I dunno. Shirt and pants?"

"So, fully clothed. At what point did he take off his clothes?"

"I don't remember. After the first week? Uncle Henry was in between jobs or house moves or something. So, he was staying with us for the whole summer."

"And what about the rest of the household. Where were they when you were having all those enemas?"

"Dad would have been at work. Yeah, the enemas were always in the morning and afternoon. I don't know where he was on Sundays. Maybe church? Sometimes he'd go to Mass by himself."

"And what about your mother? Where was she?"

I shrugged. "I don't..." And then the memory erupted. It must have been another one of those repressed images. It was hard to examine it and stay focused on therapy. I must have zoned out a bit, because I only distantly heard Dr. Brown's voice...

"Cate? You with me? What are you seeing?"

"It's Mother. I hear her coming up the stairs. Can't see her, because I'm on my belly on the newspaper. But I see her shoes. And I can also see Uncle Henry's clothes, neatly folded in one corner of the hallway. Mother's shoes walked across the hallway and into her bedroom."

"Did she say anything to you or your uncle?"

"No. But I remember something else. I asked her something afterward."

"What was your question?"

"I asked her why Uncle Henry took off his clothes to give me the enema. She told me it was to keep clean. She told me he had complained about what a mess I'd made of things after the first few enemas. Exploded all over everything. And he didn't want his clothes to get soiled."

"So, it was all your fault?"

I gulped air. "I said, 'It wasn't my fault, Mother! I couldn't help it. It hurt so much. I couldn't always make it to the toilet in time.'"

"And how did she respond?"

"She slapped my face. Hard." For the first time in this crazy session, I started to cry.

"I'm sorry," Dr. Brown said, shoving a box of Kleenex across the table separating my couch from his easy chair.

As I blew my nose, I repeated, "She slapped me! She saw a grown man, naked, with her naked nine-year-old daughter. And she blamed *me*. Slapped me! And she was the one who set the whole thing up. By asking Uncle Henry to give me all those miserable enemas."

"And this went on for how long?"

I shrugged. "A couple of weeks. I think. I'm not sure. I zoned out a lot. Especially after he got naked."

"Was anything else different about those naked enemas?"

"You mean, like rape?"

"Whatever you remember. And, by the way, even if your uncle did nothing more than what you just described, that counts as sexual abuse in and of itself."

"I just don't remember. It was all so unpleasant, so scary, I wanted to be anywhere else. And I was pretty good at... Wait a minute! I just remembered something else. It was a dream I had only a few weeks ago. Of Uncle Henry. Taking care of me when I was sick."

"Tell me about it."

"In the dream, I had a stomach ache, and Uncle Henry was trying to get me to swallow a spoonful of medicine. He was smiling and cajoling me, but I wanted none of it. Because the medicine was yucky brown and smoldering. But he kept coming at me, despite my protests. So I distracted myself by looking at pictures on the wall. And before I knew it, those pictures flew off the wall and hit Uncle Henry. And made him really, really mad. The dream really unsettled me."

"Why?"

"Because part of that dream may have been reality. I think I did move those pictures one time when I was getting an enema. And caused Uncle Henry to get hurt. And get mad."

"How did he express his anger?"

"I don't know. My brain is fogging up again."

"That's okay. You've remembered a lot. And since repressing memories is a self-protective instinct, there's no need to push yourself further than you're comfortable going. Whenever you..."

I raised an index finger. "Wait. I just got something else. The time when I made the pictures fly off the walls was the last time I experienced the enema."

"Your uncle stopped giving them to you after that incident?"

I whimpered. "No. There were more. But I wasn't in the room. I would just look at those pictures on the wall. Instead of making them move, I went to where they were."

"Where was that?"

"Some pretty meadow. And I would just stay there until it was all over."

Dr. Brown nodded. "Sounds like a much healthier place to be. You had no problem coming back to yourself?"

"I see myself kinda phasing back into consciousness, or whatever you'd call it, while buttoning up my shirt or pulling on my pants. Then I just went downstairs, while Uncle Henry cleaned up the newspapers and put the enema bag away."

"At what point did you make that sketch, the one that triggered all those memories?"

"It would have been in college, when I was doing nude studies. I must have done the sketch from memory, outside the classroom. Maybe in my dorm room."

"Were you aware at the time that you were sketching your uncle?"

"Don't think so. But I have no doubt that sketch is of Uncle Henry. For one thing, the skin is saggy. We didn't have any old models. How I could replicate it years later is beyond me."

"Visual images can stick in one's head. Look at how vivid dreams can be. Maybe that's where …"

"Wait! I'm getting a fuzzy image right now. I'm on that miserable newspaper as a little kid, and I risk looking up as I wait for the nozzle to go inside me. That's when I first saw the mole. I knew what it was, because there was a neighbor down the block who had a gross looking one on her neck. But I'd never seen a penis before. And it scared me. The mole made it even worse, somehow."

"Do you recall how you felt when you were making that sketch."

I shook my head. "I must have zoned out when I did it."

Dr. Brown nodded wearily then looked at his watch. "We've run over a bit, Cate. There's so much to talk about. And we'll get there, eventually. Meanwhile, let me suggest something to help you process all this. Your art. Whether or not you were 'zoned out' when you made that sketch of the mole and penis, it sounds like your brain was helping you handle something that was too painful to remember outright. For someone like you, art therapy can be very helpful."

"Funny, before all this surfaced, I was going to tell you about some of the painting I've been doing in the past week or so."

"Excellent. I look forward to hearing about it. Meanwhile, keep painting."

340

Thirty-Three:

Lassiter Brown, M.D.
Session Notes, 29 December 2022

Last session 21 December 2022

Recorded with patient approval. Main focus: newly surfaced memory of sexual abuse in childhood. Likely trigger for multiple dissociative episodes—starting decades earlier and continuing to this day.

General observation: Cate's demeanor frazzled, although generally well-groomed. Lots of self-soothing tics (tugging at braid, smoothing pillow, kneading dog's fur). Apologizes repeatedly for jumble of words, not always in chronological order, as she jumps from different incidents/memories.

New memory involves series of enemas at age 9, administered by maternal uncle in sexual/sadistic context. Both naked. Not clear whether more overt sexual abuse involved. One vivid memory is of seeing flaccid penis with ugly mole. Patient reports she learned to "zone out" after the first few enemas. Did she dissociate because abuse escalated? Or because of the seemingly endless series of treatments (2X a day for several weeks). Dissociation of limited duration. Cate reports "coming to" almost immediately after enema was over.

During her account of sexual abuse, Cate experiences a new memory, involving her mother, who was clearly aware of what was going on. The mother passed right by daughter and uncle, when both were naked. When Cate later asked the mother the reason for no clothing, the mother had an instant rationalization: so Cate wouldn't "dirty" the uncle's clothes. Did mother see daughter as "dirty" for triggering her brother's unhealthy sexuality? Was mother herself a victim of brother's sexual abuse, especially since he was significantly older and "helped raise" her? Was she jealous of Cate, as a rival for Henry's sexual attention? Does this sexual context color the entire mother/daughter relationship and explain the mother's constant criticism, dismissiveness?

Cate expresses anger at Mother, for enabling the abuse. Expresses fear of uncle, but not anger. Perhaps because he was something of a stranger in whom she had no expectation of trust? His long visit the summer she was 9 was the first opportunity to get to know him. She reports being too young to remember earlier visits.

Follow-up questions: Were there subsequent visits/abuse by Uncle Henry? Was the father aware of abuse?

Patient reports catharsis from artwork. Briefly reports how angry some recent paintings appeared. Art also provides a nonthreatening way of processing painful memories. Sketch she made (years later, from memory) of uncle's penis is obvious example, even if she was unaware who her subject was at the time. I encourage Cate to continue exploring art therapy. Once again I suggest medication to ease general anxiety and minimize the risks of triggering a dissociative episode. Concerned that new episode could prove more disruptive than her recent "time travel"—i.e., dissociating from reality while she immerses herself in memories of her past.

THIRTY-FOUR:

PORTRAITS, LIGHT AND DARK

1t's amazing my steering wheel didn't break on the ride home from Dr. Brown' office. I kept slapping it whenever I thought of Mother.

"And I was worried that I'd messed up your life. So worried, I went through all that work to go back and correct any wrong I'd done. Did you ever worry about messing up *my* life? You did not! Because your precious brother could do no wrong. Never mind that you saw exactly what that pervert was doing. You actually made excuses for him and laid the blame on me! What's more, you set the whole enema thing in motion. Did you get your jollies knowing I was being tortured and humiliated? How could a mother do that do her daughter? And what kind of idiot was I for diligently taking care of you when you were sick and old? Putting my life on hold for the woman who betrayed me, reviled me. What's wrong with me? No, what was wrong with *you?*"

After that rant, I glanced at the rearview mirror and saw Hecuba's bug-eyed expression. "Sorry, girl. You're a good, good girl. I'm not angry with you."

Anger wasn't the predominant emotion triggered by memories of Uncle Henry, I suddenly realized. When I thought of him, I felt fear and disgust and impotence—and the need to shut down those memories as soon as possible, lest they result in an unintended trek back to my childhood home in the late 1980s. Despite my earlier vow never to try bending time again, revisiting that era wasn't wholly without appeal. What if another time trek wreaked total havoc on Henry Purcell's life? Now that could be fun, couldn't it? No. Sadly, no. Reliving all that misery and humiliation and physical pain just wouldn't be worth it.

But I could paint vengeful havoc onto my canvases. Probably not what Dr. Brown had in mind when he prescribed art therapy. So what? I slapped the steering wheel again.

Once home, I made short work of dinner. A bowl of kibble for Hecuba. Canned soup for me. Then I went straight to work.

I picked up my charcoals and promptly dashed off a new penis portrait. This one made the actual mole look downright tame. The sketched appendage now looked like it was two seconds away from disintegrating into a pool of pus.

But that disgusting image wasn't satisfying enough. So, I retrieved some boxes containing family photos and dug out several of Mother at various ages. My rendition of her, this time executed with pastels, deviated broadly from my reference photos. Under my hand, her face became every bit as repellent as her brother's loathsome penis. Her face sprouted colorful, suppurating sores. Her teeth were rotting. Her cracked lips oozed brownish fluid. And she leaned on a rickety cane, as she looked beseechingly, helplessly out into the real world, with the sure knowledge that no help would come.

That bit of handiwork didn't bring the satisfaction I sought, either. I felt ... not guilty but disgusted and a little dirty, as if those sores on both subjects could somehow contaminate me.

My hands still twitched to create something. This time, I wanted to conjure something that might soothe me. I went back to the box of photos. So many of them were of Blackie. My sweet spaniel. Often the sole comfort of my childhood. I picked up a charcoal pencil, and Blackie slowly came to life on my sketchpad.

"Where were you, puppy, that miserable summer when Uncle Henry visited?"

As the charcoal moved across the paper, I remembered something telling. Immediately after breakfast, Blackie would scuttle down to the basement. And stay there most of the day. Did you recognize the evil that was Henry Purcell? Blending and rubbing the charcoal, I filled the spaniel's chocolate eyes with worry. The likeness was remarkable. Unfortunately, it neither satisfied nor soothed me.

I tried again, this time switching to oils, a medium that was better-suited to the multilayered portrait hovering in the shadows of my brain. Oils might have a shot at conveying the complexity of emotions I had in mind. I began with a green and umber wash, vaguely reminiscent of vegetation. Slowly, Blackie's lustrous eyes, attentive long ears, and raised muzzle emerged from the background. I painted him in profile, head raised as he gazed at some distant point. The eyes and posture signaled intensity, concern, worry, love. There was also something heroic about the little dog's front paws bracing as if ready to spring toward whatever challenge, threat, or adventure awaited. This was a dog that might have given Uncle Henry pause. But it was still my Blackie. After all, wasn't there an element of heroism in just being there, day after day, consoling me in my bleakest hours?

Which brought me to the subject of my father. No, he hadn't protected me against the Henry Purcells of this world. Or against Mother. But he had been a quiet, soothing presence. I began with a warm, autumnal wash. In the center of the canvas, I detailed the front porch stairs from my childhood home, where Daddy often rested after finishing some household project. I quickly brought to life his well-veined hands, dangling over his knees. But the face would not emerge from the shadows; there was only the suggestion of gentle eyes, turning down at the outer corners. The impression was of a kind man, in danger of disappearing into the background. It felt right to leave the painting unfinished, with a vignette effect.

"Oh, Daddy, no wonder you died so young. You look so weary."

By now, I was as weary as my subject. But the uncomfortable emotions that had plagued me earlier were drained out of me. I groaned at the wall clock, which told me it was two in the morning. I wasn't looking forward to the half-hour of cleanup before I could go to bed, but I was confident I would sleep soundly.

348

A sound sleep it was, even if it lasted just six hours. I awoke energized. One reason was my eagerness to return to painting. The other was the briskness of the air. It smelled like snow. The weatherman was right. For a change. And that meant handling a bunch of chores in case the power went out.

As I fed Hecuba, I noticed something on my back porch: a modest stack of firewood. "Roy, bless him!" I marveled that he had piled the wood outside my door without making a sound. Well, good, that was one less thing to worry about. If we lost power, I'd have a well-fed woodstove.

As I munched on cereal, I looked at the portraits from the previous night. The horrors that were Uncle Henry and Mother elicited gasps. But I would not destroy them, as I had that very first sketch of penis and mole. No, these might prove useful the next time I felt powerless and pitiful. They altered nothing about my past but would remind me of one way I could take power, be in control, create different realities. Who needs to bend time when you can wield a paintbrush or a charcoal pencil?

The portrait of Daddy made me sad. I wished I'd had the chance to know him from an adult perspective. A Psychology 101 teacher once said every parent should live long enough for his children to forgive him his failings. And every parent should live long enough to respect his children as fully-fledged adults with their own unique virtues and flaws. At the time, that sounded wise. Then again … Mother had lived long enough, but neither one of those potentials was ever realized.

It would have been different with Daddy, I told myself.

Looking at his kind eyes reminded me of another kind face. I hadn't done right with my first effort to capture Aaron, but maybe I could do better now. I took out my pastels and began anew. Before I put pencil to paper, I recalled some of the conversations we'd had on that bus to and from middle school. I couldn't exactly remember what we discussed. What I mainly remembered were the emotions that went with the words: grumpiness over an upcoming test, exuberance over the coming Christmas break and, most important, some sense of belonging. Aaron had been the only contemporary willing to give me the time of day.

The Aaron emerging on my sketchpad was not the chubby, bespectacled adolescent who happily shared time and space with me. Instead, it was the lean, still-bespectacled college boy who had shown such kindness in my hour of need. During my earlier effort to sketch him, I'd downloaded some photographs of the middle-aged Aaron to help recall facial features. Surprisingly, I didn't need those images this time. Aaron was firmly inside my head.

Emerging from a blurry blue background was a face wearing a startled smile, as if a welcome friend had just interrupted his studies. An unseen electronic screen was reflected in Aaron's glasses. The image radiated kindness combined with a sleeping vigor and just the hint of mischief.

I was on a roll. For my next sketch, I would accomplish two things at once: fulfill my sudden need to surround myself with visions of kindness while also getting a start on the commissions for Mrs. Ashwood.

After pulling on my parka, I dumped several charcoal pencils into one pocket, tucked the sketchpad under one arm, and whistled for my wolfhound. As I expected, Roy's truck was parked outside the barn. Hecuba loped toward it.

"Oops, forgot something. You stay, hound of mine," I shouted. "I'll be right back. Stay!" Hecuba obediently halted her charge and sat, as I turned back to the cottage.

Minutes later, I reappeared with a tote bag over one shoulder. It carried not only my art supplies but a thermos. Hecuba didn't wait to be released from her sit-stay. She levitated, spun around once just for the heck of it, and headed for the three-board fence enclosing the horses. I broke into a run as she vaulted it.

"Hecuba H. Hellhound! Don't you be scaring the horses like that," Roy scolded, as the white mare scurried out of the barn.

"Sorry!" I panted.

By the time I caught up with the canine interloper, Roy was thumping the dog on her rump. Hecuba reciprocated by thumping Roy's thigh with her long tail.

"Hope the beast didn't scare that mare too bad," I called.

"Aw, she's skitty about everything. The other guys just stomped their feet a bit and kept right on eating."

"Thanks for bringing by that stack of firewood."

"May need it if the power goes out. Sure looks like snow, don't it?"

I fished the thermos out of the tote bag. "Brought some hot cider. Thought you might need to warm up."

Roy took my offering and grinned. "Thanks. Could use it, day like today. What's that you got in your other hand?"

I held up my sketchpad. "I wanted to rough out some horse scenes for Mr. Ashwood. Oh, that's right! I haven't seen you since Lavinia's call. She's commissioned me to paint some scenes around the place, to make her husband less homesick down there in Florida."

"That a fact?" Roy poured steaming cider into the thermos cap.

"He especially misses the horses. So, I thought I'd do some sketches down here. You mind if I draw while you work?"

He overturned an empty metal water trough. "Got a seat for you and everything. Hope you don't mind the smell."

Shaking my head, I sat down, flipped open the pad, and began drawing.

"Mnm, mnm, mnm. Your fingers be just skipping over that paper. Like they got a mind of their own."

"Sometimes they do. When I'm having a good day."

Roy recapped the thermos and picked up his muck rake. "You got any plans for New Year's Eve?"

"No, it's not a holiday I've ever paid much attention to." I smudged some of the charcoal strokes with my middle finger.

"I hear ya. Never could see the point of getting all drunk and rowdy with a bunch of strangers. Missus and me? We're usually fast asleep by midnight."

I nodded in agreement. Also in approval of my surreptitious sketch of Roy. I began a second portrait on another corner of the same sheet.

"New Year's Day? Now that's another thing." He dumped a shovelful of straw-spiked manure into the cart attached to an all-terrain vehicle.

"That's a holiday you *do* celebrate?" I began roughing in the bay gelding currently snuffling Hecuba's tail.

"You gotta start the year right. Can't remember a New Year's Day without Hoppin' John."

"That's for good luck, yeah? My father sometimes made it when I was a kid."

"I used to make it, too. Not bad, if I do say so myself. But the missus, her Hoppin' John is the best ever." Roy paused to lean on the rake. "Mnm, mnm, mnm." He shook his head downright reverentially.

I flipped to a new page, which my pencil attacked frantically.

I badly wanted to capture Roy in this exact posture, before he resumed raking.

Maybe an hour passed, with each of us absorbed by our individual labors, while we exchanged the occasional comment. Satisfied with my collection of sketches, I closed the pad, rose, and stretched my fingers. Looking around, I muttered, "The camaraderie of the barn."

"What's that now?"

"I was just taking it all in: the horses, the dog, our conversation, even the earthy smells."

"You gonna show me what you been drawing there?"

"Not a chance. These are just rough plans. Maybe I'll show you what they turn into. If they're any good."

"I expect they will be… Hey, look! Snow's started." He pointed toward the barn opening, where fat flakes floated as much up and sideways as down.

"Brr! I'm getting cold just looking at those first few flakes."

"You stay warm, dry, and upright, you hear?"

"I'll sure try." I slapped my thigh to summon Hecuba.

Roy nodded as he cranked the engine. Over the ATV's unmuffled roar, he yelled, "I'll put the thermos on your porch when I'm done. Sure was nice of you."

What a difference a day can make! This time yesterday, I was filled with anger and gloom. But the combination of art therapy and Roy therapy had put my head in a much sunnier place. The dog's reaction to the snow sure helped. As I headed uphill toward home, Hecuba ran several circles around me, each one punctuated by her slamming on furry elbows, while her tail whirled maniacally.

By the time we reached the cottage, the flakes were training down purposefully. I knew I should jump on my storm preparations, but I was eager to play with my rough sketches.

After briefly toweling my still bouncy hound and filling a small cup with water, I pulled out my acrylics, ripped my recent sketches from the pad, set them on the end table beside my easel, and positioned a new canvas board on the easel's lip. I closed my eyes briefly to summon Roy's essence. This would be another vignette, focusing on just the top third of his body, with his left forearm leaning on his rake. With his right hand, he mopped sweat from his brow. The handkerchief cast half his face in shadow, but his lopsided grin lit up the painting.

After some time, I stepped back, holding my wet brush upright in one hand, while the other rested on my left hip. "Almost there." I sat down again, smudging here, streaking there, as brush and fingers magically brought the diverse layers into a cohesive whole.

The next time I stood, I gasped to see that night had already fallen, along with half a foot of snow. Hecuba chuffed impatience.

"Yes, yes. I know. It's past time for your dinner. Let me clean up first."

Another half-hour passed before my work site was orderly. After filling Hecuba's bowl, I pulled some pedestal candles and matches from the cupboard then dashed to the bathroom to fill the tub. In case a power outage knocked out the well pump. While the water ran, I hauled in some of Roy's firewood, complete with kindling, and stuffed some pieces in the wood stove. Then I shut off the tub faucet and positioned a bucket next to the tub. I'd have plenty of water for flushing the toilet if the power went out for long. Only then did I return to the kitchen and open the fridge. As I mulled over dinner ideas, however, the kitchen lights flickered, faded, flared, then died.

"Darn!"

I groped around for the candles and matches. Once I had sufficient illumination, I brought one of the candles to the living room. I wanted to see if my second impression of my recent efforts was as sunny as my first. Roy was right. My fingers do have a life of their own. Artwork often goes places you didn't intend at the start. But I liked where Roy's portraits had ended up. Then I inspected the portraits of Blackie and Daddy and Aaron by candlelight. They, too, had developed lives of their own. They, too, had turned out better than my original plan.

The candlelight didn't illuminate my sketches of Uncle Henry and Mother. I shivered, fantasizing that those images could snuff the flame if I brought the candle too close to them. "Nope, you're gonna stay in the darkness. Not gonna let you extinguish the lightheartedness of this day." Candle in hand, I pivoted sharply and headed back to the kitchen. The cheery glow seemed to intensify with every step.

THIRTY-FIVE:

RUMINATIONS OF A SNOWY NIGHT

Thanks to the wind, the cottage got downright chilly in short order. I fired up the woodstove and lit more candles. And for the millionth time in the past few days, I gasped when I realized how much time had passed. It was eight o'clock.

As soon as I headed for the kitchen to grab something to eat, Hecuba bolted upright from her post-prandial nap. She stood vigil at the kitchen entrance. Surprisingly, her vigil didn't last long. She abruptly swiveled her muzzle toward the front door, flicked her ears in several directions, and finally exited through the dog panel. One minute later, the howling began.

Flashlight in hand, I hurried to the doorway. In the white LED beam, Hecuba sat alertly, nose aimed at the black sky. She exhaled another long howl, rising in both volume and pitch before diminishing. Several more crescendos and diminuendos sounded as I pulled on my rubber boots and walked outside. My stomach promptly pitched when I realized what had triggered those howls: a snowman trudging ponderously up the long drive.

A disabled motorist? Ted Bundy? Another look at my dog suggested the approaching snowman was not a serial killer. Despite the howls, Hecuba was not displaying aggression or fear.

As the apparition came closer, her tail dusted a cautious arc in the snow. I took a deep breath, shook the snow from my head, and walked toward the intruder. In the swirling snow, I had no idea whether I was looking at an adult or child, a man or woman.

"Can I help you," I called in a disconcertingly thin voice.

"Cate?"

A woman's voice. Somehow familiar. Not Ted Bundy.

Hecuba rose and walked toward the woman. Her tail transitioned from a half-staff wobble to a metronomic wag. She nosed the hem of the woman's snow-crusted jacket.

Recognition finally kicked in. "Ruth? Is that you?"

The snowman panted, "You have the longest damn driveway I have ever seen."

I sped toward her and began dusting flakes and ice balls off her jacket.

Ruth laughed, pointing at my own snow cover. "Maybe we can wait till we get to the house before trying to shake ourselves dry?"

"Duh," I said, embarrassed.

Hecuba loped uphill, turning around impatiently several times to urge the chatting humans to hurry up.

Inside the cottage, Ruth protested as I unwound her sopping wool scarf. "Oh, hon, that's gonna make a mess on your floor."

"Not to worry. I've got a tarp nearby. Was using it to protect the floor from my painting." I pulled the tarp from underneath the sofa and spread it on the floor in front of the woodstove. Then I positioned an old wooden chair close to the heat and draped it with Ruth's scarf. "Gimme the rest of your stuff and we'll dry it here, too."

"But your chair!"

"It's an ancient kitchen chair. Beaten up to begin with and has so much lead enamel on it nothing will penetrate the wood. Better take off your socks, too. I'll get you a pair of my wool raggs, so you won't get cold."

Now barefoot, Ruth rubbed her hands by the stove while I disappeared into my dark bedroom and Hecuba sniffed the wet outerwear.

"Finish your story," I called from the hallway, socks in hand.

Retreating to the sofa to don the socks, Ruth said, "I need something first. Got any scotch?"

"Will bourbon do? I picked up a pint the other day when I was shopping. I used to drink it when I was young."

"Bourbon will do just fine. And, hon, you're still young. You don't know it, of course. When I was in my forties, I thought I was ancient. Little did I know."

As I headed to the kitchen, Ruth yelled, "Two fingers!" So I splashed a generous amount of amber liquid in two rocks glasses and returned to my guest.

"Ahh," groaned Ruth with pleasure, after her first sip. "Okay, as I was saying, I wasn't about to play New Year's Day hostess to my obnoxious sister-in-law if I had a broken front tooth." She waved an exculpatory palm. "Arnie can't stand her, either. So judgmental. Anyway, I didn't want to wait until next week to get my busted cap fixed. Hurt like the devil, too. My dentist tries to keep some time open for emergencies, so I called this morning. He was able to squeeze me in near the close of business today. His staff was not happy. They were looking forward to an early start to the New Year's weekend." She took another sip as I settled next to her. Hecuba joined the party, sprawling over our feet.

"His office is right off his house, about ten miles down this very road. A very twisty road, let me tell you. Well, I don't have to, do I? A very twisty road, made none the easier by darkness and eight inches of snow. VeeDOT, by the way, has lived down to its expectations. Lord only knows how many hours since the last plow came through.

"Mind you, I'm a decent snow driver. And my sturdy little SUV has four-wheel drive. So I was doing okay. Hardly any other cars. Never got above twenty miles an hour. I might have made it all the way home, if not for that miserable deer."

"Oh no! You hit a deer?"

"Relax. Bambi's fine. But I had to brake hard, which spun me in some lovely circles. And eventually into a ditch. A good way off the road, which I hope means my car won't get slammed by the next snowplow. But I'll need a tow truck to pull it out. You think Triple-A will make calls tonight? Or maybe Arnie could come fetch me."

"Oh, Ruth, no! It's still coming down awfully hard. You don't want him out in this mess. Stay here. You can call Arnie to let him know you're okay. And he can help you sort things out tomorrow. Hopefully, the roads will be decent by then."

Ruth nodded and gulped more bourbon. "Thank you, hon. I really wasn't looking forward to any more adventures tonight. Had a real sinking spell when I got out of the car. No bars on my phone. No lights visible anywhere. Except then I saw this tiny yellow glow. Started walking in that direction, using my cellphone for illumination. My spirits lifted when I spotted that ancient sign pointing uphill: 'Ashwood Family Cemetery.' I remembered Morwenna talking about some Halloween excursion to that cemetery, right on the same property where you lived. The rest is history. Except for how long your goddammed driveway is. All of it uphill!"

"Guess it's a good thing you spun out where you did, huh?"

"Hmmpf!"

"Look, I haven't had dinner yet, and you must be famished. The fridge has some ready-to-eat goodies. How does chicken salad sound?"

"Like Nirvana."

"Why don't you call Arnie while I'm throwing things together? If you need to use the bathroom, I've got a couple of flush buckets standing ready. No electricity. No well pump."

"Oh, hon, on our little farm, we're well-versed in the use of flush buckets."

Fifteen minutes later, I was shooing Hecuba to a distant corner of the living room while I laid an overflowing tray on the coffee table in front of the sofa.

"Dig in." I handed Ruth her bowl of chicken salad then topped up her drink. "So, I meant to ask earlier: What was that yellow light you saw?"

"Your cottage. In all that darkness, candlepower really stands out, shimmering through the leafless hardwoods. As I slogged up that goddammed driveway, this place looked like a cheery jack-o'-lantern. Wasn't totally sure it was your place but figured I'd throw myself on the mercy of whoever occupied it. By the way, Arnie says we're out of power back home, too. Fluffy is just beside herself. No lights. No mom. But he's got a roaring fire going. And he's in good spirits, because his sister called to say she won't be able to make it this weekend. Doesn't like driving on slippery roads, even if they've been plowed. My silver lining, huh?"

"Glad that worked out for you. And I'm pretty happy myself. With you here and everything so cozy, I feel like I'm getting an early start to the New Year. Maybe the best start I've ever had."

Ruth reached over to pat my knee. "That's more than a little sad, hon."

"Oh, gee, I wasn't throwing myself a pity party. Does all the hoopla surrounding the New Year ever live up to anyone's expectations? What I meant was that it feels so cheerful—the storm, the candlelight, the warmth from the woodstove, sharing a meal with good company. Comfortable and safe."

"Safe? Odd choice of words."

I *did* feel safe. And that feeling was particularly welcome to someone who'd spent quite a lot of life feeling *unsafe*. Of course, I wasn't about to get into all that and destroy the happy vibe. I just shrugged and said, "I guess I'm just thinking of the years gone by."

"Nostalgia? The holidays will do that to you."

I coughed. "No, it's not nostalgia. I'm not missing one single thing from my past. The present is pretty nice." Now I reached out and patted *her* knee. "But the turn of the year makes you more aware of the passage of time, the choices made back when, things that might have gone differently."

"Regrets?" Ruth's eyes narrowed.

"Not exactly. Ever since that conversation we had about killing Hitler, I've thought about all the consequences that can come from taking action. Any action. How interesting that your college friend said he wouldn't go back in time to kill Hitler. Not because he shied away from assassination, but because he worried he might make things worse."

She nodded. "The law of unintended consequences."

"Funny, I never knew there was a term for it until my shrink mentioned it." As soon as that noun left my mouth, I sucked in my breath. How easily I had shared that secret!

"You see a shrink? Good for you. I always wondered what that would be like. Having a sounding board might be nice. But I'd be cowed by all the work involved."

I chuckled. "I know what you mean. Mine assigns homework."

"See? That would bug me. What if I flunked?"

"You? But you're so ... normal."

"I'm just a little insulted." Ruth laughed.

"No, no, no. I didn't phrase it right. You just strike me as someone who has it all together. You're grounded, have a good sense of humor, healthy relationships. Bet you could handle just about anything that came your way. Look at how you handled the accident and being stranded. I would have been a basket case."

"Good Lord, I was lucky!"

"See? Right there! You're focusing on the positive. I'd be obsessing about how close I came to ... well, really bad things happening."

She shrugged. "Maybe age provides perspective. You should have seen me when I was juggling the responsibilities of two active little kids, Arnie, and teaching. *I* was the basket case. Short-tempered, constantly worrying that I was handling it all wrong. And you know what? I didn't enjoy the girls' early years. That's such a shame. Wish I could get that time back."

"Really? What would you do differently?"

"I dunno. Maybe quit my job so I wasn't always so frazzled. Maybe be more upfront about asking for Arnie's help. Maybe just give myself the slack to make mistakes."

"I wonder what unintended consequences you might trigger if you could go back and do all that."

Ruth raised her eyebrows. "I can't imagine any consequences at all, apart from improving my comfort level."

"Yeah, but who knows? Maybe if you had quit your job, some school kid would have had a far less productive life because you weren't around to push him in the right direction. Or maybe, if you had been there twenty-four-seven for your daughters, they'd be less independent and have fewer achievements today."

"Hmmpf. That feels like a stretch. Okay, what would *you* change?"

Darn. I'd let myself in for that and didn't really want to go there. But I came up with a harmless but still true response. "I used to think I should have been more assertive. Stood up for myself more. Called people out for bad behavior."

"Sounds reasonable. But you *used* to think that? Meaning you no longer do? Why?"

I groaned. "Well, there was this one homework assignment for Dr. Brown. That's my therapist. I thought about a few incidents. How I might have changed the dialogue. You know, putting all those 'I shoulda said' afterthoughts into action."

"And?"

"I was overwhelmed by all the different consequences that could have played out. Not all of them good. Some were quite disturbing, with me going so overboard that the punishment didn't fit the..."

"Big deal. You indulged in a few murderous fantasies. We all do that."

"We do? Well, anyway, I didn't care for the results. There was still this strong urge to undo wrongs. Make the world a better place, but I'm not..."

"Oh, hon, you're putting a lot on your shoulders. You're not God. And even He doesn't always feel an obligation to right wrongs."

"Huh?"

"Look at the television news. Look at history. God lets all sorts of atrocities happen, without raising one finger to stop them."

I blinked. "But you're a believer."

"Yes, I am. What's more, I'm one of God's chosen people. And just look at the awful things that happened to his chosen people over the millennia."

"So, what do you do with all that?"

Ruth splayed her hands. "Why do we need to do anything? Who said life is supposed to make sense? Look at all the mysteries of nature. I doubt science can explain all of them. And some are pretty damn nifty. We already know—most of us by the time we hit adulthood—that life's not fair. Why should it be logical?"

"But, but…"

"See, this is what comes from all that homework with your shrink." She gently rapped my crown. "All that stuff churning around up there. Too much introspection will drive you nuts."

"So, what are we here for?"

Ruth sighed. "I supposed the goal is to live as decently and usefully as possible, while preparing the next generation to do the same. More than that I'll leave to the philosophers and theologians. Not that they have all that much of a handle on things. God, how I hated those two philosophy courses I stupidly signed up for a million years ago!"

"You know what's weird, though? With all that introspection about changing things in my past, I easily envisioned consequences for other people but saw no change in my own life path. I got the creepy feeling that whatever I did or didn't do, I'd be exactly where I am today."

"How can you possibly know that?"

"Because I lived … I dunno … I just have this strong feeling. Besides, none of that would have changed the fact that I was the only one around to step up as my mother's caretaker. And put my life on hold for nearly a decade."

"Ouch. I sure hope I don't burden either of my girls like that. But I still don't see how you can be so sure. For all you know, you might have taken a different route to work one day and bumped into someone who would change your life completely.

For the better. Some stud muffin with pots and pots of money. My goodness, you're young enough that could still happen. Never can tell what bright new opportunity or person might enter your life."

"With my luck, it'd be a serial killer."

"Good Lord, stop that! You're being morose. And all this speculation is giving me a headache. I need another drink." She held up her nearly empty glass. "You could use one, too."

I rose, refreshed Ruth's drink, and placed the empty salad bowls on the tray. "Lemme dump this in the kitchen. Back in a jiff."

When I returned, Ruth pursed her lips in a frown. "Was I too outspoken? Arnie always tells me I talk without thinking. Especially when I've had a few. It's just that I hate seeing you get down on yourself."

"Don't worry about it," I said sitting. "I was being self-indulgent and whiny."

"Oh, swell! Now I've got you criticizing yourself. Not my intention at all. After being a mother all these years, I just want to fix things. At least in the here and now." She paused, reaching down to pet Hecuba who had returned to her usual perch by the couch. "I'm glad you have this beast. Not merely for the protection she affords. She's such a calming influence."

I smiled first at Hecuba then at Ruth. "Yup, sure is."

"Well, see? My prescription is to take a lesson from Hecuba here. You don't see her overthinking things. She lives in the moment. With not a care in the world, as long as she gets two square meals a day and the occasional tummy rub."

Hecuba rose abruptly, bumping into our shins in her haste. As she trotted toward the dog panel, her long tail fanned an unmistakable fart at Ruth.

"Was it something I said?" Ruth asked, pinching her nostrils and giggling.

Thirty-Six:

Burning Ears

Ruth's visit made me feel like part of the human race again. Nevertheless, I was glad to have my solitude back the next afternoon, when Arnie's mechanic friend came by to pull her car out of the ditch and see her safely home. My newfound memories from childhood were demanding attention. I was also feeling pressure to focus on Mrs. Ashwood's commissions. I figured I could do both once I was alone again.

So, back inside my head I retreated. I made a list of possible themes for Harland's mementos. I also enumerated some emotions that badly needed purging on canvas, just for myself. Anger. Despair. Shame. Guilt. Did I say anger?

My plans went awry, however, for lack of energy. Energy to confront difficult emotions. Energy to paint scenes around the estate. What I wanted to do, what I did have the energy to do, was revisit the portrait I'd made of Aaron. It was good but deserved to be fleshed out. Aaron deserved to be fleshed out. Not only because he had rescued me from the frat party disaster. Not only because he had been a welcoming presence in middle school. But of all the memories that had been bubbling up lately, his stood out as unique. He had been someone I could count on.

As I pored over the most recent sketch of him, I wondered if people could tell when we're thinking about them. Does their spine tingle happily when someone has kind thoughts of them? Do their ears burn, as that saying goes, when others talk about them? Do their muscles contract painfully when someone has an angry memory of them? Do the molecules that once were Mother and Uncle Henry whirl in their graves when I remember my childhood?

How ironic that a hermit like me would spend so much time thinking about other people. Do other people think of *me*? Does Aaron ever recall the girl who sat next to him on the school bus? Better he remember me *that* way than as the college girl so badly in need of his help.

As I set a new canvas board on my easel to start a comprehensive portrait of Aaron, I doubted anyone ever thought about me much at all. It wasn't like I had any accomplishments worthy of discussion. My appearance certainly didn't turn heads. And my hermit lifestyle, wrapped around my own internal thoughts, didn't improve the odds of getting noticed.

Ruth slapped Arnie's hand before it could steal a walnut from the bowl. "That's for Cate!"

"Aw, c'mon! You know how much I love your banana nut bread. Least you could do is make two, so we could have a loaf for ourselves."

"Don't have enough bananas, and I'm not venturing back on

those roads before some serious melting. Probably won't happen until classes start back up on Tuesday."

"*If* classes start back up. Fauquier closes school at the drop of a hat."

"Nah, the temp's gonna be fifty on Tuesday. At most, there'll be a late opening. At any rate, I want to have this thank-you gift ready for Cate first thing."

"You girls have fun Friday night?"

Ruth paused her mixing. "Not sure you'd call it fun. We got into some heavy subjects. But it was warm and cozy, and I was well-fed and … watered. Slept like a baby on her sofa."

"What heavy subjects?"

"Stuff like free will and predestination and whether God has any plan at all for us."

"Who won?"

"It wasn't a debate, silly. Just an exploration. She does a lot of that. Lives inside her head. Too much. You know, she reminds me of Joanie sometimes."

"Our daughter's not neurotic," Arnie chided.

"Who said Cate was neurotic?"

"Struck me as a scared rabbit. And *that's* not Joanie."

"No, but they both overthink things. Remember that time Joanie went nuts when you foolishly recited that old saw about cracks in the sidewalk?

"Step on a crack? Break your mother's back," Arnie recited in childish singsong.

"Joanie rushed home after school one day expecting to find me flat on the floor, paralyzed. She had done the unthinkable: inadvertently stepped on a crack. I think it was two months before she stopped walking head down whenever she was outdoors, for fear some crack would pop out of nowhere."

"Christ, Ruth, the kid was seven at the time. Big deal."

"It *was* a big deal for her. Joanie has always been sensitive, thinking about consequences, planning every move down to the nth detail. Too smart for her own good. That's Cate, too."

Arnie shrugged. "I'm just glad she put you up. Glad you spun out on that particular stretch of road."

"Me, too. But I tell you, there's more to that girl than meets the eye."

"Joseph Francis Scanlon! We're moving in three days. The packers are coming tomorrow, and you have done absolutely nothing."

"Isn't that why we have packers, babe? So we don't have to do anything?" Joe favored his wife with his most ingratiating, dimple-studded smile. When that didn't have the intended effect, he reached out to tickle her belly.

She swatted his hand away so forcefully that she connected with a stack of personal papers and sports trophies on the dining table. The assortment thudded onto the floor. Pointing at the mess, she said, "This is all your crap. I hauled it up from the basement, along with your camping shit, your golfing shit, your fishing shit, and all the other shit you never use. Figure out what you want to save. Now! If you don't, I'll throw it all out. Every last bit! I'm telling you, Joe, I have packed my last fucking box."

Joe clutched at his chest and bugged out his eyes in imitation of a heart attack. "Not my trophies, Debbie! C'mon, babe, you know I suck at making decisions."

Debbie rolled her eyes and stomped out of the room.

Joe sighed and lowered himself onto his haunches, wincing at the crackle and pop in his right knee. He looked around to see if Debbie was in earshot, with the unfulfilled hope that the reminder of football-damaged knees would earn sympathy points. Groaning, he focused on the mess before him. "Why don't I just dump it all in one of those packing boxes?" Then he raised his head and yelled, "Hey, Debs? Where are the boxes?"

"By the goddammed bookcase!" she bellowed from the next room.

"After locating the folded cardboard, he puzzled over how it transformed into a box. On his third try, he succeeded. "I guess I'm supposed to tape it together," he mumbled. Then more loudly: "Babe, where's the tape?"

"Right in front of you, you moron!"

"Oh."

Awkwardly, Joe hunkered down on his butt, taped the bottom

box tabs closed, and began tossing items willy-nilly inside. Ten minutes later, he finished. Lifting the box proved more challenging than packing it. "Finished!" he called, just as Debbie returned, carrying another full carton to stack in one corner.

"Did you mark what it contains?" she asked.

"With what?"

Debbie grabbed a Sharpie pen from the table and threw it at him. Then something on the floor caught her eye. "You forgot to pack that." She pointed to a large manila envelope.

Opening the envelope, Joe squinted at the photograph inside. He waved it at his wife. "Bet you didn't know I was an ace in physics."

Debbie leaned forward. "Who's that with you?"

"My partner for the science fair project. Can't remember her name."

"It's right there, dumbass, on the exhibit behind both of you. 'Catherine Devine and Joseph Scanlon, Scientific Applications for Moiré Patterns.' What are moiré patterns?"

Joe shrugged. "Beats me."

"Lemme guess. The project was the girl's idea, and you just tagged along for the ride."

"Nuh-uh! She was one tough cookie. Made me do research at the library. Made me haul all that crap into the exhibit room, too."

"What's her secret?"

"Huh?"

"How'd she manage to put you to work? God knows, I haven't been able to."

Joe shook his head sorrowfully. "She threatened to take my name off the project and tell Old Man Hofstadter she did everything herself. Jeez, I woulda flunked! And if I flunked physics, that woulda been the third strike. No graduation. Buh-bye, football scholarship."

"What were you doing taking physics in the first place?"

"I needed another science credit, and one of the guys on the team said physics was cool. He said all you did was drop shit from second-story windows to see how fast it fell. And one time, we dropped bananas into liquid nitrogen then shattered them with hammers. Way cool! But the rest of the time, not so much."

Debbie grunted then examined the photo more closely. "She's hardly your type."

"What's my type, babe?"

"Dumb blonde with tits. Like what I used to be before I had two kids and wised up."

Joe glanced at the photo. "No, she sure wasn't my type. I thought she was a little sweet on me, though, but I guess I was wrong. Too smart."

"Outsmarted *you*, huh?"

"What can I say? I'm all about looks, not about books." He flashed a full-toothed smile.

"Gimme a fucking break!" Debbie stomped out again.

Joe crumpled the photo and lobbed it toward a nearby wastebasket. And missed.

The framed portrait stood propped up against the kitchen wall. Pressing an index finger to her lips, Nell Washington stared hard at it. Roy stood beside her. He, too, gazed at the painting but repeatedly stole eager glances at his wife as he awaited her reaction.

Nell finally broke the silence. "The painter is that woman who rents the gatehouse?"

Roy nodded. "Sad little white gal."

"Looks like your sad little white gal got herself some talent."

"You think? Sure looks good to me. But what do I know?"

"Well, I don't know beans about art, but May taught me a few things. From those fancy paintings she got hanging in that fancy-ass house she and Will bought in Leesburg. Now I'm not saying I liked the ones that look like the artist spilled his paint bucket. But some others, well, they grabbed me. So, May, she asks why. I could tell she was getting into teacher-mode."

"You raised yourself one smart daughter, and that's a fact."

"I sure did. She wouldn't let me get away with saying something dumb, like the colors were pretty. No sir. She kept prodding, asking how the paintings made me feel. Finally, I realized they made me want to meet the folks in those pictures. They seemed warm and kind, God-fearing. May gets this big smile on her face. 'Exactly,' she says. 'These paintings show not just the outside, but the inside of people.' This one does, too, Roy. This gal's got some kinda X-ray vision. Can see inside your soul."

"Truth be told, I always thought she was a bit tetched. Not lock-up crazy, but tetched like some of them old-time prophets. Folks who kept hearing God talking to them."

"That a fact?" Nell raised her eyebrows. "She's religious, then?"

"Danged if I know. Don't think she goes to church. Not regular, anyways."

Still staring at the painting of Roy and the horses, Nell mused, "I wonder if art is one way God talks to us."

"You think?"

"By that foolish grin on your face and the way your chest is all puffed out, what I think is there'll be no living with you for the next month or so."

"Maybe only for the next week or so, now that I got something in common with that King Charles fella. He ain't the only one got his portrait painted."

Nell shook her head. "Gonna be a long week."

Thirty-Seven:

Taking Control, Brushstroke by Brushstroke

The snowstorm forecast for the second week in January raised my hopes. Maybe I could plead icy roads as an excuse to dodge my next therapy session. But no such luck. VeeDOT, under fire for its poor performance in the late December storm, had plows and sand-trucks out in force. So there I was, parked on Dr. Brown's sofa once more, with Hecuba at my feet.

"You look troubled," was my therapist's opening line.

I punched the pillow on my lap. "It's just that dredging up all these emotions and memories is no fun."

"Give me an example of an emotion that's uncomfortable to explore."

"All the anger I've been feeling toward my mother, because she knew about the naked enema drill."

"Sounds like a perfectly reasonable reaction. Does it not sound reasonable to you?"

"Yeah, but isn't it weird that I feel so much more anger toward her than toward Uncle Henry? Not that I'm letting him off the hook, the creep. Mother didn't directly hurt me. Yet I feel so betrayed by her."

"But you don't feel betrayed by your uncle?"

"I didn't know my uncle. Not really. So I had no expectations of him. Expectations that would be betrayed. Sure, he was a blood relative. But I supposedly have a bunch of cousins in Florida whom I've never met. And I wouldn't automatically expect good behavior from them just because we share some DNA."

"That's the adult Cate talking, someone who learned to distrust people at an early age. How did you feel as a child? Were you wary of the largely unknown Uncle Henry, when you learned he would visit your childhood home? Did the nine-year-old Cate decide to wait and see whether he would prove trustworthy or scary?"

I wrapped my braid around my hand and thought. "All I knew of him at that point was how Mother looked up to him. Darn, she worshipped him!"

"And did her positive feelings predispose you to worship him, too?"

"Not at all! If anything, I was skeptical. Even at that young age."

"So you didn't trust your mother's word. Interesting. How did your father feel about Henry?"

"I got the feeling he didn't like him much. Maybe because Daddy felt second-best in my mother's affections, what with his business failing and the constant financial strain. Why does any of that matter?"

"It might not. I'm just trying to get a sense of family dynamics. Were there other visits from Henry after that summer of the enemas?"

"No. I never saw him again."

"Why is that?"

"Well, he moved pretty far away. Someplace in the Midwest. I remember Mother exchanged Christmas cards with him. His had postmarks from … Illinois, maybe?"

"So, your mother stayed in touch with him? But no more visits? She didn't invite him again, and she didn't travel to see him?"

"No. Her health would have gotten in the way of traveling to Illinois. She didn't even go to his funeral. He died not long after Daddy."

"Isn't it odd that a woman who 'worshipped' her big brother didn't attend his funeral? What was the cause of death?"

"Some kind of cancer. He was sick for a while."

"But your mother never got together with him before he died. Why is that, do you suppose?"

I hit the pillow again. Hard enough that Hecuba lifted her muzzle from my ankles and stared at me with concern. "Because of her health? Because she didn't have the money to travel? I don't know. Where are you going with this?"

"Is it possible your mother had conflicted feelings about her brother? Something more complicated than 'worship'? Abusers typically have a long record of hurting children. Given Henry's age when you were nine, it's unlikely you were his first victim. Is it possible he abused your mother when she was little and he was in a pseudo-parental role?"

"Never thought about it. Then why would she have looked up to him?"

"It's complicated. Victims often rewrite history, often want to please their tormentors. As I'm sure you know, the cycle of child abuse often plays out from one generation to the next. So most abusers, including the people who enable abuse—as your mother did with you—experienced similar harm themselves."

"What? So that gives my mother a pass? And if someone abused Uncle Henry as a kid, he's got a pass to get naked with me?" I was yelling.

"Is it possible that her minimal contact with the brother she supposedly adored was, on some level, a way of protecting you? Making sure Uncle Henry never had the chance to victimize you again? How would that make you feel?"

"Too little too late!" I asserted, raising my voice again. "Okay, Dr. Brown, I've got a question for *you*. If most abusers were abused as kids, what percentage of abused kids grow up and choose *not* to hurt kids? Their own or others?"

"An excellent question. There's a lot of research explaining why the cycle of abuse continues to the next generation. But I'm not aware of studies explaining why or how other abuse victims stop the cycle."

"Here's an idea. I could never, ever do to a kid what Uncle Henry did to me. I'd kill myself before giving into any urge like that. And I wouldn't be able to live with myself if I knew a kid was being abused, and I did nothing to stop it. And I'm no heroine!"

"I believe you. The first part, I mean. As for you not being a heroine, I dunno. After all, Cate, you've already saved one kid from an oncoming truck. And it takes a lot of courage to examine repressed memories of sexual abuse. To see it for how wrong it was. To see how wrong your mother was to enable it. Even to challenge some of the suppositions I've tossed out here."

My anger eased somewhat. "Can you really equate the two threats? If that truck had hit Marcy Boone, she would have been dead or maimed. Sexual abuse isn't gonna kill you or maim you. Most of the time. So why does it feel so bad?"

"A mentor once told me that physical abuse breaks bones. Sexual abuse breaks the spirit. Or is that too simplistic for you?"

I shrugged. "All I know is I don't like feeling this way. Angry. Unvalued. With so little control over my life."

"Aren't you taking control by being here, talking about what happened? Aren't you taking control every time you pick up a paintbrush? How's the art therapy going, by the way?"

My angry outbursts were giving me a headache, and my energy for therapy was flagging. Reporting on my recent artwork was something I did have the energy to do, however. So, we talked for a while about the commissions offered by Lavinia Ashwood and about the two extremes in my paintings and sketches. I described the angry, violent abstracts and the diseased images of my uncle and mother. And I contrasted those pieces with the gentle portraits of my childhood dog, Roy, and Aaron. I told him both extremes made me feel a bit better about myself, but I didn't understand why.

Toward the close of our session, Dr. Brown commented, "I wish I could put a paintbrush in every patient's hands."

Thirty-Eight:

Lassiter Brown, M.D.
Session Notes, 10 January 2023

Devine, Cate. Last session 29 December 2022

Recorded with patient approval. Main focus: continued discussion of recently resurfaced memory of sexual abuse at age nine. Abuser, "Uncle Henry." Enabler, "Mother."

General observation: Cate is well-groomed, highly articulate, accompanied by dog, very agitated. Twisting braid, punching pillow, even being somewhat rough in kneading dog's fur. Anger is dominant emotion.

Most of anger is directed at mother for witnessing abuse, rationalizing Henry's behavior, blaming Cate for an "explosion" of fecal fluid thus requiring Henry to remove his clothes. Underscores self-image (apparently encouraged/invented early on by mother) of Cate as defective, "dirty," thus deserving of mistreatment.

Acknowledges anger at uncle, "the creep," but feels no sense of betrayal there, since she didn't trust him to begin with. Her mother's "worship" of Henry apparently made Cate wary. Sign of distrusting mother even before enema abuse? NB: Explore possible reasons.

Anger is also directed at me for suggesting alternative narrative regarding mother: i.e., that she may have been abused by Henry and thus became predisposed to abusive behavior (otherwise, she'd have to confront what he did to her). Cate is also angered by my speculation that Mother may have belatedly acted to protect her—by making sure Henry never visited again. Interestingly, Mother, although exchanging letters with her brother over subsequent years (only Christmas cards?), didn't attend his funeral or visit him during his long illness. My timing in introducing this idea was premature. Wound still too raw. NB: Look for more appropriate time to raise this theme again, in hope Cate may feel some show of love from her aloof and judgmental mother.

Discussion of Cate's continuing art therapy has calming, positive effect. She describes two extremes represented in recent artwork: "violent" (in terms of color?) paintings vs. soothing portraits of "kind" elements in Cate's life, including several from childhood. Interesting that she describes her recent portrayals of mother and Henry as "diseased." Suggests some awareness that their behavior was unhealthy. Next task: see herself as healthy.

Once again, I raised the subject of anti-anxiety and/or anti-psychotic medication. Explained that goal is to prevent potentially disruptive dissociative episodes, triggered by anxiety. Patient remains resistant. So far, no sign that her dissociative episodes place her in any danger. But now that long-repressed anger is surfacing, watch for any signs she might hurt herself or others.

Thirty-Nine:

Rescuing Persephone

Yet another drama was playing out on the periphery of my crosswalk.

"Gimme my hat!" shouted the red-faced Nicu as Tobey Drinkwater spun a knit cap above his head. The smaller boy jumped for it repeatedly. Several adolescents jeered on the sidelines.

I was preoccupied stopping a line of cars as I beckoned children to cross. But out of the corner of one eye, I could see Tobey's maddening smirk.

Finally, after the last of the children had crossed, Hecuba and I marched toward the confrontation. I promptly snatched the pompom atop the rotating cap. Tobey lunged toward me to retrieve his trophy but froze when my giant wolfhound snaked her neck forward, growled softly, and fixed dead yellow eyes on the adolescent.

I pressed the cap into Nicu's hand and aimed my own glare at the thief.

"Hey, he dropped it," said Tobey, whose wide-eyed shock quickly morphed into an unctuous smirk. "I was just shaking the dirt off it." Turning to his posse, he muttered, "Not that a dirty little Gypsy would notice one more piece of shit." His homeys snorted their appreciation.

"Move it along."

The posse sauntered toward the school, but Nicu stayed at my side. Tobey turned and shouted at him, "Remember, I'll be happy to take care of your pussy. Really good care!"

Looking down at Nicu, I asked, "What was that all about?"

"I need your help. Really bad." He shrugged off his—undulating—backpack.

"You got something inside that pack?"

Nodding woefully, he unzipped the top a few inches. Black furry ears poked through. "I didn't realize Percy climbed into my pack. I guess I left it open on the floor and didn't find out till I was on the bus. She started meowing. Really loud. What am I gonna do? I'll get in trouble if I take her inside. She'll get in trouble if I leave her behind. Get lost, run over … or worse."

"What's worse than getting run…? Oh, Tobey."

Nicu bobbed his head up and down. "He said he'd make Percy a science experiment. Dissect her. Can you take her? Please?" He fished out the mewling kitten and thrust her at me.

Sighing, I tucked the cat under one arm. She squirmed as Hecuba's nose prodded the tiny black rump.

"Hecuba H. Hound, stop that! And settle down there, kitty. Ouch!" The frightened kitten tried to claw her way to freedom. "Empty your backpack," I ordered Nicu.

"What?"

"I need to contain Percy somehow. Just stuff the contents into your pockets."

394

Nicu spilled out everything on the ground. He pulled the ripcord to tighten his jacket waistband, partially unzipped the jacket, and crammed a notebook, book, pencils, and an eyeglass case inside the front opening. He held one hand against his belly to secure the contents and with his other hand retrieved the one item that remained, a small cooler bag.

I dangled Percy over the open backpack, dropped her inside, and managed to close the zipper before she could escape. "Look, Nicu, I can put the cat in my car and hope Hecuba doesn't eat her. But I've got a class in an hour and won't be able to get clear until ten-thirty at the earliest. Got another class this afternoon, so it's not like I can keep checking on Percy."

Nicu bit his lip then shouted, "I know! I'll pretend I'm sick and need to go home. My mother can pick me up. But I'll need an hour or so to make it believable."

"Make what believable?"

"My rash." He grinned.

"Huh?"

"I'm allergic to pine trees. The sap, I guess. I'll snag a branch from that tree over there and stuff it in my pocket. After I'm in class a while, I'll ask to go to the boy's room so I can rub the needles all over my arms. The red spots usually pop up within fifteen minutes."

"You've pulled this before? You don't go into shock or anything, do you?"

"Nah, just itches like crazy and looks bad. I can tell the nurse

I'm feeling woozy, too."

"Okay, but how about your mother? She'll figure out what's going on, certainly by the time you two retrieve Percy. Won't she be angry with you?"

"She won't rat me out. She doesn't like *gadjo* schools anyway. She'd home-school me except she can't get permission. Her English isn't good enough. But I don't think she could be here before eleven. Could you meet us then?"

Mentally, I calculated how much time it would take to clean up after class. "Yeah, okay. That should work. Tell your mother to drive to the staff parking lot. I'm the only Jeep."

"I know where you park."

"Great. Now skedaddle before the bell rings."

Nicu nodded and dashed for the school entrance, by way of the big pine tree. I watched with admiration as he stopped to tie his shoe, a complicated maneuver because of all the stuff inside his jacket. While crouched down, he discreetly broke off a small, low-hanging branchlet and stashed it into a pants pocket.

"Got some experience ripping stuff off," I chuckled to myself. "Oops. Just because he's a Gypsy doesn't mean he's a thief, Cate. But he's a resourceful little thing."

Was that resourcefulness born of hard times? An immigrant family would inevitably face all sorts of challenges in a strange, new country. There were more than a few Tobey Drinkwaters in this world, after all.

With Hecuba at my side, I trudged to my Jeep and placed the wriggling backpack inside. "In you go, kitty." Before I closed the hatch, I opened the pack's zipper just a bit, so the cat wouldn't suffocate. Then I turned to Hecuba. "Okay, puppy let's take you for a walk."

As I locked the car, I heard rhythmic swishing behind me. Turning around, I saw Morwenna speed-walking, her arms creating friction as they brushed against her quilted jacket.

"Crap!" she said. "If you're done with crosswalk duties, the final bell must have already rung. What the hell. Might as well take a breather if I'm already late." She leaned against the Jeep and panted.

Smiling at her, I noticed my stop-sign resting against one tire. "Darn. I forgot to stash it inside." When I opened the hatch, the backpack was now lying on its side, zipper fully open. "Lord love a duck! She's escaped!"

"Who's escaped?"

"Nicu's cat! Help me look for her?"

Morwenna lifted the edge of her glove to view her watch. "Ah, screw it. In for a penny, in for a pound."

Seeing no cat on the back deck, I closed the hatch and motioned for Morwenna to enter the back seat, while I slipped behind the wheel. With all doors and windows closed and Hecuba chuffing in protest outside, we contorted ourselves into ridiculous postures peering under floor mats, probing between seats, poring through various compartments, and exploring the carton in the back seat. It contained my father's army blanket, a snow brush, collapsible shovel, old-fashioned flashlight, and a metal tin.

"What's this?" Morwenna asked, shaking the tin.

"Emergency rations if I get stuck in the snow. You're not gonna find a kitten inside."

"What a girl scout you are! Hmm, what *will* I find inside?"

"For heaven's sake, Morwenna, we're looking for a cat!"

Her lips pursed in an exaggerated pout. "I was hoping for a chocolate bar."

"Jeez! There *is* a chocolate bar inside, and you're welcome to it. If you find Percy."

Hecuba pressed her nose against the passenger window, whined, and stared intently at the center console. Ears cocked, she angled her head.

Following her gaze, I opened the lid covering the small storage compartment. Percy levitated out of it and draped herself over my lap. "How'd you get in there?"

From the back seat, I heard, "Mystery solved. Now do I get my reward? I was running so late, I didn't have any breakfast."

"Have at it. How the heck am I gonna keep this one secured?"

"Mm! Goddess, this is so good." Morwenna waved the remaining half of the chocolate bar. "Why don't you make a bed for her with this blanket I found? Maybe she won't wander around if she's comfy."

"Worth a shot. Pass it to me, will you?"

As she handed the rolled blanket through the two front seats, Morwenna asked, "So what's Nicu's cat doing in your Jeep?"

"Long story." I unrolled the wool and loosely folded it onto the passenger seat. Percy immediately crawled onto it and curled into a tight ball. "The kitten got into his backpack without him knowing. He found out on the school bus. Tobey Drinkwater found out, too, and threatened to hurt the cat."

"Little shithead would, too. How'd you enter the picture?"

"Nicu begged me to take Percy. He's gonna fake being sick so his mother has to pick him up. When she arrives, we'll make the transfer."

Morwenna giggled. "Sounds like a spy story: The old maid crossing guard, whom no one would ever suspect of anything shady, has an illicit rendezvous with the Romanian Gypsy."

I narrowed my eyes. "I'm feeling a little shady right now, Morwenna."

"Aw, c'mon. I'm just teasing. How's Nicu gonna fool the school nurse?"

"Rub pine needles over his arm to get a rash. He's allergic."

"Kid's got game. Well, enough of this frivolity. Gotta take my forty lashes from Principal HO. My kids are probably bouncing off the walls." As she exited, she received a thorough sniffing from Hecuba. "I ate it already. All gone!" Morwenna flipped her empty hands.

The kitten was already snoring. I eased myself out of the car and whispered to Morwenna, "Good luck with Heather. I'm gonna squeeze a dog walk in before my class."

After my art class was done and I'd cleaned up, I bolted for the parking lot. Halfway there, I stopped to decipher the odd sound. It was Hecuba, howling from inside my Jeep. "Darn it! I hope she hasn't eaten Percy!" I exclaimed, breaking into a run.

I saw a pompom bobbling outside the front passenger window. Beneath it was Nicu's round face, grinning at Percy, now staring up at him, front paws positioned on the arm rest. Too large to jump into the back seat, Hecuba was spinning with frustration on the deck.

Nicu walked around the Jeep and waved at me, then pointed to the white minivan parked nearby.

"Good timing," I said, as I motioned to Hecuba to settle down. The dog stopped spinning, but her tail wagged up a storm.

Nicu slipped off his jacket and rolled up one jersey sleeve. "See?"

"Yikes! That looks awful!"

"Just itchy." He vigorously scratched the rash.

Nadja Radulescu exited her minivan and appeared by his side. She swatted his hand away from the rash. "Don't scratch. Put jacket back on." Then she turned to me. "You a nice lady to take

400

the little *muca*. Keep it safe. Help out Nicu."

"A cat, Mama. It's a cat."

Nadja nodded. "He takes a cat to school and that's bad. But this Tobey boy, he takes a knife to school. And that's okay?" She folded her arms and scowled.

I gasped, "Tobey had a knife?"

Nadja shoved her son's shoulder. "You tell her what this Tobey says."

"I already told her. He said he was gonna dissect Percy."

Nadja nudged him again. "No. You tell her what he *does*, too."

Nicu sighed. "He pulled out a switchblade, flipped it open, and waved it around."

"Lord love a duck! That kid needs to be put on a leash. You should tell the principal what happened."

"Pah, they don't listen to no Romany kid. Nicu just gets into trouble."

"You got that right," Nicu agreed, rubbing his arm against his side.

Nadja cuffed the back of his head. "Enough scratching, you!" Then, looking at me, she added, "How I keep him safe from this Tobey?"

"The staff already knows Tobey's a troublemaker, so he's on their radar. I can keep watch at the crosswalk, but unless you make some kind of formal complaint..."

"I know what I like to do to him," Nadja growled.

I nodded in sympathy. "Well, at least Persephone here is safe and sound. Let's get her out of the car. Oh, and the backpack, too."

Nicu dashed back to the front passenger door and as soon as I clicked it open, picked up the cat and cuddled it to his chest. "You have a good nap, Percy? You're a good kitty."

Nadja turned her attention to the deck, where Hecuba was panting in frustration. "This is the dog Nicu talks about, yeah? He don't lie. That's one big dog."

"Tallest dog in the world." I beamed at my wolfhound.

"This Tobey don't mess with you if you have big dog like this, huh?"

"Like I been telling you, Mama."

As I opened the hatch to grab Nicu's backpack, Hecuba vaulted outside and promptly sniffed each Radulescu butt.

Laughing at the greeting, Nadja took the backpack. "Thank you. And I thank you if you ... how you say? If you keep an eye on this one?" She thumped her son's head.

"Ow!" Nicu protested.

"Sure," I said. "He's a good kid."

Nadja smiled for the first time. And dropped about ten years in age. Her frown quickly returned as she said, "Sometimes."

FORTY:

A WORK IN PROGRESS

After Hecuba and I claimed our usual spots in Dr. Brown's office, I took a big breath before beginning. Nothing came out of my mouth.

My therapist raised an eyebrow and said, "Looks like you're bracing for something difficult."

I nodded. "It's just that I'm tired. I'm tired of dredging up painful history. I'm tired of picking at scabs. I'm tired of coming here. I know it's been useful, but therapy feels a bit like I'm running away from life."

"That's a new take." Dr. Brown slid his reading glasses down his nose to eye me skeptically.

"Well, you can analyze your life, or you can live it."

"You really think it's that cut and dried? Socrates would disagree."

"Huh?"

"You know, his line about the unexamined life not being worthwhile."

"I don't think Socrates had someone like me in mind when he said that. Because examining is all I ever do. Which doesn't leave much time for actually *living* my life."

He shrugged and was about to make a comment, when I raised my palm.

"With all the thinking I've been doing about Mother," I continued, "something new occurred to me. You've probably heard me say how I put my life on hold to take care of her the last decade of her life?"

"Sounds familiar."

"Well, that's not the whole truth. Her illness and dependency gave me an excuse to closet myself away from the world, the world I'm scared of, the world I've been scared of since childhood. And I'm still coming up with excuses for hiding out. Look at my job. You know, I probably feel more in sync with my duties as a school crossing guard than I do as a part-time art teacher. Why? Because I'm not a very good art teacher. I really don't want to spend my time finger painting. So, I don't make the effort to connect with the kids. I'm just sleepwalking through every class, with minimal preparation and effort."

"Does that realization have anything to do with your return to painting and sketching on your own time?"

I nodded vigorously. "It has everything to do with it. It's funny, because all the time I spend inside my head gives me the source material for artwork. Ironically, when I'm translating what's inside my head onto a canvas, I feel really alive. I don't feel arthritis pains. I don't feel overwhelmed by a zillion worries and doubts. Yet, I'm in touch with my emotions, the bad ones and the good ones. And amazingly enough, I'm in touch with the wider world— the world of clashing colors and confusing, scary images. The world of chaos. But all that chaos doesn't scare me off, at least when it comes to my artwork."

"Why do you think that is?"

My fingers groped the air, in search of the right words. Looking at my moving hands, I smiled and said, "My fingers are looking for a paintbrush to grab." I imagined the solid way the brush fills the space between thumb and forefinger, the plumpness of bristles loaded with paint, the fluid arc my entire forearm makes when the brush moves across the canvas. "Because that's when I'm in control. I'm choreographing the chaos, wrestling it into some kind of meaningful order. In the process, I may be understanding the outside world a tiny bit better."

"That's a compelling description."

"It's a compelling feeling, one I want to experience more and more. I have zero interest in wielding glitter guns and dunking leaves in tempera and praising some kid's stick drawing. Isn't that awful? For the first time in ... maybe forever, there are activities that excite me. So I want to make time for them. And that means cutting back on the other stuff."

"Like therapy? Like your day job?"

"Yes, like therapy. But no, I won't be quitting my day job. I like having a roof over my head. But who knows, maybe these commissions could lead to something bigger? Heck, even if they don't, I need the empowerment of artwork, *real* artwork."

"How you structure your therapy sessions here has always

been up to you. It's just a matter…"

"And you know the best thing?" I interrupted. "I'm getting better. In the past few weeks, I can't tell you how many iterations I churned out of Aaron, the guy who rescued me from that frat party disaster. And finally, I came up with a worthy portrait, but only after I stopped trying to hunt down photographs of him. Sure, if you can't have your model sit down before you, photographs can serve a purpose. They're good references for figuring out the shape of someone's nose, the color of their eyes, the contours of their hairline. But that's craftsmanship, not art. So, I went back inside my head to conjure Aaron's essence, at least my impression of it. And it's good. Really good. Nothing about it suggests photographic reality. It's more evocative, with some stylistic sense of the painter painting him. Kind of a blend of both our energies. Yet Aaron would recognize himself. At least I hope he will."

"Come again?"

"I dredged up an address for Aaron and plan to send him the portrait."

Dr. Brown's eyes widened. "What do you hope will come of your gift?"

"He'll be so awed by my gesture he'll offer me a million dollars to serve as his company's artist in residence. Either that, or he'll realize how fond he always was of me and will ask me to marry him."

My therapist struggled manfully to maintain a calm expression, until he noticed the smirk on my face.

"Sorry," I said. "I couldn't resist. No, all I want to do is repay an old kindness, touch his life, however briefly, in the same positive way he touched mine. If I hear not one word from him, that's okay. If this sparks some response, that's okay, too. It would be nice to have some communication, however infrequent, with someone I was fond of."

"Reasonable goals. And it's nice to see you taking the initiative, even if my gut tells me your decision to end therapy is premature. After all, this is only our sixth session, Cate. And only our second since those repressed memories surfaced. Plus, I have continuing concerns about your dissociative episodes, especially without benefit of medication that could ease likely triggers." He paused and raised both palms. "But, as I said, it's up to you. Just remember, I'm here if you decide you need to hash more things out."

"Thank you for being so understanding. As for those dissociative episodes, I don't plan on ever, ever traveling around in time again. It just isn't worth it. Too much can go wrong."

He sighed. "I guess I don't have to urge you to keep up with the art therapy."

I grinned. "No, you don't. I kinda see myself like a canvas. No, make that 'canvases,' plural. I expect getting my metaphorical self-portrait right will take multiple tries. Consider me a work in progress."

408

FORTY-ONE:

LASSITER BROWN, M.D.
SESSION NOTES, 24 JANUARY 2023

Devine, Cate. Last session, 10 January 2023

Recorded with patient's permission. Main focus: patient's desire to end therapy.

General observations: As usual, Cate is well-groomed, highly articulate. Much less angry than at last session, more focused. Minimal tics, including the usual braid pulling and manipulation of pillow.

Cate expresses weariness at the therapy process, at confronting difficult memories and questioning her coping methods. Sees psychotherapy as an excuse to avoid living. When I challenge the idea that living life and examining life can play out concurrently, she seems skeptical. Notes that her tendency to "live inside my head" already consumes enormous time and energy. Therapy only increases that drain. I remind her that, while she's in charge of the duration and pace of therapy, we're still at an early stage in the process (only six sessions since autumn 2022). I repeat my concerns about the potential for major disruption from her dissociative episodes, which have been manifesting lately in her self-proclaimed time travel (when her focus on past events temporarily divorces her from her current reality). I repeat my recommendation for medication to ease the anxiety that triggers those episodes. Patient remains adamant about ending (or at least suspending) therapy. I remind her I'll be available for more sessions if she changes her mind.

Cate reports a recent (encouraging) insight: Over the years, she has concocted numerous excuses for running away from her life (her words, more or less), and she doesn't want to do that anymore. She cites her caregiving role for her ailing mother. Also implies that her day job as part-time (elementary school) art teacher is another avoidance tactic: Avoiding the challenges of an artistic career more in line with her academic background? Avoiding the fear that she isn't as artistically gifted as she would hope?

Art therapy (producing her own work on her own time) continues to exert a positive influence, help her deal with uncomfortable realities, make her feel "in control" of her life.

NB: keep this file open

FORTY~TWO:

HISTORY REPEATS ITSELF

"**1** will not second-guess myself. I will not second-guess myself."

That was my mantra after ending my sessions with Dr. Brown. Decisiveness was never my strength, and my therapist's skepticism about my decision didn't boost my confidence any. Still, it was nice to get out from under the pressure of coming up with grist for therapy. And so far, I hadn't taken any detours in time or "dissociated" from my current reality.

It would have been nice to have some magic switch I could turn off, to keep childhood goblins out of sight. Then again, I sometimes chose to bring them into the light, to stare them down. Without much success. Nevertheless, their existence wasn't weighing on me quite so much. And when gloom did descend, I'd commit my dark emotions to canvas or sketchpad.

It was a rare night when I did not paint. Yes, I was feeling pressure to come up with ideas for the Ashwood commission. But those themes figured in less than half of my efforts. Both the goal-oriented and free-wheeling projects made me feel more alive than I ever had. Maybe my re-entry into the world of art would keep me sane.

Still… I couldn't stop looking over my shoulder, waiting for the next dark surprise. Was that just a bad habit in need of purging?

Maybe the purge would work if I filled enough canvases with the amorphous dread inside my head. I was developing quite the stack of abstracts airing out dark emotions. Those emotions sometimes found their way into my commissioned works, too—sometimes making the painting better. One example began with the old still site on the Ashwood property. An appropriate theme, I thought, because it evoked the centuries-old history of that part of Fauquier County, the defiant "Free State." One Sunday afternoon, I set up my easel in the tree-shaded cavity some Ashwood ancestor had chosen for his moonshine factory. The brickwork was largely intact. Even the copper pipes remained. The spring that serviced the moonshiners was now dry for more than half the year. But the site's original function remained obvious.

That Sunday afternoon was blessed with golden February weather, coaxing crocuses out of the leaf duff, however prematurely. But you wouldn't know it from my painting. Warm hues did not dominate the color scheme. No, my paintbrushes kept dipping into the palette's blue, gray, purple, and green pools. I hadn't realized just how cold green could be, until I painted wraiths emerging from the moss-choked brickwork, partially obscured by swirling mist. The semi-corporeal moonshiners kept watch on their site with a hint of menace.

As the unsettling wraiths emerged, I shivered, despite the sunbeam warming my back. This time it was a satisfying shiver, because I was the architect of that spooky chill. The more I looked at the work on my easel, the more I liked it. The better I felt about myself.

The good feeling lasted into Monday. Despite the morning frost, my shoulders glowed with sunshine, and my nostrils welcomed spring-like humidity in the air. I exchanged smiles and waves with some of the kids I beckoned through the crosswalk. My smile lasted all the way into the building, as I headed for my morning art class. Until I spotted Nicu.

The youngster was staring forlornly at the main hallway's bulletin board. His round face crumpled, like a balloon slowly losing air. The source of his sadness was a photo of his kitten, Percy. Nicu had apparently used a bathroom break to post the photo, with the caption: "Missing Cat," followed by a phone number.

"Oh no, Nicu! Has Percy gone missing?"

"Since yesterday. We started letting her out in the backyard to do her business. She's really good. Doesn't stay outside long, especially when it's dark. I think she's scared of the dark. So she comes back quickly when I call her. But not last night. I called and called. Nothing. Mama and I took flashlights and walked up and down our road calling for her. This morning, I jiggled her bowl of kibble. But no Percy. Do you think some wild animal ate her?"

I patted his shoulder. "I dunno, Nicu. Maybe she just got diverted by some interesting smells. At least it wasn't too cold last night. And it will be downright balmy today."

My pitiful attempt to inspire hope didn't sweep the clouds from the boy's face. So I added, "Good idea, putting up posters.

I bet someone took Percy in for the night. But they didn't know where she lived. Did you call the pound?"

"Mama was gonna call this morning."

"Maybe you'll have some happy news when you get home."

I didn't believe that any more than Nicu did. He glumly walked away. I was no less glum as I headed for my class. The spring themes I had in mind for my first-graders seemed utterly inappropriate. It felt hypocritical extolling robin redbreasts and daffodils.

My dark mood lasted throughout the workday. I regretted leaving Hecuba at home, in deference to the rainy forecast that never materialized. There were no happy chuffs to cheer me as I approached my Jeep. Worse, the everyday sight of idling school buses took on a sinister aspect in my dark mood. I would have painted the line of buses as a yellow dragon, belching smoke while hungrily waiting to fill its belly with children.

"I guess my artwork isn't always conducive to sane..." I mumbled before being diverted by something that was definitely *not* an everyday sight.

The children I'd recently shepherded across the county road were faced away from the yellow dragon. Several bus drivers left their idling vehicles to beckon their passengers onboard. Instead of complying, many kids rushed toward a field between the buses and the woods, in back of the main school building. Walking toward the scene, I saw four adolescents. Three waved handmade signs: "Disappearing Act" and "Fireworks" and "The Incredible Master Magicko." A fourth boy wore a black cloak and black fedora. Despite the hat's low tilt, I readily recognized Tobey Drinkwater.

Master Magicko was not waving a sign. He was waving something small, black, odd-shaped, and struggling.

"It's a cat!" shouted one member of the impromptu audience.

"He's going to make it disappear!" shouted another.

"Is that Percy?" I whispered to myself. It was hard to identify the creature for sure, because it was wearing something that looked like old-fashioned hair curlers.

Some teachers approached, talking over one another as they tried to make sense of the bizarre spectacle. "Are those ladyfingers wrapped around the cat?" "My God, he's gonna blow up the kitten!" "No, it's just an act." "Nah, that's not a real cat."

The onlookers, myself included, made no effort to intervene. We were all temporarily frozen in place. That changed when Nicu arrived at the bus line.

"No!" he screamed, running toward the magician, who was now pumping the struggling kitten up and down with one hand, while the other waved a cigarette lighter.

"Get away, filthy Gypsy," shouted a Drinkwater cohort, as he dropped his sign.

"And now I will make the cat disappear!" Tobey proclaimed.

The smaller boy stopped running long enough to fish

something out of his pocket. A slingshot. One member of Tobey's cheering squad rushed at him. Out of nowhere, a burly bus driver tackled the henchman from the sidelines, before the adolescent could slam into Nicu.

None of which deterred the cloaked magician. He pumped the firecracker-festooned cat in the air multiple times. Then he lit the cigarette lighter. Several adults shouted, "Drop that lighter right now!" But none of us intervened physically. Were we worried about causing more harm to Tobey's hostage? That's exactly what it felt like: a hostage situation, with none of us sure what to do. And most of us still frozen in time.

In the midst of all the shouting and confusion, Nicu bit his lower lip, his face radiating intense focus. He loaded something into his sling and slowly, deliberately pulled it back.

Thwock! The magician yelped, dropping both cat and lighter. Cupping a hand over his right ear, he crumpled to the ground. Meanwhile, the driver who had tackled one of Tobey's buddies, was sitting on the squirming adolescent, effectively im-mobilizing him. Two other adults, one of them a male teacher, literally collared the other two members of the Drinkwater posse to keep them from going after Nicu, who dropped his weapon and dashed toward the cat. Nicu's movement further terrified the already panicked kitten. Despite the firecrackers impeding her movements, Percy succeeded in scrambling frantically away from Nicu, away from the crowd. She circled around the buses and headed for the woods.

I finally unfroze. "No, no, no!" With all the intensity I could muster, I focused on the fleeing cat. I envisioned Percy abruptly stopping her flight into the trees, pivoting one hundred eighty degrees, and coming right to me.

And that's more or less what happened. The kitten stopped so abruptly that her hind paws collided with her front paws, a move reminiscent of a Roadrunner cartoon. For a yard or so, she slid backward on one side before righting herself and heading away from the trees ... and right into my outstretched arms.

My interception was less than elegant. The cat had no idea what was happening, why she had ended up where she was. She panicked even more, claws flailing wildly. But I had a firm grip on her. My quilted jacket took most of the slashes, but my wrists and hands got well-bloodied. Turning away from the onlookers, I forcefully pressed the struggling animal against my chest. Not forcefully enough to smother her, I hoped, but enough to restrain those flailing limbs. Eventually she wore herself out, stopped flailing, but panted wildly, probably in shock.

I used the pause to claw through the netting holding half a dozen ladyfinger firecrackers against Percy's torso. It looked like the kind of mesh bag used for supermarket onions.

I was so focused on my task that I didn't notice the crowd gathering around me. I was also unaware of the blood flowing from my nose, until one little girl cried. "Eww! The cat scratched her nose. Bad kitty!"

I had no shortage of scratches. None of them was on my nose. No, this eruption of body fluids had nothing to do with a bad kitty. It was my body's typical reaction to psychokinesis.

After freeing the panting cat from her cruel vest and stuffing it in my pocket, I readjusted my grip and looked for Nicu. He was not among the children gathered around me. Looking farther afield, I saw an angry Heather holding his upper arm and pushing him toward the school building. Then I spotted Tobey, sitting on the ground, moaning as Felicia, the kindergarten teacher, gently daubed drops of blood from the side of his face.

The contrast between Tobey's and Nicu's treatment was infuriating. I blurted out, to no one in particular, "Are you kidding me? The animal abuser gets coddled while the kid trying to save his pet gets treated like a criminal?"

Heather must have heard, because she turned in my direction and glared across the many yards separating us. I glared back then jumped when a hand gripped my shoulder.

"Hon, you gotta take care of yourself." It was Ruth, pointing at my bloody face, hands, and jacket. Then she pointed to a small animal carrier on the ground by her feet. "I found this tucked under a picnic bench. Lots of black hairs inside. Must be how the little bastards transported the kitten. I threw a towel inside. Let's see if we can wrap the kitten in it and get her into the carrier. Sound like a plan?"

420

I nodded, grateful that someone was doing something sensible. Percy came to life again, claws flailing, but we managed to wrap her in the towel. That quieted her enough for us to stash her into the carrier. I suffered only one more scratch. Ruth, wisely wearing gloves, accomplished the task without injury.

"Swathing," she chuckled, looking down at the closed carrier, now back on the ground. "Works with cranky babies, too."

"Glad you showed up. You wouldn't believe how hard her little heart was beating. And all that panting. I hope she's gonna be okay."

"She's a young, healthy animal. Probably just needs a little quiet time to recover. Now let's get *you* okay. I'm looking at a lot of blood here." Ruth whipped a handkerchief from her pocket and daubed at my face. "Jesus, those sharp little claws did a number on your nose. Gotta get reinforcements." She handed me the handkerchief and fished around in her purse. "I know I have a pack of Kleenex in here somewhere."

I was grateful not only for the solicitude but also for her routine assumption about the blood coming out of my nose.

"Ah, found it," Ruth said, pressing the tissue packet into my hands.

"Thanks. What's going on with Nicu and Heather?"

"Probably telling him he's suspended. Tobey will get suspended, too, of course. I overheard Heather saying she would have both families pick up their kids. I guess she's afraid a new ruckus could break out on one of the buses."

"Why should Nicu be suspended?"

Ruth shrugged. "He brought a weapon onto school property."

"A lousy slingshot?"

"Coulda taken out an eye."

"Who cares!"

"Now, now." Ruth patted my blood-spattered arm then looked at her watch. "Uh-oh. Better hit the road before the dog groomer closes. Gotta pick up Fluffy. Why don't you take the cat to Nicu? Just don't mouth off too much at Heather, okay?" She grinned then added before walking away, "That was one hell of an interception you made."

Picking up the carrier with one hand while pressing a wad of Kleenexes against my bloody nose with the other, I looked toward the main building, in hope of spotting Nicu. After a minute, he emerged from the central entrance, with Heather still imprisoning his upper arm. She released it and motioned that he should stand still at the curb. As I began walking toward them, I realized I'd have to pass Tobey, now standing much farther down the same sidewalk. He was in the custody of Roger Brown, a far less solicitous teacher than Felicia. Roger's large hand lay heavily on Tobey's shoulder. Sullen adolescent eyes tracked my movement. As I drew near, he muttered, "Bitch! You and that filthy Gypsy spoiled my act! I'll get you for this!"

Roger shoved Tobey's shoulder and shook his head apologetically at me. I shook my head back in disgust and continued toward Nicu and Heather.

As I deposited the cat carrier at the boy's feet, he beamed. But when he took a step toward it, Heather restrained him.

"Why can't the boy see his cat? Make sure she's okay after that ordeal?" I asked. "Is he under house arrest or something?"

"He assaulted a student," Heather said tightly.

I pulled one of the firecrackers from my pocket, waved it, and shouted, "He stopped a sadist! Don't you read the newspapers? Kids who abuse animals go on to even worse crimes if they're not stopped early on. Crimes like rape and serial killings."

"Here, take him." None too gently, she shoved Nicu in my direction. "You can wait with him, right here, until his mother arrives. I've got better things to do than babysit this one. I can only imagine all the calls waiting for me from parents wondering what happened to their school bus. All because of this ridiculous cat drama." Before she strode off, she cocked a finger at Nicu and said, "Two weeks of suspension, young man. And I'll need a sit-down with your parents before you can come back. I've already texted your mother to set it up."

"Cat drama?" I whispered, incredulous.

Nicu ignored me. He crouched down, waggling a finger through the bars of the crate. "You're purring, Percy! You okay, girl?"

"I don't think she was injured. Just scared. But maybe you should take her to the vet for a checkup."

The boy nodded and stood up, still smiling at the cat. When he finally looked at me, he exclaimed, "You're a mess!" He pointed to the blood stains on my jacket and around my nostrils.

I laughed, triggering another small spurt from my nose.

"Sorry Percy did that to you. She didn't mean it. She was just scared. But why'd she run to you, not me? Did you do something to make her come to you?"

"Who knows where a panicked cat will bolt? I guess I was just at the right spot at the right time."

Nicu squinted suspiciously. "Just like when you rescued Marcy, huh?"

I shrugged.

Nicu continued. "I woulda never seen Percy again if she got into those woods. She woulda been eaten by something."

"I doubt there are any cat-eating monsters in the woods." I hoped I sounded convincing.

Nicu crouched down again to coo at Percy, while I kept vigil on the county road, now filled with departing school buses—as if my vigilance would make Nadja Radulescu's minivan show up sooner. Even under Roger's surveillance, Tobey was far too close for comfort, and I was impatient to leave all this tense energy behind.

Elsie Drinkwater's Mercedes rolled up to the curb. If any words were exchanged as Tobey slouched inside, I didn't hear them. Roger waved at the departing sedan then headed toward the staff parking lot.

I continued my vigil. Nicu was oblivious to the passage of time. He was happily whispering to Percy, while I repeatedly checked my watch. Finally, I spotted what looked like the Radulescu car pulling into the schoolgrounds. Sighing with relief, I looked down at Nicu and said, "Why'd you have to name the cat Persephone?"

"Huh?"

"The original Persephone got kidnapped, too. And taken to the underworld."

"What happened to her?"

"A goddess went after her, to make sure she was okay."

"Just like you did with Percy, huh?"

I snorted derisively. "Yeah, that's me. A goddess."

FORTY-THREE:

SUN AND SHADOW

It was childish of me, but I took satisfaction from the fact that the Leeds Manor community did not share Principal Hayes-O'Meara's dismissive attitude about the "ridiculous cat drama." None of the chatter cast Nicu and his slingshot in a bad light, unlike Tobey.

I was even more pleased that my role did not figure much in the chatter surrounding the "incident on the green," as Percy's near immolation came to be known. Used to seeing me in the company of a wolfhound, students and teachers apparently assumed I just had a way with animals, explaining why Percy had made a beeline for me.

The "ridiculous cat drama" radically changed one young life, hopefully for the better. Two weeks after the incident, the parents of Jason Stillwell, one of Tobey's cohorts, transferred their son to a regional military academy with a strong academic record. The Stillwells had long worried about Tobey's dark influence on their son. The abuse of a kitten was the last straw. The family doted on their own cats and dogs, and Mrs. Stillwell was an active member of the Virginia Federation of Humane Societies. She was horrified at her son's involvement in Tobey's cruelty. Jason, who lived near the Radulescus, had been the one to grab Percy that night she went missing. He had stashed her in one of his family's pet carriers.

Jason's fate didn't have much impact on Tobey, however. According to the rumor mill, he promptly recruited a replacement, someone named Sam. The new cohort was far more useful, because he was old enough to have a driver's license. Several teachers had seen Tobey riding shotgun with an older teen, who looked stoned out of his mind.

Clearly, the Drinkwaters were not reining in their troubled son since Heather decreed his two-week suspension. But one member of his extended family appeared unhappy at the lack of discipline and the leniency of the school's reaction.

That piece of information came my way during one early March day, when the temperature hiked above seventy. I decided to take my lunch to the school's picnic area. Enjoying the sun at my back, I munched on my tuna sandwich in tranquil solitude, accompanied only by the John Irving novel I was reading—until the swat to my right hip.

"Scoot over," Ruth said, dumping a tote bag on the opposite side of the bench's tabletop. "I'm saving a place for Morwenna. She's got an update about the incident on the green. I'll mess it up if I tell it, so let's wait for her."

I scooted over and smiled as Ruth extracted a plastic tub from her tote. "Mm, that smells good," I commented.

"Got plenty. You want...?" Ruth interrupted herself to wave vigorously at Morwenna, slurping from a straw as she exited one of the main building's side doors.

Morwenna waved back and picked up her pace. As she deposited her iced tea on our picnic table, she scowled at Ruth. "You better not have spoiled my story."

Ruth raised her palms defensively. "Not one word. Tell Cate about that interesting parent-teacher meeting."

Settling onto the bench, Morwenna flung her silk scarf over one shoulder, out of harm's way, and began.

"Okay, you know that Heather wanted to scold both the Radulescus and Drinkwaters in person before their kids returned to school, right? She made Alison and me attend that little gathering. Nicu is in Alison's class, and Tobey's in mine. Alison and I figured our main job was to make sure school personnel outnumbered the family members.

"Well, that plan didn't quite work, because *three* members of Team Drinkwater showed up. Number three was Elsie Drinkwater's brother, a state trooper, in full, knife-creased uniform. I don't mind telling you, that boy heightened the interest level of an otherwise ghastly sit-down, in more ways than one. You know, men in uniform don't normally turn my head. All that patriarchy stuff can be a real turn-off. But this is one man in uniform, I wouldn't mind…"

"Morwenna, tick, tock," Ruth said, pointing to her watch.

"Okay, okay. I'm getting there. Turns out that the bodacious Trooper Mike has no love for the male Drinkwaters. He acted frosty toward Daddy, the county supervisor. And I later heard he banned Nephew Tobey from ever stepping foot in his house. I got the impression he doesn't want the little bastard anywhere near his kids. Interesting, no?"

"You know why?" I asked.

Morwenna shook her head and took a big gulp of tea before continuing. "You should have seen the body language at that meeting. Trooper Mike parked between Sister Elsie and Supervisor Drinkwater. The two siblings had their legs crossed toward each other. Mr. Drinkwater's chair was a couple of feet away."

"Tell Cate about the shiner."

"Oh, damn! I should have led with that. Elsie Drinkwater clearly had a bruise under one eye. Covered with makeup, but you could still see it. Now, I know she's a drunk, and drunks fall down a lot. But I sensed that mouse came from … wait for it … sonny boy."

"How do you know it wasn't the husband?" I asked.

"Somewhere in the course of the discussion, Elsie mentioned how distraught Tobey was after the incident on the green. She said he got particularly agitated that evening."

"That doesn't prove anything."

"There's more. Elsie's brother interrupted her with 'Distraught? Agitated? More like violent.'"

"Yikes!"

"Mom looked down, embarrassed, and Trooper Mike patted her hand and said in a low voice, "I'm sorry, Elsie, but you know it's true."

"How did Heather react?" Ruth asked.

"She didn't. Too hell-bent on her own agenda. I'll give her props for doing some clever troubleshooting, actively discouraging either family from seeking any kind of legal remediation. She said there was plenty of guilt to go around, and any charges or court suit would likely trigger countercharges and countersuits, and cost everyone a lot of time and money. The subtext, as I read it, was 'don't even think about suing the school system.'

"Supervisor Drinkwater interrupted to pontificate about the zero-tolerance policy concerning violence on school grounds. He reminded everyone that his son had been the victim of assault. Heather nodded, smiling that sly smile of hers, and added, 'Of course, the first act of violence on school grounds was Tobey's, when he committed the crime of animal abuse. And I definitely have zero tolerance for that.'"

"Good for Heather," Ruth said.

"Then Trooper Mike eyed everyone in the room and said flatly that there would be no legal action. Period. Then he said the staties would beef up their routine patrols in this section of the county."

"I don't understand."

Morwenna shrugged. "I guess the idea is to show the flag, so any kid who's up to no good will think twice. But I also sensed an underlying threat, like Trooper Mike was warning Drinkwater

Senior to keep Junior in line."

Ruth turned to me and chuckled, "Wouldn't you love to be a fly on the wall for that family's next Thanksgiving?"

"What were the Radulescus doing during the meeting?"

"The mother was trying hard to keep up with the conversation. Her English isn't great. The father scowled a bit. But basically, both kept their heads down. I thought Mrs. Radulescu was gonna pee her pants when the meeting broke up, and Trooper Mike walked over to her. Guess what he did? Shook her hand and her husband's hand."

"Did Drinkwater Senior make nice with the other parents?" Ruth asked.

"Nope. But the missus made a half-assed nod in the Radulescus' direction. After that, Heather took me aside for 'a word.' She expressed concern that Tobey's suspension would set back his studies. Goddess knows, the kid isn't the sharpest pencil in the box to begin with."

"Does she expect you to give Tobey special tutoring?" I asked, eyes wide in disbelief. "And is anyone concerned about how the suspension affects Nicu?"

"Heather couldn't give a rat's ass what either kid learns. Her message, as I understood it, was to make damn sure Tobey passes fifth grade and gets his ass out of here."

Ruth nodded sadly. "In other words, dump him and his problems on the middle school. Lord, I'm glad I'm retiring in a few months."

"When does Tobey return?"

"Monday. Can't tell you how much I'm looking forward to it."

"Are you worried about your own safety?"

"I've managed to handle him so far. Handle, mind you. Not teach. Now that his homeys have been diminished and chastised, he'll have less backstopping when he mouths off. So maybe the classroom atmosphere will improve."

"Wow. You should get hazardous duty pay."

"I know! Right?"

Ruth elbowed Morwenna. "Maybe you can get Trooper Mike to shadow you."

"Now there's an idea! My, my, that's one large shadow I could happily bask in."

I grinned. "Can you bask in a shadow?"

"Details, details," said Morwenna, rising from the table. "Our time in the sun is almost up. Once more unto the breach, ladies."

FORTY-FOUR:

CALL OF DUTY

Maybe it was the brief, depressing return of winter in mid-March that made me look over my shoulder more than usual. The weird dreams didn't help. I never claimed to be psychic, but Lord love a duck, my claim to psychokinesis was presumptuous enough. I began to wonder if the vague threats in those dreams might come true. The gist was that I needed to be on alert. That shirking some duty could bring disaster. In several dreams, the warning came from Hecuba—sometimes barking like Lassie reporting Timmy in the well, sometimes delivering a highly articulate lecture. In one lecture, she repeated a dream-theme from weeks earlier: I was the reincarnation of the goddess Hecate, and it was no accident that I had landed the job as a school crossing guard. I should take those duties seriously. It was not a small job, Hecuba explained patiently, her golden eyes appraising me. Mine was not a small life, she said, claiming that there *was* no small life, that it was up to us to make something out of whatever circumstances presented themselves.

I woke up in the middle of that dream relieved to hear Hecuba snoring her usual canine snores on the floor near my bed. "Quite the lecture, hound of mine," I called to her. She responded with a sleepy tail thump.

It saddened me that Dream Hecuba had focused on my

crosswalk job as significant, but not my re-immersion into the world of art. My artwork certainly felt significant to me. The five paintings and sketches sent to the Ashwoods received rave reviews. Harland was particularly fond of the ghostly moonshiners. Lavinia was less pleased, as she confided in one phone call, because rather than soothing her husband's homesickness, the painting only heightened his eagerness to head north.

It was just as well that the Ashwoods had advanced their northbound plans to early April, because I wasn't sure I'd have any more artwork to send them in Florida. Oh, I had plenty of ideas. The Ashwood acres were so varied, so filled with flora and fauna that they presented constant inspiration. But lately, as I sat at my easel, the planned themes changed radically before too many brushstrokes.

As the horses frolicked in the sun-filled pasture before me, the scene on my canvas changed into the Ashwood graveyard. Another plan to portray the handsome split-rail fence marking the road frontage morphed to portray some unknown, three-way crossroads where menacing shadows undulated just beyond the gray mist. One painting, featuring Roy grooming Sophie, suddenly included me, watching on the sidelines, while one hand, one shoulder, and part of my face seemed to be vanishing. That theme repeated itself in two charcoal self-portraits, one set in the crosswalk, the other in the classroom. The charcoal outlines were broken, and once again, several body parts were melting into another time and place. The most disturbing work began with a wash for a soothing nature scene but soon morphed into a hideous collage: orange enema bags competing for attention with screaming (literally) red dildos, brown blobs of peanut butter, splayed pale legs—naked but of indeterminate gender—and penises resembling the greenish-black stinkhorn mushrooms Roy once pointed out at the edge of the woods.

I would never inflict the more troubling works on anyone else. They were difficult for *me* to view. But view them I did, almost maternally. They said nothing good about the sanity of the artist, but there was something healing about extracting those images from inside my head. Dr. Brown might not agree.

One late afternoon, when Hecuba developed labored breathing, I feared that this was the other shoe dropping. "Not my dog!"

I spotted the remains of a bag of walnuts on the kitchen floor. After making brownies for the school's "Spring Fling" bake sale the previous day, I must have left the bag with the remaining nuts on the kitchen counter, certainly within reach of a hound as tall as Hecuba. A handful of walnuts wouldn't pose risk to the average dog, but my wolfhound was allergic, a condition pre-dating her adoption. Until now, I'd managed to keep her far away from nuts of any kind and was ignorant of how an allergic reaction looked. A frantic call to the vet reassured me. Somewhat. Was her nose swollen? Were her eyelids puffy? Yes and yes—how had I missed that? Was she struggling or panicked? No. Did I have any Benadryl on hand? Yes, in preparation for my annual battle with the spring pollen count. Dr. Fry figured out the proper dosage and said the swelling should decrease half-an-hour or so after dosing, and her breathing would return to normal. He warned that I might have a very sleepy hound, perhaps through the evening. A harmless side-effect of the antihistamine.

The vet didn't sound alarmed, so I calmed down, especially after seeing that Hecuba's respiratory problem did not interfere with her appetite for pills wrapped in cream cheese. I counted down the minutes until her face unpuffed. and she no longer sounded like a roomful of walruses. She was indeed sleepy. I re-sisted the urge to poke her every five minutes to make sure she was breathing. Finally deciding to let her sleep it off, I returned to the commission theme I'd just started, in hope of finishing with-out the canvas taking bizarre detours.

It was to be another rendition of the Ashwood cemetery. The first version had the lightness of watercolor. The latest version would be heavier, in oil, with a heavier message, focusing more on the gravestones than the scenery. I wanted to suggest an ominous portal between Planet Earth and the Underworld. Since I no longer had the original painting, I was working from memory. That usually wasn't a problem. But something was wrong with the staggered row of tombstones. The perspective was off. I needed to see the actual scene, now, while some daylight remained. I glanced at my watch then at the sleeping Hecuba. "I'll be back in an hour, puppy. I'll leave the dog panel open in case you need to pee."

Hecuba didn't stir as I grabbed sketchpad and pencil then pulled my jacket from the wall rack. As I hiked up the path, purple clouds rolled in and with them the likelihood that darkness would descend sooner than anticipated. So, once parked on the bench overlooking the graves, I wasted no time. It took four sketches before I came up with the right perspective. By then, I was relying on the dim glow of the sun, dropping below the western hills. With perfect timing, I closed up my sketchpad just as the hills swallowed the sun. Squinting at the weakly iridescent hands of my watch, I was stunned to learn that two hours had passed. I hadn't thought to stuff a small flashlight in a pocket, and full darkness was a few minutes away.

"What a dummy, I am! I'm gonna break a leg stumbling over a rock." That worry kept my footsteps short and halting, as I fixed my eyes on the ground, not on the dim yellow glow of my porchlight, barely penetrating the trees along my path.

Before long, I heard voices. Was the talk coming from a car moving up my neighbor's long driveway, on the other end of the Ashwood graveyard? Then I saw a small white glow, too weak to come from headlights. It had to be a flashlight. And it was too close to my own footpath to be on the neighboring property. Someone was walking up the second dirt path that connected the cemetery with the Ashwood residence. Had the Ashwoods returned home a month early?

No. The voices I heard sounded young. I caught the word "dude," an unlikely vocabulary choice for the septuagenarian Ashwoods. I turned back uphill to follow the intruders.

"…wacked, man…" Though deep, the voice sounded frightened.

"Calm down!" another voice croaked, in that broken pitch typical of adolescent boys.

The frightened, older one uttered something in protest.

"Here, Sam … Percocet. It will…"

"You said … practical joke … buddies … he's not…"

"He's not what?" the younger voice was shouting now.

"Breathing? Scared…"

"Fuck's sake! What a pussy! He's breathing fine." Even louder volume.

"Didn't … up for this." The older male was whimpering.

"No? Well, you sure signed up for Mom's Percocet. Time to earn those pills, Sammy."

I snuck behind a nearby tree as a sliver of moonlight separated two clouds on the eastern horizon. My heart was thumping so hard. Surely the intruders would hear it. I wished I had my phone with me. I could call nine-one-one, instead of just standing frozen in the darkness. Unsure of what to do, I continued uphill, tucking behind trees, spying.

440

I could make out not two people, but three. The shouter was roughly my height. The whimperer—Sam?—was considerably taller. They were dragging a third boy between them. I assumed it was a boy, but a hood concealed his face. He was upright, but unable to walk properly. He didn't look fully conscious. He looked like their prisoner. Could I run back to the cottage and call the police before the intruders tackled me? I hadn't seen any weapons, but there were two kidnappers and just one me.

The trio entered the graveyard. The conversation was muffled. I heard stumbling footsteps. Then the distinct sound of a zipper opening or closing.

"What are you doing, dude? Oh, jeez, this is wacked!" whimpered Sam, now standing on the sidelines as the other kidnapper shoved his victim over the very bench I had peacefully occupied just a half hour earlier. The victim's hands were tied at his belly.

I watched in horror as the kidnapper who wasn't Sam roughly pulled down his prey's jeans. Then the underpants. Then he kicked the victim's legs apart. And paused to look for Sam.

"Take the fucking picture, Sam!" the predator said, as he extracted something secured by his belt.

In the camera flash from Sam's phone, I saw a long stick. What was it? For just an instant it changed before my eyes. For just an instant I thought I was looking at a tube connected to an enema bag. For just an instant I smelled peanut butter.

"Now for the money shot, Sam."

"I don't wanna do this no more, Tobey."

Tobey?

With the next camera flash, I saw what looked like a police nightstick in Tobey's right hand. The weapon prodded the victim's rectum.

"Noooo!" I wailed.

Both assailants turned in my direction. Only briefly. Maybe they would eventually come looking for whoever had screamed. And incapacitate me. For now, however, Tobey had a higher priority: the semi-conscious boy bent over the bench.

My options were few. Hiding was pointless, since the intruders knew someone was nearby. I could run for home, in hope of calling the police before the intruders caught up with me. Or I could try to do the right thing, right where I was. Snippets from those recent dreams popped into my head. No, I would not shirk my duty.

My brain tried to move the nightstick, make the weapon fly out of Tobey's hands. For psychokinesis to work, I needed a clear view of the object to be moved remotely. But my eyes were fried from the two flashes.

If I couldn't move the nightstick, I would have to move time, just like I did when that truck was bearing down on Marcy Boone. I had sworn never to tinker with time again. But ... never say never.

So, I imagined slowing the reality enveloping Tobey, while fast-forwarding myself a minute or two into the past. My focus was intense. My heart rate slowed. My brain felt on fire. I sped toward the scene of the crime. My speed so startled Sam that he crumpled to the ground, in excruciatingly slow motion. Illuminated by the cellphone screen on his lap, his mouth stretched into a bigger and bigger O. His protracted scream startled an owl in one of the trees overhead: "hoo ... hoo ... hoo," it protested, at about one tenth the pace of its normal cry. A cloud that had been rushing to obliterate the moonlight slowed to a near standstill.

With sufficient light—and time—to zero in on the assailant, I grabbed his collar. His efforts to resist my onslaught were so slow that I easily pulled him off his victim. As I tried to wrench the nightstick from his hand, he fell, heavily, on top of me—the nightstick jabbing into my ribs before rolling slowly onto the ground. I heard a pop then a sickening hiss. A sharp, sharp pain and what may have been a lung collapsing rendered me unable to keep manipulating time. I was no longer moving at accelerated speed. Tobey and I flailed at each other and rolled over before he pinned me, aiming a fist at my face. I managed to turn my head, receiving only a glancing blow. That's when I saw the fallen nightstick. I made a grab for it. Tobey grabbed faster.

He straddled me, his knees squeezing my injured ribcage, so my breathing became even more labored. "You gonna pay, bitch." I clawed at him ineffectively as he raised his weapon with both hands to crash it into my skull. His grin was the last thing I saw before passing out, for lack of oxygen.

I came to, breathing raggedly, but breathing. Tobey was no longer on top of me. Someone was screaming, "Call it off! Call it off!" Soprano screams.

I struggled onto my right side, for a better view. My first sight was Sam passed out on the brown grass. Then I turned toward the screamer. It was Tobey, lying prostrate and flapping his palms against the ground, as if signaling submission in some impromptu wrestling match.

Tobey was pinned, all right. By Hecuba.

My scream must have disrupted her Benadryl slumber, sending her out the dog panel and up the hill. Her weight advantage may have been minimal, but her vaulting ability was worthy of Olympic gold. I figured one-hundred-ten pounds of flying wolfhound would be sufficient to knock over a good-sized man. And once her prey was on the ground… Nevertheless, she hadn't gone for the kill. Yet. Her posture was tense, muscular, all-business. Her jaws encircled the side of Tobey's neck. Waiting. I could just make out some spots on his shirt. Blood? She would draw more blood if Tobey squirmed. As clouds parted once again, moonlight illuminated her yellow eyes, glowering at the boy. She emitted a long, low growl.

Tobey sobbed, "Help me!" His shudders made Hecuba's teeth

dig into the flesh more deeply.

"Good … girl, Hecuba! Hold … him," I gasped. "Don't move … Tobey. Or those big … white teeth…will sever … artery. You'll … bleed out … before … ambulance…"

The boy stifled his sobs. Hecuba maintained her hold.

As I lay there so helpless, my brain scrambling for ideas of what to do next, something moved behind me. I braced, waiting for a blow. Had Tobey's cohort come to? No. Sam's legs were still in my front field of vision. They remained stretched on the ground, completely still. Zoned out on Percocet, perhaps.

Then I realized the kidnap victim was standing over me, nudging my back with his sneaker toe. His tethered hands awkwardly held onto his still-unzipped jeans so they wouldn't fall. He shook his head vigorously, to toss off the "hood" I'd seen earlier, actually a canvas tote bag. He grunted with frustration. Only then did I see the handkerchief gag. In the next second, as that curly dark head shook off the tote bag completely, I recognized Nicu. Of course.

As I tried to sit up, something inside my jacket pocket bruised my hip. Something quite useful, I realized gratefully. When you teach art to kids, you're always picking up the odd pair of craft scissors. Earlier in that very long day, I'd been cutting Easter eggs out of card stock for my students to color in the next art class. I wasn't using the blunt-tipped scissors made for little kids. No, indeed, this was a pair of Fiskars, sharp enough and strong enough to cut the zip-tie imprisoning Nicu's wrists.

"Bend ... down ... Nicu. Gonna ... cut that." I motioned toward his wrists.

He nodded, dropped clumsily to his knees, and extended his hands. Cutting the plastic took more force than anticipated. But one painful minute later, Nicu's hands were free. The first thing they did was zip up and button his fly. Only then did he pull off the gag. No stranger to humiliation myself, I understood his priorities.

"Gonna get his cellphone," Nicu said, pointing toward Sam.

He had to pass Tobey and Hecuba on his none-too-steady path. Worried that Tobey might try something, or Hecuba might be startled by Nicu's dizzy gait, I called out to my dog. I hoped I sounded both authoritative and soothing: "Good ... girl! Hold ... him." Tobey whimpered softly. Hecuba adjusted her grip and growled again.

Nicu staggered slightly as he bent forward to pick up Sam's cell. When he returned to me, he asked, "Should I call nine-one-one?"

"Gimme." I reached for the phone. Despite my halting speech, I needed to convey important information. It took a long time, but I managed to identify myself and my precise location. I said I needed an ambulance, was seriously injured. Nicu probably needed one too, since he looked dazed. I even reported Sam's possible overdose. I described the crimes: trespassing by two intruders, kidnapping, attempted rape of a young boy. With all the precision I could muster, I added, "Rapist is ... pinned ... by my dog. Don't ... hurt ... dog. Don't ... hurt dog." Gasping from talking so long, I was about to hang up when I added, "Wait. Have evidence ... cellphone photos."

Panting, I looked up from the phone to see Nicu waving something. "Just found these over there. Tobey must have dropped it. A bag of zip-ties. How about I tie them both up? Hecuba needs a break."

I nodded. "Tie him ... tight."

Nicu began with Tobey's ankles, well clear of Hecuba. I heard the satisfying noise of the plastic ratchets engaging. The next thing I heard was Nicu, "Can't reach his wrists. Dog's in the way."

"Tobey?" I winced at my effort to project my voice. "Gonna call ... off ... dog. Don't ... try ... anything. She ... will kill. Wolfhound ... bred ... to bite ... heads off ... in battle."

Just then Hecuba repositioned her grip, snarling when Tobey whimpered.

If Tobey had doubted my words, he had new reason to believe them. "Not gonna move," he whispered. "Swear to God!"

FORTY-FIVE:

NEVER SAY NEVER

"Up for a visit?"

I looked up from my sketchpad to see Morwenna at the door of my hospital room. She was holding a large fruit basket.

"Sure!"

"Good Goddess, girl! If you were any paler, Hollywood would snap you up to play Morticia in the next go-round of *The Addams Family*."

I chuckled then winced, laying a hand protectively over my ribcage. "Don't make someone with broken ribs and a surgical incision laugh."

"Just how many did you break anyway?"

"Only two. But one of them was a compound fracture that ruptured my spleen, hence the bleeding, hence the pallor."

"Your spleen? I thought you had a punctured lung?"

"Fortunately, no. It just collapsed for a while. Reinflated all by its onesies, no doubt saving me some ghastly procedure."

"Hope none of that means you can't eat goodies, cause buried beneath all this healthy fruit is a box of the most sinful Belgian chocolates. They're from me. The basket is from the whole school staff. To express our gratitude."

"Thank you, especially for the chocolates. No dietary restrictions. But why gratitude?"

"Thanks to you, we no longer have to look into Tobey Drinkwater's lying, smirking, dead eyes," Morwenna said, plunking the oversized basket on a cabinet.

"You always seemed to handle him well."

"Not without girding my loins."

I nodded sympathetically. "It's scary to see evil in someone that young."

"Evil is exactly the right word. Oh, we pussyfoot around it. Talk about counseling and family troubles. And Goddess forbid his parents sue us because we hurt the little psycho's feelings. But that kid's a blight. He needs to be locked far away from other kids, teachers, even his own mother. She may have mixed feelings now, but I'll bet Elsie Drinkwater is relieved sonny boy's in custody. All because of you, our heroic Guardian of the Crosswalk." Morwenna bowed, dramatically rotating her right wrist from forehead to stomach.

"I wasn't heroic. I just got angry."

"I wish someone had gotten angry enough to take action a lot sooner. Hope the Romany kid will be okay."

"Well, look at that! The Leeds Manor troops are assembling, I see," called a flower-bearing Ruth from the doorway. She waved at Morwenna then marched to the opposite side of my bed to plant a kiss on my cheek. As she thumbed away a spot of lipstick, she frowned. "Awfully pale. Heard you needed a transfusion."

"Yeah, but they expect I'll heal up just fine. Thanks for the flowers. They're gorgeous. And thanks for coming. It's good to see you."

Realizing she was still encumbered by the huge bouquet, Ruth spun around to scan the room. "Aw, damn. Lemme see if one of the nurses can scare up a vase. Back in a jiff."

"The school's not gonna be the same without Ruth," Morwenna sighed. Then she brightened. "But one personnel change is coming that will gladden all our hearts."

"Don't keep me guessing."

Morwenna parked on the edge of my bed and adopted a confidential tone. "Heather's been taking heat for her handling of the Drinkwater mess. She could probably weather the storm if she'd just shown some regret. But she smart-mouthed a reporter the other day, which infuriated the superintendent. The word on the grapevine is that Principal HO will be forced to resign at the end of the school year. All because she won't bend her knee to the school board. I thought her survival instincts were more finely tuned."

"I had the impression you got along fairly well with her."

"Unlike Heather, I can make nice with anybody if I have to. Especially a boss."

"Wonder who the replacement will be."

Morwenna giggled. "I'll let you in on a little secret. I'm gonna throw my hat in the ring. I've heard they're thinking of hiring from inside. For a change."

"Yeah? That would be a definite improvement."

Ruth returned, holding a vase full of flowers. "What would be a definite improvement?"

Shooting me a cautionary glance, Morwenna said, "School without psycho Tobey."

"Oh, Lord! You can say that again." Ruth placed the vase next to the fruit basket and stole a chair adjoining the unoccupied second bed. "I heard the Drinkwaters are striking a deal. Tobey might avoid juvie hall, or worse, if they commit him to a private psychiatric facility."

Morwenna groaned. "Private? So he weaves a few baskets at some cushy hospital and gets sprung when he cons his doctors?"

Ruth's hands gestured downward. "Easy, girl. We're not talking short-term incarceration. That boy needs serious head-shrinking. And the shrinks would report regularly to the state."

"I wonder if someone that broken can ever be fixed." I shuddered.

"I wonder if it's worth the effort to try," Ruth added.

"Shit!" Morwenna interrupted, looking at the wall clock opposite my bed. "I'm running later than I thought. My Wiccan group is due at my house in just half an hour. Sorry for the short visit, but at least I verified you're still among the living. And now I better hit the road."

She rose, wound her ubiquitous scarf around her neck, and blew a kiss at me. "See ya Monday, Ruth," she added at the doorway.

Ruth waved. "Go, go. You don't want to piss off a bunch of witches."

I laughed then groaned. "Darn! This is getting old."

"It's gonna take a while yet. When I busted a rib from an ice-skating fall, I banned Arnie from telling any jokes for a whole month. I remember how much it hurt to laugh. Or sneeze."

"And let's not forget coughing," I added.

"Oh, damn, I almost forgot." Ruth raised an index finger then rummaged in her oversized purse. "I've got another present for you." She extracted a sorry looking cellphone. Its screen was cracked, and the back was stained reddish-brown. "This has been sitting in the school's lost-and-found station since last fall. Heather was gonna toss everything that hadn't been claimed at the start of the year. Can you imagine forgetting you lost a phone?"

"Kids. I've seen some really nice jackets sit in lost-and-found for months without getting claimed. And how many times do you see a solitary shoe there? Who walks out of the school with just one shoe?"

Ruth rolled her eyes. "Too true. Anyway, Heather made a half-assed effort to identify the owner, but the phone's a burner. No Internet. No personal information. And the temporary phone number had expired."

"Why would a kid have a burner phone?"

"Arnie says it can be a cheap way of giving your kid an emergency phone for a short period of time. No contract, for one thing. Some parents use short-term burners to determine whether the kid can be trusted to handle a permanent cellphone responsibly. Without losing it.

"I didn't know all that when I retrieved it. But I saw the camera lens and figured I might be able to identify the owner from the photos. The battery was dead as a stone by then, of course, but Arnie worked some magic. He was doubtful because the thing had clearly been stuck in the mud for a while. Look at the red clay stains! But he finally got it to take a charge. Basic phone functions no longer work. It won't take any new pictures. But Arnie could pull up the shots already taken. Not many, and most were of pets, even a squirrel or two. But one critter I did recognize: your Hecuba."

"Hecuba's on it?"

"Yup," Ruth said, fidgeting with the phone. When she looked up, she saw the alarm on my face and added, "Don't worry. No one was stalking you. Some kid must have snapped Hecuba in the crosswalk. You can just make out the bottom of your safety vest on the side there." She turned the screen around to show me.

"But that's not what I wanted to share. I found one video, too. Shaky, but you'll get a kick out of it. Here, just hit the start button." She handed the phone to me.

I hit the button. There I was, sternly waving some kids back from the curb. All but one complied: Marcy Boone. Then I started running, at my usual clunky pace. Then it looked like someone had hit a fast-forward button, with my arms and legs blurred from running so fast. Everything else was at normal speed. Off in the distance, you could see a few kids walking into the school. They certainly weren't moving fast. But I looked like Jesse Owens on methamphetamine. The oncoming truck entered the frame, and it was approaching me at a much slower pace than I was approaching it. Then everything started shaking, probably because the photographer was moving too fast toward the scene, but you could just make out my feet levitating onto the running board on the passenger side, before the video ended. When I looked up at Ruth, my mouth was agape.

"That was one helluva sprint you made, kiddo. Didn't realize you could run that fast."

I scanned her face for irony. None. She actually thought I was capable of an Olympic sprint. She hadn't grasped the huge disparity between my speed and the truck's speed.

"I just thought you might want to have it," Ruth added. "In thirty years, when you're ancient of days, you can look back at your athletic youth."

I nodded dully, looking down at the phone. "I can keep this?"

"Sure. If you don't want it, it goes in the trash bin."

"Gee, thanks, Ruth. I think I will hold onto it."

The visit continued for another five minutes, but I wasn't much of a conversationalist. I was too preoccupied with what that video meant.

"Okay, that's enough." Ruth said, rising from her chair. "I can see I've tired you out. You need your rest. Do you have your cell-phone here?"

Confused, I raised the burner in my hand.

"No, silly, I mean your own phone."

"Oh, yeah. Roy the caretaker brought it to the hospital yesterday, along with my sketchpad and some other things. He's been taking care of Hecuba, too."

"Nice guy. I know you have my number in your phone. So you're gonna call me as soon as you know when you'll get sprung. I'll take you home. And I'll make damn sure your larder is fully stocked for your recovery."

"No, Ruth! That's awfully nice, but I wouldn't want you to miss work or go out of..."

"I'm picking you up, and that's final." She pivoted sharply, heading for the door, and gave me a backhanded wave before exiting.

I replayed the video several times before laying the phone on the table-tray by my bed. I wasn't sure how I felt, as I tried to parse the "why" of my life. I now had some validation of my bizarre talent: moving objects, even time, with my brain. But to what end? Sure, thanks to psychokinesis, I'd dodged a few weapons. That came in handy. And moving time had served a strong moral purpose on two occasions: saving two children.

But more often than not, I ended up in worse shape after making use of my special gift. Questioning my sanity. Coping with embarrassing and occasionally health-endangering eruptions of body fluids. And here I was, hurting in a hospital bed, minus one spleen. That dramatic splenic bleed was probably the price the universe exacted for bending time. Some "gift."

It certainly hadn't advanced my career, financial status, or romantic prospects. Contrary to what I'd told Dr. Brown, I did harbor a tiny hope it would. I hoped I would hear from Aaron, for example, after sending him that portrait. Reconnecting with him would have provided some small justification for traveling back and forth in time to make sure I hadn't screwed up his life. But … "crickets," as the kids say.

And to be painfully cynical, what difference did my time-bending rescues of Marcy and Nicu make in the grand scheme of things? Were they destined to do great deeds for the world? It was hardly likely Marcy Boone would come up with a cure for cancer. And as fond as I was of Nicu, I couldn't see him bringing peace to the Middle East.

"So why?" I asked aloud.

"Ah, the question that keeps psychiatrists in business," said a voice in the doorway.

"Dr. Brown? What are you doing here?"

The psychiatrist smiled and said, "I can leave…" And made a

goofy feint to exit.

"No, no. You just surprised me. How did you even know I was here?"

"You've created quite the buzz around here, Cate. I was checking on a patient admitted for a psych evaluation when I heard two nurses chatting about this gigantic service dog who pretty much filled the hallways yesterday. When I overheard 'Irish wolfhound,' I had to check the admissions list. I doubt there are two Irish wolfhounds in Fauquier County. And there was your name. I didn't know Hecuba was a service dog."

"She's not." I said, motioning for him to sit at the bedside chair. "Roy, the guy who brought her here, has a friend who trains service dogs. He persuaded him to lend out one of their official vests. He knew Hecuba would behave well. He also knew she was sad and worried. He's been taking care of her since I was hurt. He works at the estate where I live. Roy also knew I'd be missing my dog and worrying about her. Visit really perked me up."

"Not a small achievement after what you went through. A splenectomy, broken ribs, collapsed lung, transfusion? You look amazingly well after all that. And I gather the boy you saved is okay, too. Thanks to you."

I nodded. "One of the nurses was nice enough to update me on Nicu. He had a concussion, so they kept him here in the hospital that first night, for observation. His kidnappers had hit him with a rock. What's wrong with people anyway?"

458

"Wish I knew. I've got some time right now if you'd like to talk about it. Off the clock. You've been through a lot, both mentally and physically."

I certainly didn't have the energy for a therapy session. But his input about my recent discovery would be welcome. I strained to reach for the beaten-up phone on the table.

"Here, let me get it," Dr. Brown said, handing the phone to me.

"No. I want you to see something on it. Swipe the screen to bring up the last thing I watched. Play the video."

He did as asked. His expression morphed from mild amusement to confusion to intense concentration. He hit the play button again. Squinted as he watched. He viewed it a third time before laying the phone down.

"Could this be AI?" he said at last. "Forgive me, Cate, but you couldn't run that fast if you were twenty years younger. Nobody can run that fast. And the video can't be on fast-forward because other people are moving at a normal pace."

"You're observant. As you can see, I overtook a truck that was probably doing at least twenty miles an hour. And the other night, I covered a good quarter mile in record time to tackle a miserable little psycho before he could rape Nicu." Gingerly folding my arms over my chest, I waited for his reaction.

"You're saying you moved time in both cases?"

"Got a better explanation?"

He shook his head. "There are all sorts of ways videos can be manipulated. Where'd you get this?"

"From the lost-and-found station at my school. It's a burner some kid never claimed after dropping it in the mud and cracking the screen. I can't see some tech wizard getting his hands on the phone and screwing with the video. Can you?"

"Maybe he uploaded it on the Internet and…"

"No Internet connection for this phone. Besides, how would the altered video get back on this burner, sitting in a lost-and-found box for months?"

"I'm stumped. None of this makes sense."

"No. There's no logical explanation explaining how or why the video could have been manipulated. And there's no logical explanation explaining how an ordinary woman could manipulate time. I guess the question is: Which version makes more sense?"

"I honestly don't know. But I do know I wouldn't call you ordinary, Cate."

I snorted. "Just weird, huh?"

"No. What I meant was that you've done some extraordinary things. In the past few months alone. Saved two children. And as I told you once before, you summoned the courage to explore all sorts of dark issues in your past. Found the energy to reinvent your life as an artist. Nothing about that is ordinary."

"Do you think it's at least *possible* that I might be able to move time, under special circumstances?"

He shrugged. "Never say never."

I smiled. "Thank you for that bit of doubt. Maybe I'm not so crazy, after all?"

"I never thought you were crazy. You were certainly troubled. For good reason. And if you decide, after all this, that you'd benefit from resuming our therapy sessions, you know how to reach me."

"Never say never," I grinned.

"Hope to hear from you. Our sessions were nothing if not interesting." He grinned back, rose, and raised a palm in farewell.

FORTY~SIX:

STANDING AT THE CROSSROADS

rue to her word, Ruth picked me up at the hospital two days later. During the drive home, she regaled me with amusing anecdotes about school, Arnie, Fluffy, her girls. After settling me into my sofa, she dashed back to her car and hauled in bags of groceries. Then she bustled about the kitchen to make lunch.

As we ate our chicken salad sandwiches, a knock sounded at the door. Ruth sternly ordered me to stay put, while she checked. As arranged over the phone, Roy had brought Hecuba home. I heard Roy insisting he would bring the wolfhound inside himself, still on her leash. "She might knock you over, little bitty thing like you."

Even Roy had his hands full keeping the dog in check as she joyously strained toward the sofa. "You sit down right there, Hecuba H. Hound," he ordered. "Don't you be giving Miss Cate a new hurt."

Hecuba complied, without even looking at the sandwiches on the coffee table. She scooted her butt closer to me so she could lay her long muzzle, ever so gently, over my lap. I stroked the smooth channel between her golden eyes, as she looked up at me worshipfully. "I'm so sorry to worry you, puppy. After you were so, so brave." My eyes were tearing up.

Ruth and Roy stood on the sidelines like proud parents, palms folded over their stomachs and broad smiles on their faces.

When Roy broke the silence, there was a catch in his voice. "Well," he began, clearing his throat. "I'd best get back to work and leave you two gals to catch up."

"Why don't you join us?" Ruth said. "We've got tons of chicken salad. I can whip up a couple of sandwiches for you in no time flat."

He shook his head, "Naw. I promised the horses some extra grain today. To celebrate the homecoming."

As he approached the dog, to remove the leash and chain collar, I extended my hand toward him. "How can I thank you for everything you've done these past few days? For Hecuba. For me. Really, I can't find the words."

He grasped my hand firmly with both of his. "It was an honor. You just heal up, quick as you can. And you need anything, you let me know. Okay? And Hecuba, you take good care of your mistress." He stroked her shoulders. She thumped her tail on the floor, but did not move her head from my knees.

Ruth showed Roy out then joined me on the sofa. She tried her best to jolly me through lunch, urging me to have dessert, another glass of iced tea, sharing the latest joke popular with her third-graders, showing me pictures of Fluffy on her cell. But she was fading almost as fast as I was. Despite the happy re-union with my dog, I was exhausted, sore, and more than a little depressed. Not even Ruth could nudge me into a better state of mind.

After tidying up in the kitchen, she urged me to call her if I needed anything. With a worried look on her face, she left.

I was still obsessing about all the questions that had troubled me in my hospital room. I leaned into the sofa back, propped my legs up on the coffee table, and beckoned Hecuba onto the seat cushions. I'd never seen her climb up so quietly, gently. She gave me a thorough sniffing, before nestling against my hip, her nose and bony paws overhanging the seat. With a sigh of contentment, she closed her eyes. It wasn't long before she began snoring softly.

The snores morphed into muffled barks. Her paws twitched, her tail thumped a few times, and some white slobber trickled from her muzzle. Chasing bunnies, no doubt.

"This is the noble beast who watched over ancient crossroads with some goddess?"

Which was more ridiculous? That Hecuba, the same dog who would joyously roll in the disgusting remains of a dead squirrel, was an immortal or at least a regularly reincarnated companion of the gods? Or that I was her divine mistress? Viewed logically, both possibilities were ludicrous.

There's that word again. Logic. Hadn't Dr. Brown's commitment to logical, scientific explanations annoyed me? Yet here I was, looking for logic to explain the belief in reincarnation. Expecting some logic behind ancient myths. Searching for the logic in my time travel—not just the how, but the why. What compelling purpose did my special talent serve? How did it serve my mission in this life? Assuming I had some mission.

But the more I thought about it, what was so illogical about a reincarnated goddess having a ho-hum life? Just how stellar was the life of the original Hecate? In her supposed incarnation as guardian of crossroads in the British Isles, she must have spent a lot of time cold, wet, and hungry. Were she and her faithful hound dependent on the meager offerings fearful travelers would leave for her?

And what was so great about Hecate's life in ancient Greece? Sure, she had a special talent other gods didn't have. She alone could traverse all three spheres of Heaven, Earth, and Hell. But what did all that wandering get her? Those weren't exactly recreational trips. She was usually doing someone else's bidding, like when she trudged down to Hades on a mission for Demeter.

I had a lot more in common with Hecate than I realized. In a way, we both had/have small lives, and maybe our lives didn't/don't serve some great universal plan. Maybe there is no universal plan. Maybe we just do the best with what we have. And that's how we discover our purpose in life.

Isn't that exactly what Hecuba told me in that dream I'd had a week or so earlier? There was honor in duty, in trying to do the right thing. Whether it was guiding schoolchildren safely across a county road or stopping a predator like Tobey Drinkwater. And yeah, maybe I had to have my own history of sexual abuse to spur me into action on Nicu's behalf. A good example of making good use of one's circumstances, even the lousy experiences.

I thought suddenly of Roy. The world would never applaud him for mucking out stalls or taking care of a modest country estate. Although the Ashwoods certainly appreciated him, his pay probably was as lackluster as mine. But Roy was good at his job. He had probably rescued countless dogs, and he certainly made life easier for at least one of their owners. Who knows, maybe he would have been revered as a god in another dimension, with exactly the same life circumstances. Most important, he appeared to feel good about himself.

Was that all there was to it? Whether goddess or earthly human, the idea was to derive satisfaction from being good at something and trying to do the right thing? I had done the right thing with Nicu. And it did make me feel good about myself. Maybe I'd never use my special talent again. But it was there if needed. Just one of the varied circumstances shaping my life.

Did *you* feel good about yourself, Hecate? For saving Persephone? For keeping weary travelers safe from the monsters that lurked in ancient woods? I hoped so. Right then and there I decided on my next art project: honoring the goddess Hecate. Maybe in a whole series of works. If that meant honoring myself as well, so much the better.

I closed my eyes. As the first outriders of sleep embraced me, I smelled the skunk cabbages that had popped up weeks earlier along the path leading to the Ashwood cemetery. Not exactly a pleasant aroma, but the yeasty, mustardy notes were reassuring. As was the humid, mulchy scent of a landscape awakening to spring after months of arid sterility. As was the fragrance of wild onions, pushing their green tips out of the ground.

Even as those scents filled my nostrils, I knew this was just a dream. Not some feat of psychokinesis bending time and space to put me on that path. It was a lovely dream, reassuring me that all the Tobeys of the world could not desecrate this spot. It had been washed by rain, baked by sun, swept clean by wind.

As Dream Me reached the grave markers, I spotted Hecuba calmly waiting. We stood side by side, surveying the woods and hills and pathways. I freed my hair from its braid and let the wind play with it. How it glinted, as sunbeams caught the white and silver streak newly emerging at one temple.

I pivoted. Hecuba rotated with me. A gust tossed my hair this way and that. How curious! It was entirely white now. As I raised my hand to clear the strands from my eyes, I noticed how peppered my skin was with brown, tan, and gray spots. I smiled at the crenellations that marked my forearms.

I turned another hundred-plus degrees. The hair blowing in the wind was now so richly black it had dark blue highlights. So lustrous, it seemed to have a life of its own. The hands that tossed the strands over my shoulder were unblemished, creamy, and smooth.

The landscape seemed to change with every rotation, too. It was no longer the Ashwood cemetery. Maybe it was that venue, from centuries earlier. Or, maybe it was some primeval forest in the British Isles or Greece or Italy. The trees were taller and stouter than the ones on the Ashwood property. Against the dark background of the deepwood, pathways were clearly delineated. They intersected at the precise point where Hecuba and I stood. Three paths.

Which one would I take? Which one felt right? What felt right was to stay precisely where I was, my faithful dog at my side. Honoring my current circumstances, whatever they might be. I would continue standing watch for whatever might come out of the woods. I could handle whatever emerged, whether blessing or curse.

Looking down at my feet, I noticed a pile of small stones, dusted by snow. And over there, nearly buried in bright, autumnal leaves was a palm-sized pouch, made of coarse linen and tied off with hemp. I picked it up, untied the string, and smiled at the small cluster of sweetmeats inside. And what was that over there, by the spring-green grass poking through the mulch? A musical instrument of some sort? Ah, a mouth harp. Of course.

Offerings all. For me. The goddess of the crossroads.